JUPITER'S CIRCLE

CHARACTERS CREATED BY MARK MILLAR AND FRANK QUITELY

MARK MILLAR
WRITER

WILFREDO TORRES
ARTIST (CHAPTER 1, 2, 3, 6)

DAVIDE GIANFELICE
PENCILS & INKS (CHAPTER 3-PAGES 8,13,14,21, 4, 5)

FRANCESCO MORTARINO
INKS (CHAPTER 3-PAGES 8,13,14,21, 4, 5)

IVE SVORCINA
COLORS

PETER DOHERTY
LETTERS · DESIGN

FRANK QUITELY
COVER & CHAPTER ILLUSTRATIONS
(COLOR CHAPTER 5 BY NATHAN FAIRBAIRN)

NICOLE BOOSE
EDITOR

PETER DOHERTY & DREW GILL
PRODUCTION

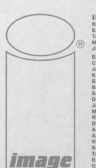

IMAGE COMICS, INC.
Robert Kirkman – Chief Operating Officer
Erik Larsen – Chief Financial Officer
Todd McFarlane – President
Marc Silvestri – Chief Executive Officer
Jim Valentino – Vice-President

Eric Stephenson – Publisher
Corey Murphy – Director of Sales
Jeremy Sullivan – Director of Digital Sales
Kat Salazar – Director of PR & Marketing
Emily Miller – Director of Operations
Branwyn Bigglestone – Senior Accounts Manager
Sarah Mello – Accounts Manager
Drew Gill – Art Director
Jonathan Chan – Production Manager
Meredith Wallace – Print Manager
Randy Okamura – Marketing Production Designer
David Brothers – Branding Manager
Ally Power – Content Manager
Addison Duke – Production Artist
Vincent Kukua – Production Artist
Sasha Head – Production Artist
Tricia Ramos – Production Artist
Emilio Bautista – Digital Sales Associate
Chloe Ramos-Peterson – Administrative Assistant
IMAGECOMICS.COM

CHAPTER 1

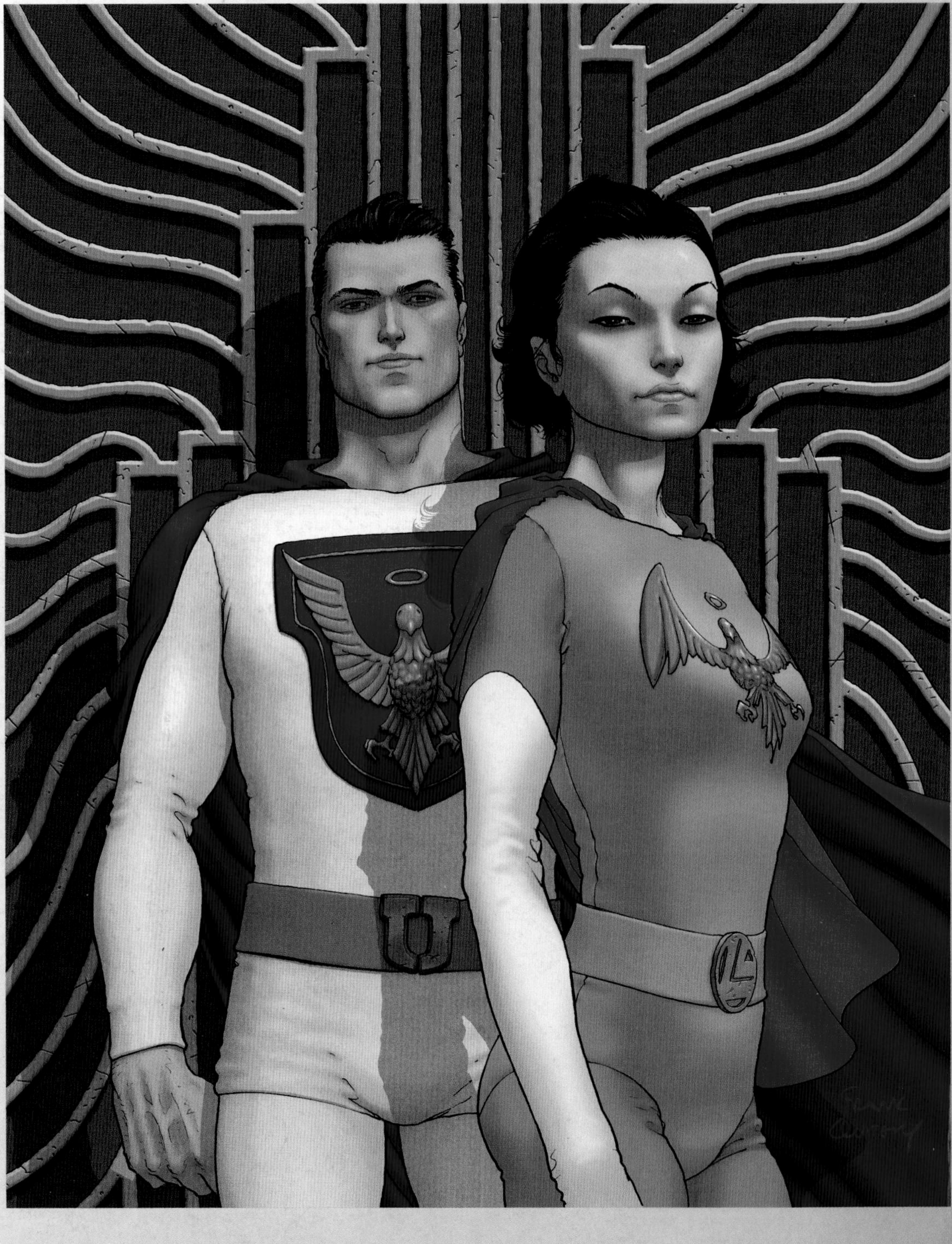

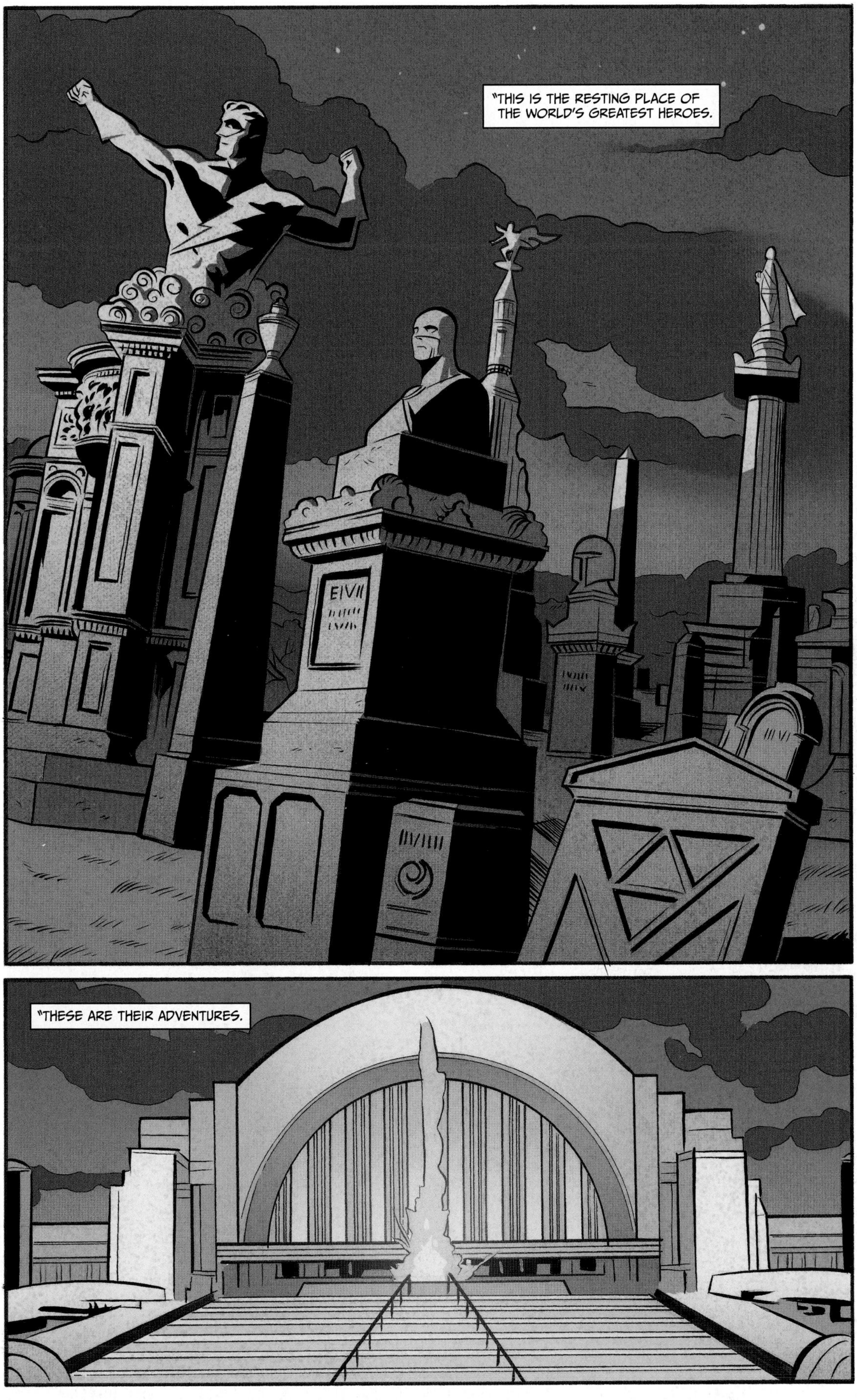
"THIS IS THE RESTING PLACE OF THE WORLD'S GREATEST HEROES.
"THESE ARE THEIR ADVENTURES.

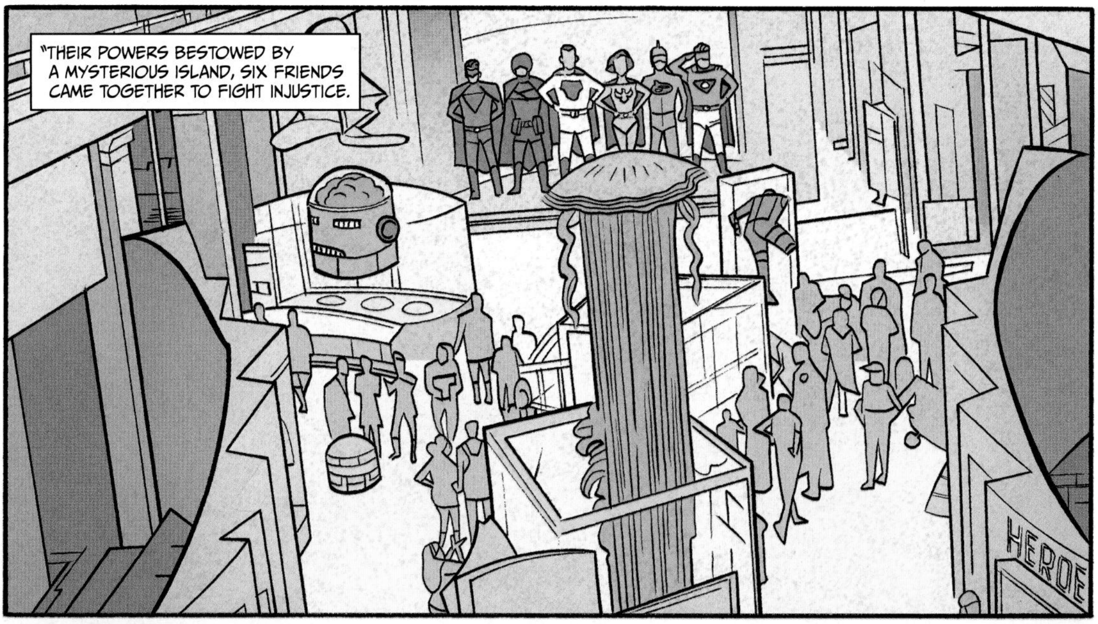
"THEIR POWERS BESTOWED BY A MYSTERIOUS ISLAND, SIX FRIENDS CAME TOGETHER TO FIGHT INJUSTICE.
HEROE

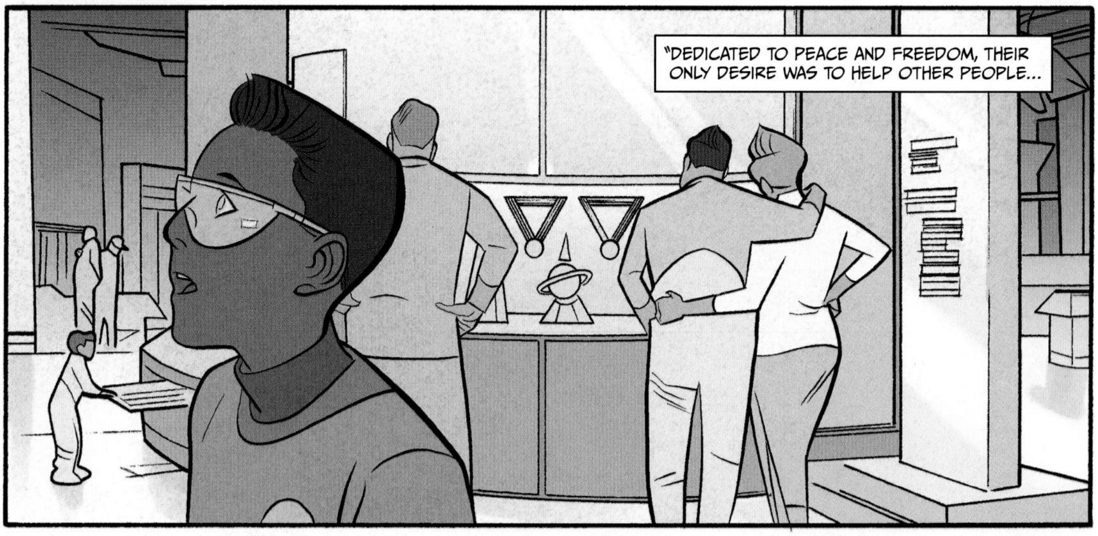
"DEDICATED TO PEACE AND FREEDOM, THEIR ONLY DESIRE WAS TO HELP OTHER PEOPLE...

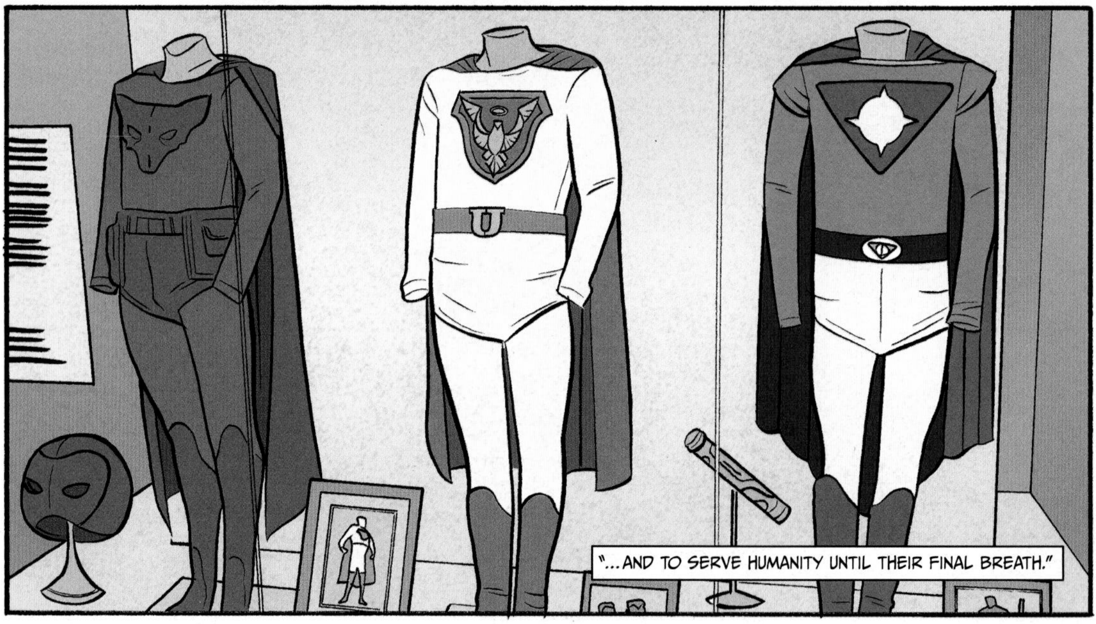
"...AND TO SERVE HUMANITY UNTIL THEIR FINAL BREATH."

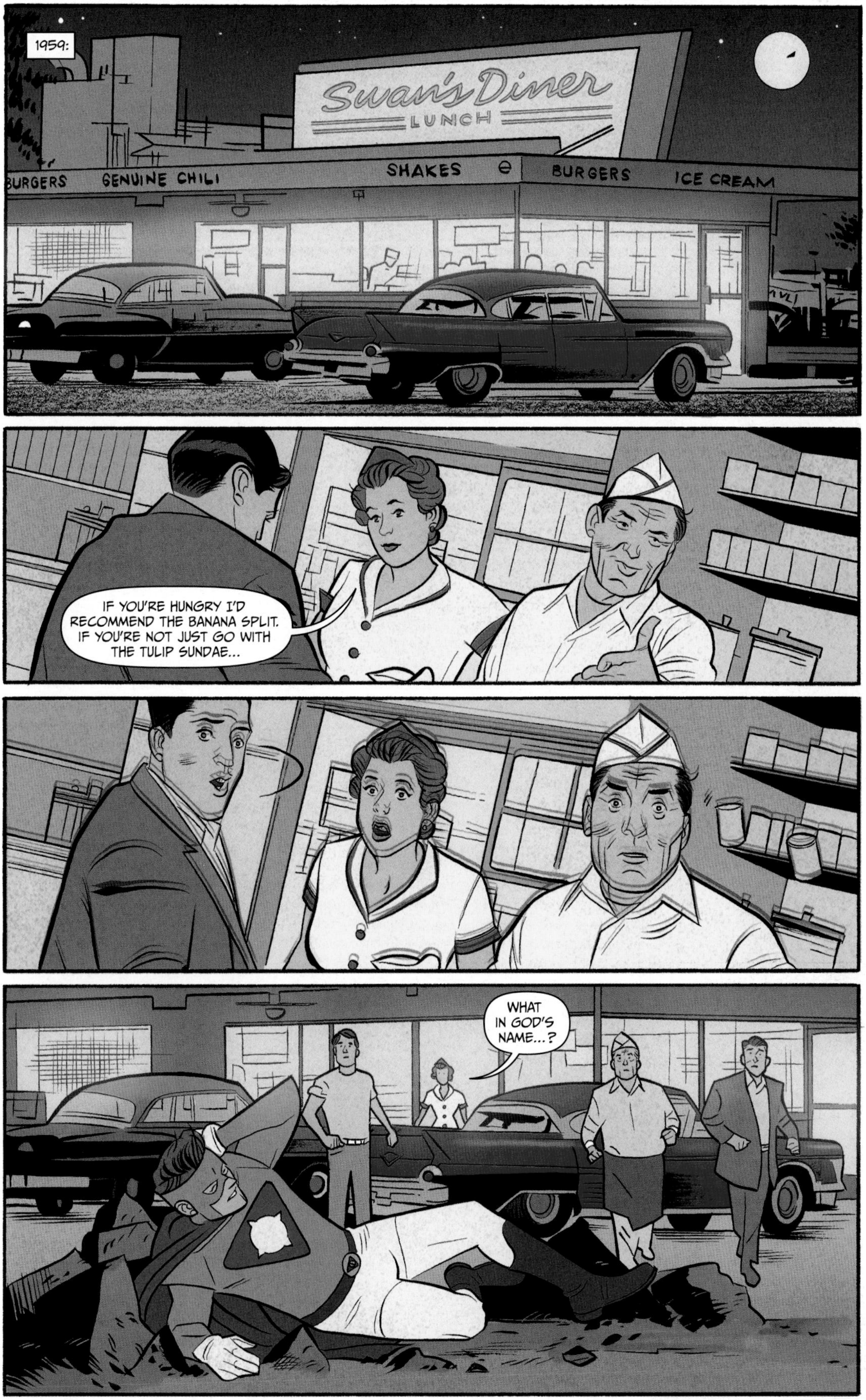
1959:
Swan's Diner
LUNCH
BURGERS GENUINE CHILI
SHAKES
BURGERS ICE CREAM
IF YOU'RE HUNGRY I'D RECOMMEND THE BANANA SPLIT. IF YOU'RE NOT JUST GO WITH THE TULIP SUNDAE...
WHAT IN GOD'S NAME...?

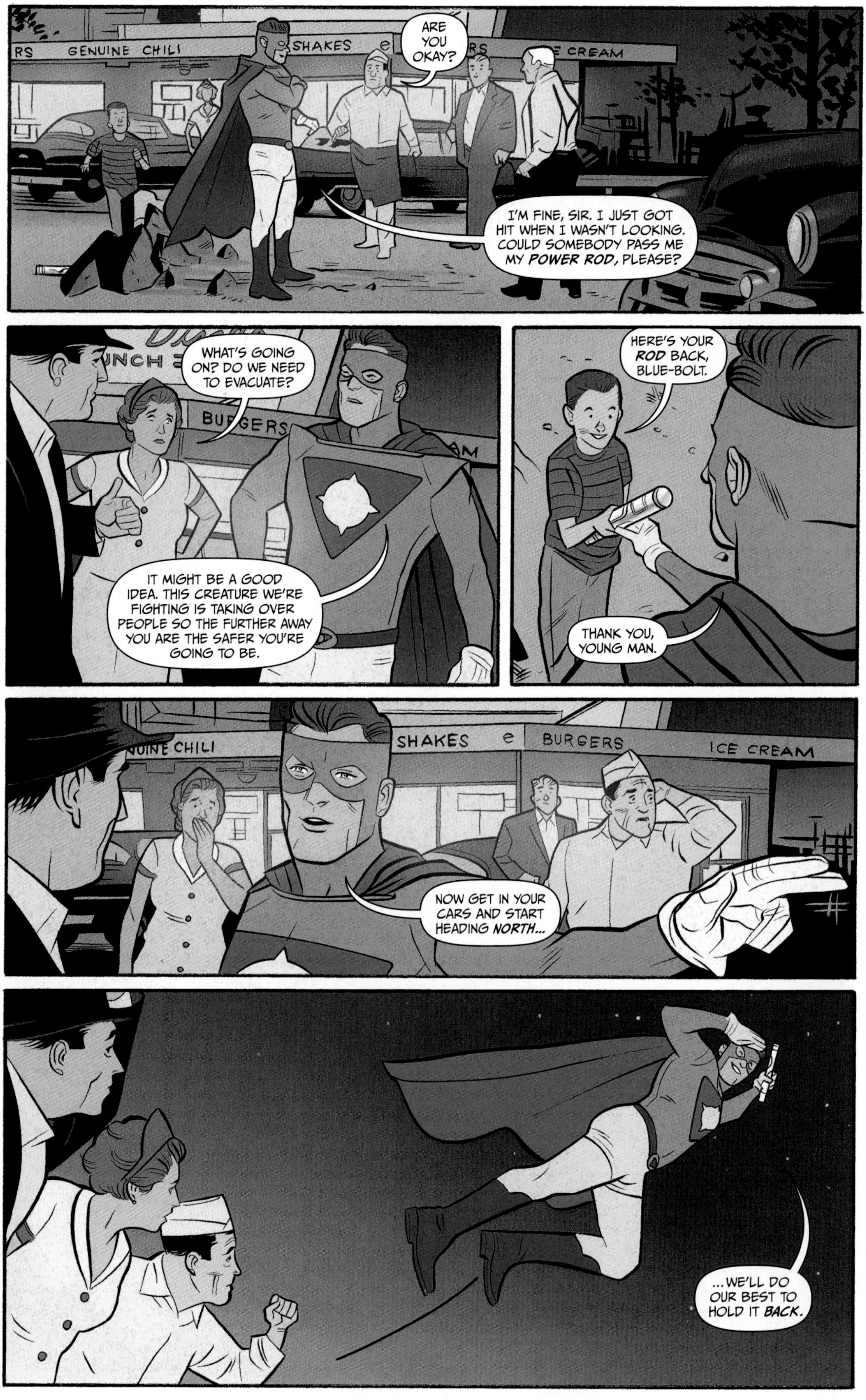
RS GENUINE CHILI
SHAKES
E CREAM
ARE YOU OKAY?
I'M FINE, SIR. I JUST GOT HIT WHEN I WASN'T LOOKING. COULD SOMEBODY PASS ME MY POWER ROD, PLEASE?
UNCH
BURGERS
WHAT'S GOING ON? DO WE NEED TO EVACUATE?
IT MIGHT BE A GOOD IDEA. THIS CREATURE WE'RE FIGHTING IS TAKING OVER PEOPLE SO THE FURTHER AWAY YOU ARE THE SAFER YOU'RE GOING TO BE.
HERE'S YOUR ROD BACK, BLUE-BOLT.
THANK YOU, YOUNG MAN.
NUINE CHILI
SHAKES
BURGERS
ICE CREAM
NOW GET IN YOUR CARS AND START HEADING NORTH...
...WE'LL DO OUR BEST TO HOLD IT BACK.

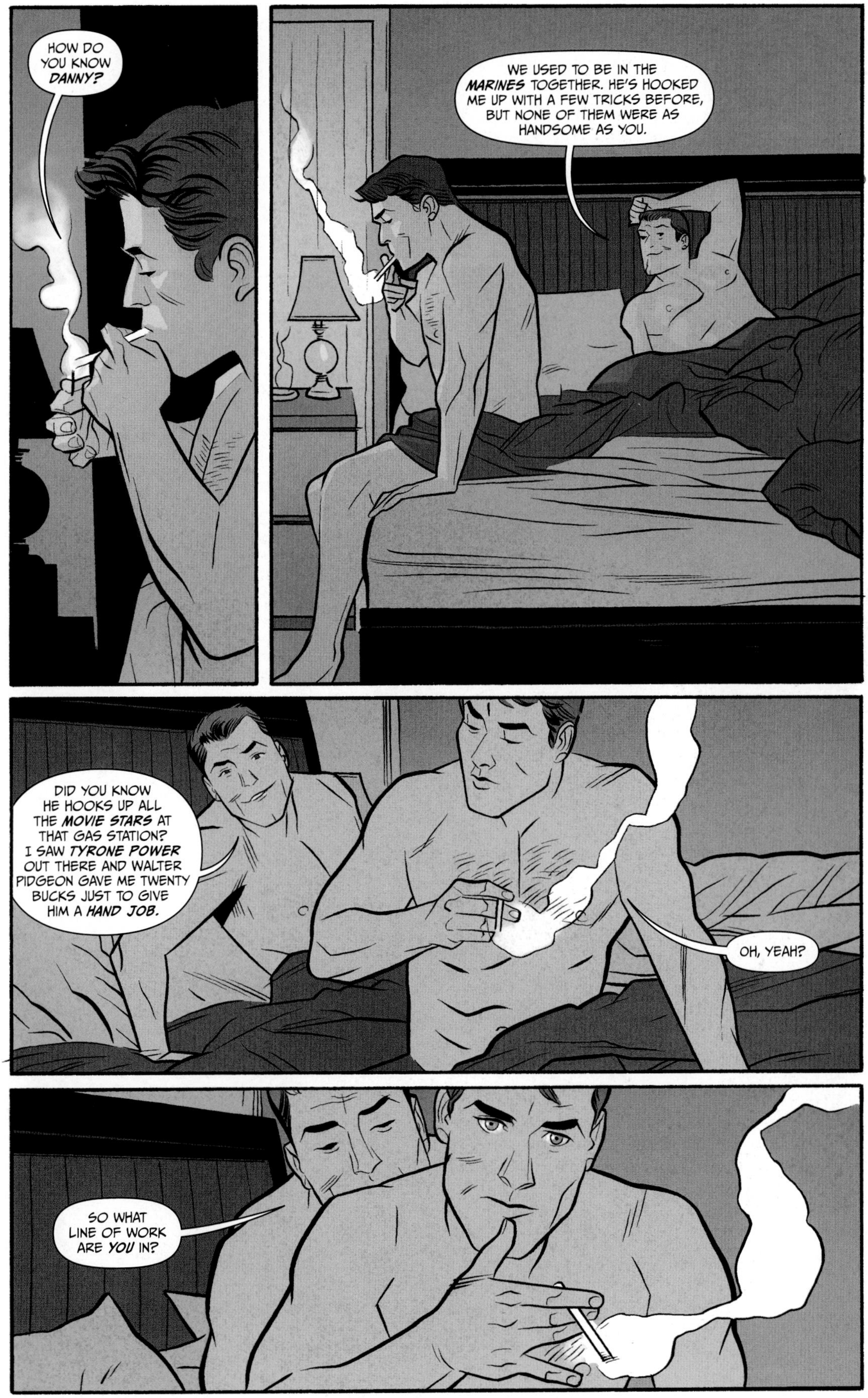
HOW DO YOU KNOW DANNY?
WE USED TO BE IN THE MARINES TOGETHER. HE'S HOOKED ME UP WITH A FEW TRICKS BEFORE, BUT NONE OF THEM WERE AS HANDSOME AS YOU.
DID YOU KNOW HE HOOKS UP ALL THE MOVIE STARS AT THAT GAS STATION? I SAW TYRONE POWER OUT THERE AND WALTER PIDGEON GAVE ME TWENTY BUCKS JUST TO GIVE HIM A HAND JOB.
OH, YEAH?
SO WHAT LINE OF WORK ARE YOU IN?

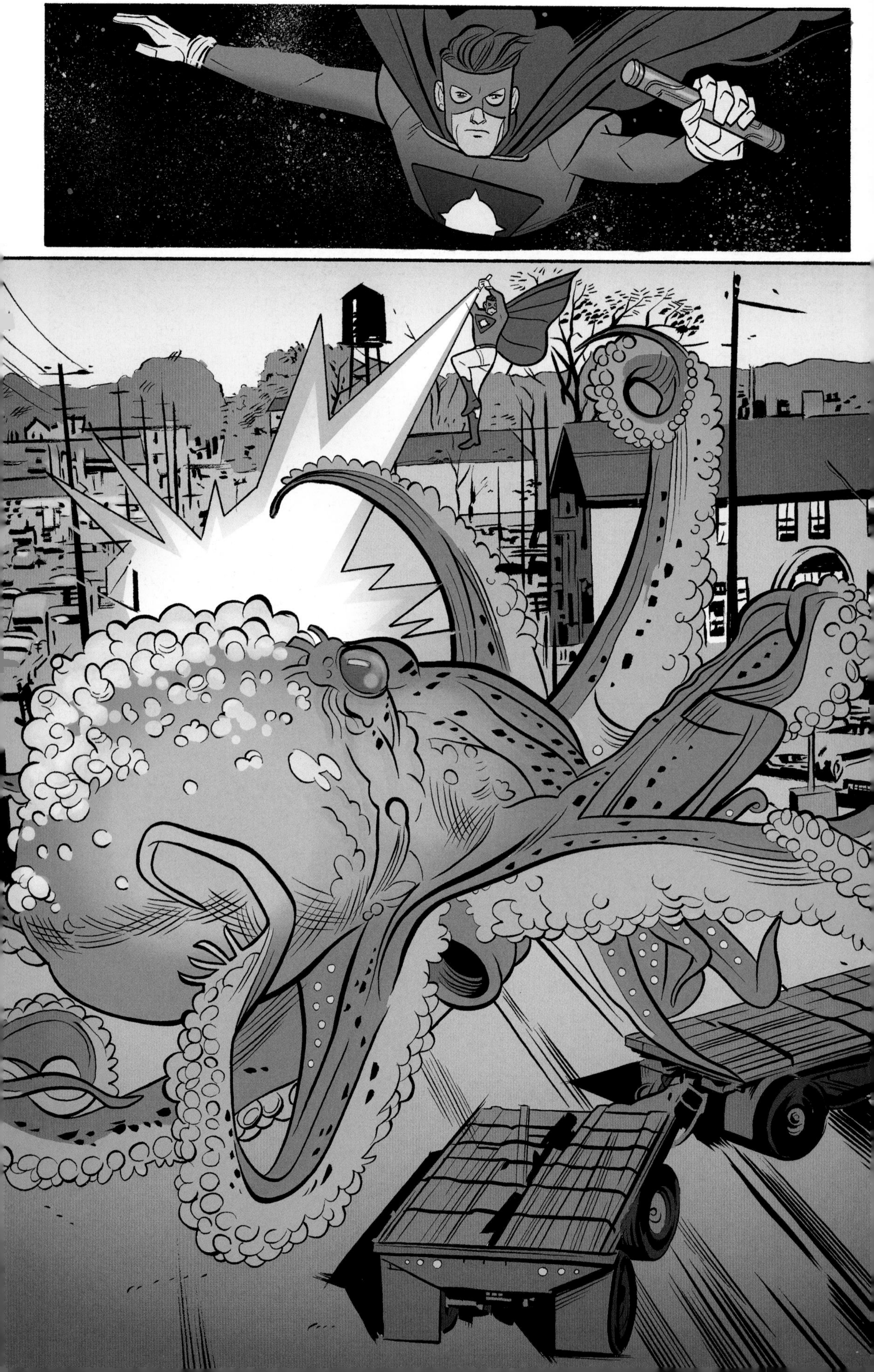

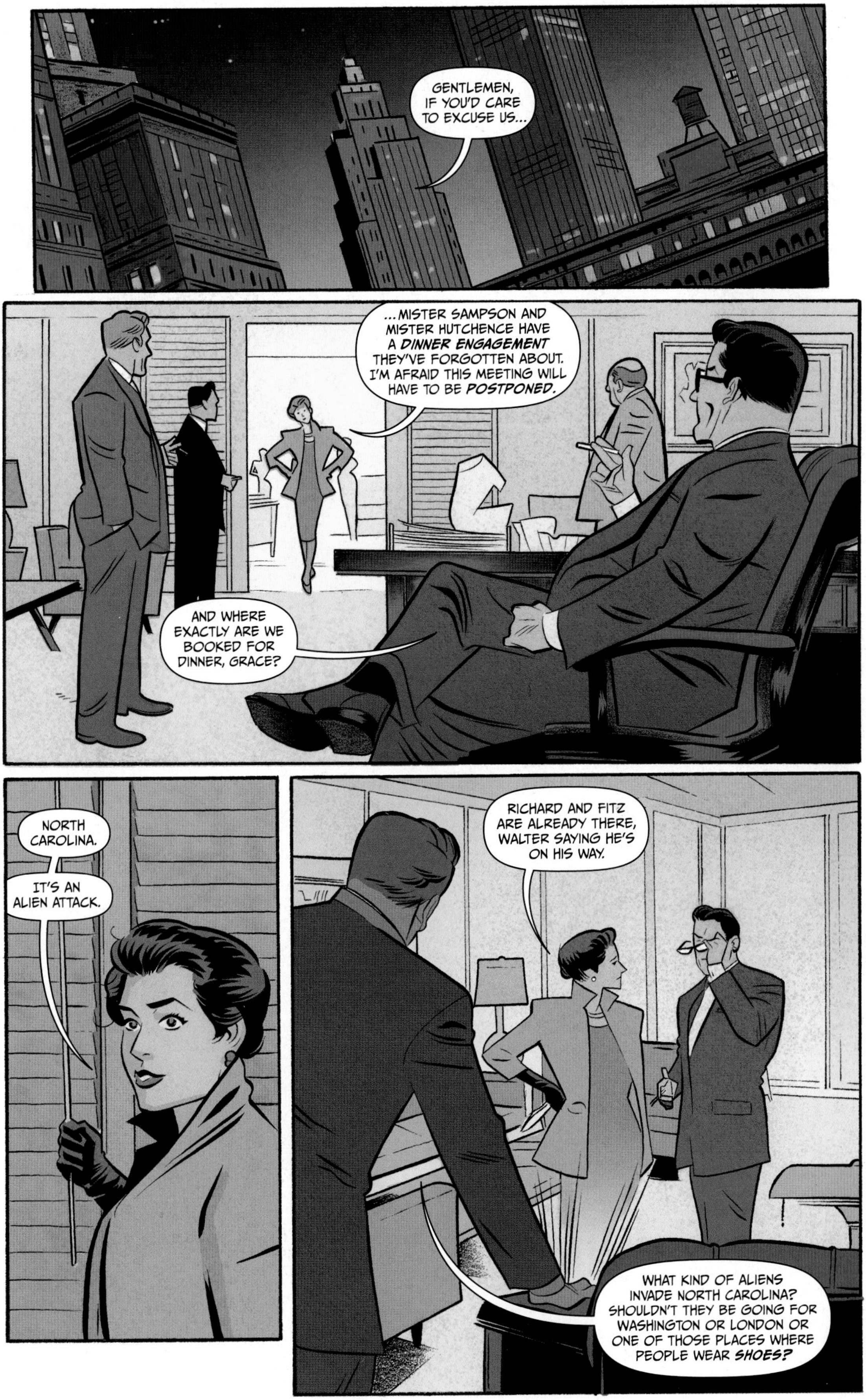
GENTLEMEN, IF YOU'D CARE TO EXCUSE US...
...MISTER SAMPSON AND MISTER HUTCHENCE HAVE A **DINNER ENGAGEMENT** THEY'VE FORGOTTEN ABOUT. I'M AFRAID THIS MEETING WILL HAVE TO BE **POSTPONED.**
AND WHERE EXACTLY ARE WE BOOKED FOR DINNER, GRACE?
NORTH CAROLINA.
IT'S AN ALIEN ATTACK.
RICHARD AND FITZ ARE ALREADY THERE, WALTER SAYING HE'S ON HIS WAY.
WHAT KIND OF ALIENS INVADE NORTH CAROLINA? SHOULDN'T THEY BE GOING FOR WASHINGTON OR LONDON OR ONE OF THOSE PLACES WHERE PEOPLE WEAR **SHOES?**

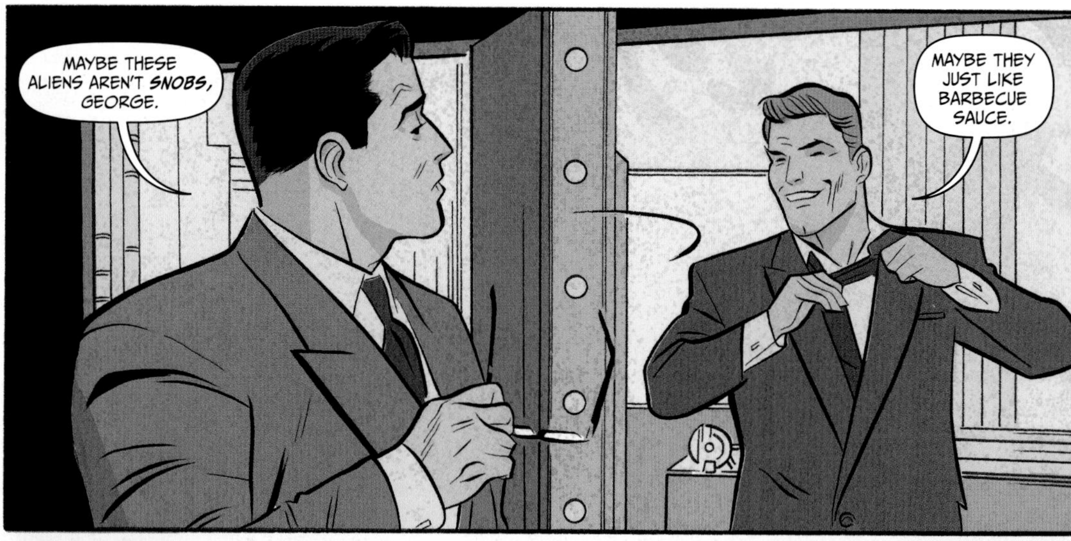
MAYBE THESE ALIENS AREN'T *SNOBS,* GEORGE.
MAYBE THEY JUST LIKE BARBECUE SAUCE.

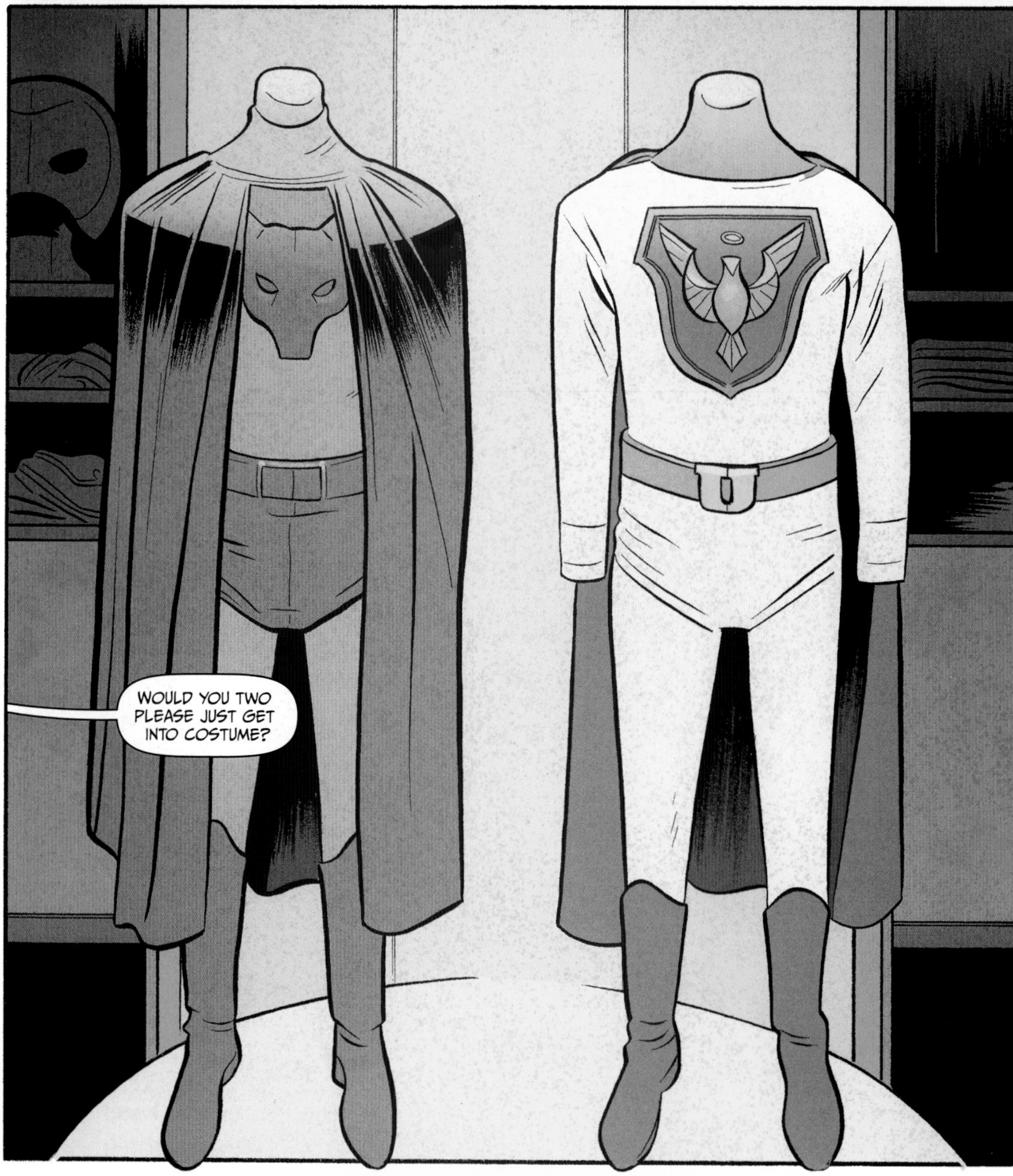
WOULD YOU TWO PLEASE JUST GET INTO COSTUME?

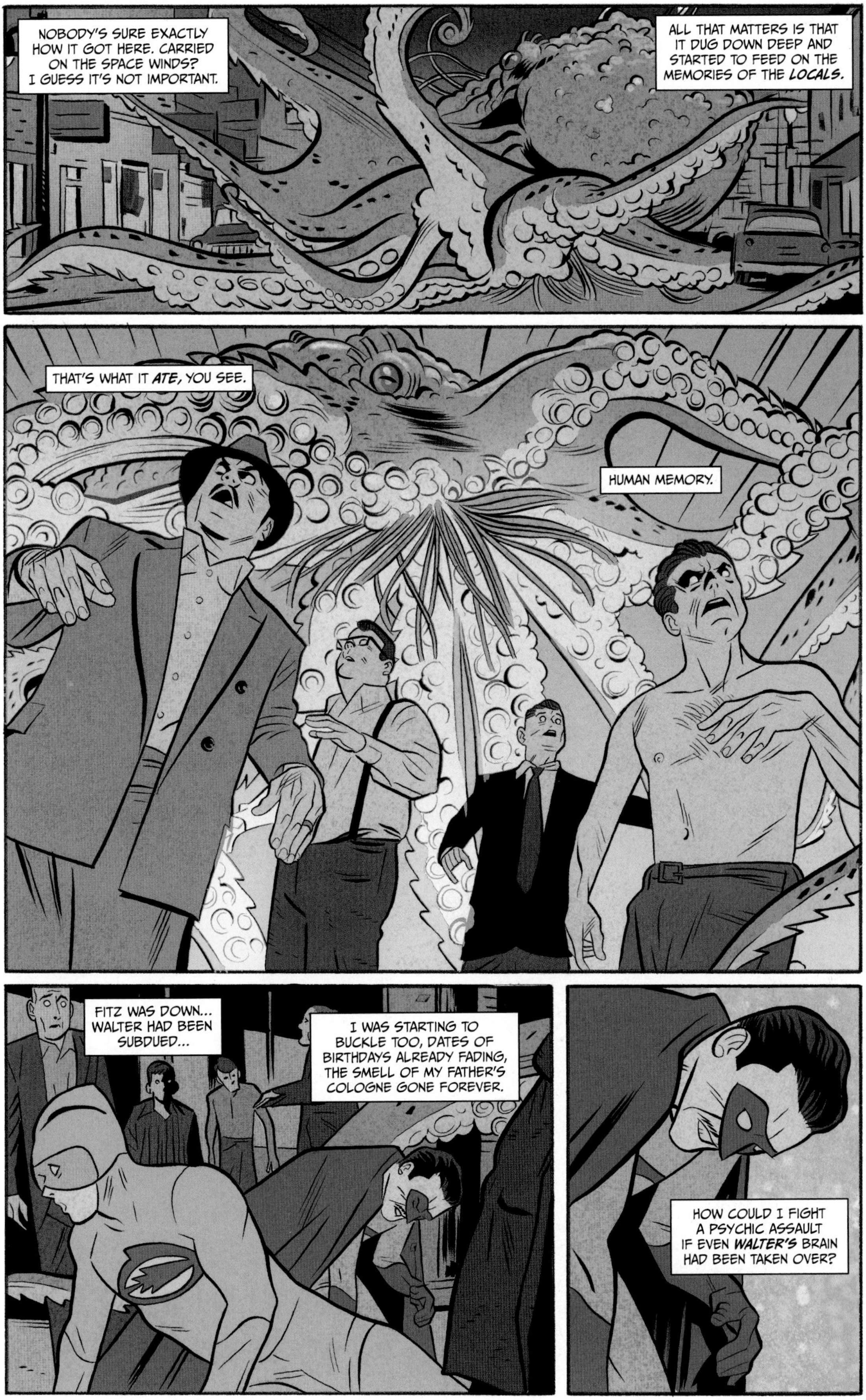
NOBODY'S SURE EXACTLY HOW IT GOT HERE. CARRIED ON THE SPACE WINDS? I GUESS IT'S NOT IMPORTANT.
ALL THAT MATTERS IS THAT IT DUG DOWN DEEP AND STARTED TO FEED ON THE MEMORIES OF THE LOCALS.
THAT'S WHAT IT ATE, YOU SEE.
HUMAN MEMORY.
FITZ WAS DOWN... WALTER HAD BEEN SUBDUED...
I WAS STARTING TO BUCKLE TOO, DATES OF BIRTHDAYS ALREADY FADING, THE SMELL OF MY FATHER'S COLOGNE GONE FOREVER.
HOW COULD I FIGHT A PSYCHIC ASSAULT IF EVEN WALTER'S BRAIN HAD BEEN TAKEN OVER?

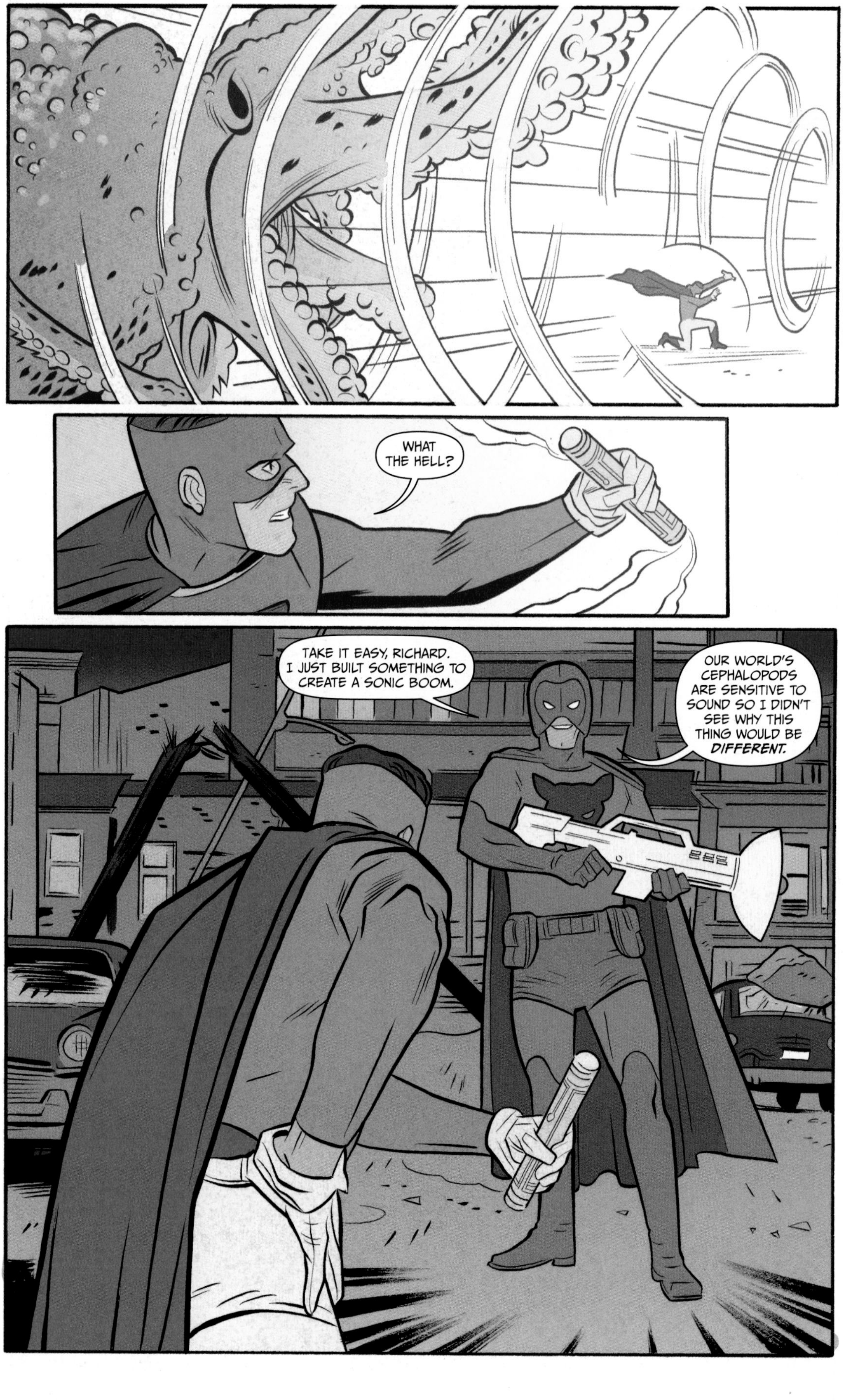
WHAT THE HELL?
TAKE IT EASY, RICHARD. I JUST BUILT SOMETHING TO CREATE A SONIC BOOM.
OUR WORLD'S CEPHALOPODS ARE SENSITIVE TO SOUND SO I DIDN'T SEE WHY THIS THING WOULD BE *DIFFERENT.*

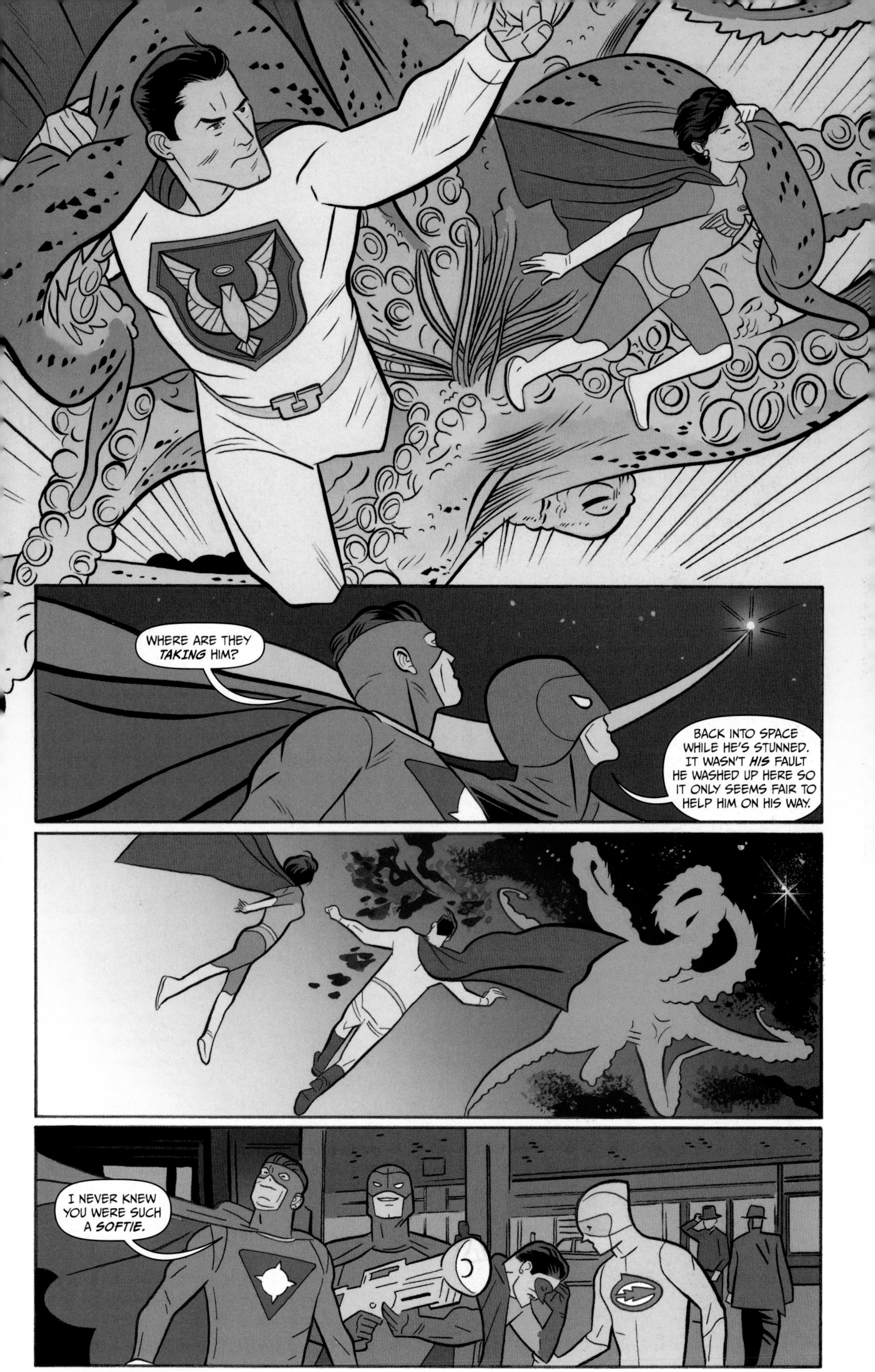
WHERE ARE THEY *TAKING* HIM?
BACK INTO SPACE WHILE HE'S STUNNED. IT WASN'T *HIS* FAULT HE WASHED UP HERE SO IT ONLY SEEMS FAIR TO HELP HIM ON HIS WAY.
I NEVER KNEW YOU WERE SUCH A *SOFTIE.*

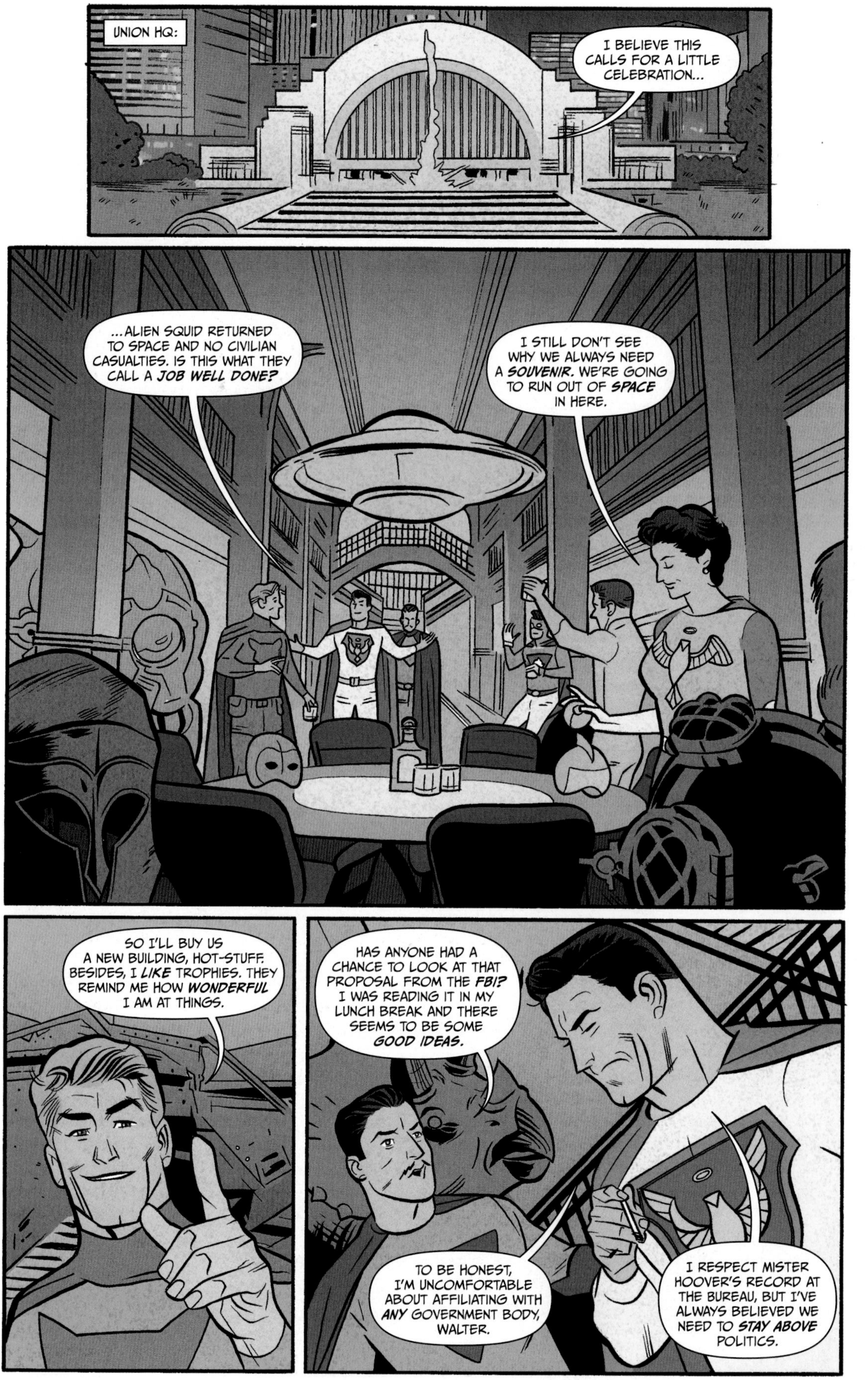
UNION HQ:
I BELIEVE THIS CALLS FOR A LITTLE CELEBRATION...
...ALIEN SQUID RETURNED TO SPACE AND NO CIVILIAN CASUALTIES. IS THIS WHAT THEY CALL A JOB WELL DONE?
I STILL DON'T SEE WHY WE ALWAYS NEED A SOUVENIR. WE'RE GOING TO RUN OUT OF SPACE IN HERE.
SO I'LL BUY US A NEW BUILDING, HOT-STUFF. BESIDES, I LIKE TROPHIES. THEY REMIND ME HOW WONDERFUL I AM AT THINGS.
HAS ANYONE HAD A CHANCE TO LOOK AT THAT PROPOSAL FROM THE FBI? I WAS READING IT IN MY LUNCH BREAK AND THERE SEEMS TO BE SOME GOOD IDEAS.
TO BE HONEST, I'M UNCOMFORTABLE ABOUT AFFILIATING WITH ANY GOVERNMENT BODY, WALTER.
I RESPECT MISTER HOOVER'S RECORD AT THE BUREAU, BUT I'VE ALWAYS BELIEVED WE NEED TO STAY ABOVE POLITICS.

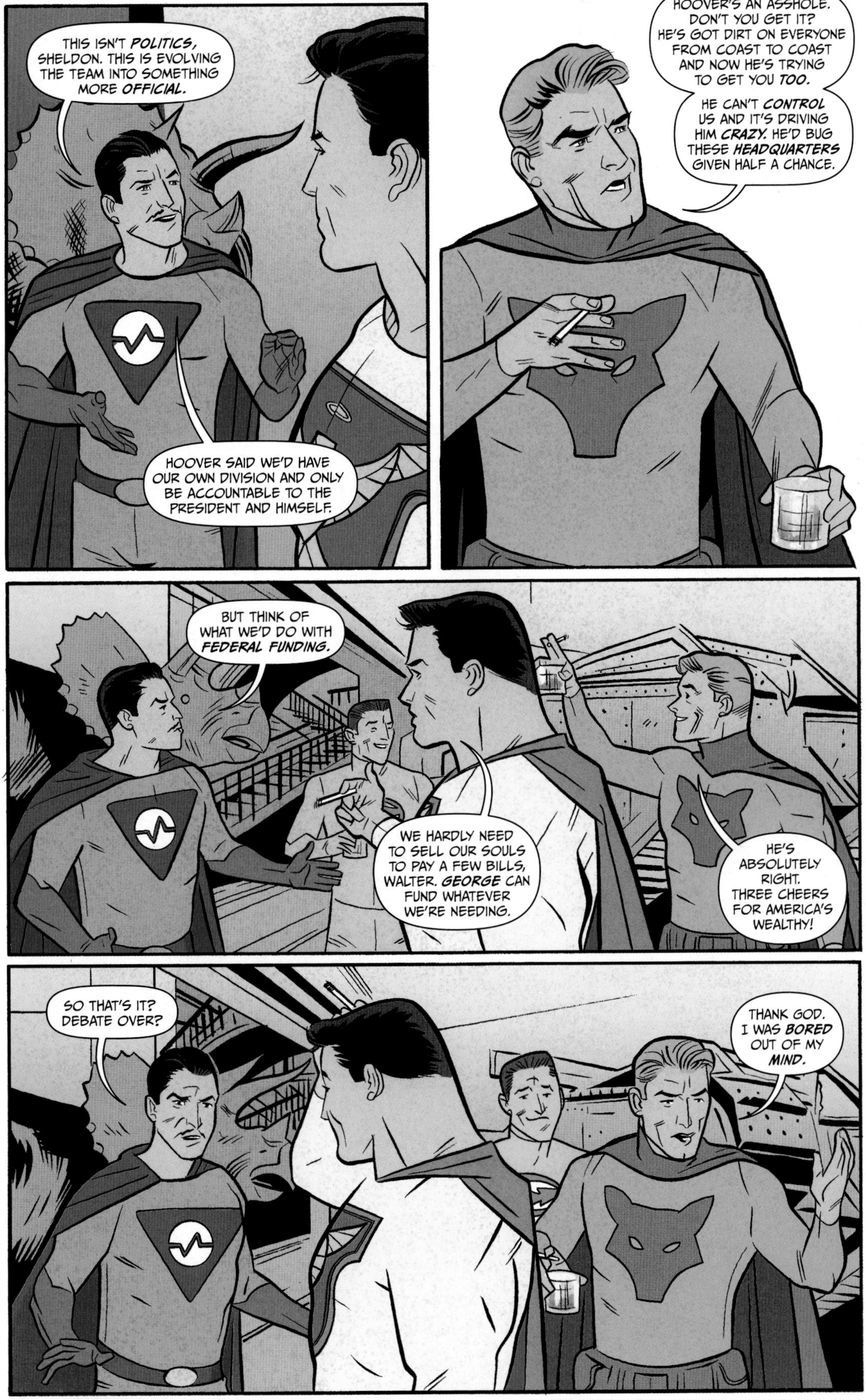
THIS ISN'T *POLITICS*, SHELDON. THIS IS EVOLVING THE TEAM INTO SOMETHING MORE *OFFICIAL*.
HOOVER SAID WE'D HAVE OUR OWN DIVISION AND ONLY BE ACCOUNTABLE TO THE PRESIDENT AND HIMSELF.
HOOVER'S AN ASSHOLE. DON'T YOU GET IT? HE'S GOT DIRT ON EVERYONE FROM COAST TO COAST AND NOW HE'S TRYING TO GET YOU *TOO*.
HE CAN'T *CONTROL* US AND IT'S DRIVING HIM *CRAZY*. HE'D BUG THESE *HEADQUARTERS* GIVEN HALF A CHANCE.
BUT THINK OF WHAT WE'D DO WITH *FEDERAL FUNDING*.
WE HARDLY NEED TO SELL OUR SOULS TO PAY A FEW BILLS, WALTER. *GEORGE* CAN FUND WHATEVER WE'RE NEEDING.
HE'S ABSOLUTELY RIGHT. THREE CHEERS FOR AMERICA'S WEALTHY!
SO THAT'S IT? DEBATE OVER?
THANK GOD. I WAS *BORED* OUT OF MY *MIND*.

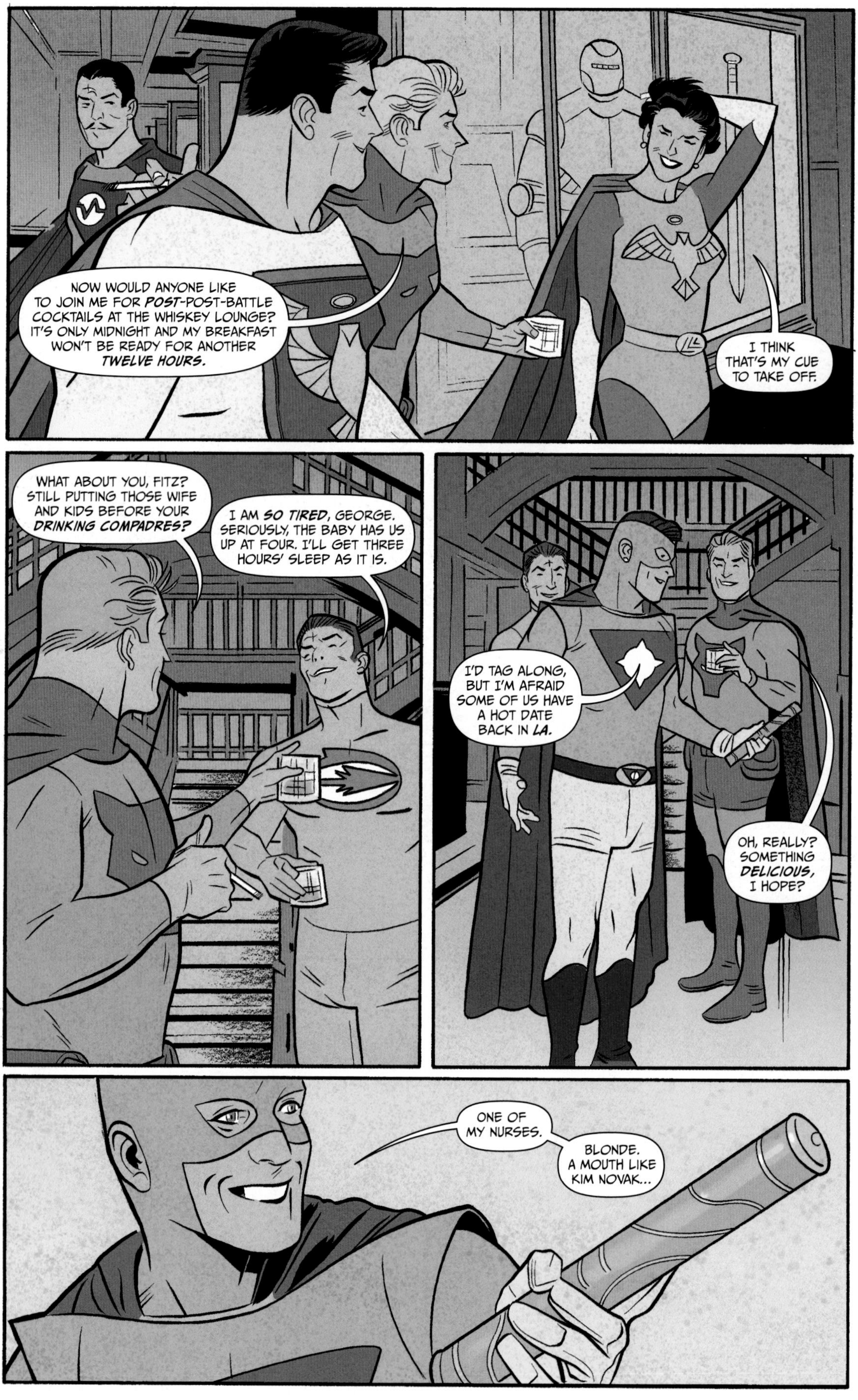
NOW WOULD ANYONE LIKE TO JOIN ME FOR POST-POST-BATTLE COCKTAILS AT THE WHISKEY LOUNGE? IT'S ONLY MIDNIGHT AND MY BREAKFAST WON'T BE READY FOR ANOTHER TWELVE HOURS.
I THINK THAT'S MY CUE TO TAKE OFF.
WHAT ABOUT YOU, FITZ? STILL PUTTING THOSE WIFE AND KIDS BEFORE YOUR DRINKING COMPADRES?
I AM SO TIRED, GEORGE. SERIOUSLY, THE BABY HAS US UP AT FOUR. I'LL GET THREE HOURS' SLEEP AS IT IS.
I'D TAG ALONG, BUT I'M AFRAID SOME OF US HAVE A HOT DATE BACK IN LA.
OH, REALLY? SOMETHING DELICIOUS, I HOPE?
ONE OF MY NURSES.
BLONDE. A MOUTH LIKE KIM NOVAK...

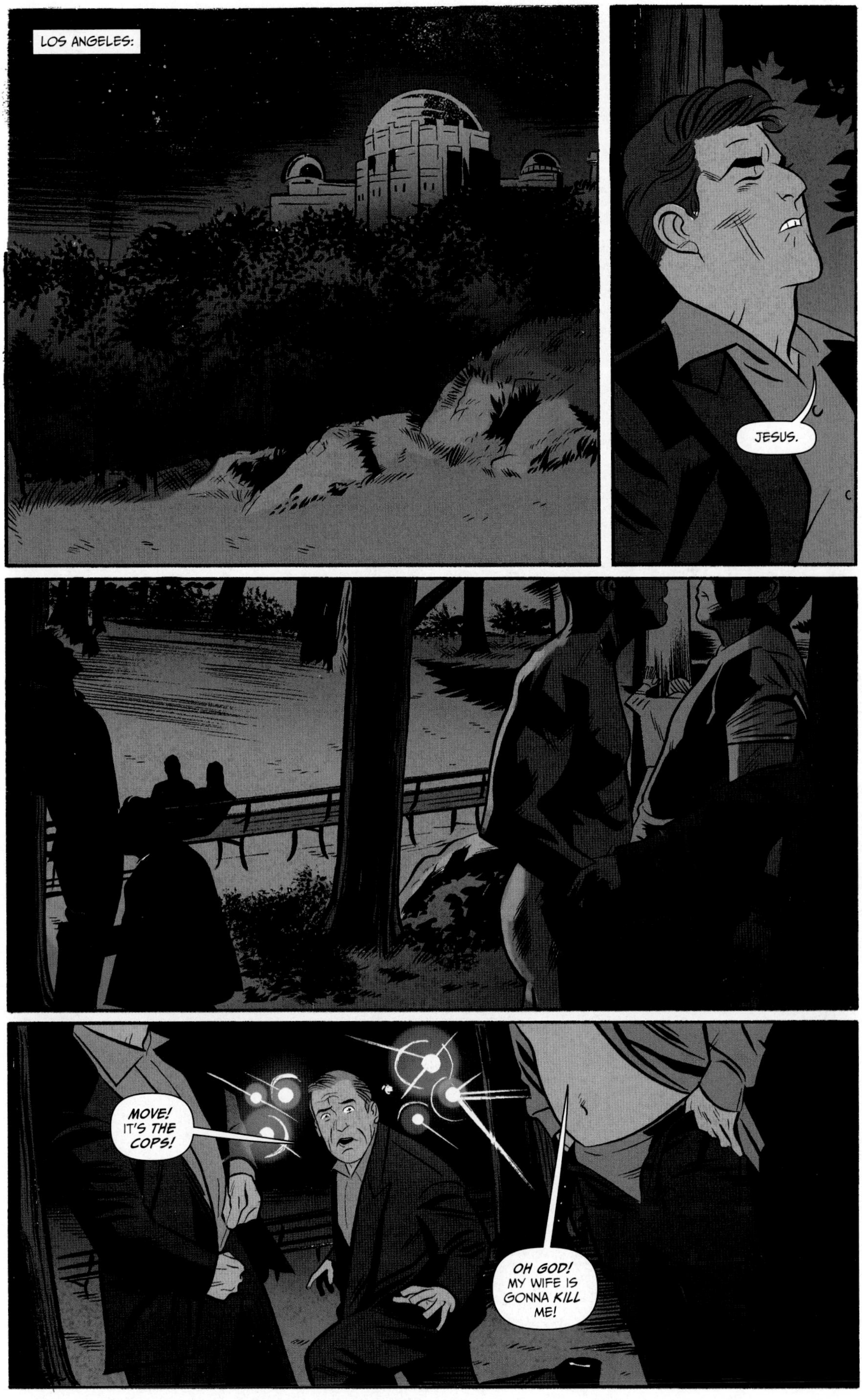
LOS ANGELES:
JESUS.
MOVE! IT'S THE COPS!
OH GOD! MY WIFE IS GONNA KILL ME!

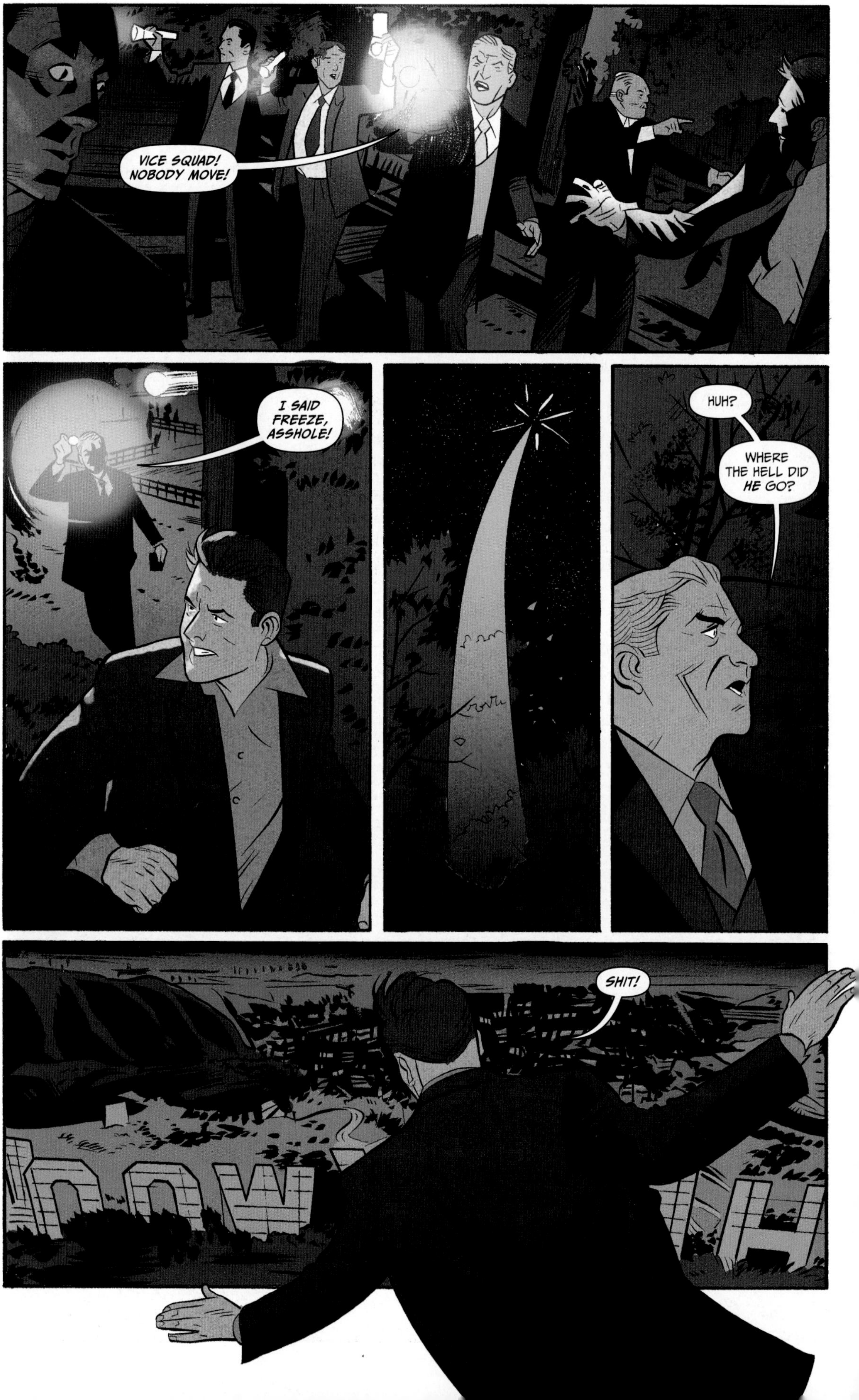
VICE SQUAD! NOBODY MOVE!
I SAID FREEZE, ASSHOLE!
HUH?
WHERE THE HELL DID HE GO?
SHIT!

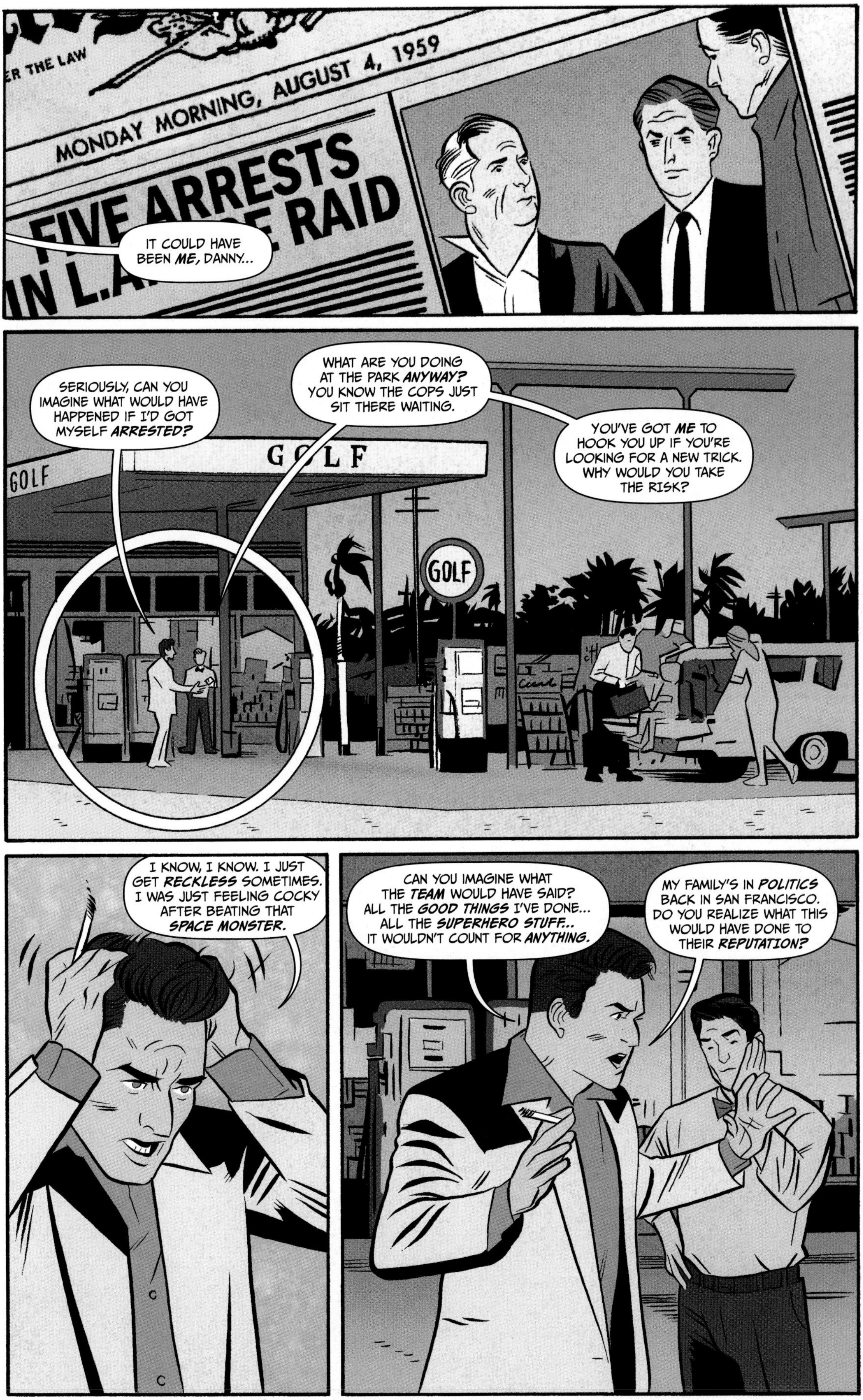

MONDAY MORNING, AUGUST 4, 1959
FIVE ARRESTS
RAID
IT COULD HAVE BEEN *ME,* DANNY...
SERIOUSLY, CAN YOU IMAGINE WHAT WOULD HAVE HAPPENED IF I'D GOT MYSELF *ARRESTED?*
WHAT ARE YOU DOING AT THE PARK *ANYWAY?* YOU KNOW THE COPS JUST SIT THERE WAITING.
YOU'VE GOT *ME* TO HOOK YOU UP IF YOU'RE LOOKING FOR A NEW TRICK. WHY WOULD YOU TAKE THE RISK?
GOLF
GOLF
GOLF
I KNOW, I KNOW. I JUST GET *RECKLESS* SOMETIMES. I WAS JUST FEELING COCKY AFTER BEATING THAT *SPACE MONSTER.*
CAN YOU IMAGINE WHAT THE *TEAM* WOULD HAVE SAID? ALL THE *GOOD THINGS* I'VE DONE... ALL THE *SUPERHERO STUFF...* IT WOULDN'T COUNT FOR *ANYTHING.*
MY FAMILY'S IN *POLITICS* BACK IN SAN FRANCISCO. DO YOU REALIZE WHAT THIS WOULD HAVE DONE TO THEIR *REPUTATION?*

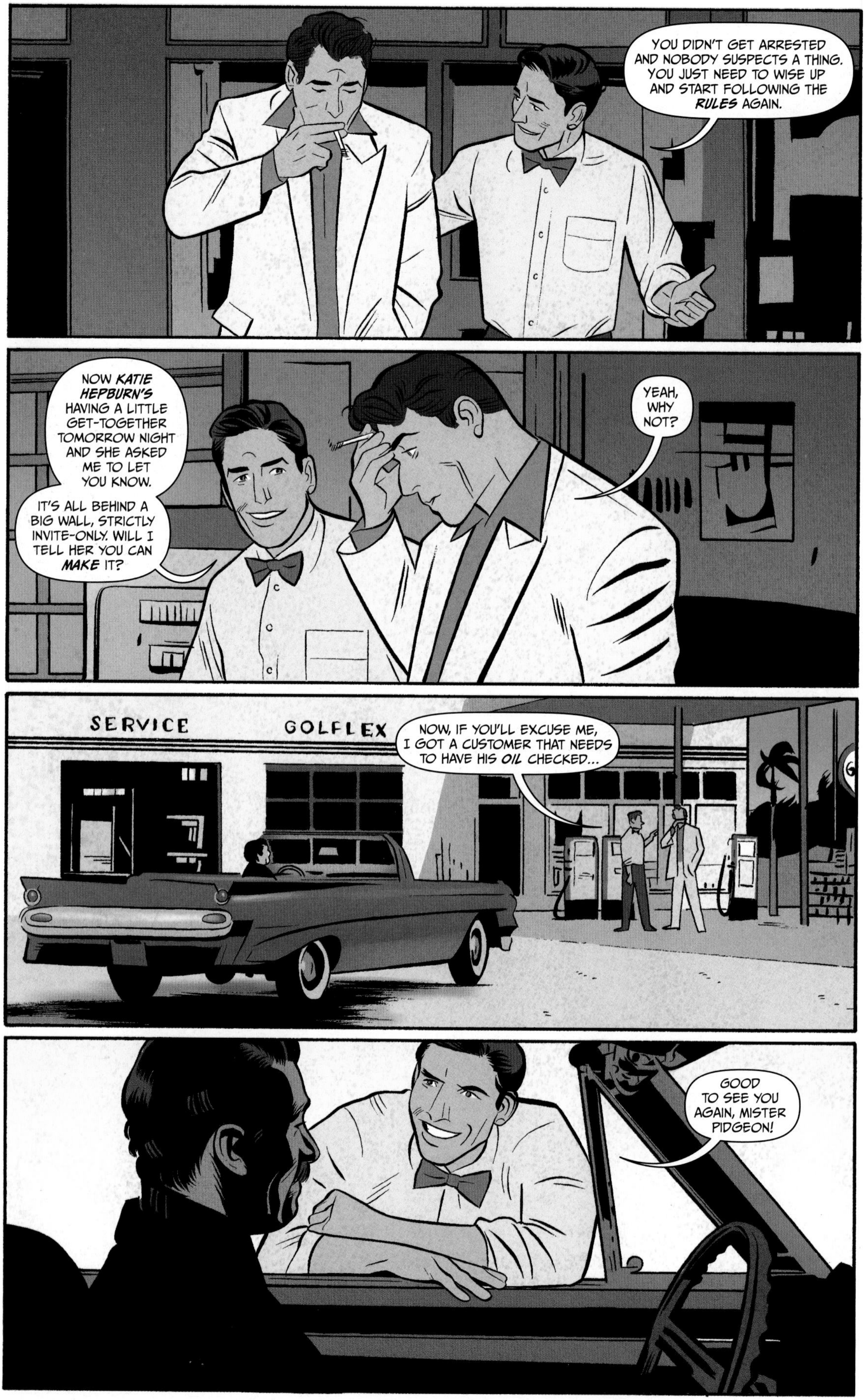
YOU DIDN'T GET ARRESTED AND NOBODY SUSPECTS A THING. YOU JUST NEED TO WISE UP AND START FOLLOWING THE *RULES* AGAIN.
NOW *KATIE HEPBURN'S* HAVING A LITTLE GET-TOGETHER TOMORROW NIGHT AND SHE ASKED ME TO LET YOU KNOW.
IT'S ALL BEHIND A BIG WALL, STRICTLY INVITE-ONLY. WILL I TELL HER YOU CAN *MAKE* IT?
YEAH, WHY NOT?
SERVICE
GOLFLEX
NOW, IF YOU'LL EXCUSE ME, I GOT A CUSTOMER THAT NEEDS TO HAVE HIS *OIL* CHECKED...
GOOD TO SEE YOU AGAIN, MISTER PIDGEON!

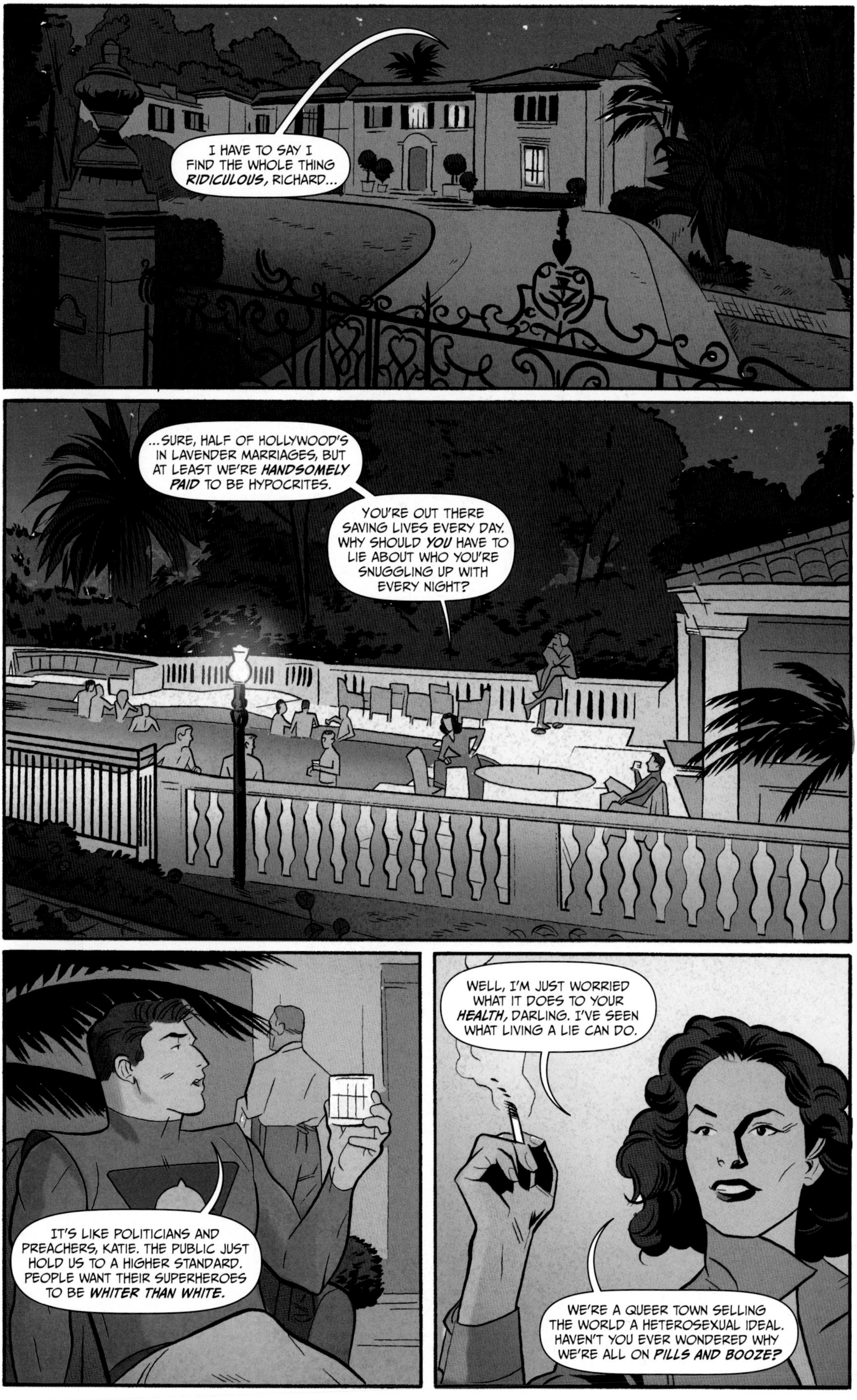
I HAVE TO SAY I FIND THE WHOLE THING RIDICULOUS, RICHARD...
...SURE, HALF OF HOLLYWOOD'S IN LAVENDER MARRIAGES, BUT AT LEAST WE'RE HANDSOMELY PAID TO BE HYPOCRITES.
YOU'RE OUT THERE SAVING LIVES EVERY DAY. WHY SHOULD YOU HAVE TO LIE ABOUT WHO YOU'RE SNUGGLING UP WITH EVERY NIGHT?
IT'S LIKE POLITICIANS AND PREACHERS, KATIE. THE PUBLIC JUST HOLD US TO A HIGHER STANDARD. PEOPLE WANT THEIR SUPERHEROES TO BE WHITER THAN WHITE.
WELL, I'M JUST WORRIED WHAT IT DOES TO YOUR HEALTH, DARLING. I'VE SEEN WHAT LIVING A LIE CAN DO.
WE'RE A QUEER TOWN SELLING THE WORLD A HETEROSEXUAL IDEAL. HAVEN'T YOU EVER WONDERED WHY WE'RE ALL ON PILLS AND BOOZE?

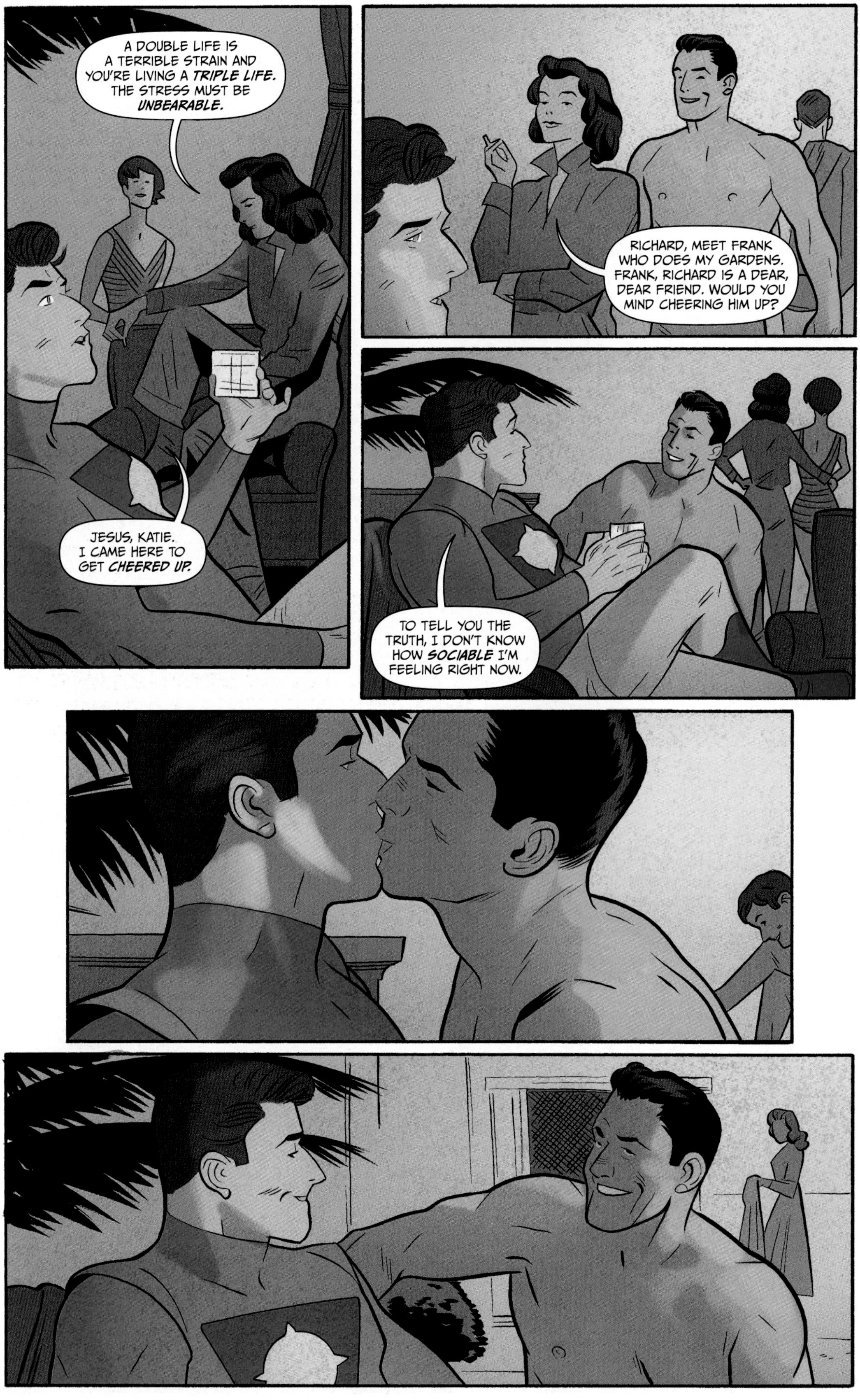
A DOUBLE LIFE IS A TERRIBLE STRAIN AND YOU'RE LIVING A TRIPLE LIFE. THE STRESS MUST BE UNBEARABLE.
JESUS, KATIE. I CAME HERE TO GET CHEERED UP.
RICHARD, MEET FRANK WHO DOES MY GARDENS. FRANK, RICHARD IS A DEAR, DEAR FRIEND. WOULD YOU MIND CHEERING HIM UP?
TO TELL YOU THE TRUTH, I DON'T KNOW HOW SOCIABLE I'M FEELING RIGHT NOW.

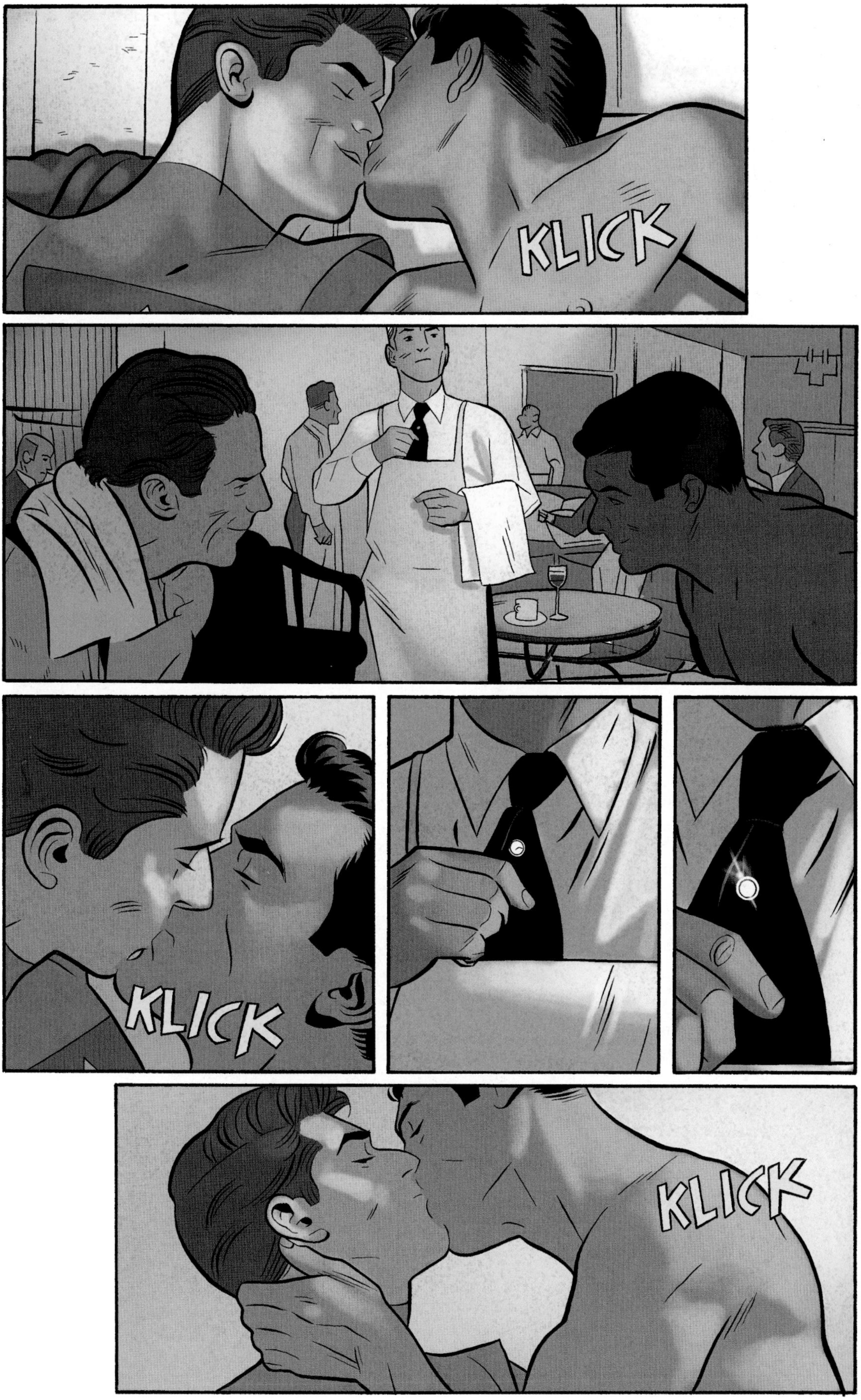
KLICK
KLICK
KLICK

ST THOMAS' HOSPITAL:

DOCTOR CONRAD, I'M FEDERAL AGENT CLYDE TOLSON. DIRECTOR HOOVER ASKED ME TO LET YOU KNOW HE'S WAITING FOR YOU IN YOUR OFFICE.

WHAT?

WELL, *SOMEBODY'S* BEEN A NAUGHTY BOY.

I WONDER WHAT YOUR FRIENDS ON THE TEAM WOULD THINK IF THEY SAW ALL THE DISGUSTING THINGS YOU'VE BEEN GETTING UP TO IN YOUR SPARE TIME.

OH MY GOD.

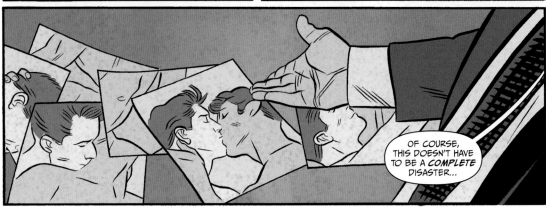

OF COURSE, THIS DOESN'T HAVE TO BE A *COMPLETE* DISASTER...

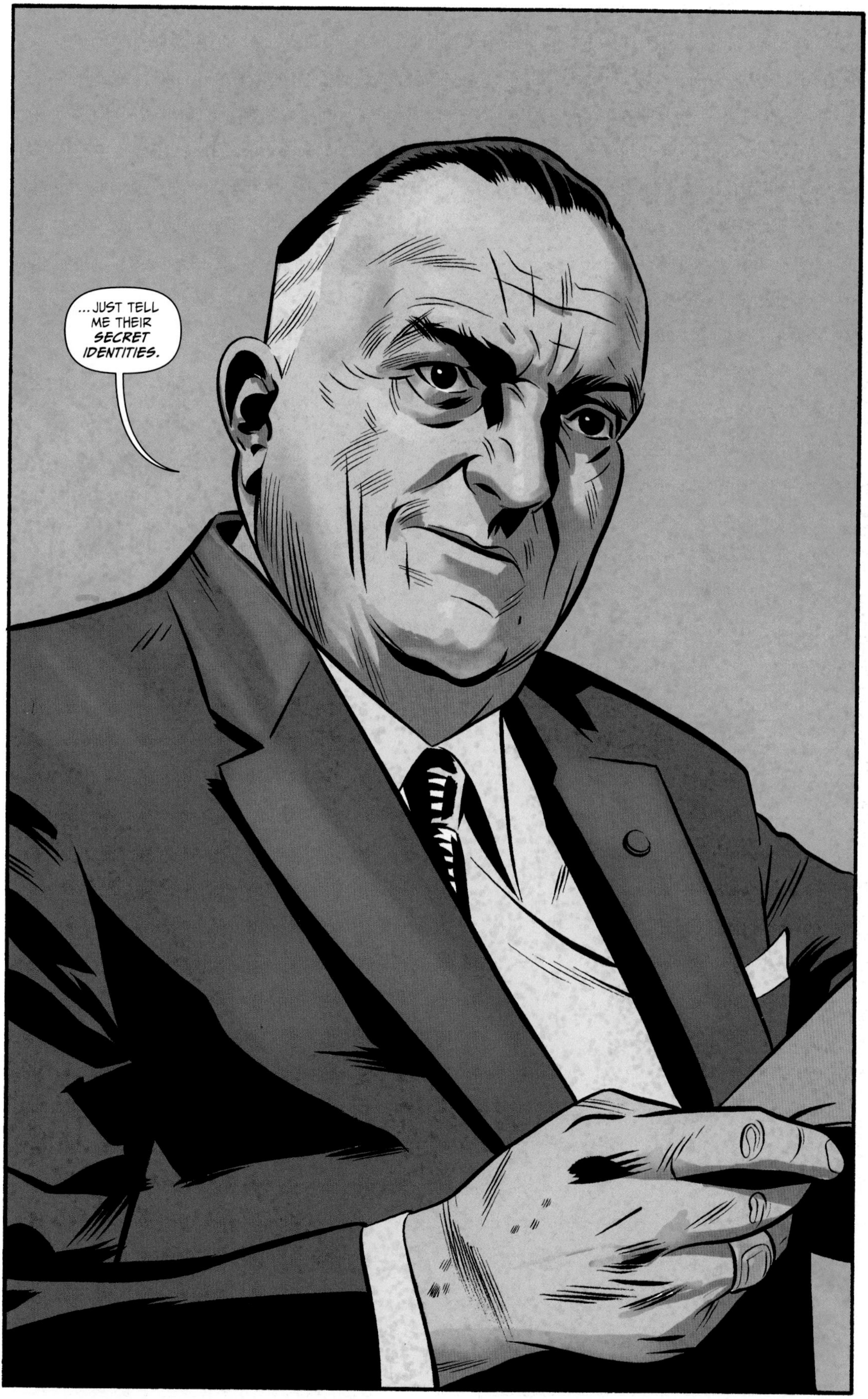
...JUST TELL ME THEIR *SECRET IDENTITIES.*

CHAPTER 2

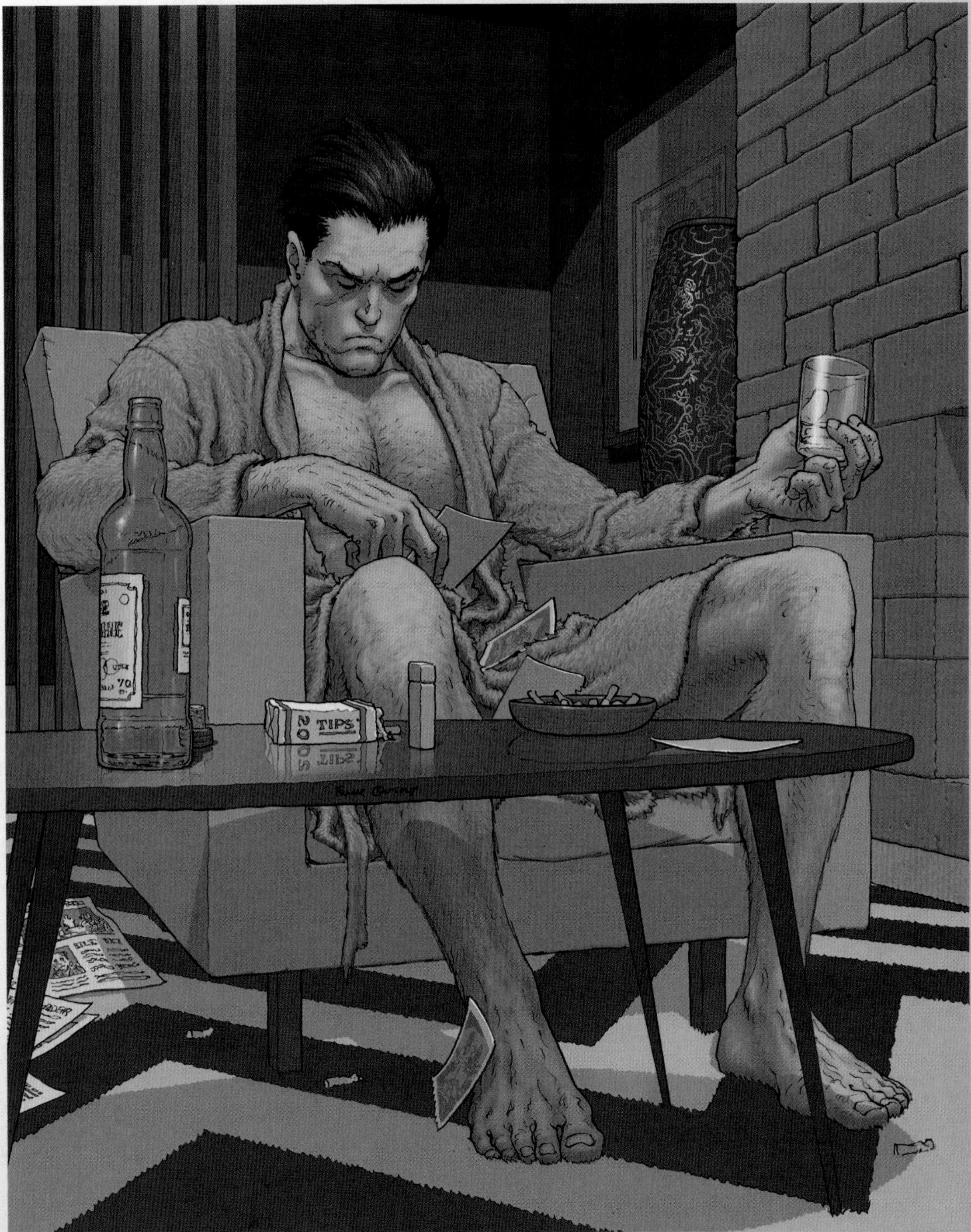
20 TIPS

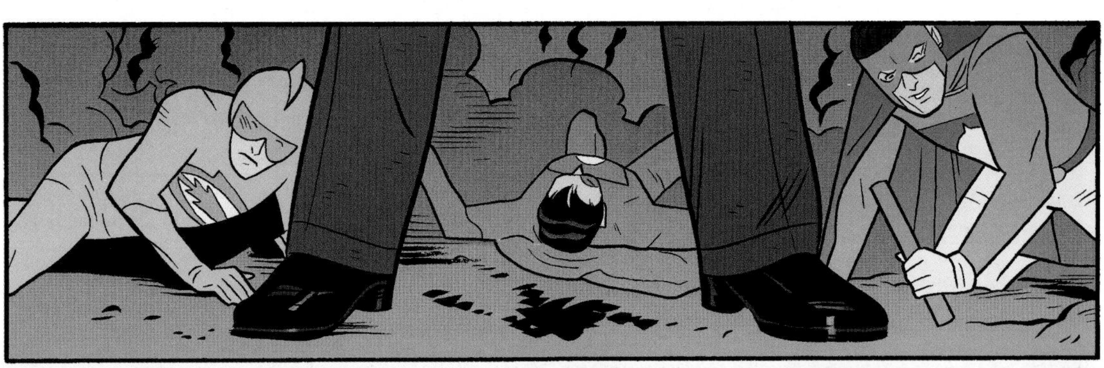

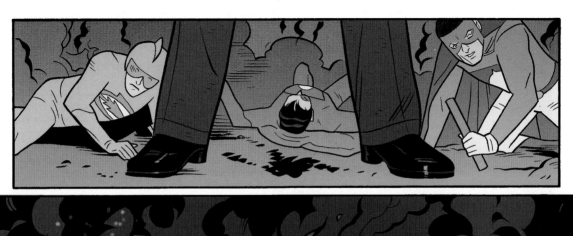

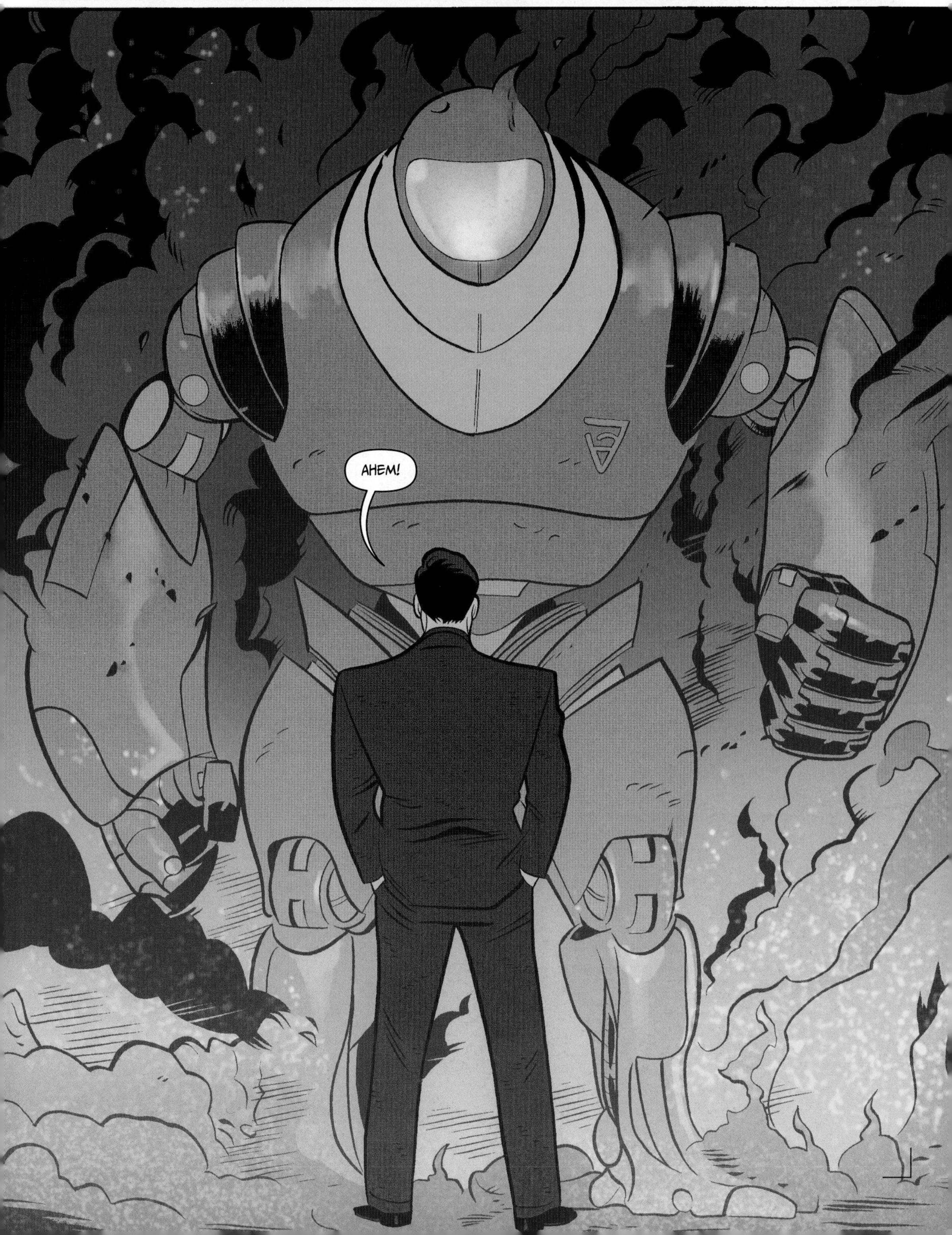
AHEM!

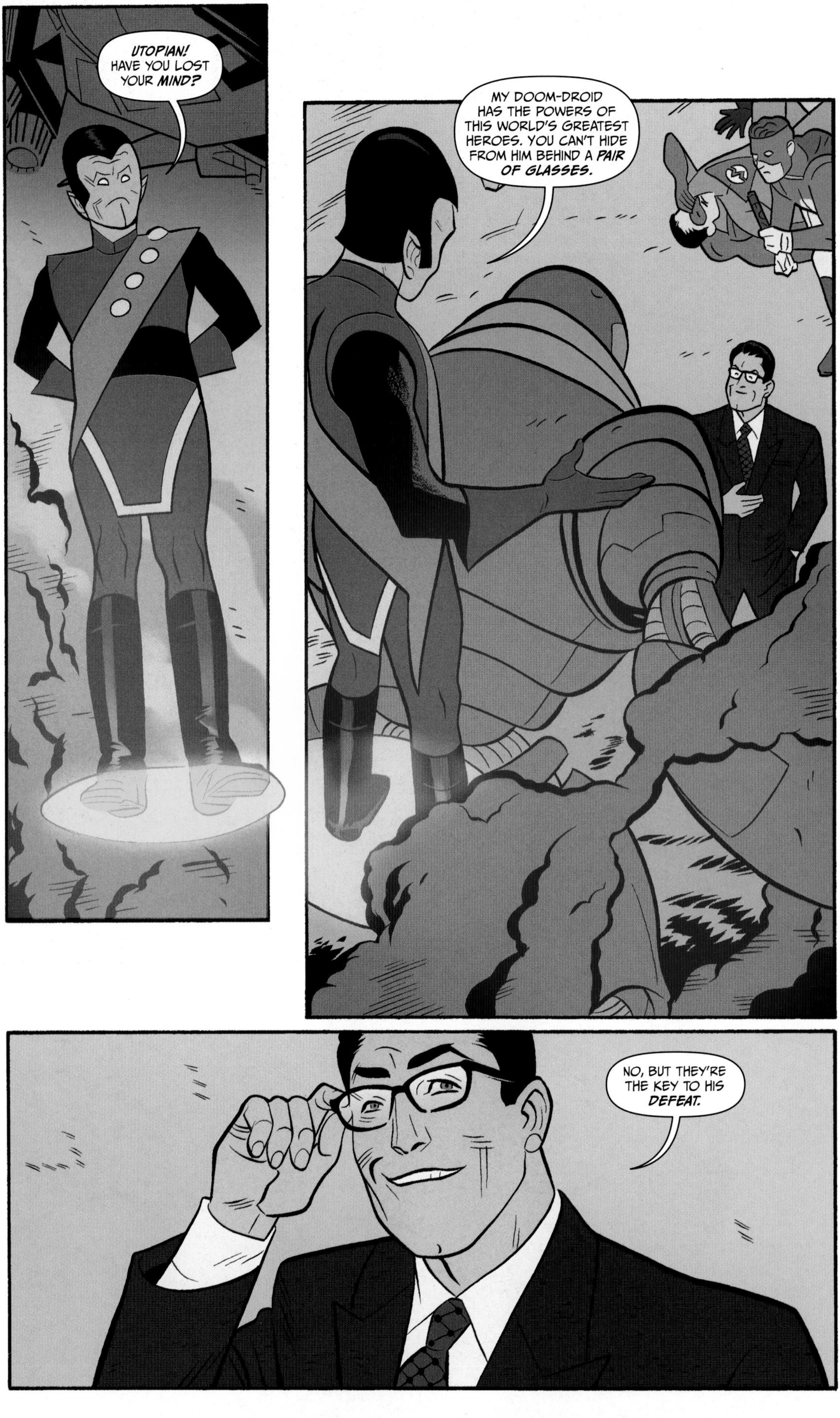
UTOPIAN! HAVE YOU LOST YOUR MIND?
MY DOOM-DROID HAS THE POWERS OF THIS WORLD'S GREATEST HEROES. YOU CAN'T HIDE FROM HIM BEHIND A PAIR OF GLASSES.
NO, BUT THEY'RE THE KEY TO HIS DEFEAT.

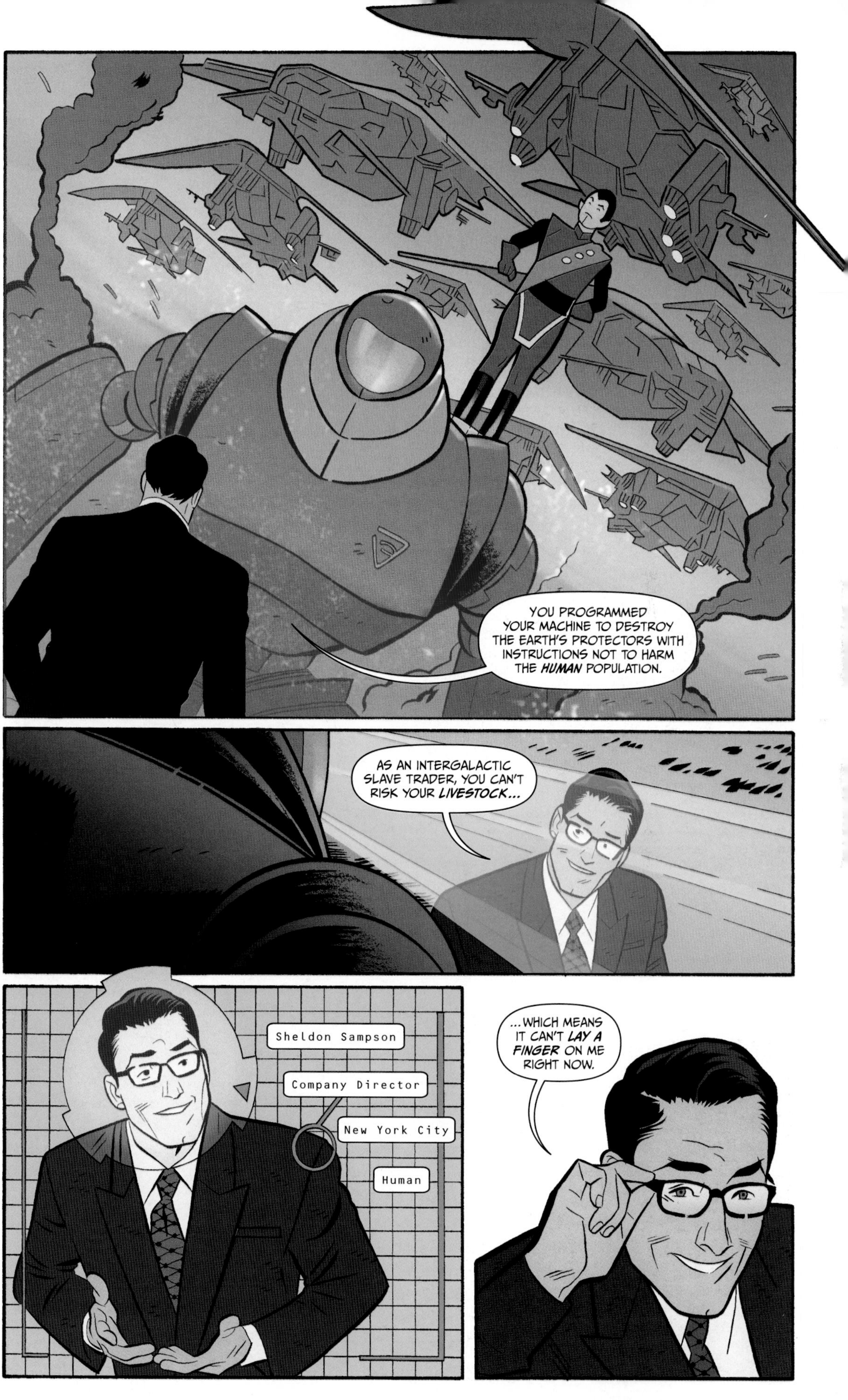
YOU PROGRAMMED YOUR MACHINE TO DESTROY THE EARTH'S PROTECTORS WITH INSTRUCTIONS NOT TO HARM THE *HUMAN* POPULATION.
AS AN INTERGALACTIC SLAVE TRADER, YOU CAN'T RISK YOUR *LIVESTOCK*...
Sheldon Sampson
Company Director
New York City
Human
...WHICH MEANS IT CAN'T *LAY A FINGER* ON ME RIGHT NOW.

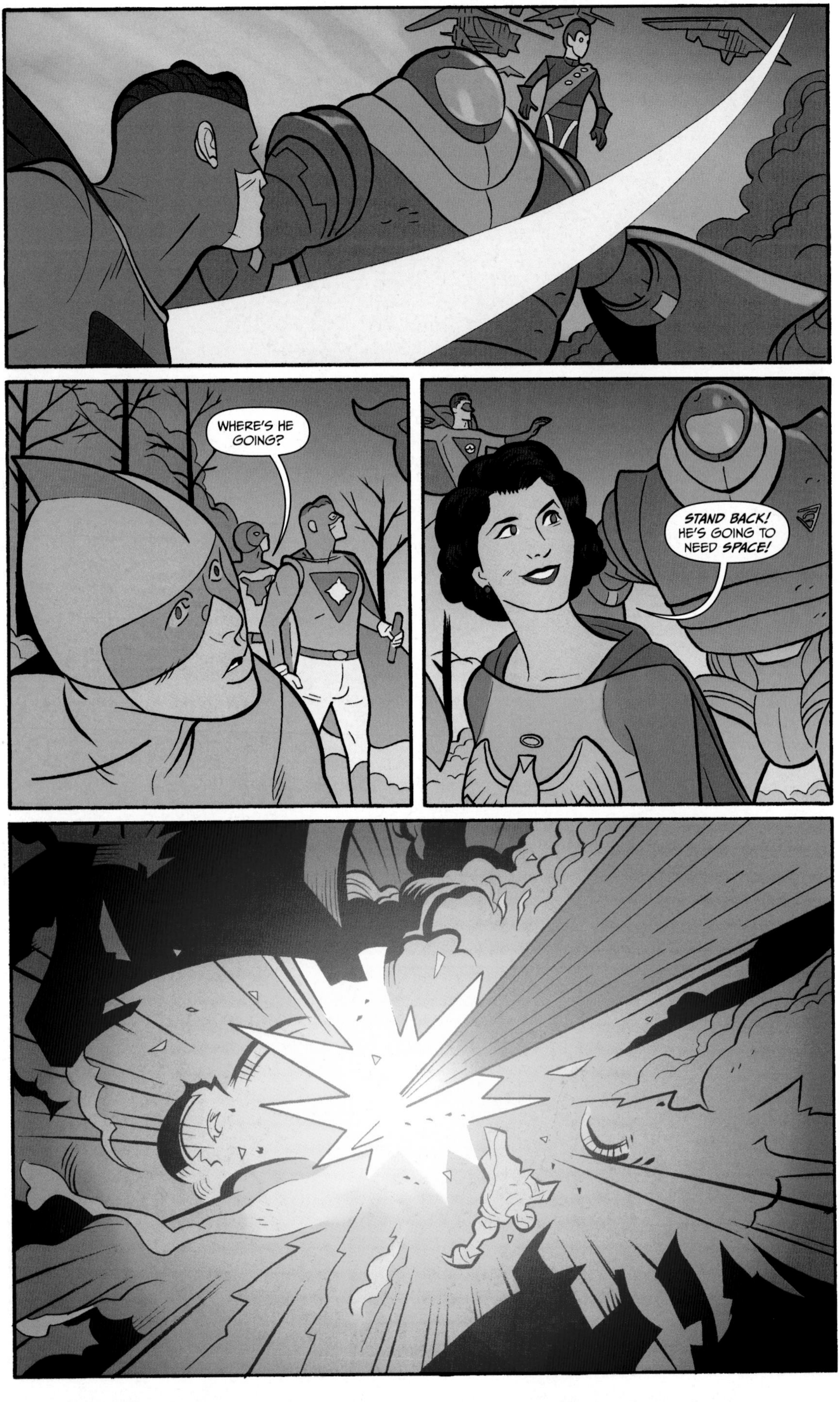
WHERE'S HE GOING?
STAND BACK! HE'S GOING TO NEED SPACE!

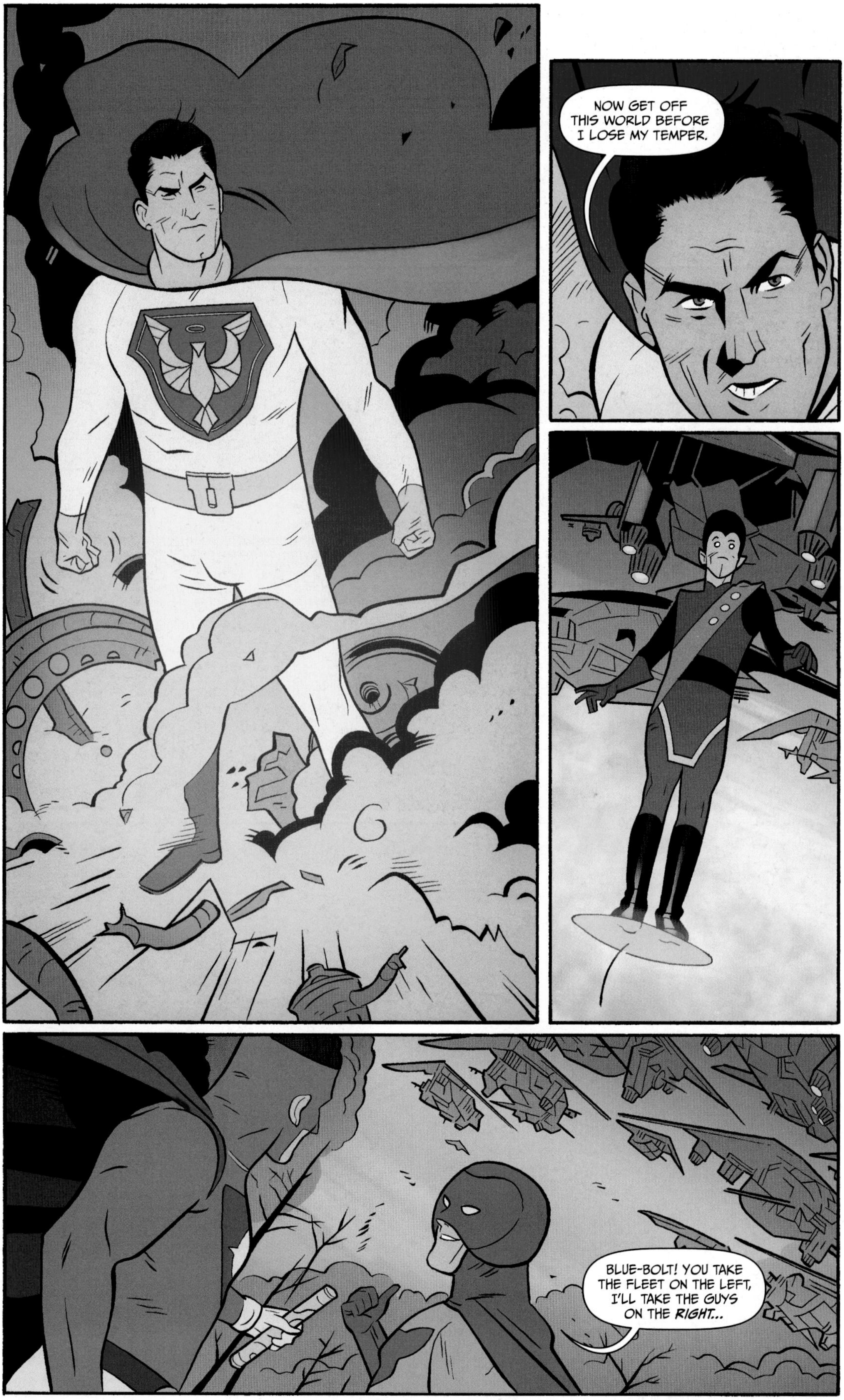
NOW GET OFF THIS WORLD BEFORE I LOSE MY TEMPER.
BLUE-BOLT! YOU TAKE THE FLEET ON THE LEFT, I'LL TAKE THE GUYS ON THE *RIGHT...*

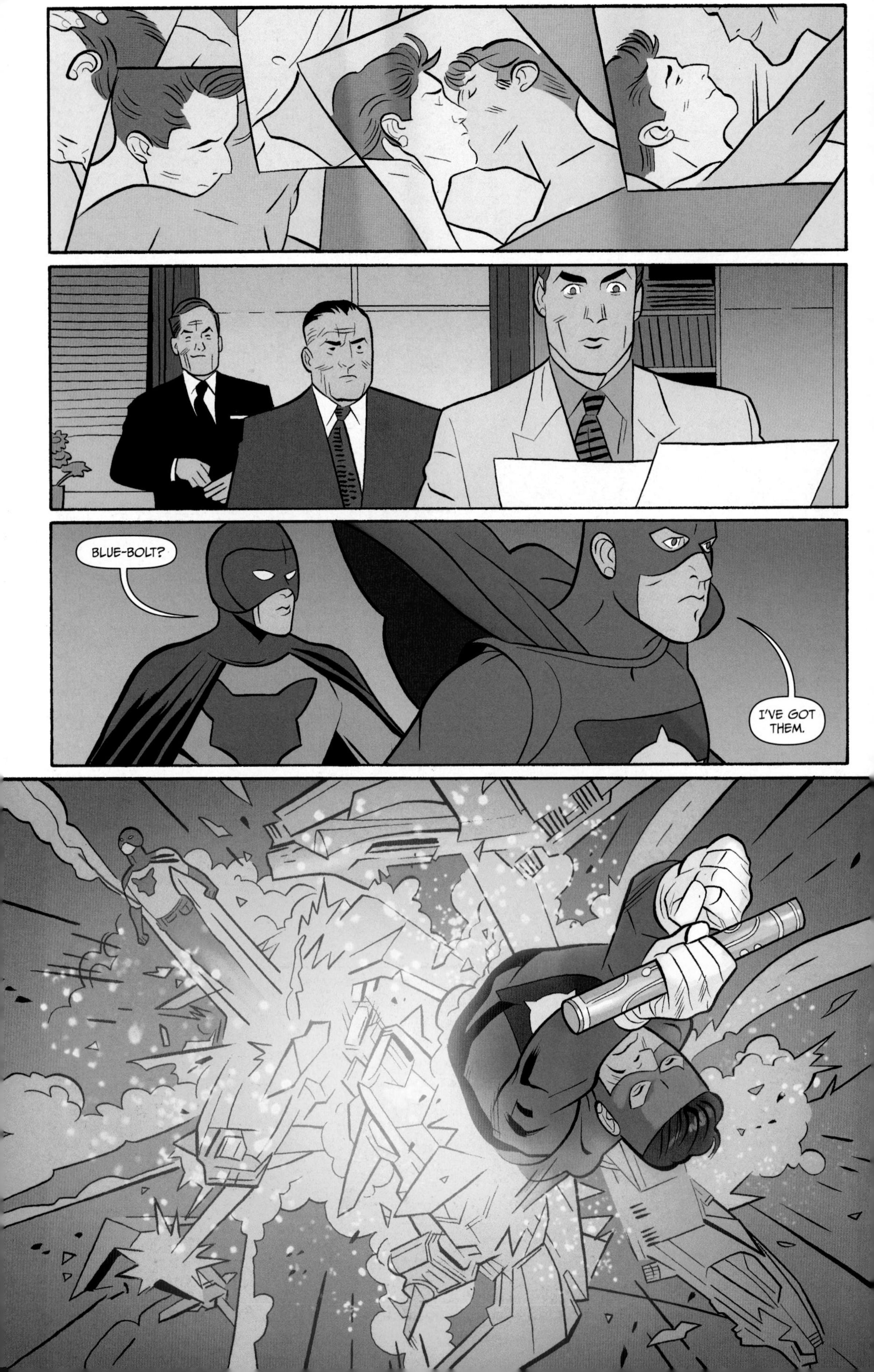
BLUE-BOLT?
I'VE GOT THEM.

UNLIKE THE REST OF THE TEAM I'VE GOT THREE DIFFERENT IDENTITIES.

THE FIRST IS A SUPERHERO AND IDOL TO MILLIONS.

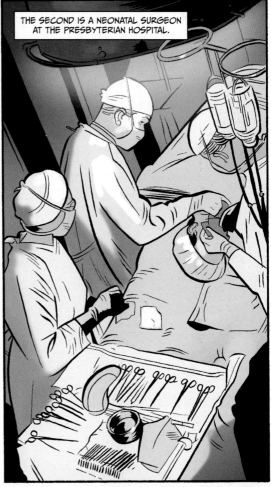

THE SECOND IS A NEONATAL SURGEON AT THE PRESBYTERIAN HOSPITAL.

THE THIRD IS A SECRET HOMOSEXUAL WHO ENDANGERS THE LIVES AND REPUTATIONS OF ALL THE PEOPLE *CLOSEST* TO HIM.

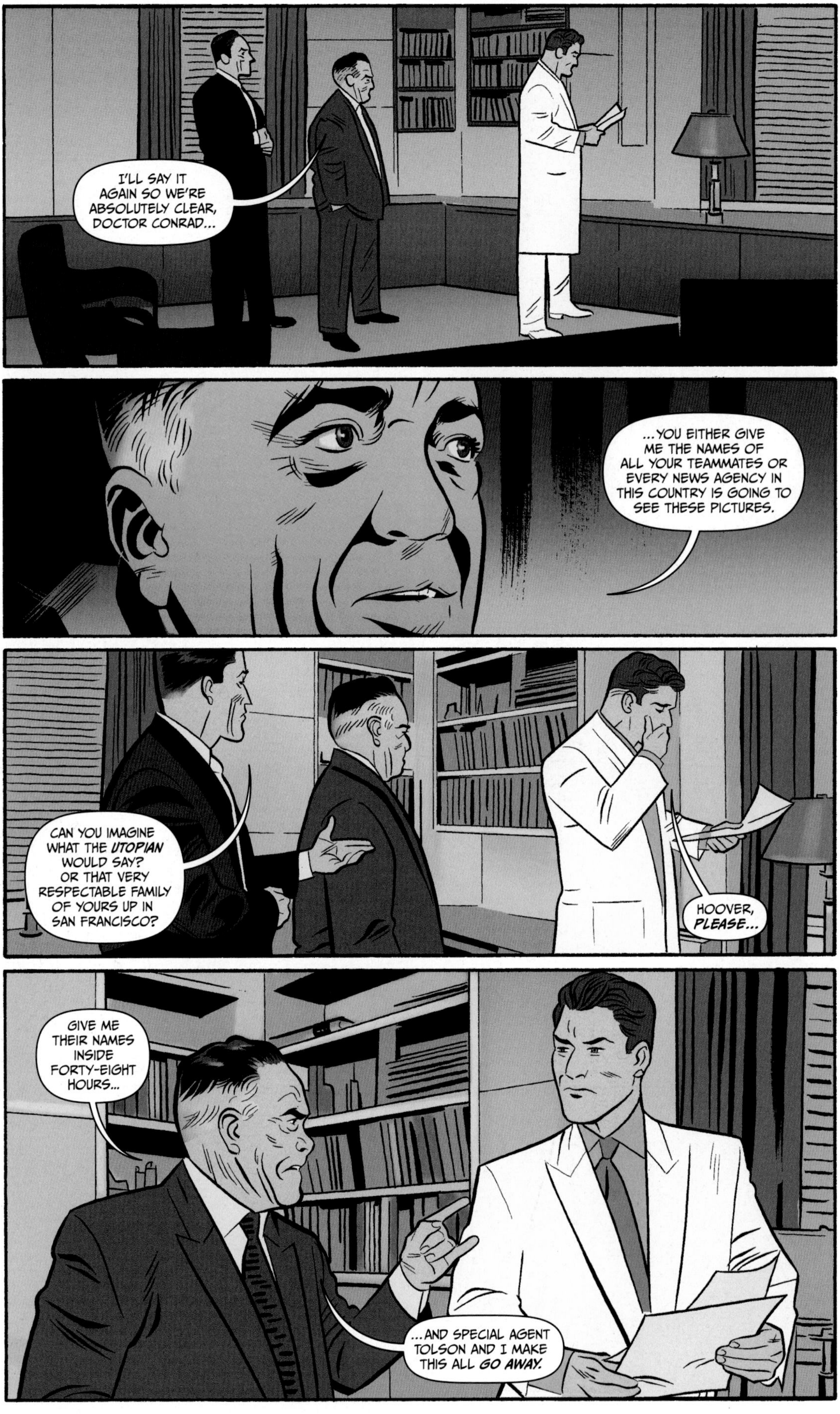
I'LL SAY IT AGAIN SO WE'RE ABSOLUTELY CLEAR, DOCTOR CONRAD...
...YOU EITHER GIVE ME THE NAMES OF ALL YOUR TEAMMATES OR EVERY NEWS AGENCY IN THIS COUNTRY IS GOING TO SEE THESE PICTURES.
CAN YOU IMAGINE WHAT THE *UTOPIAN* WOULD SAY? OR THAT VERY RESPECTABLE FAMILY OF YOURS UP IN SAN FRANCISCO?
HOOVER, ***PLEASE...***
GIVE ME THEIR NAMES INSIDE FORTY-EIGHT HOURS...
...AND SPECIAL AGENT TOLSON AND I MAKE THIS ALL ***GO AWAY.***

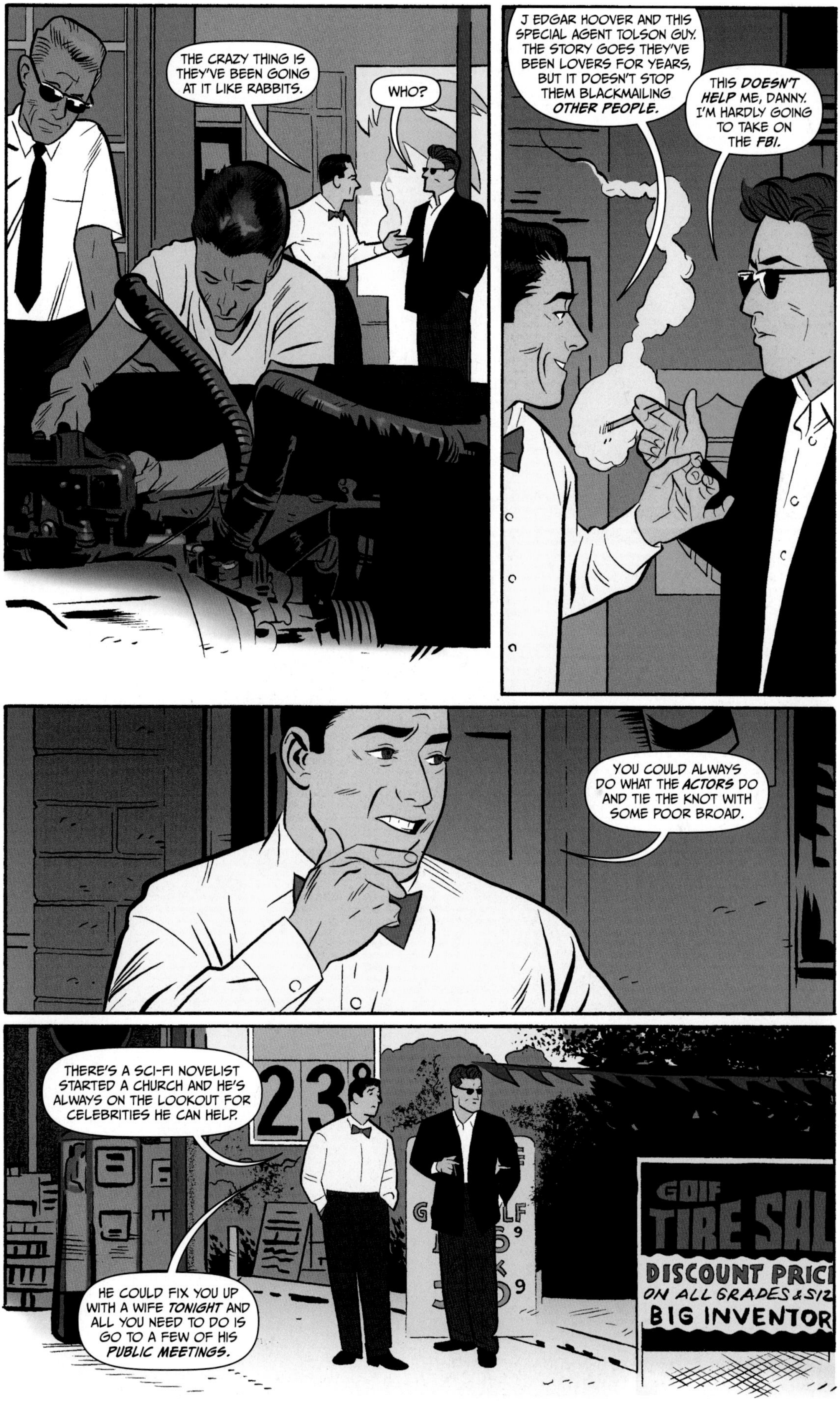

THE CRAZY THING IS THEY'VE BEEN GOING AT IT LIKE RABBITS.
WHO?
J EDGAR HOOVER AND THIS SPECIAL AGENT TOLSON GUY. THE STORY GOES THEY'VE BEEN LOVERS FOR YEARS, BUT IT DOESN'T STOP THEM BLACKMAILING *OTHER PEOPLE.*
THIS *DOESN'T HELP* ME, DANNY. I'M HARDLY GOING TO TAKE ON THE *FBI.*
YOU COULD ALWAYS DO WHAT THE *ACTORS* DO AND TIE THE KNOT WITH SOME POOR BROAD.
THERE'S A SCI-FI NOVELIST STARTED A CHURCH AND HE'S ALWAYS ON THE LOOKOUT FOR CELEBRITIES HE CAN HELP.
HE COULD FIX YOU UP WITH A WIFE *TONIGHT* AND ALL YOU NEED TO DO IS GO TO A FEW OF HIS *PUBLIC MEETINGS.*
TIRE SAL
DISCOUNT PRIC
ON ALL GRADES & SIZ
BIG INVENTOR

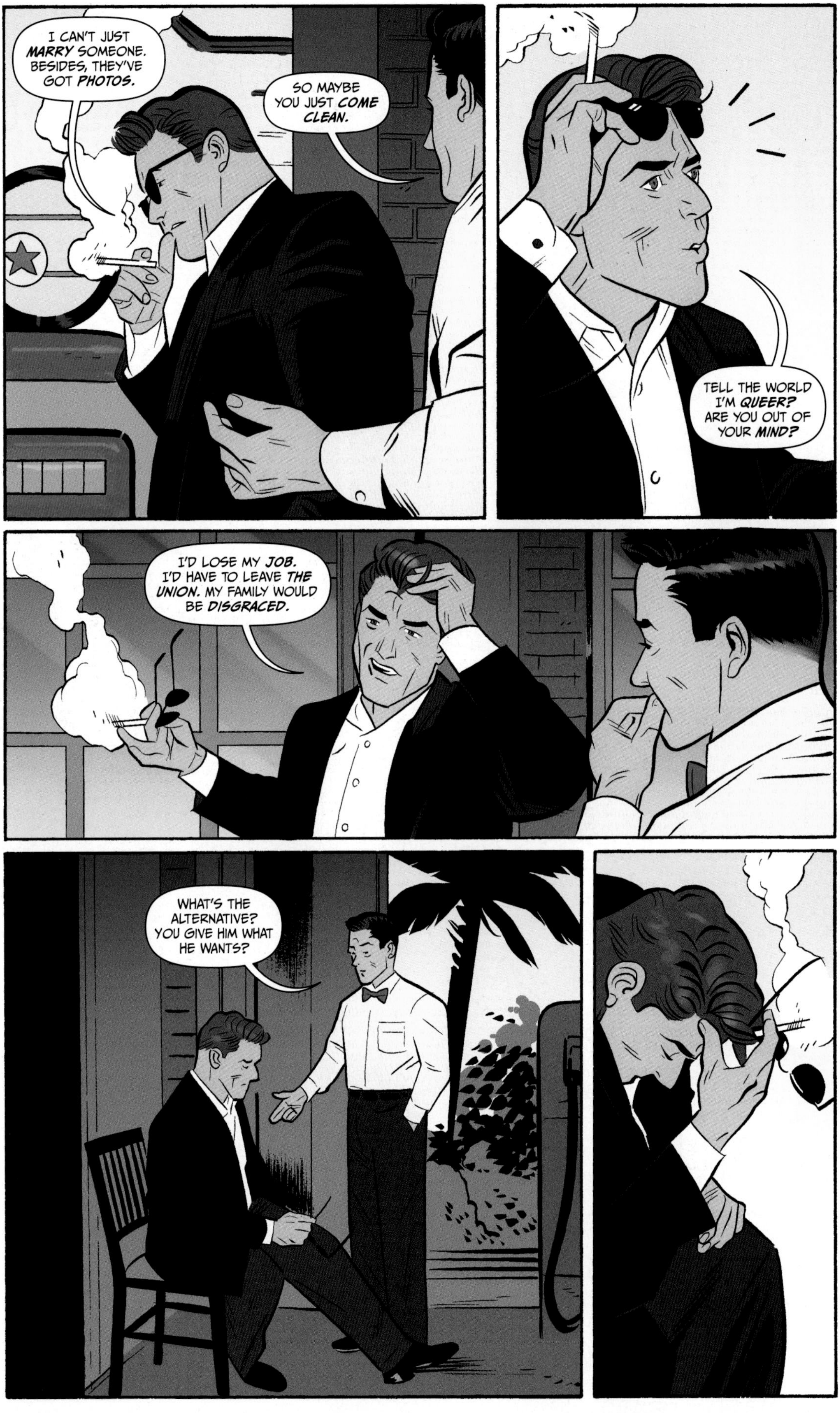
I CAN'T JUST *MARRY* SOMEONE. BESIDES, THEY'VE GOT *PHOTOS.*
SO MAYBE YOU JUST *COME CLEAN.*
TELL THE WORLD I'M *QUEER?* ARE YOU OUT OF YOUR *MIND?*
I'D LOSE MY *JOB.* I'D HAVE TO LEAVE *THE UNION.* MY FAMILY WOULD BE *DISGRACED.*
WHAT'S THE ALTERNATIVE? YOU GIVE HIM WHAT HE WANTS?

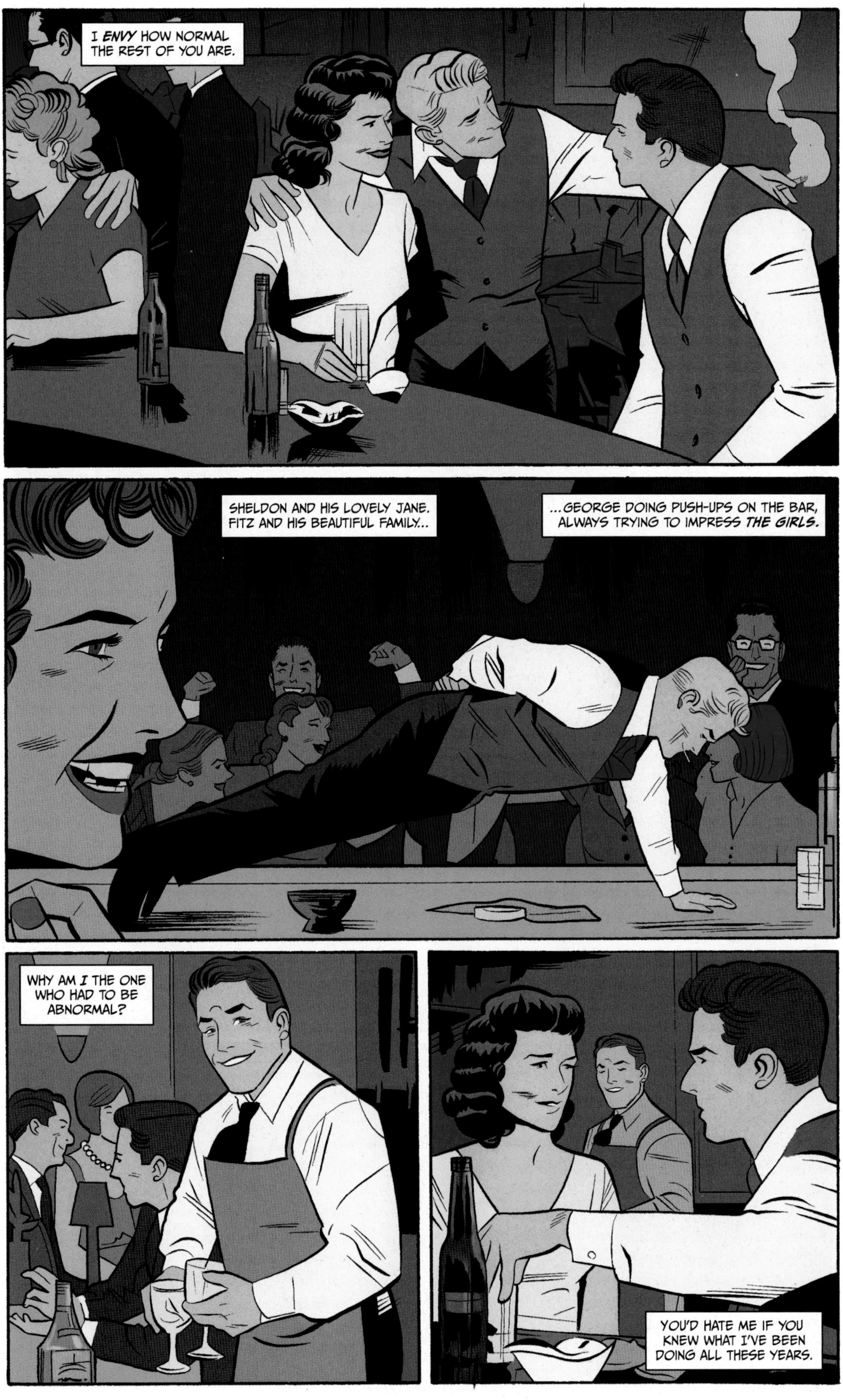
I ENVY HOW NORMAL THE REST OF YOU ARE.
SHELDON AND HIS LOVELY JANE. FITZ AND HIS BEAUTIFUL FAMILY...
...GEORGE DOING PUSH-UPS ON THE BAR, ALWAYS TRYING TO IMPRESS THE GIRLS.
WHY AM I THE ONE WHO HAD TO BE ABNORMAL?
YOU'D HATE ME IF YOU KNEW WHAT I'VE BEEN DOING ALL THESE YEARS.

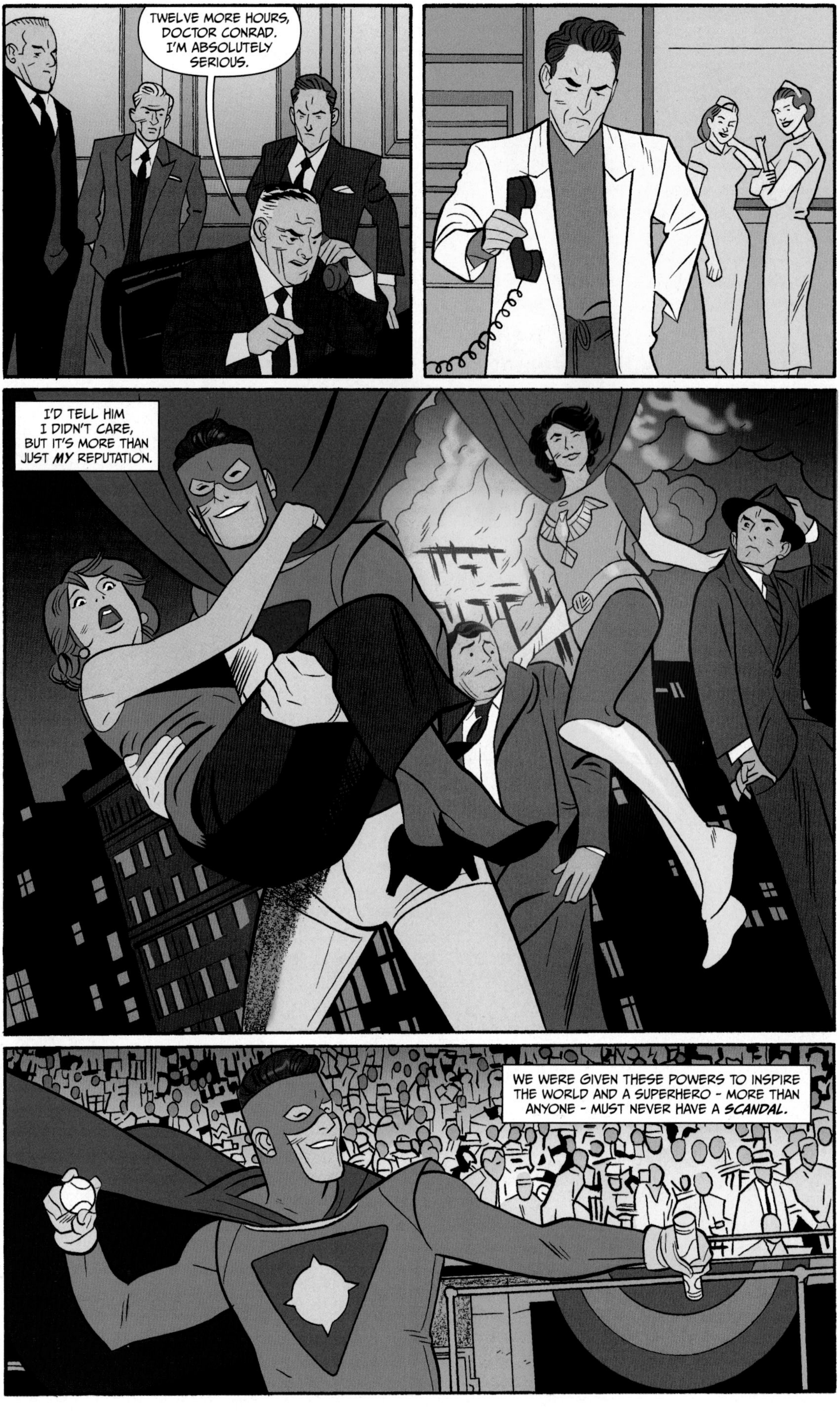
TWELVE MORE HOURS, DOCTOR CONRAD. I'M ABSOLUTELY SERIOUS.
I'D TELL HIM I DIDN'T CARE, BUT IT'S MORE THAN JUST *MY* REPUTATION.
WE WERE GIVEN THESE POWERS TO INSPIRE THE WORLD AND A SUPERHERO - MORE THAN ANYONE - MUST NEVER HAVE A ***SCANDAL.***

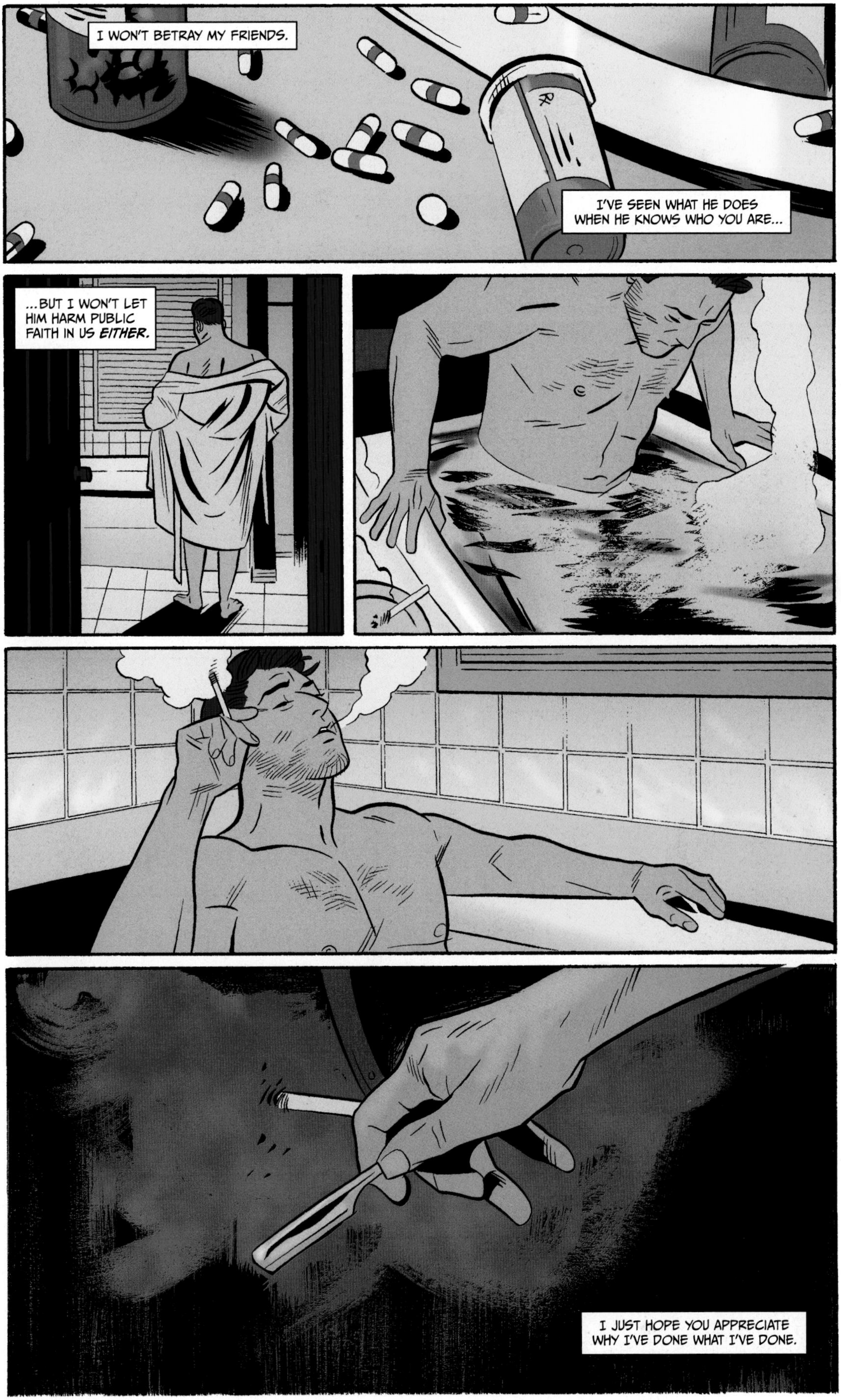
I WON'T BETRAY MY FRIENDS.
I'VE SEEN WHAT HE DOES WHEN HE KNOWS WHO YOU ARE...
...BUT I WON'T LET HIM HARM PUBLIC FAITH IN US *EITHER.*
I JUST HOPE YOU APPRECIATE WHY I'VE DONE WHAT I'VE DONE.

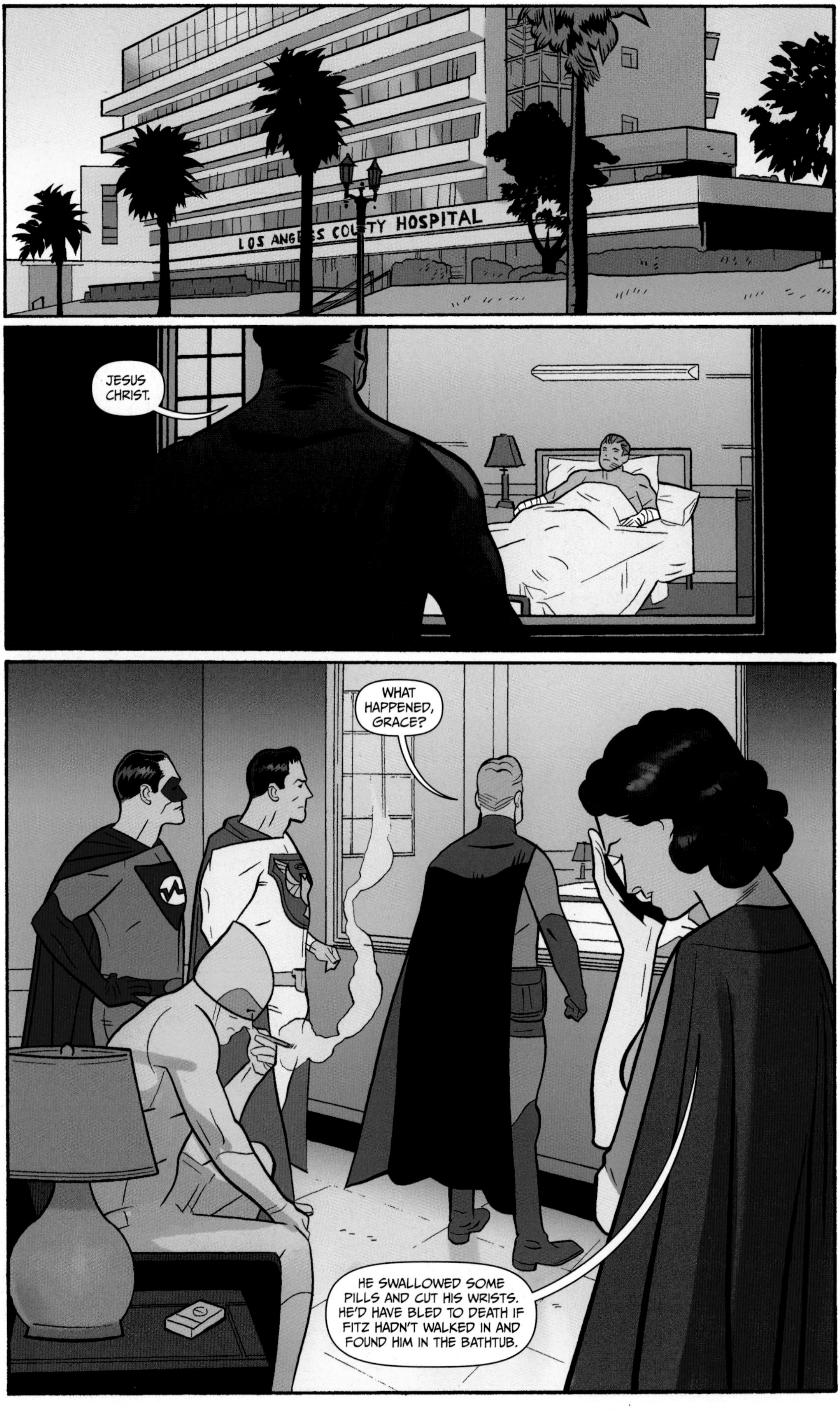
HOSPITAL
JESUS CHRIST.
WHAT HAPPENED, GRACE?
HE SWALLOWED SOME PILLS AND CUT HIS WRISTS. HE'D HAVE BLED TO DEATH IF FITZ HADN'T WALKED IN AND FOUND HIM IN THE BATHTUB.

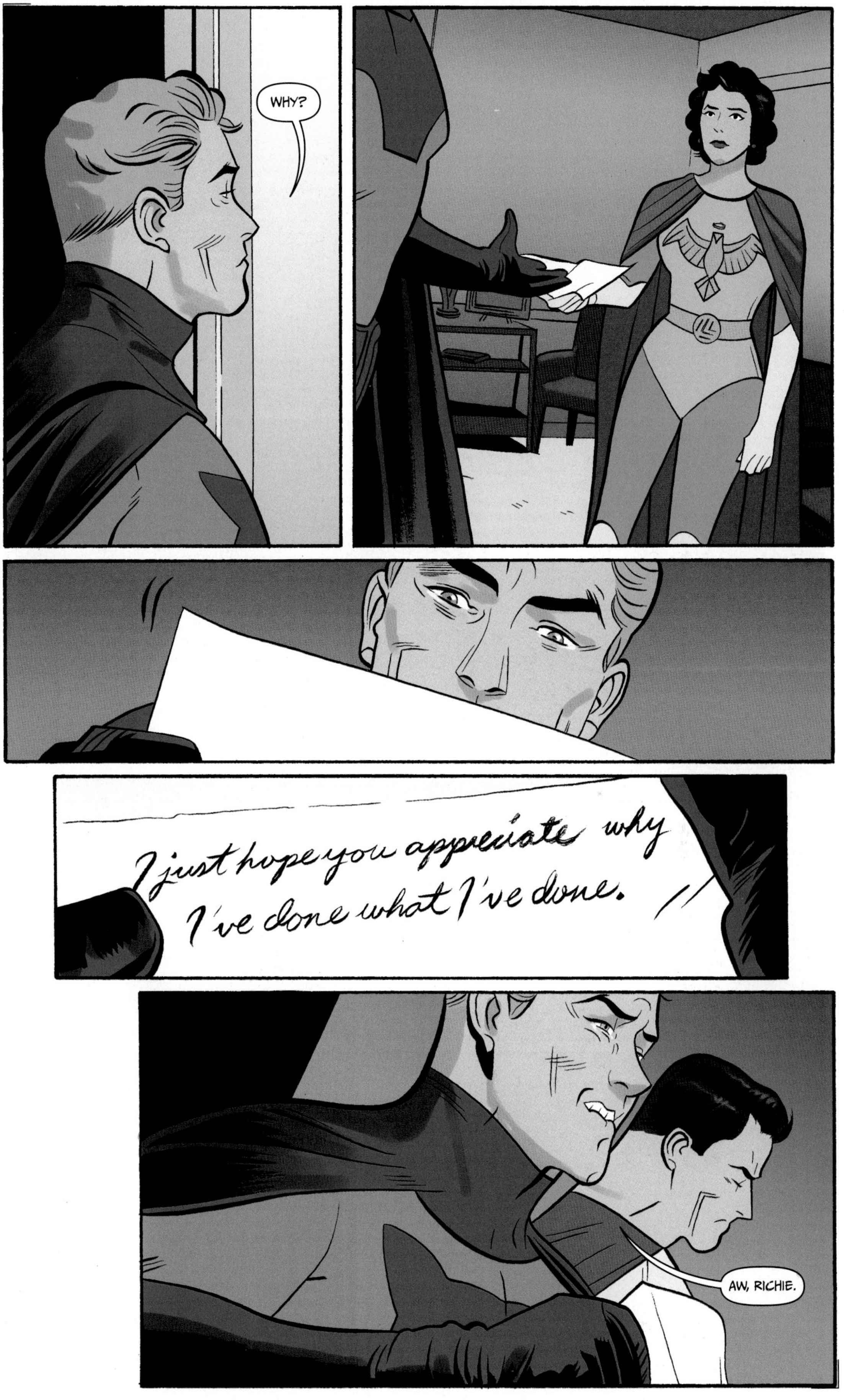
WHY?
I just hope you appreciate why I've done what I've done.
AW, RICHIE.

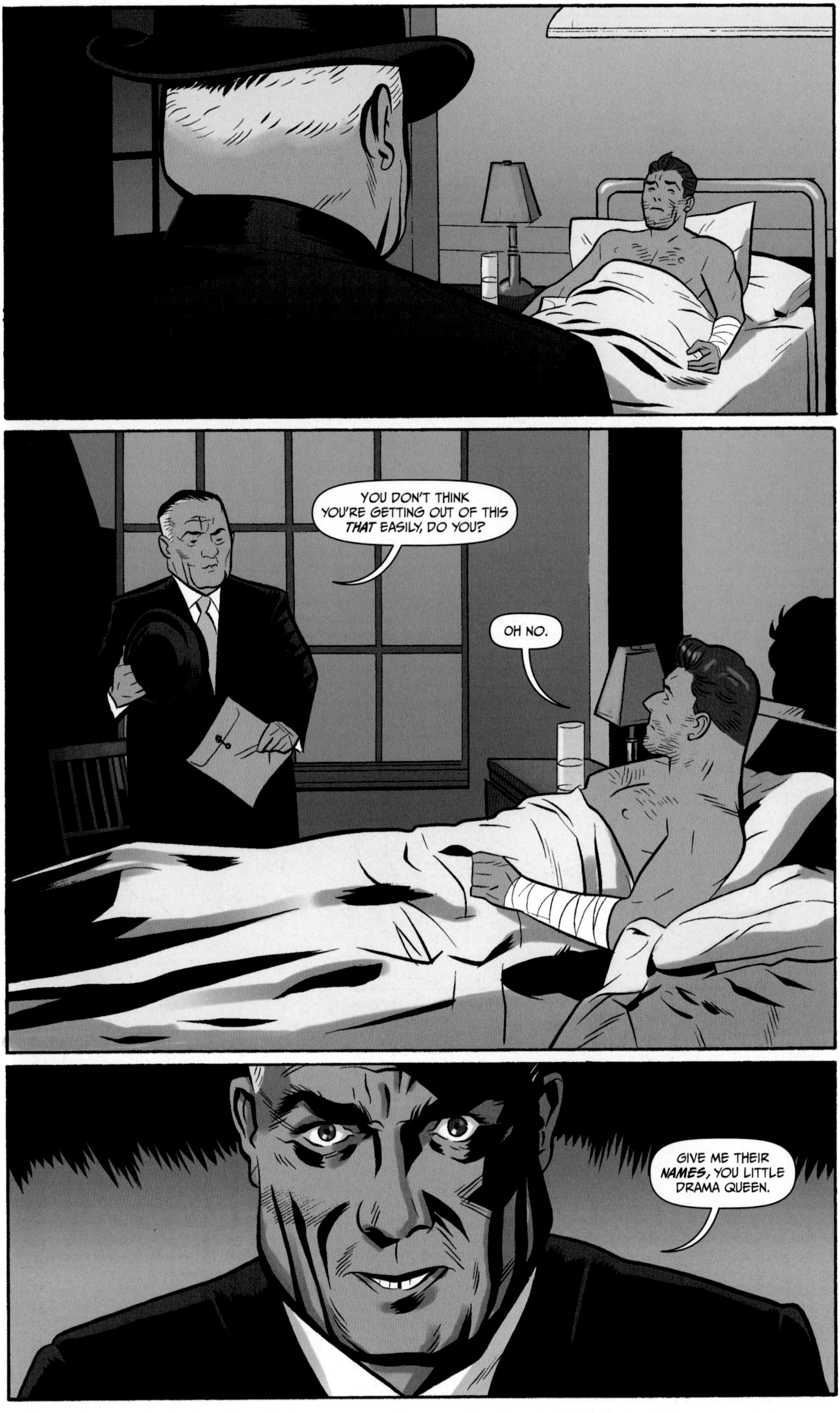
YOU DON'T THINK YOU'RE GETTING OUT OF THIS *THAT* EASILY, DO YOU?
OH NO.
GIVE ME THEIR *NAMES,* YOU LITTLE DRAMA QUEEN.

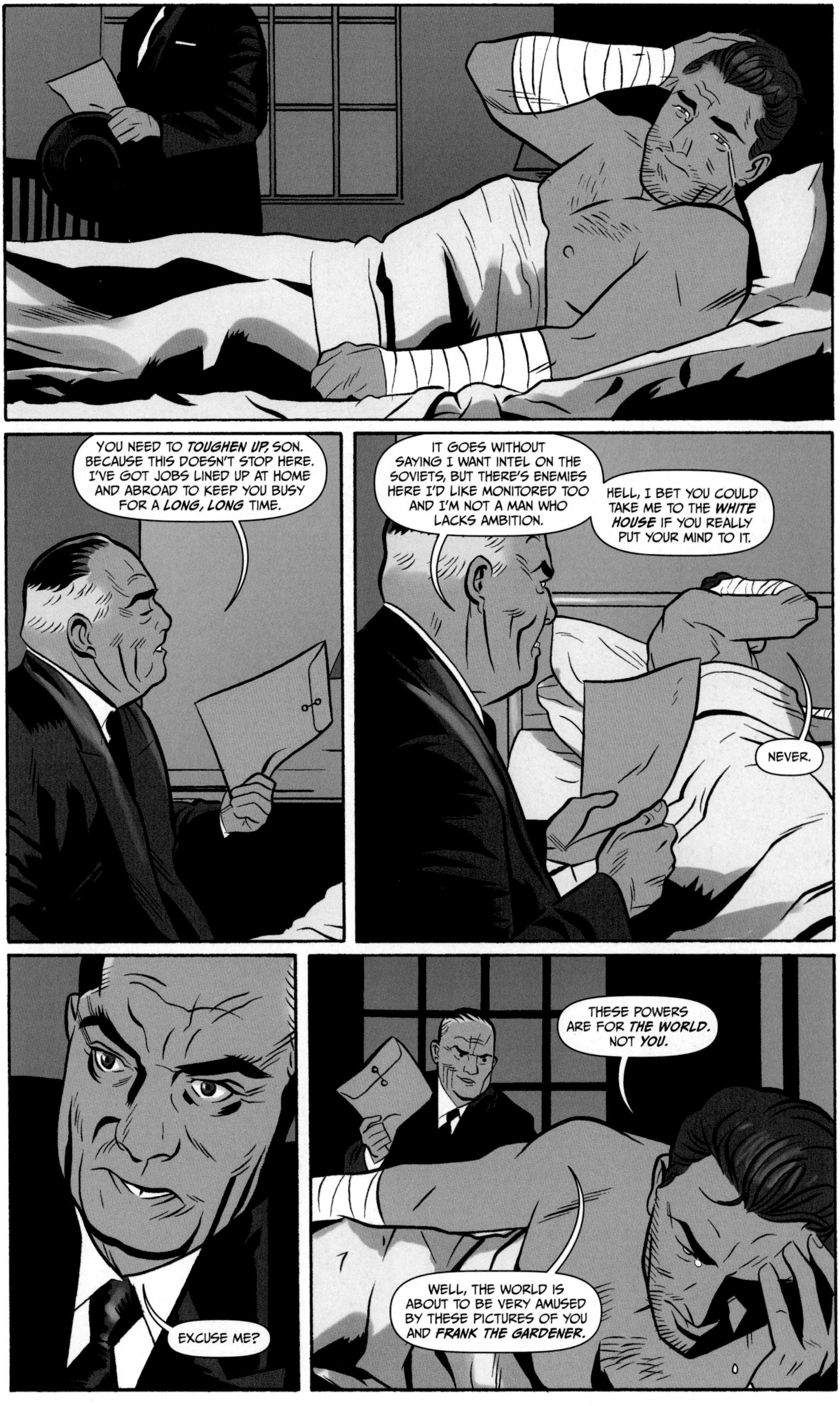
YOU NEED TO *TOUGHEN UP,* SON. BECAUSE THIS DOESN'T STOP HERE. I'VE GOT JOBS LINED UP AT HOME AND ABROAD TO KEEP YOU BUSY FOR A *LONG, LONG* TIME.
IT GOES WITHOUT SAYING I WANT INTEL ON THE SOVIETS, BUT THERE'S ENEMIES HERE I'D LIKE MONITORED TOO AND I'M NOT A MAN WHO LACKS AMBITION.
HELL, I BET YOU COULD TAKE ME TO THE *WHITE HOUSE* IF YOU REALLY PUT YOUR MIND TO IT.
NEVER.
EXCUSE ME?
THESE POWERS ARE FOR *THE WORLD.* NOT *YOU.*
WELL, THE WORLD IS ABOUT TO BE VERY AMUSED BY THESE PICTURES OF YOU AND *FRANK THE GARDENER.*

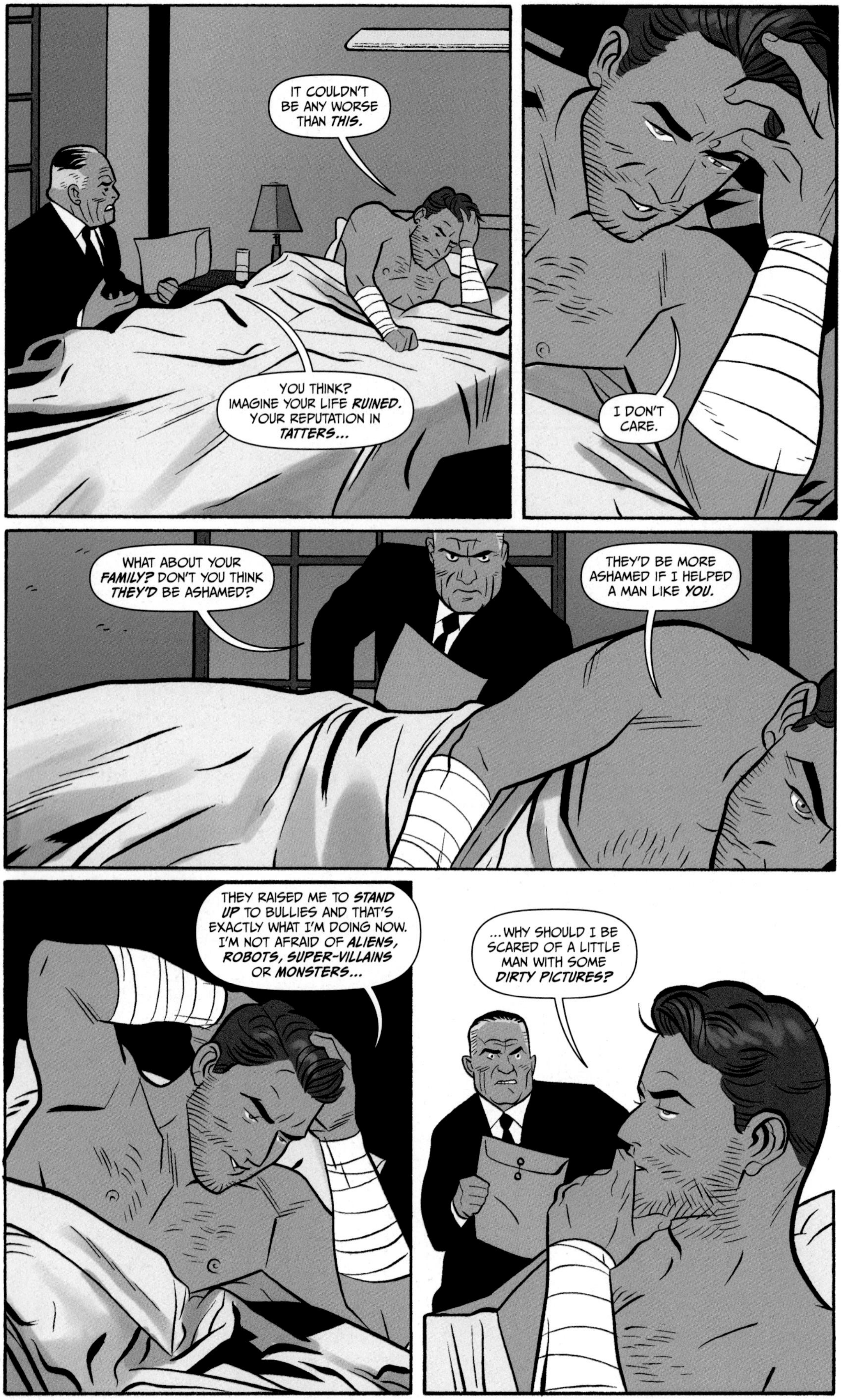
IT COULDN'T BE ANY WORSE THAN THIS.
YOU THINK? IMAGINE YOUR LIFE RUINED. YOUR REPUTATION IN TATTERS...
I DON'T CARE.
WHAT ABOUT YOUR FAMILY? DON'T YOU THINK THEY'D BE ASHAMED?
THEY'D BE MORE ASHAMED IF I HELPED A MAN LIKE YOU.
THEY RAISED ME TO STAND UP TO BULLIES AND THAT'S EXACTLY WHAT I'M DOING NOW. I'M NOT AFRAID OF ALIENS, ROBOTS, SUPER-VILLAINS OR MONSTERS...
...WHY SHOULD I BE SCARED OF A LITTLE MAN WITH SOME DIRTY PICTURES?

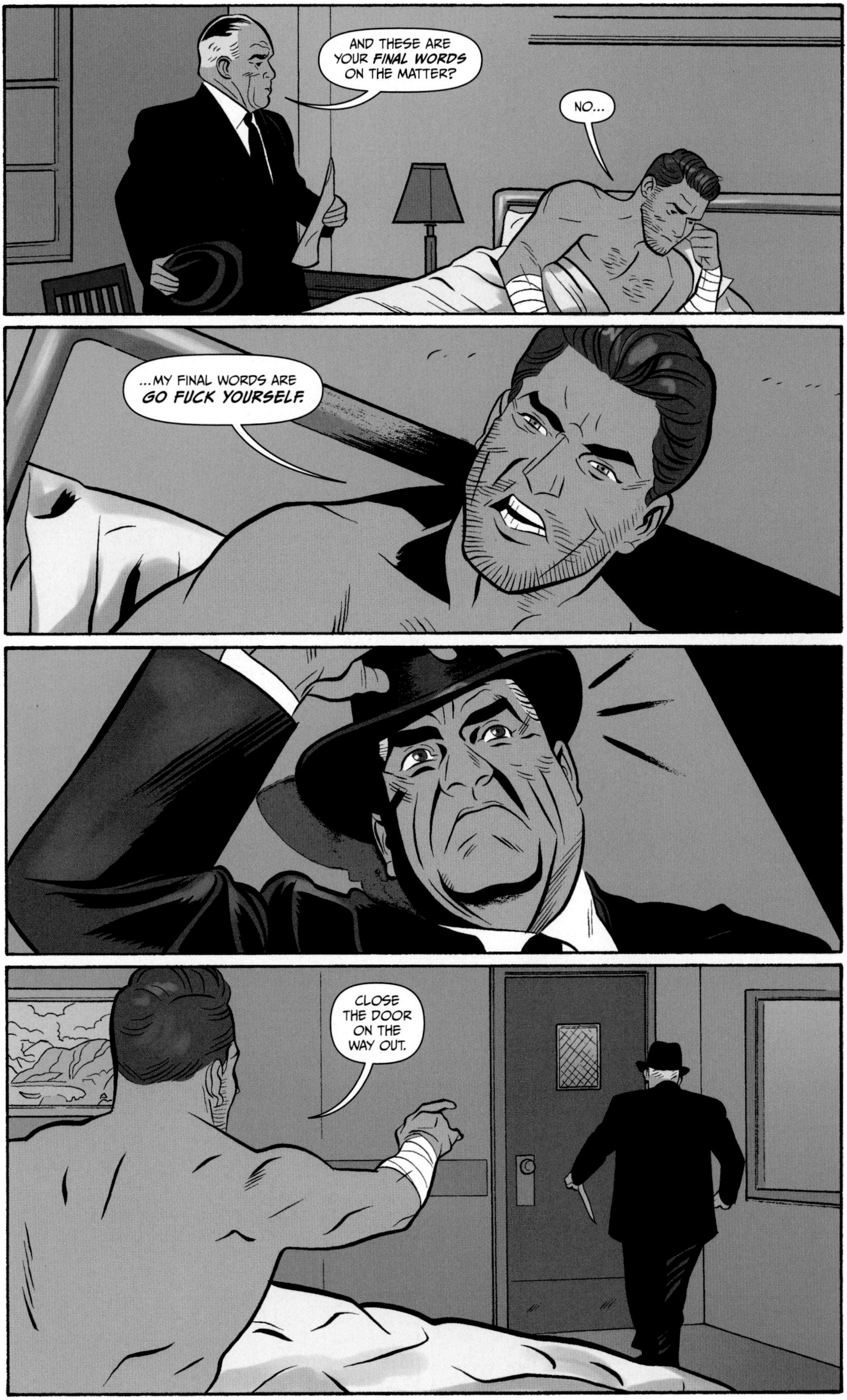
AND THESE ARE YOUR FINAL WORDS ON THE MATTER?
NO...
...MY FINAL WORDS ARE GO FUCK YOURSELF.
CLOSE THE DOOR ON THE WAY OUT.

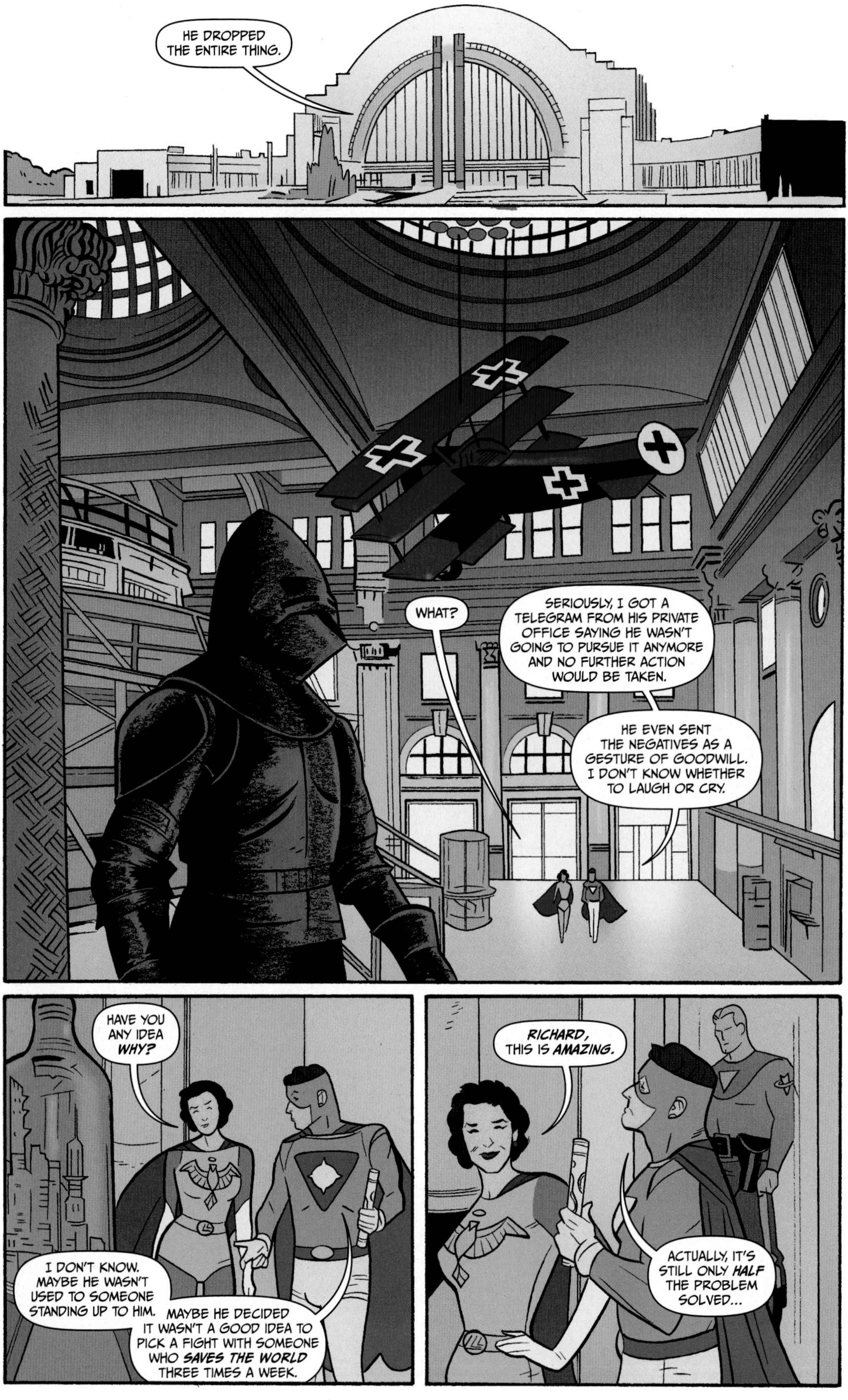
HE DROPPED THE ENTIRE THING.
WHAT?
SERIOUSLY, I GOT A TELEGRAM FROM HIS PRIVATE OFFICE SAYING HE WASN'T GOING TO PURSUE IT ANYMORE AND NO FURTHER ACTION WOULD BE TAKEN.
HE EVEN SENT THE NEGATIVES AS A GESTURE OF GOODWILL. I DON'T KNOW WHETHER TO LAUGH OR CRY.
HAVE YOU ANY IDEA ***WHY?***
I DON'T KNOW. MAYBE HE WASN'T USED TO SOMEONE STANDING UP TO HIM.
MAYBE HE DECIDED IT WASN'T A GOOD IDEA TO PICK A FIGHT WITH SOMEONE WHO ***SAVES THE WORLD*** THREE TIMES A WEEK.
RICHARD, THIS IS ***AMAZING.***
ACTUALLY, IT'S STILL ONLY ***HALF*** THE PROBLEM SOLVED...

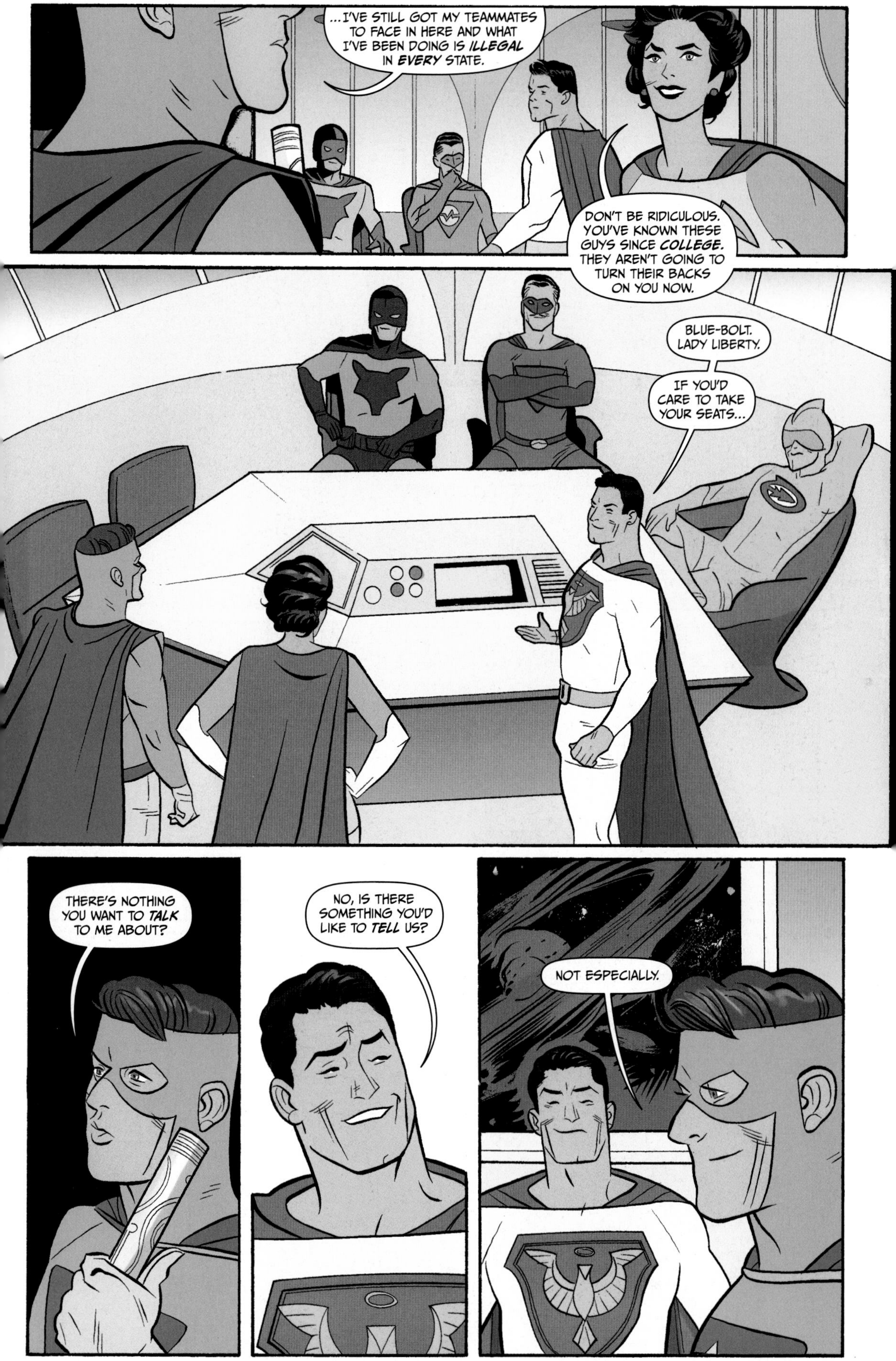
...I'VE STILL GOT MY TEAMMATES TO FACE IN HERE AND WHAT I'VE BEEN DOING IS *ILLEGAL* IN *EVERY* STATE.
DON'T BE RIDICULOUS. YOU'VE KNOWN THESE GUYS SINCE *COLLEGE.* THEY AREN'T GOING TO TURN THEIR BACKS ON YOU NOW.
BLUE-BOLT. LADY LIBERTY.
IF YOU'D CARE TO TAKE YOUR SEATS...
THERE'S NOTHING YOU WANT TO *TALK* TO ME ABOUT?
NO, IS THERE SOMETHING YOU'D LIKE TO *TELL* US?
NOT ESPECIALLY.

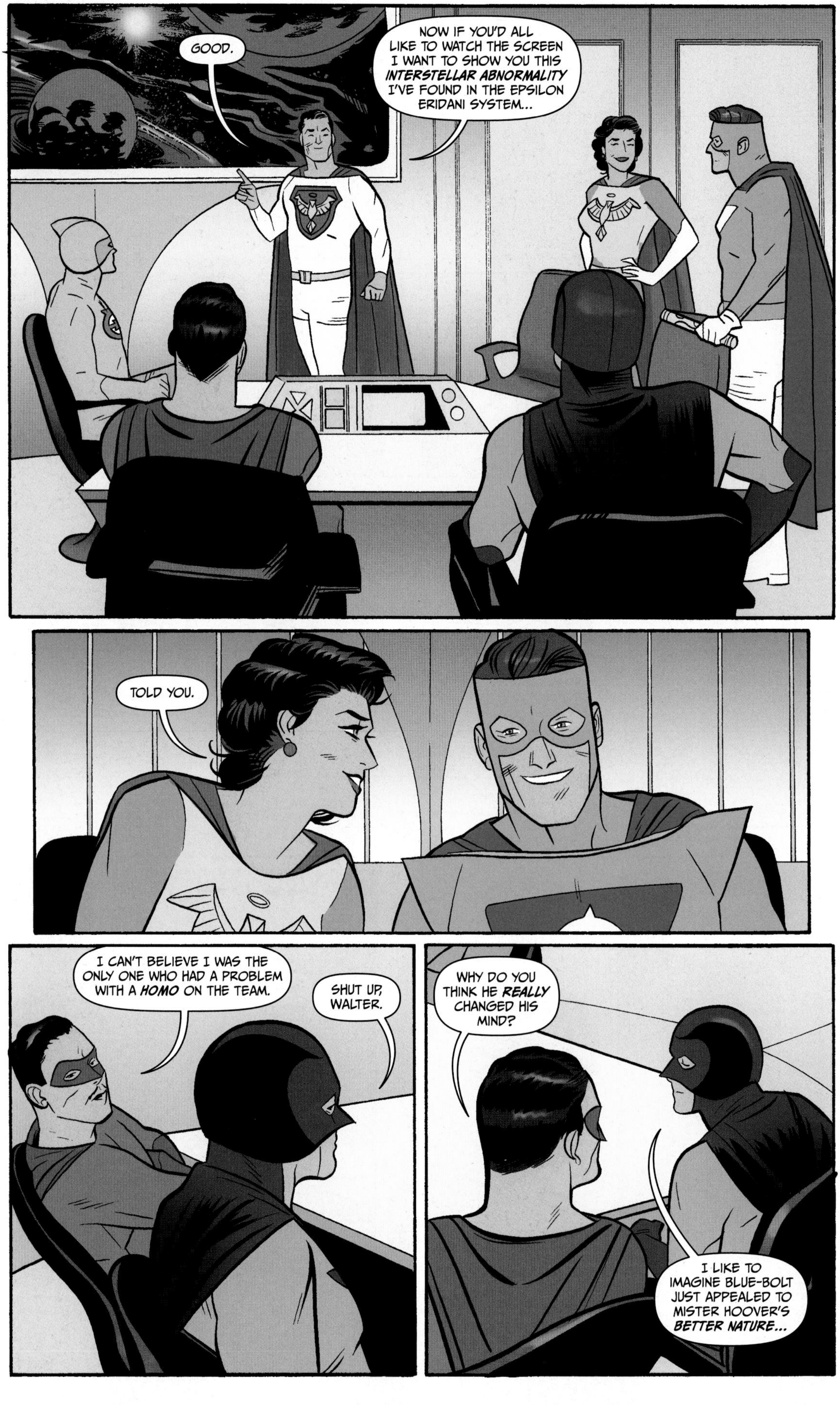
GOOD.
NOW IF YOU'D ALL LIKE TO WATCH THE SCREEN I WANT TO SHOW YOU THIS *INTERSTELLAR ABNORMALITY* I'VE FOUND IN THE EPSILON ERIDANI SYSTEM...
TOLD YOU.
I CAN'T BELIEVE I WAS THE ONLY ONE WHO HAD A PROBLEM WITH A *HOMO* ON THE TEAM.
SHUT UP, WALTER.
WHY DO YOU THINK HE *REALLY* CHANGED HIS MIND?
I LIKE TO IMAGINE BLUE-BOLT JUST APPEALED TO MISTER HOOVER'S *BETTER NATURE...*

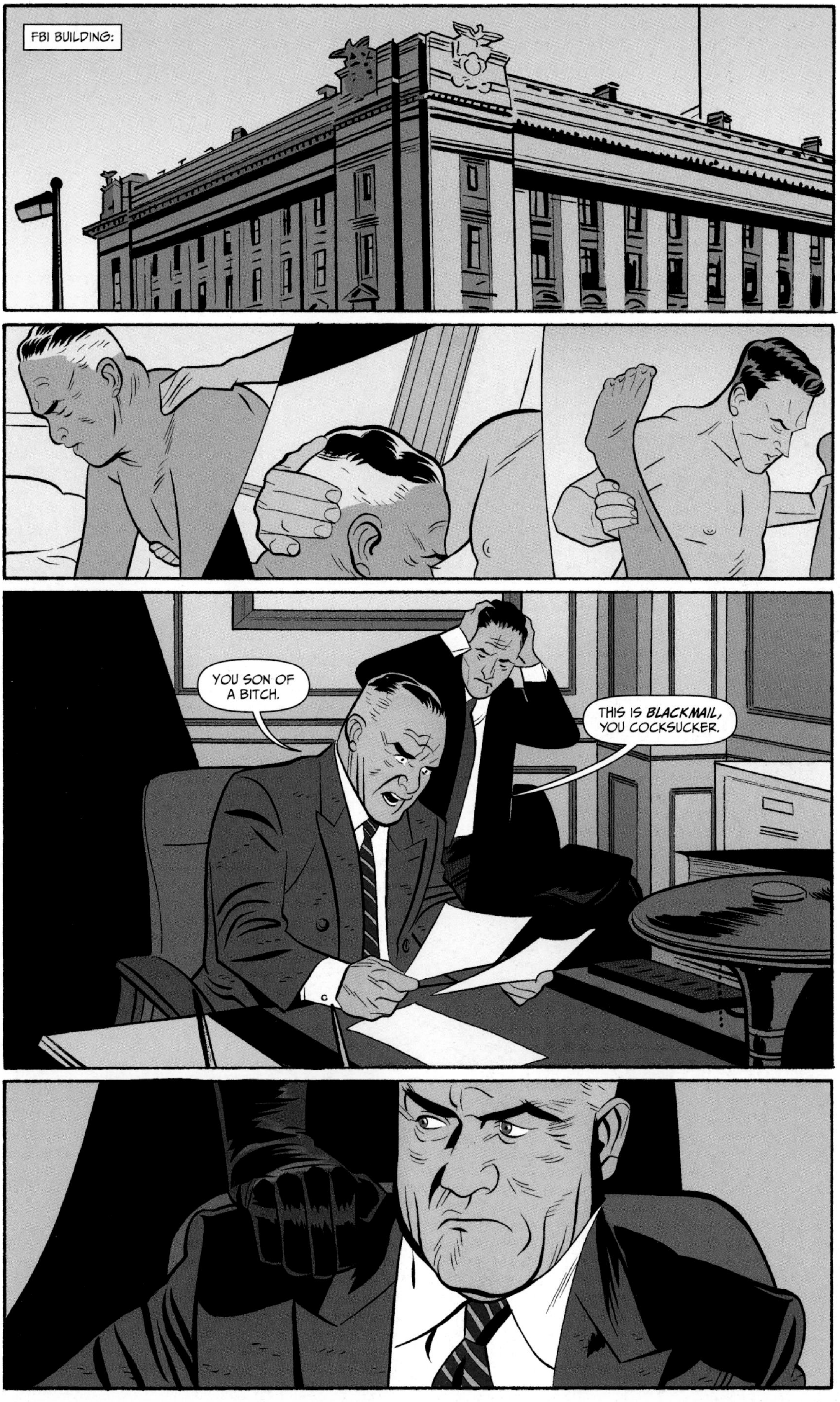
FBI BUILDING:
YOU SON OF A BITCH.
THIS IS BLACKMAIL, YOU COCKSUCKER.

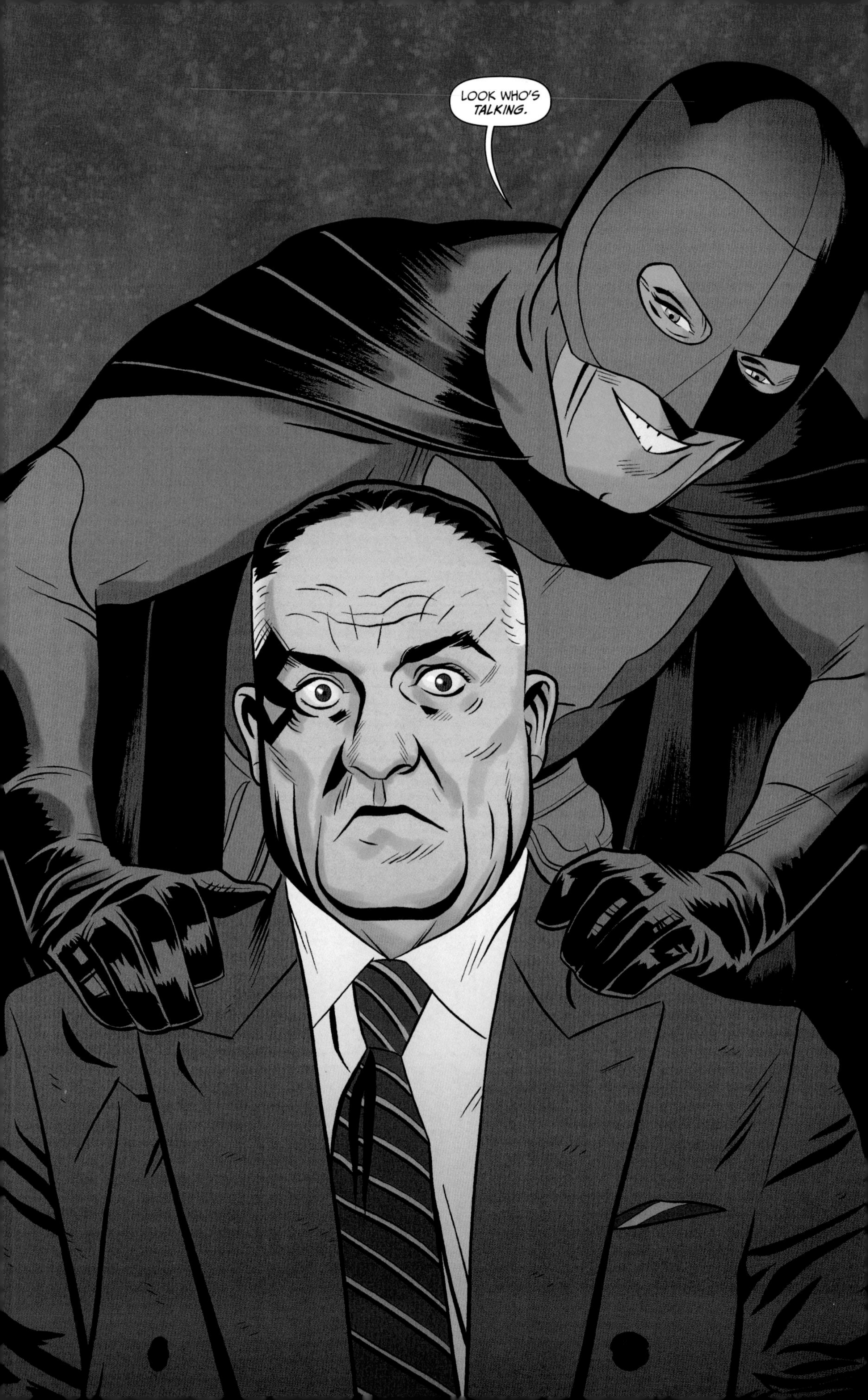
LOOK WHO'S TALKING.

CHAPTER 3

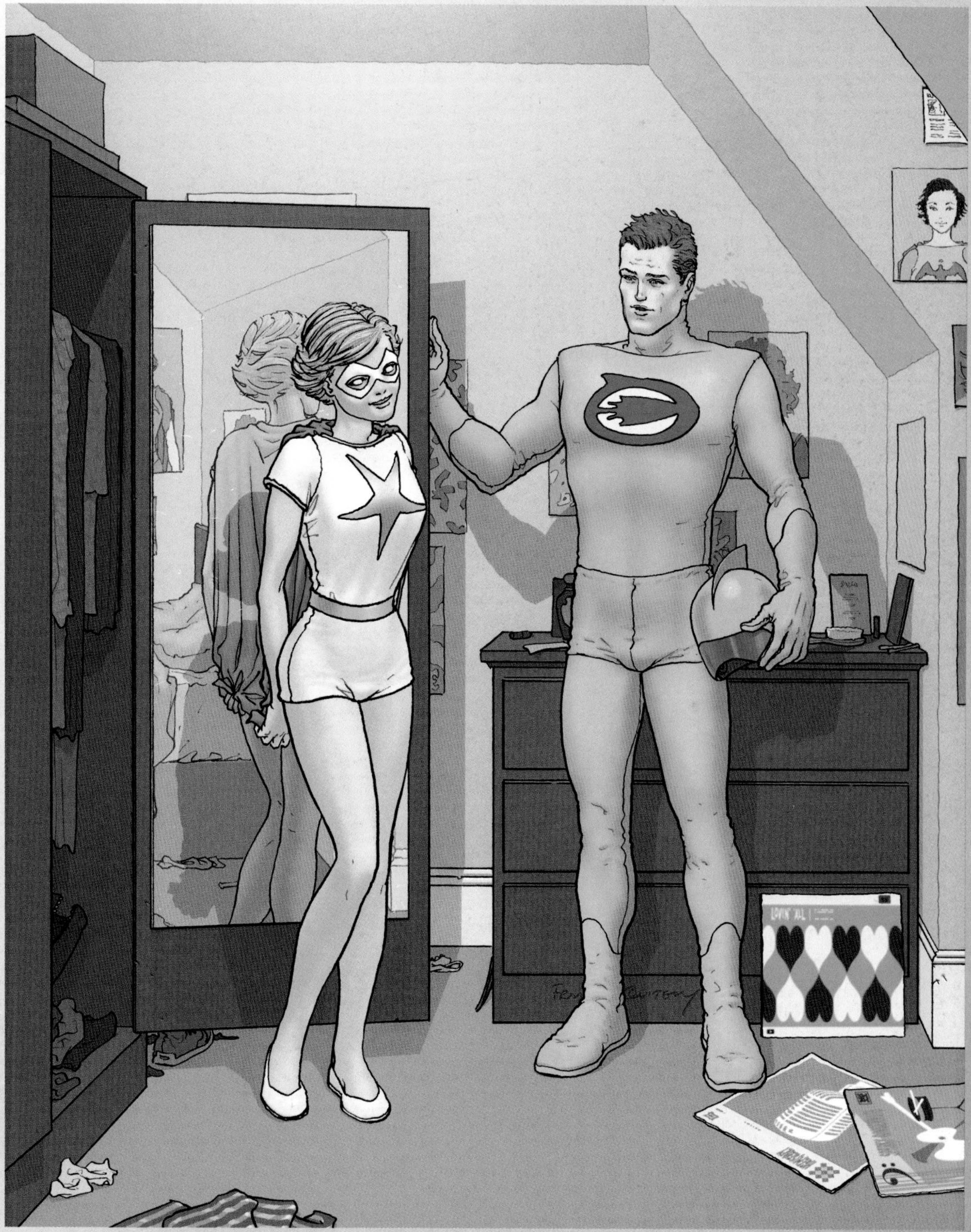

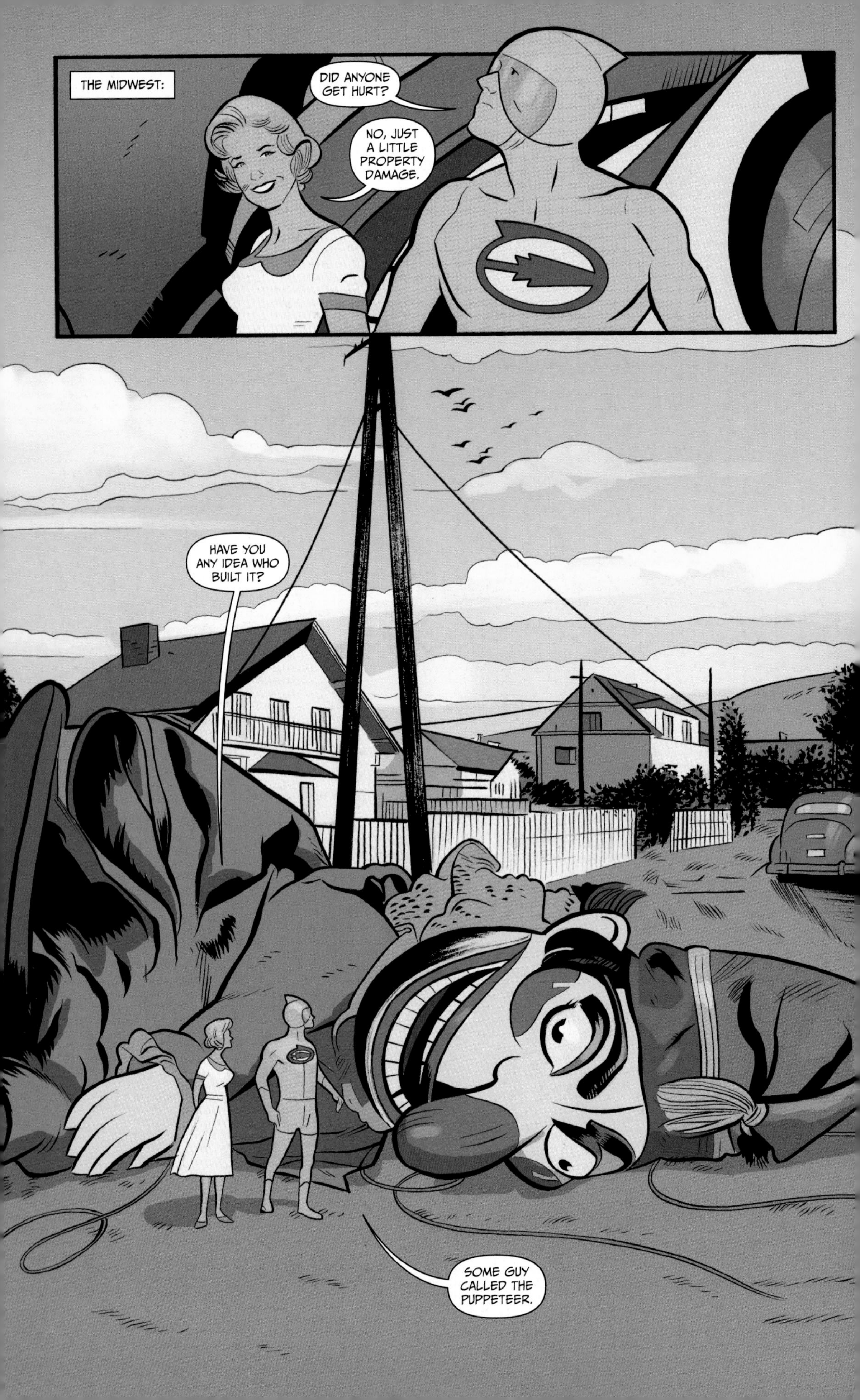
THE MIDWEST:
DID ANYONE GET HURT?
NO, JUST A LITTLE PROPERTY DAMAGE.
HAVE YOU ANY IDEA WHO BUILT IT?
SOME GUY CALLED THE PUPPETEER.

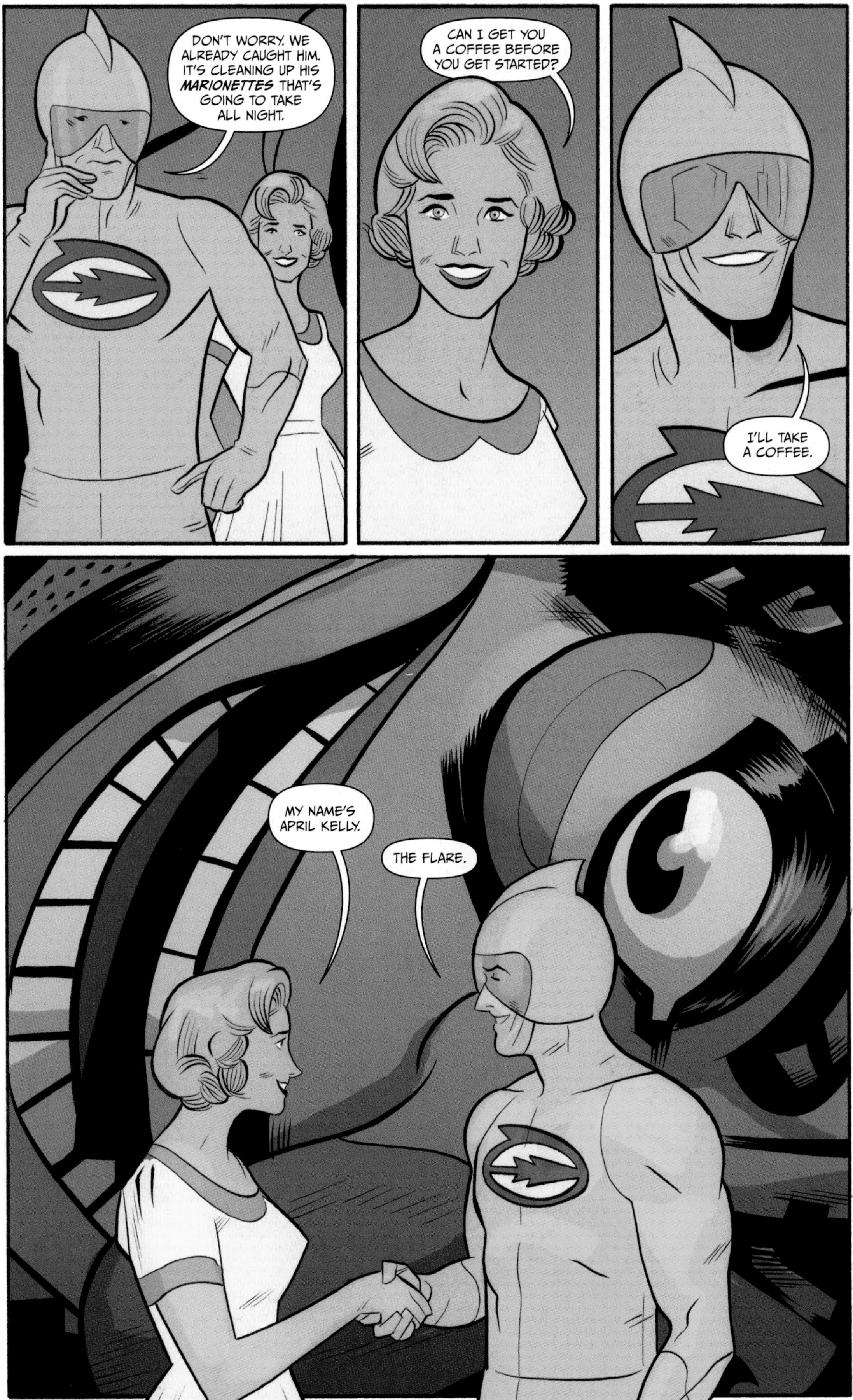
DON'T WORRY. WE ALREADY CAUGHT HIM. IT'S CLEANING UP HIS *MARIONETTES* THAT'S GOING TO TAKE ALL NIGHT.
CAN I GET YOU A COFFEE BEFORE YOU GET STARTED?
I'LL TAKE A COFFEE.
MY NAME'S APRIL KELLY.
THE FLARE.

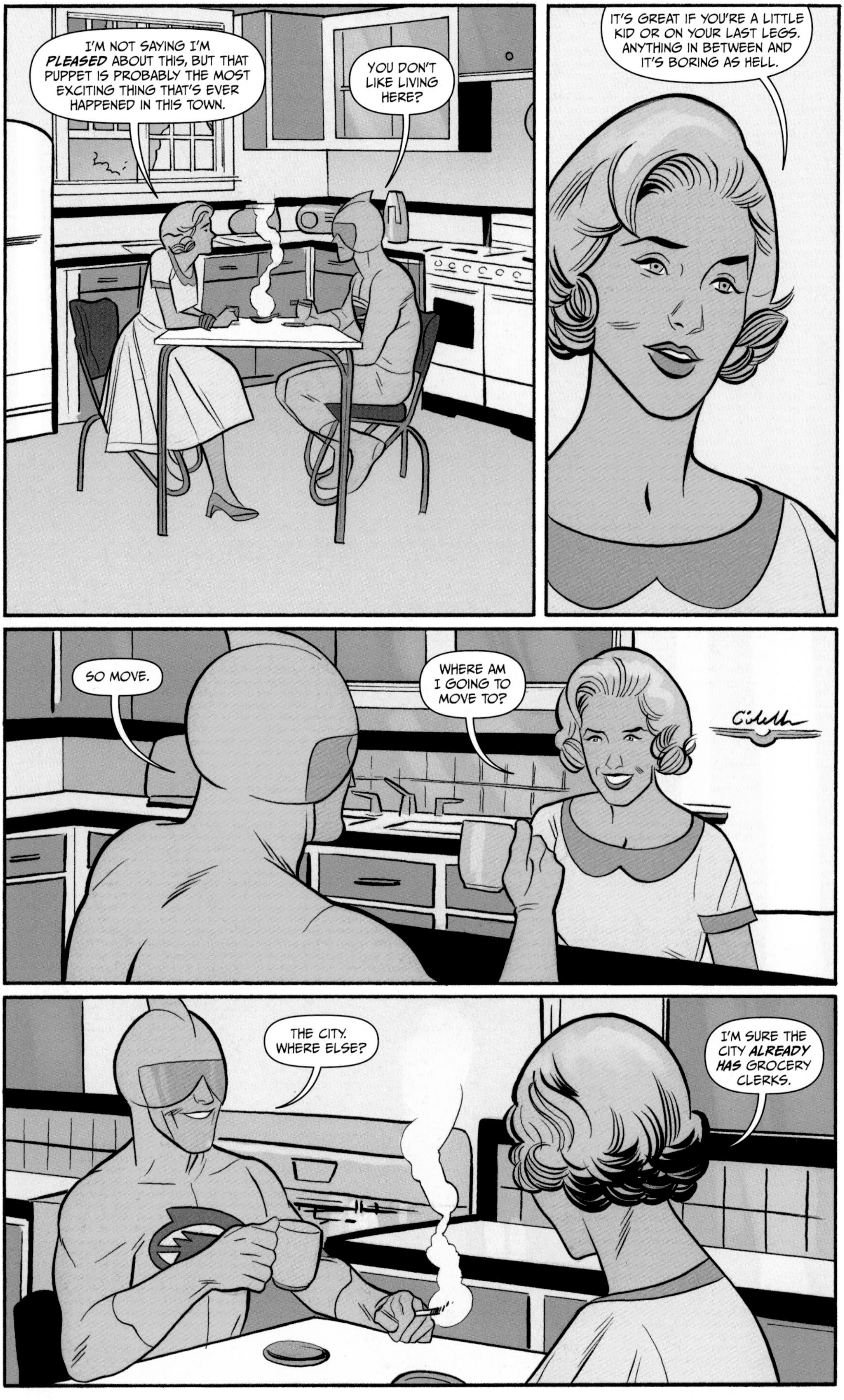
I'M NOT SAYING I'M PLEASED ABOUT THIS, BUT THAT PUPPET IS PROBABLY THE MOST EXCITING THING THAT'S EVER HAPPENED IN THIS TOWN.
YOU DON'T LIKE LIVING HERE?
IT'S GREAT IF YOU'RE A LITTLE KID OR ON YOUR LAST LEGS. ANYTHING IN BETWEEN AND IT'S BORING AS HELL.
SO MOVE.
WHERE AM I GOING TO MOVE TO?
THE CITY. WHERE ELSE?
I'M SURE THE CITY ALREADY HAS GROCERY CLERKS.

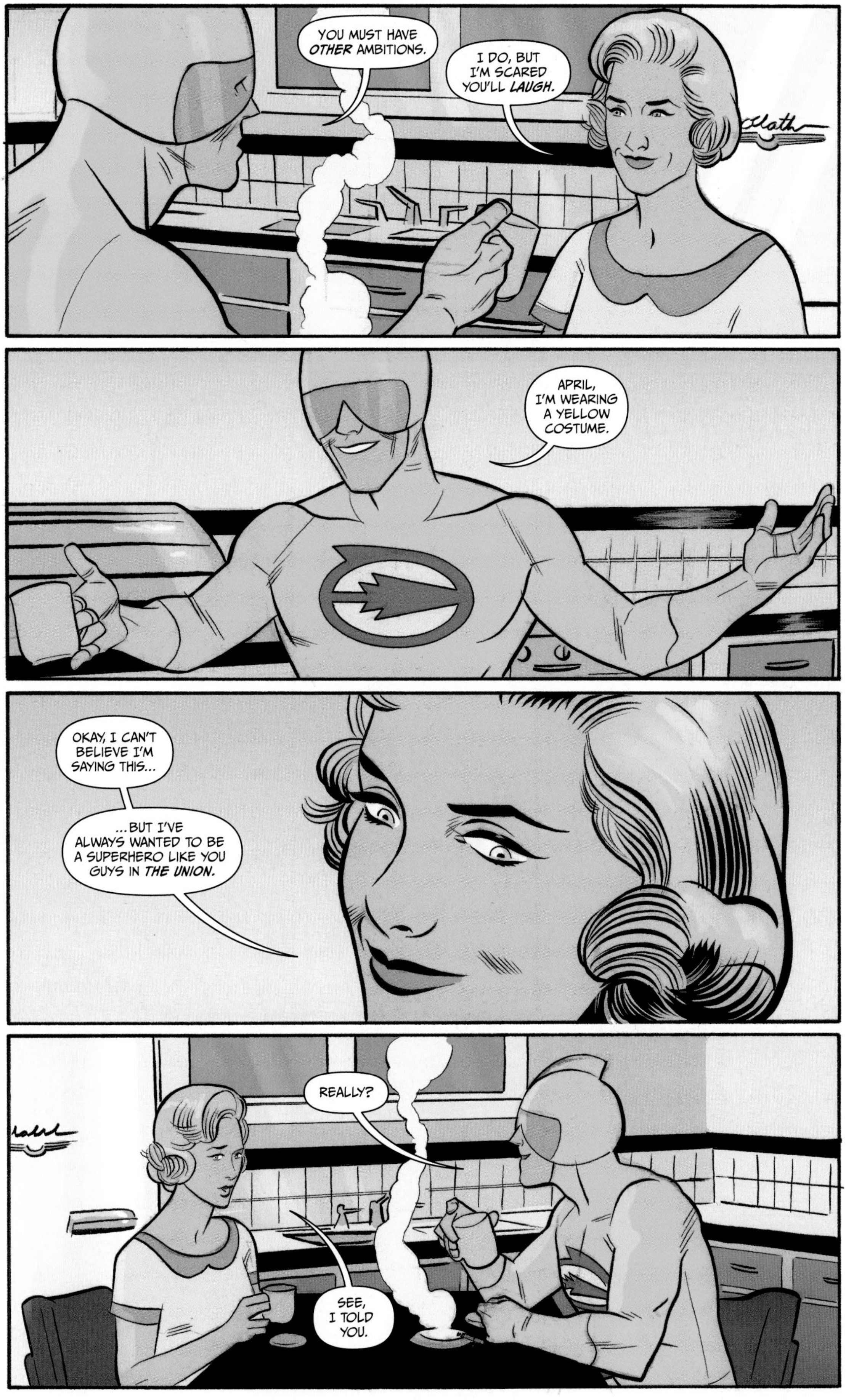
YOU MUST HAVE OTHER AMBITIONS.
I DO, BUT I'M SCARED YOU'LL LAUGH.
APRIL, I'M WEARING A YELLOW COSTUME.
OKAY, I CAN'T BELIEVE I'M SAYING THIS...
...BUT I'VE ALWAYS WANTED TO BE A SUPERHERO LIKE YOU GUYS IN THE UNION.
REALLY?
SEE, I TOLD YOU.

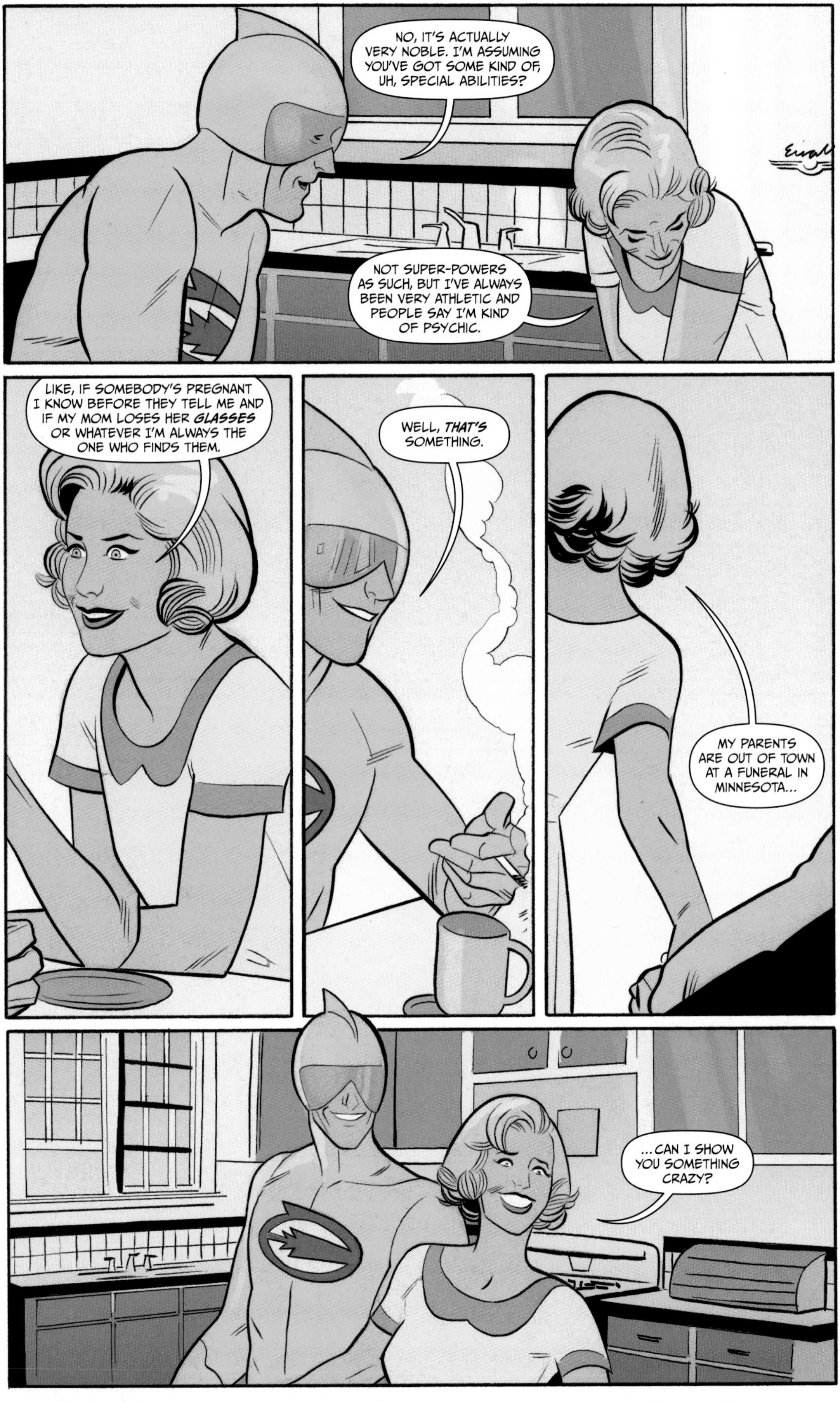
NO, IT'S ACTUALLY VERY NOBLE. I'M ASSUMING YOU'VE GOT SOME KIND OF, UH, SPECIAL ABILITIES?
NOT SUPER-POWERS AS SUCH, BUT I'VE ALWAYS BEEN VERY ATHLETIC AND PEOPLE SAY I'M KIND OF PSYCHIC.
LIKE, IF SOMEBODY'S PREGNANT I KNOW BEFORE THEY TELL ME AND IF MY MOM LOSES HER *GLASSES* OR WHATEVER I'M ALWAYS THE ONE WHO FINDS THEM.
WELL, *THAT'S* SOMETHING.
MY PARENTS ARE OUT OF TOWN AT A FUNERAL IN MINNESOTA...
...CAN I SHOW YOU SOMETHING CRAZY?

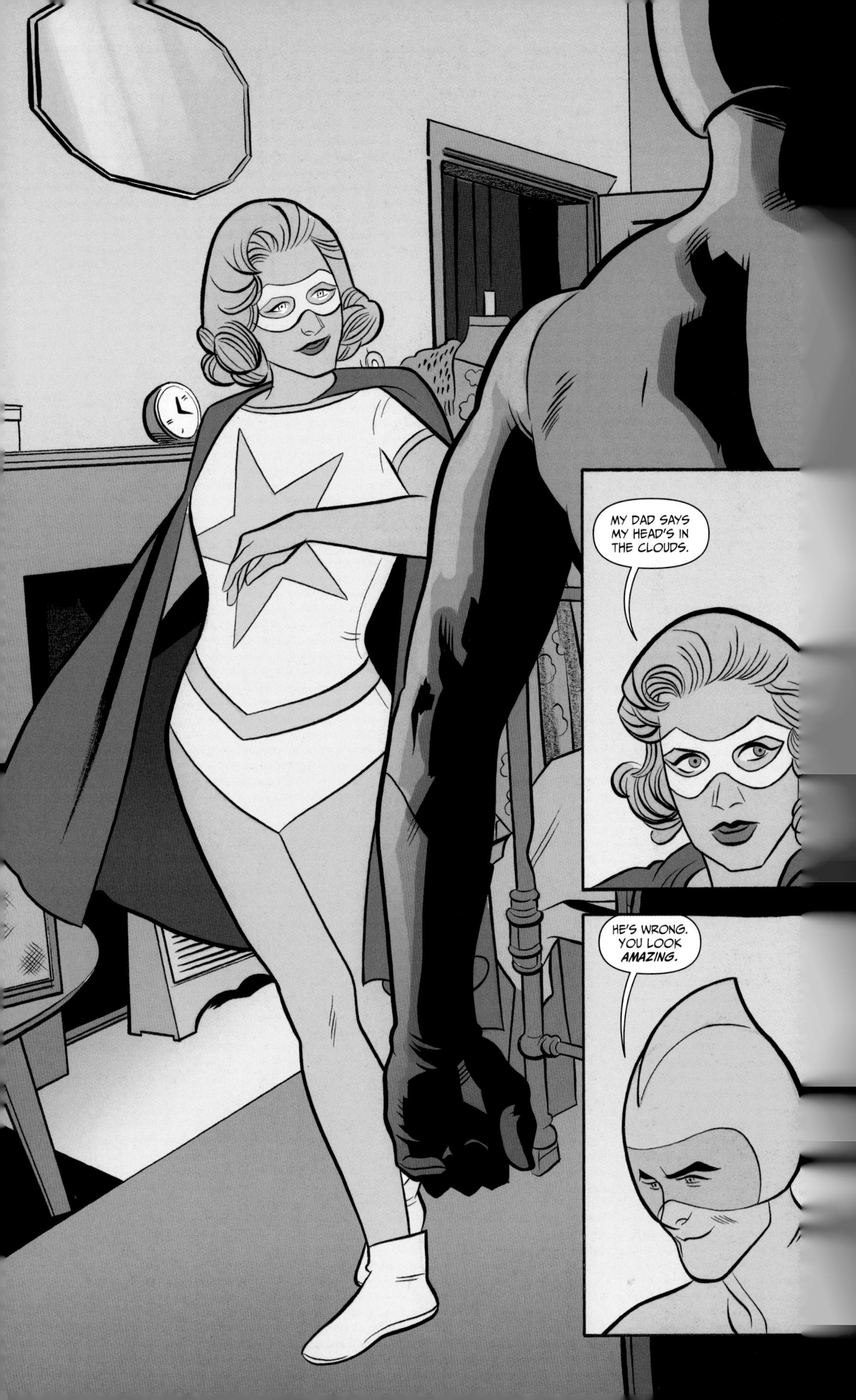
MY DAD SAYS MY HEAD'S IN THE CLOUDS.
HE'S WRONG. YOU LOOK *AMAZING.*

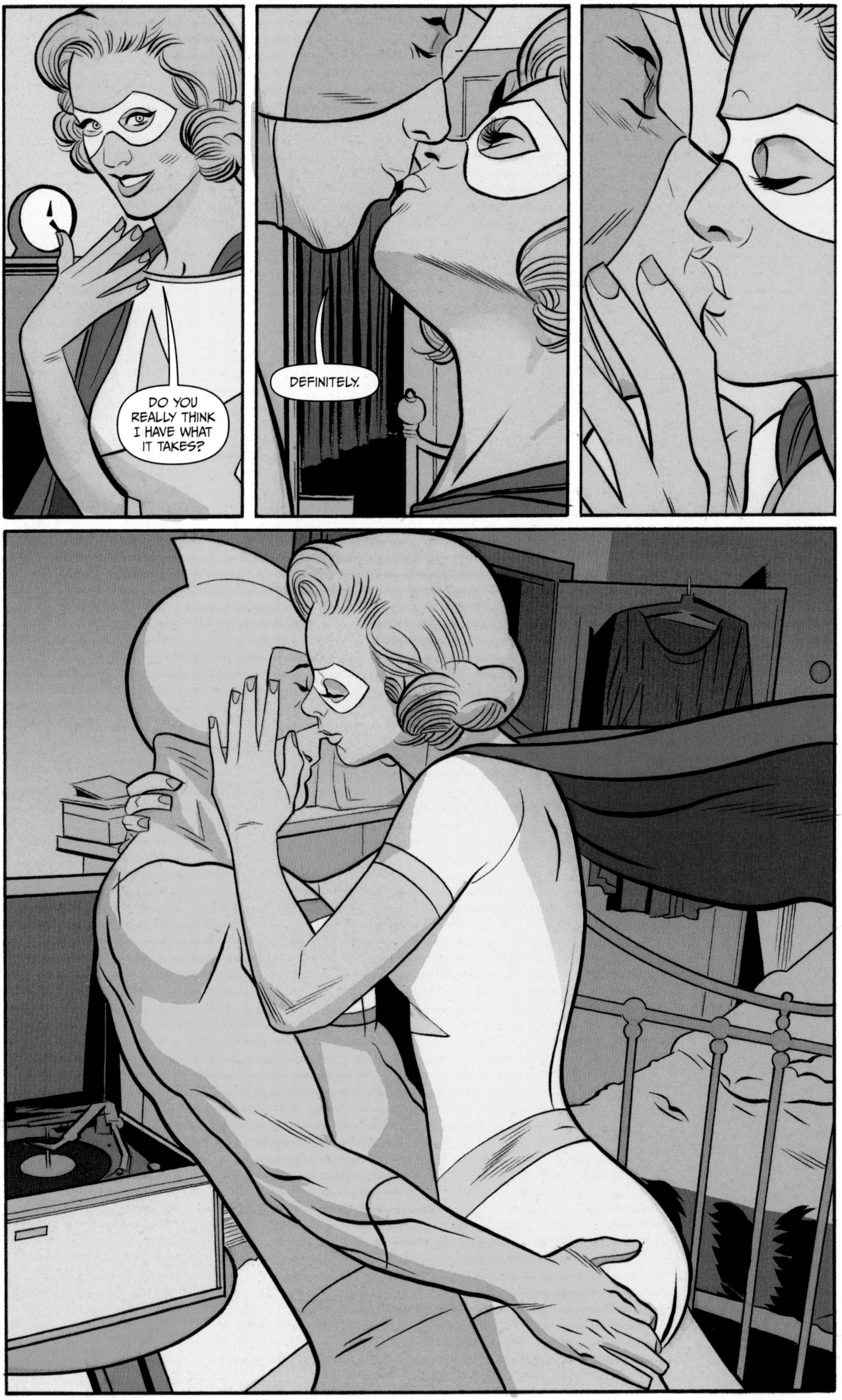
DO YOU REALLY THINK I HAVE WHAT IT TAKES?
DEFINITELY.

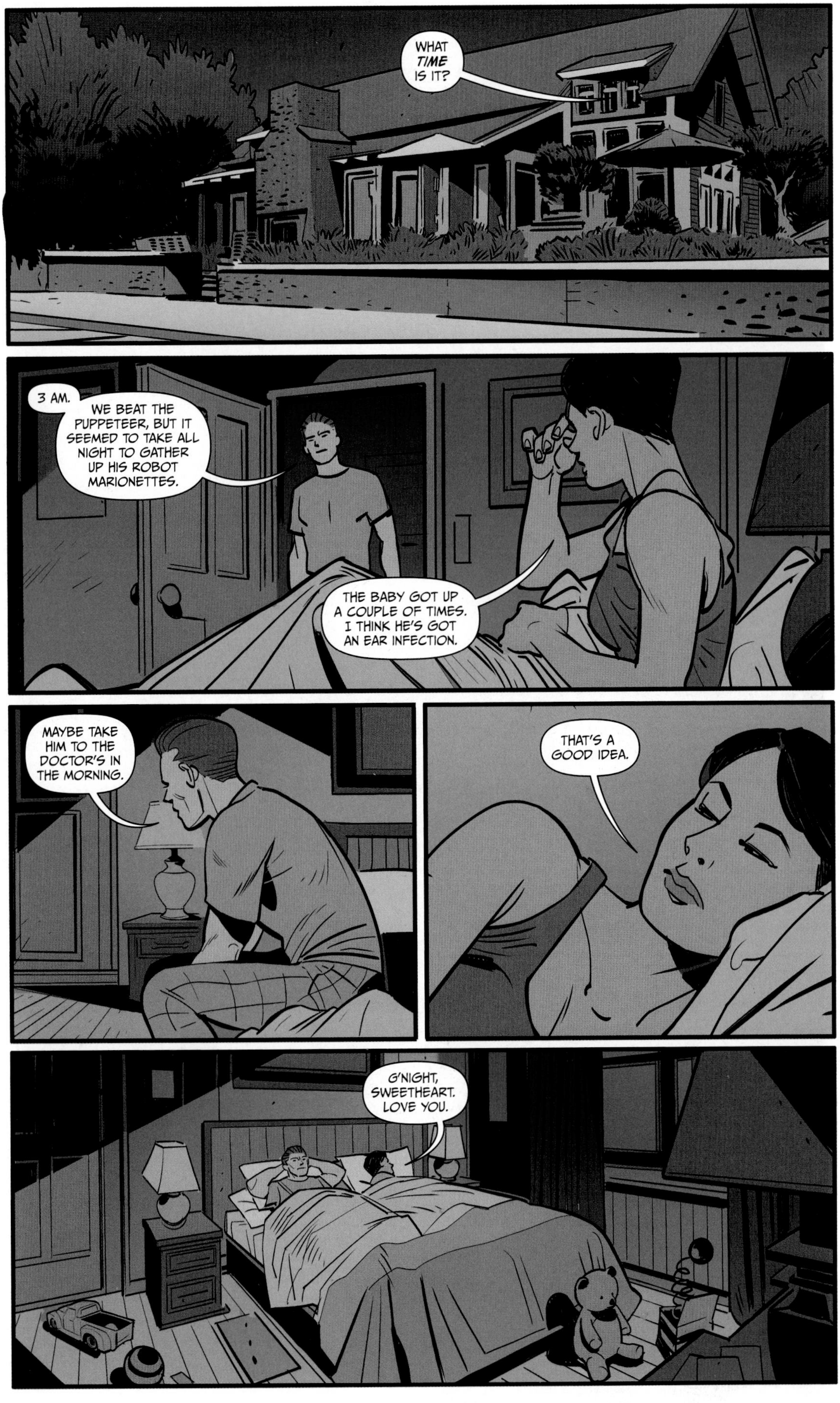
WHAT *TIME* IS IT?
3 AM.
WE BEAT THE PUPPETEER, BUT IT SEEMED TO TAKE ALL NIGHT TO GATHER UP HIS ROBOT MARIONETTES.
THE BABY GOT UP A COUPLE OF TIMES. I THINK HE'S GOT AN EAR INFECTION.
MAYBE TAKE HIM TO THE DOCTOR'S IN THE MORNING.
THAT'S A GOOD IDEA.
G'NIGHT, SWEETHEART. LOVE YOU.

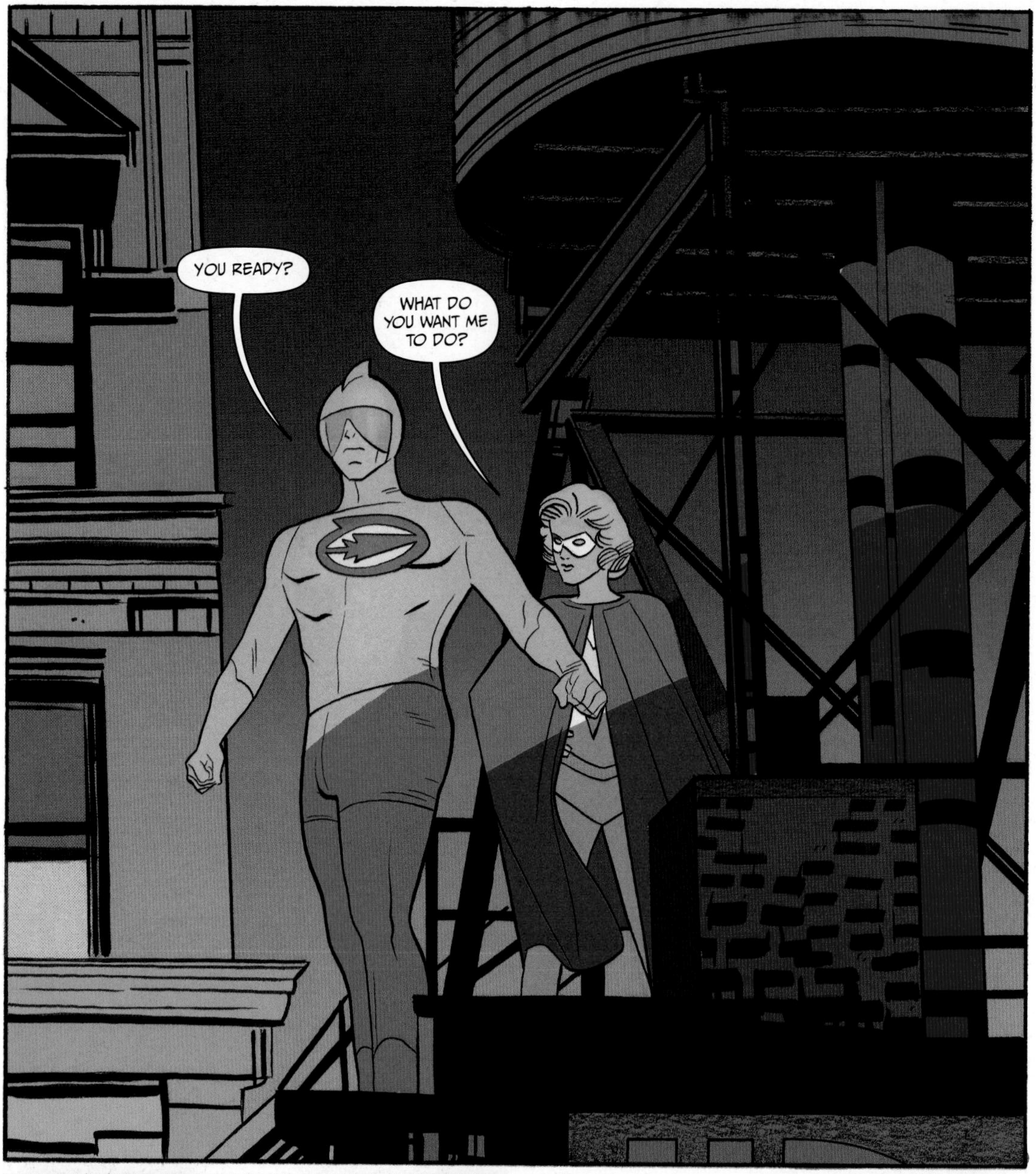
YOU READY?
WHAT DO YOU WANT ME TO DO?

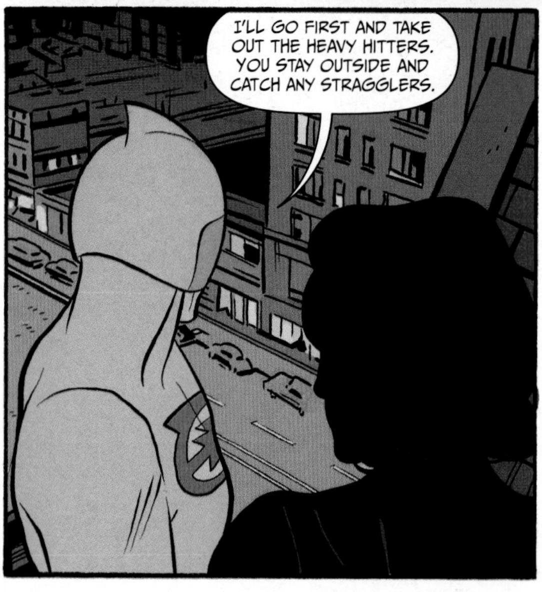
I'LL GO FIRST AND TAKE OUT THE HEAVY HITTERS. YOU STAY OUTSIDE AND CATCH ANY STRAGGLERS.

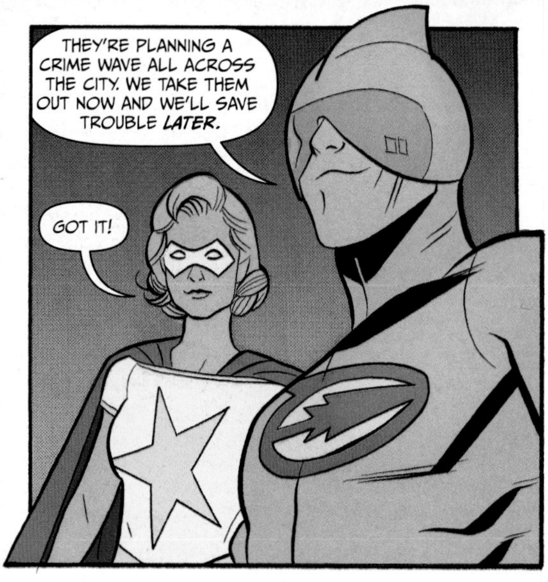
THEY'RE PLANNING A CRIME WAVE ALL ACROSS THE CITY. WE TAKE THEM OUT NOW AND WE'LL SAVE TROUBLE *LATER.*
GOT IT!

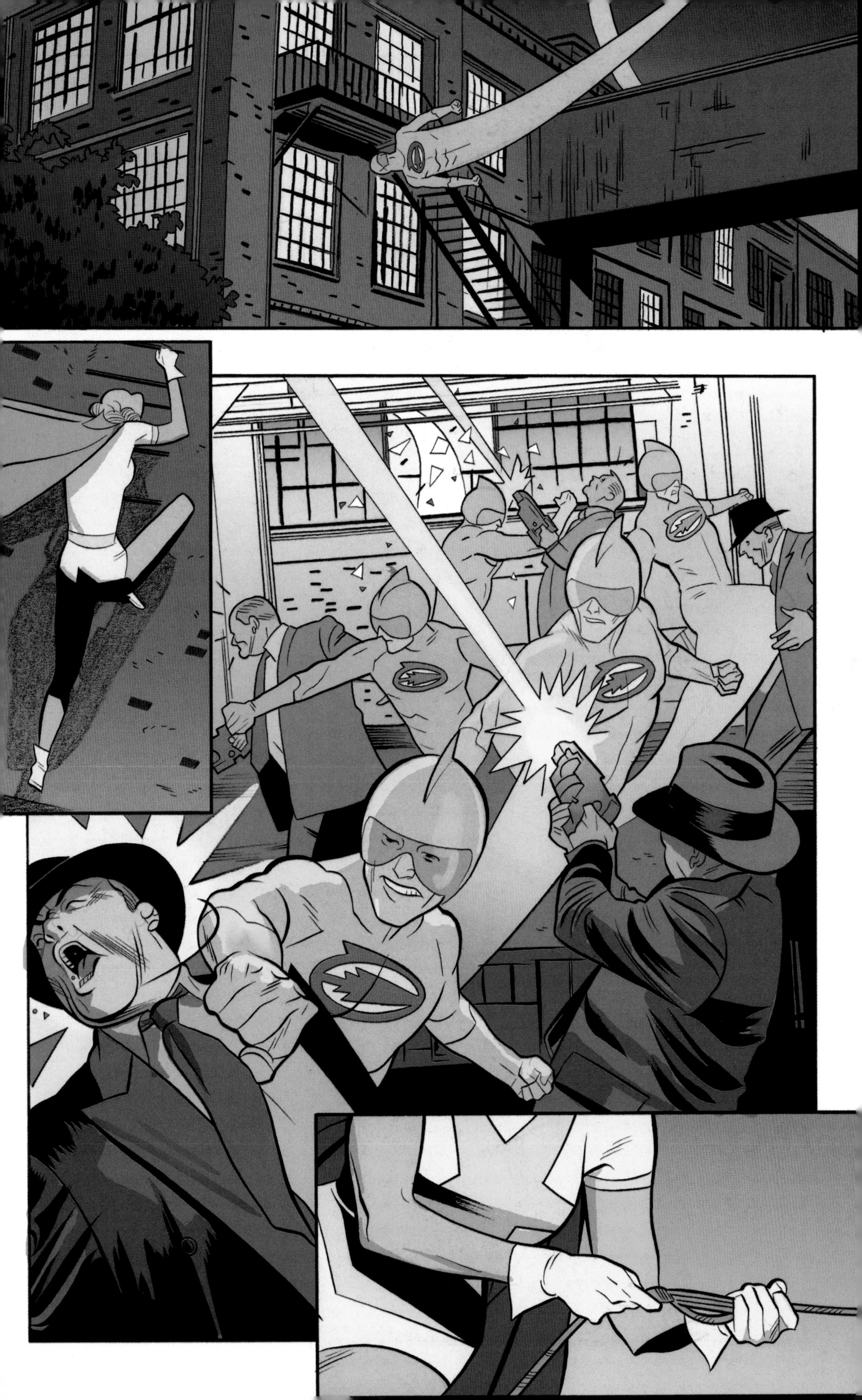

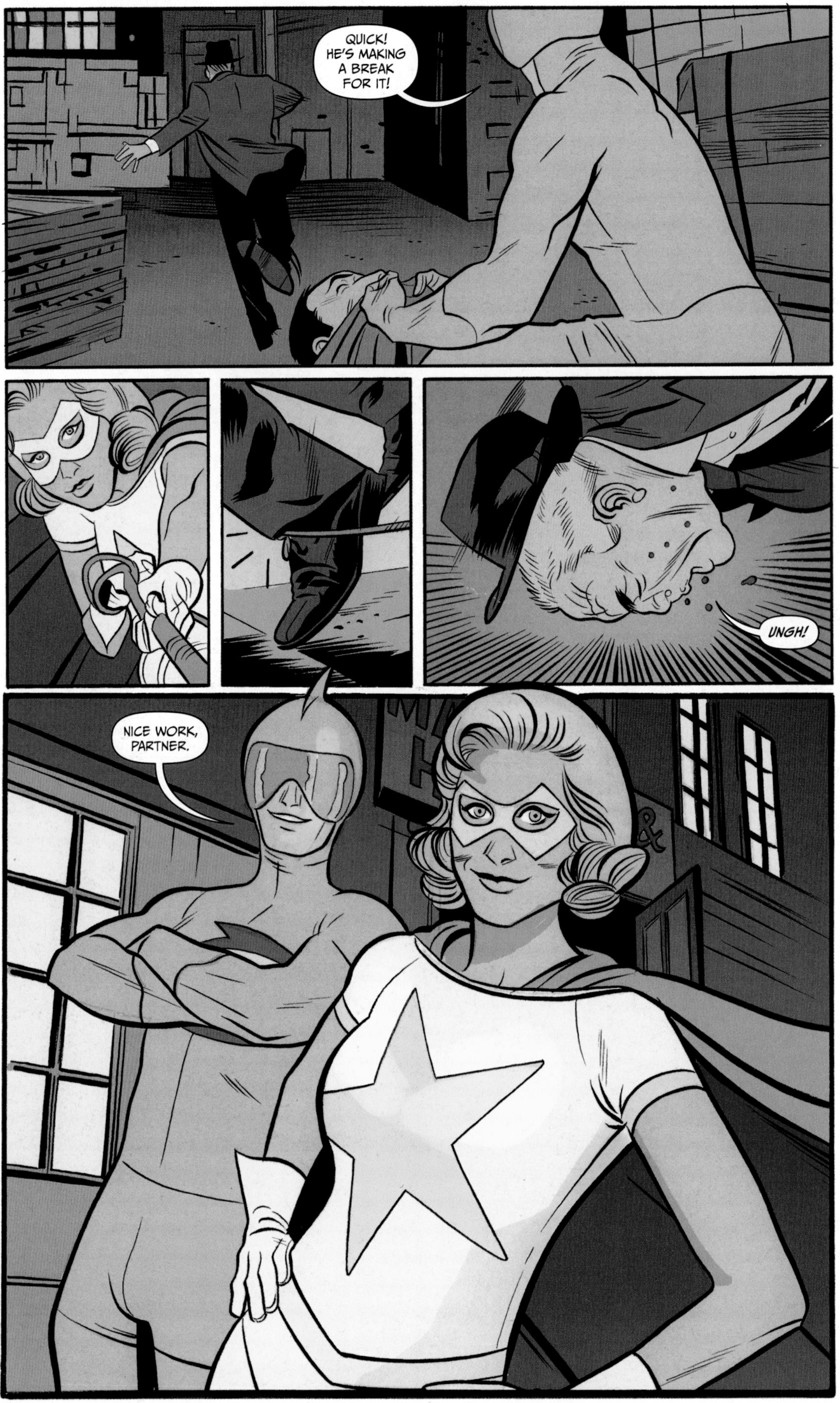
QUICK! HE'S MAKING A BREAK FOR IT!
UNGH!
NICE WORK, PARTNER.

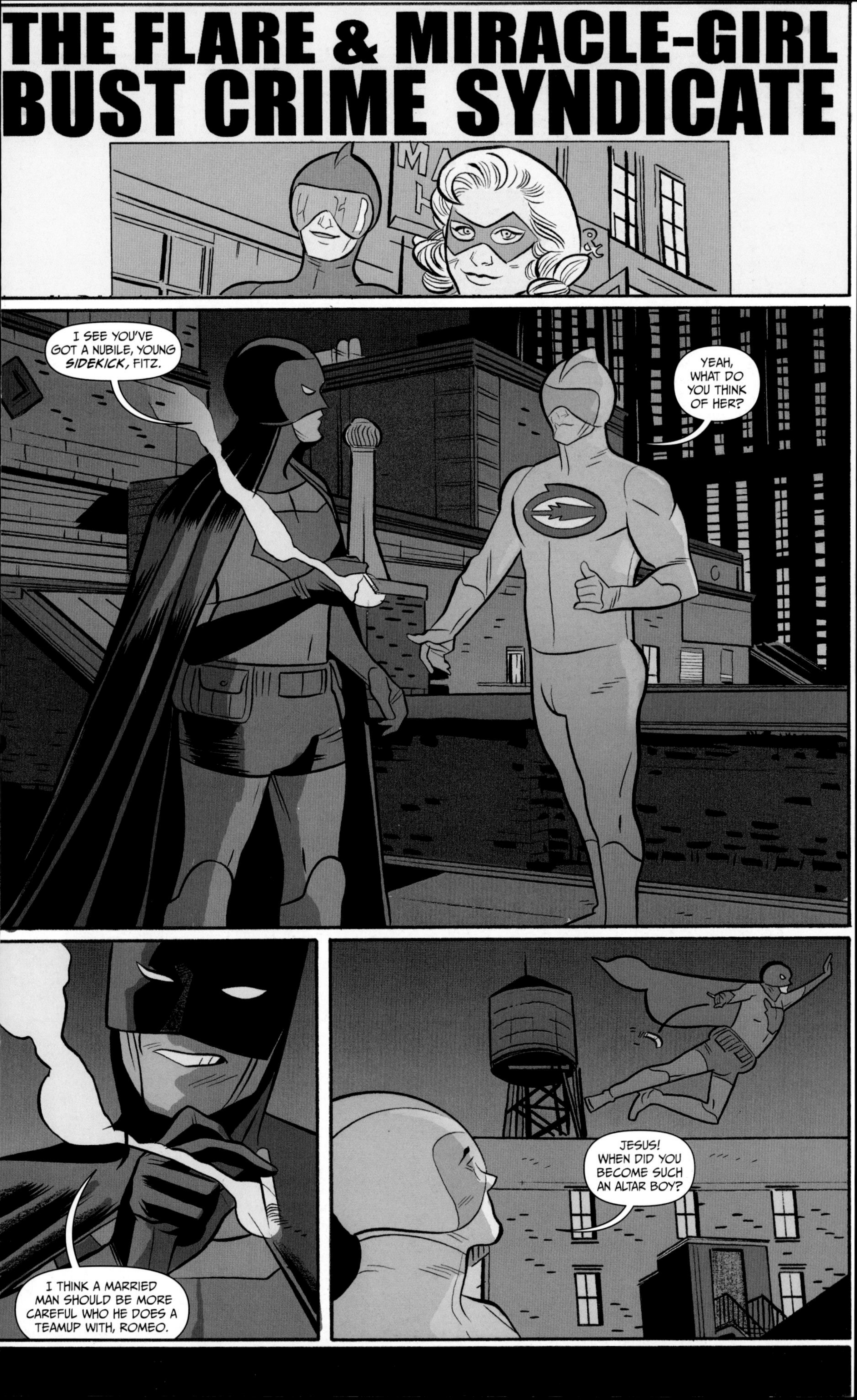
THE FLARE & MIRACLE-GIRL BUST CRIME SYNDICATE
I SEE YOU'VE GOT A NUBILE, YOUNG *SIDEKICK,* FITZ.
YEAH, WHAT DO YOU THINK OF HER?
I THINK A MARRIED MAN SHOULD BE MORE CAREFUL WHO HE DOES A TEAMUP WITH, ROMEO.
JESUS! WHEN DID YOU BECOME SUCH AN ALTAR BOY?

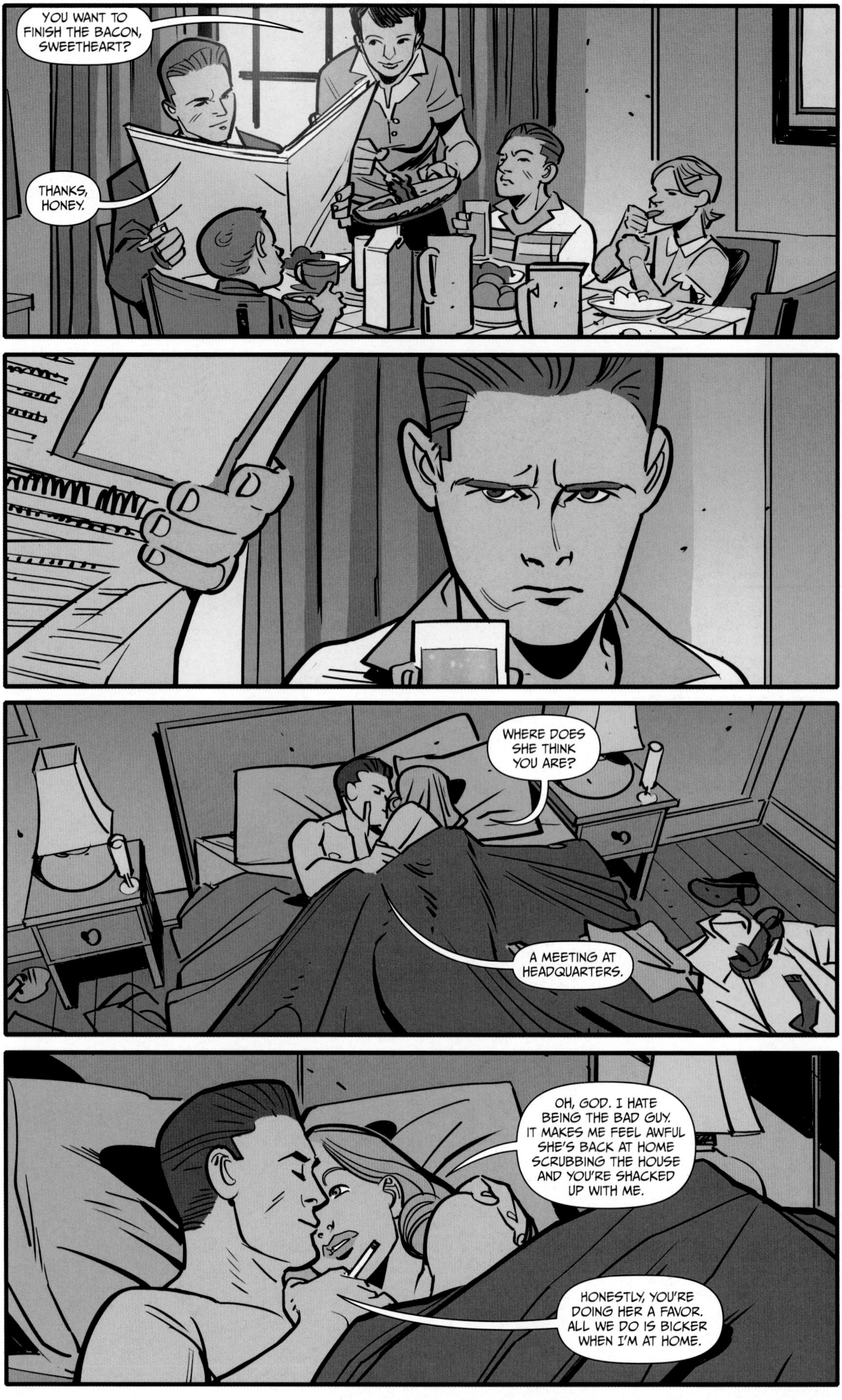
YOU WANT TO FINISH THE BACON, SWEETHEART?
THANKS, HONEY.
WHERE DOES SHE THINK YOU ARE?
A MEETING AT HEADQUARTERS.
OH, GOD. I HATE BEING THE BAD GUY. IT MAKES ME FEEL AWFUL SHE'S BACK AT HOME SCRUBBING THE HOUSE AND YOU'RE SHACKED UP WITH ME.
HONESTLY, YOU'RE DOING HER A FAVOR. ALL WE DO IS BICKER WHEN I'M AT HOME.

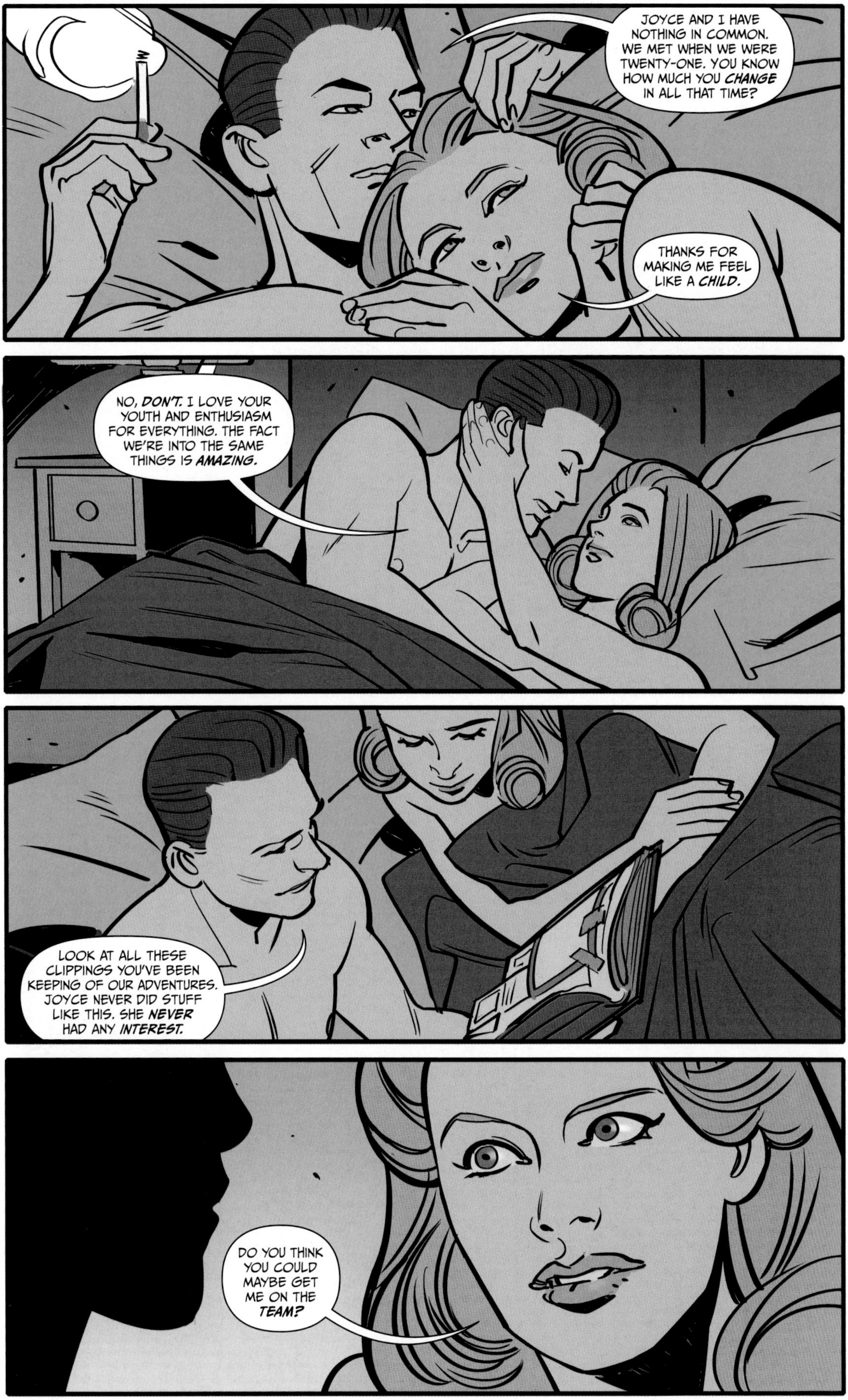
JOYCE AND I HAVE NOTHING IN COMMON. WE MET WHEN WE WERE TWENTY-ONE. YOU KNOW HOW MUCH YOU *CHANGE* IN ALL THAT TIME?
THANKS FOR MAKING ME FEEL LIKE A *CHILD.*
NO, *DON'T.* I LOVE YOUR YOUTH AND ENTHUSIASM FOR EVERYTHING. THE FACT WE'RE INTO THE SAME THINGS IS *AMAZING.*
LOOK AT ALL THESE CLIPPINGS YOU'VE BEEN KEEPING OF OUR ADVENTURES. JOYCE NEVER DID STUFF LIKE THIS. SHE *NEVER* HAD ANY *INTEREST.*
DO YOU THINK YOU COULD MAYBE GET ME ON THE *TEAM?*

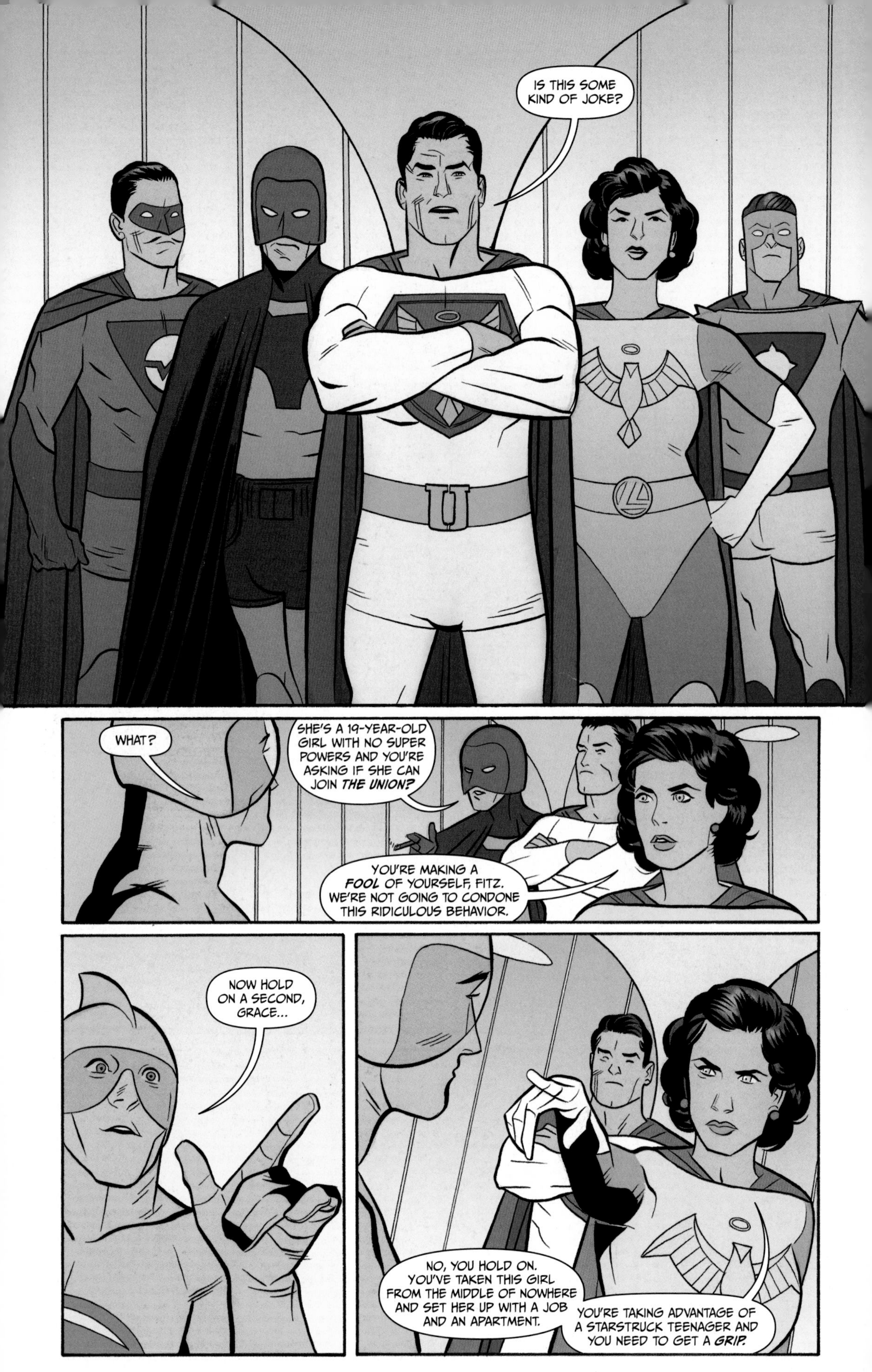
IS THIS SOME KIND OF JOKE?
WHAT?
SHE'S A 19-YEAR-OLD GIRL WITH NO SUPER POWERS AND YOU'RE ASKING IF SHE CAN JOIN THE UNION?
YOU'RE MAKING A FOOL OF YOURSELF, FITZ. WE'RE NOT GOING TO CONDONE THIS RIDICULOUS BEHAVIOR.
NOW HOLD ON A SECOND, GRACE...
NO, YOU HOLD ON. YOU'VE TAKEN THIS GIRL FROM THE MIDDLE OF NOWHERE AND SET HER UP WITH A JOB AND AN APARTMENT.
YOU'RE TAKING ADVANTAGE OF A STARSTRUCK TEENAGER AND YOU NEED TO GET A GRIP.

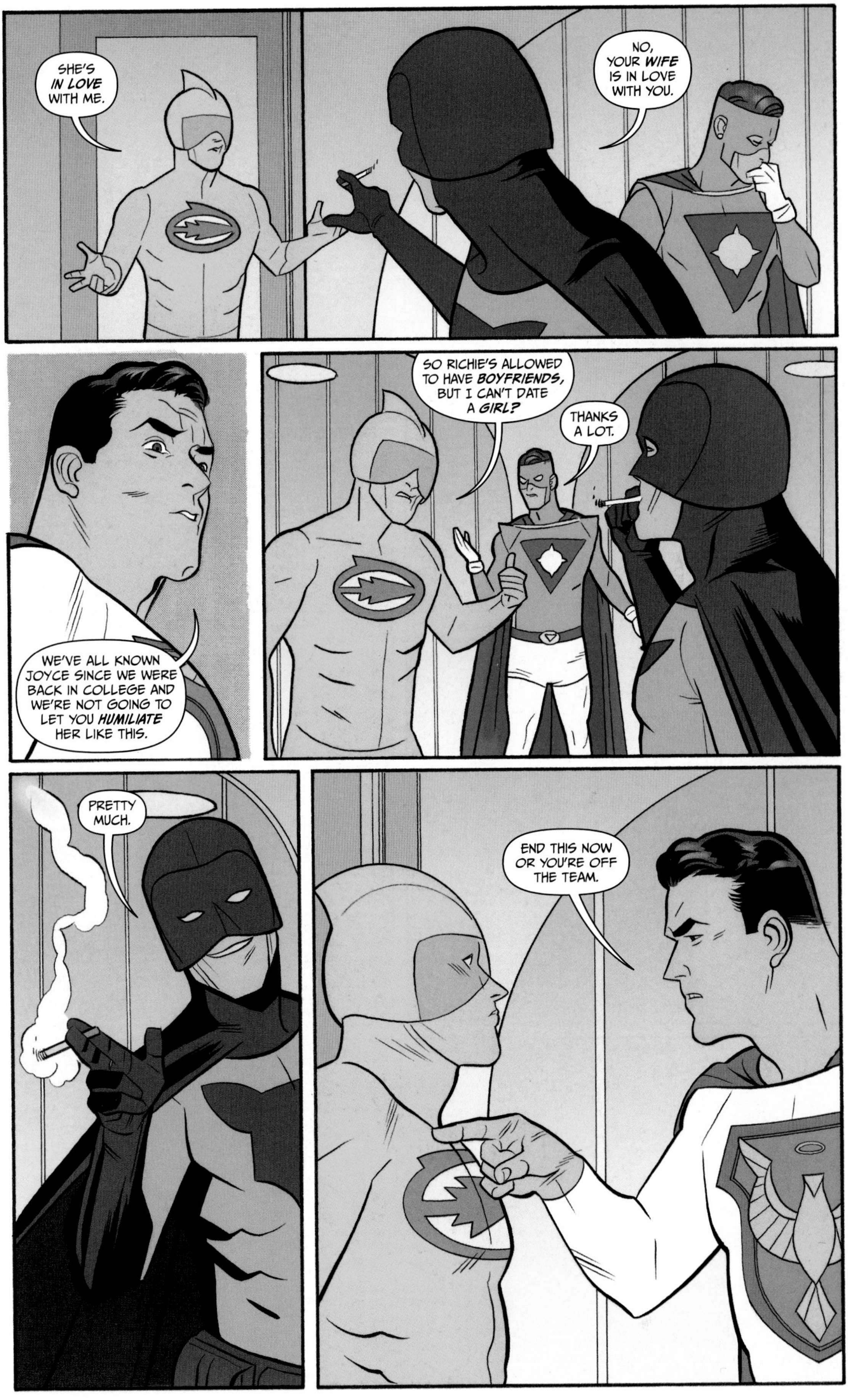
SHE'S IN LOVE WITH ME.
NO, YOUR WIFE IS IN LOVE WITH YOU.
WE'VE ALL KNOWN JOYCE SINCE WE WERE BACK IN COLLEGE AND WE'RE NOT GOING TO LET YOU HUMILIATE HER LIKE THIS.
SO RICHIE'S ALLOWED TO HAVE BOYFRIENDS, BUT I CAN'T DATE A GIRL?
THANKS A LOT.
PRETTY MUCH.
END THIS NOW OR YOU'RE OFF THE TEAM.

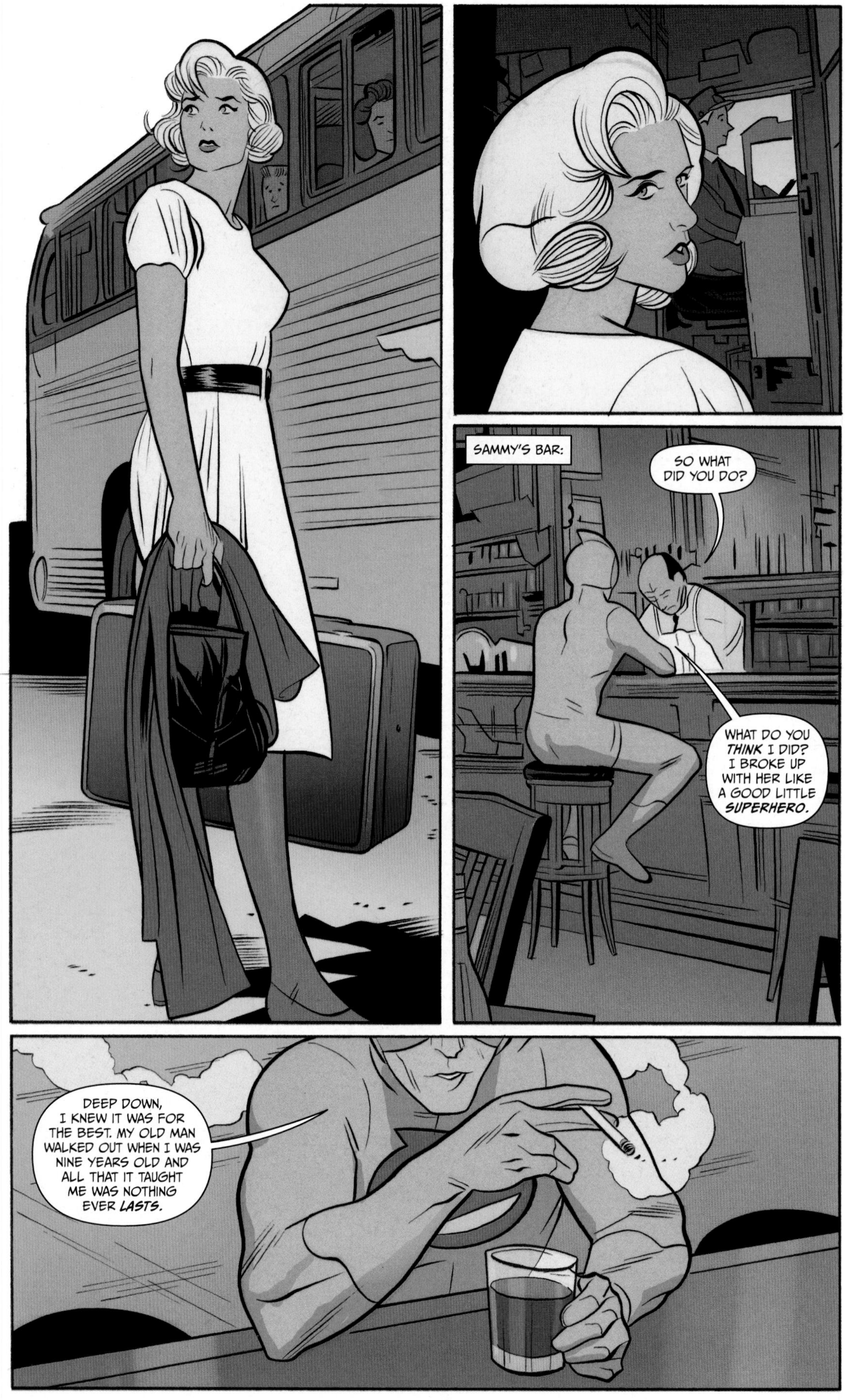
SAMMY'S BAR:
SO WHAT DID YOU DO?
WHAT DO YOU *THINK* I DID? I BROKE UP WITH HER LIKE A GOOD LITTLE ***SUPERHERO.***
DEEP DOWN, I KNEW IT WAS FOR THE BEST. MY OLD MAN WALKED OUT WHEN I WAS NINE YEARS OLD AND ALL THAT IT TAUGHT ME WAS NOTHING EVER ***LASTS.***

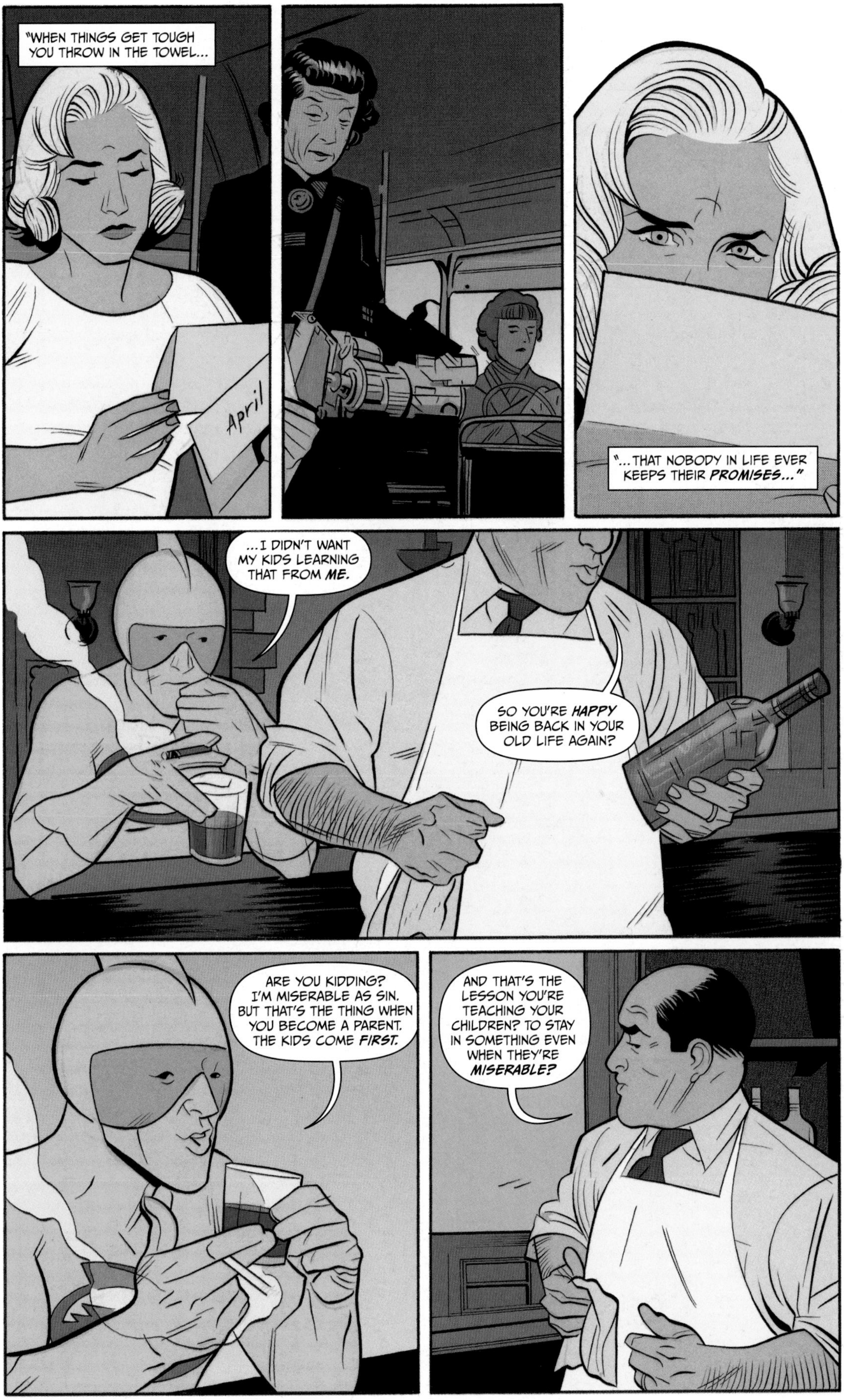
"WHEN THINGS GET TOUGH YOU THROW IN THE TOWEL...
April
"...THAT NOBODY IN LIFE EVER KEEPS THEIR *PROMISES...*"
...I DIDN'T WANT MY KIDS LEARNING THAT FROM *ME.*
SO YOU'RE *HAPPY* BEING BACK IN YOUR OLD LIFE AGAIN?
ARE YOU KIDDING? I'M MISERABLE AS SIN. BUT THAT'S THE THING WHEN YOU BECOME A PARENT. THE KIDS COME *FIRST.*
AND THAT'S THE LESSON YOU'RE TEACHING YOUR CHILDREN? TO STAY IN SOMETHING EVEN WHEN THEY'RE *MISERABLE?*

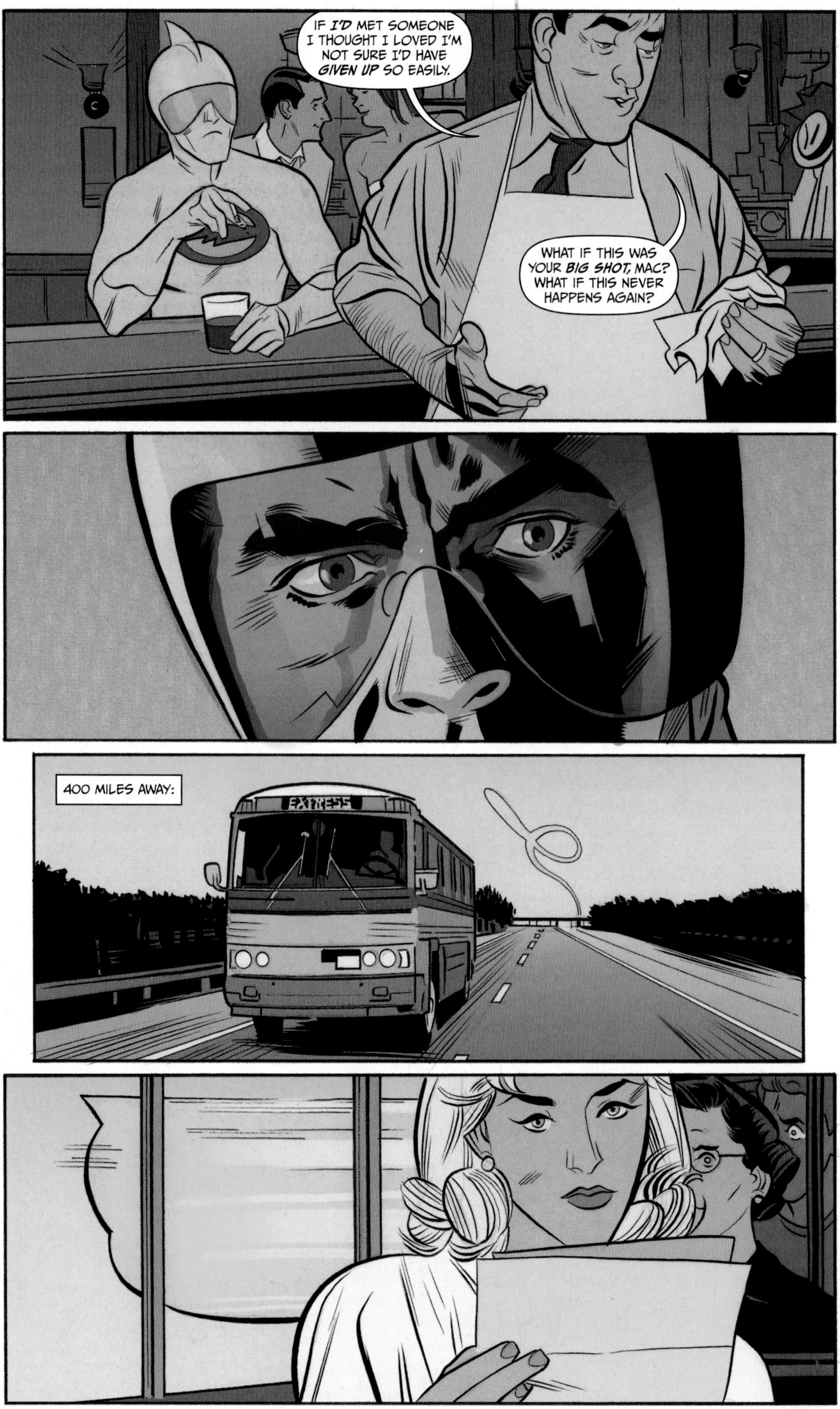
IF I'D MET SOMEONE I THOUGHT I LOVED I'M NOT SURE I'D HAVE GIVEN UP SO EASILY.
WHAT IF THIS WAS YOUR BIG SHOT, MAC? WHAT IF THIS NEVER HAPPENS AGAIN?
400 MILES AWAY:
EXPRESS

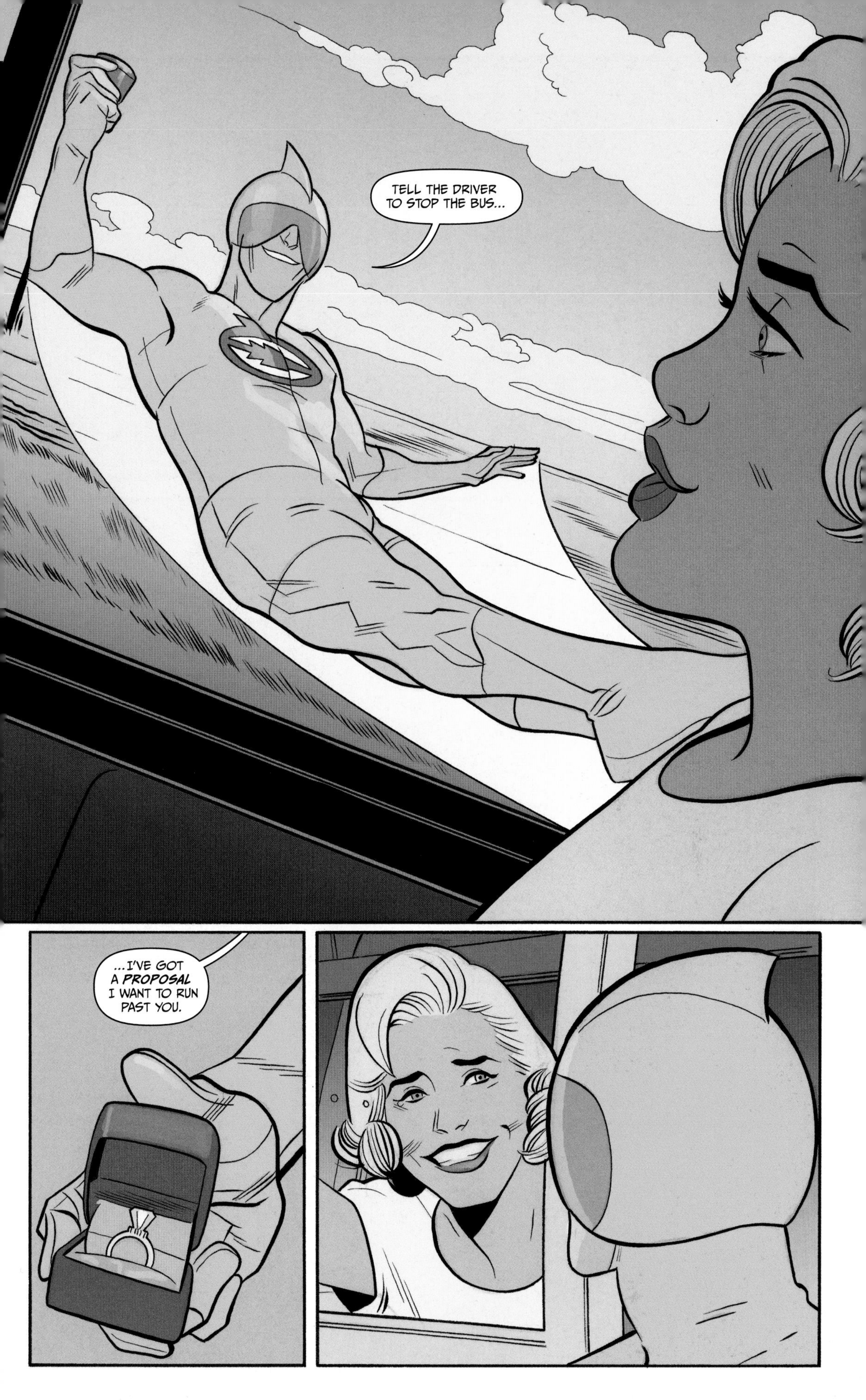
TELL THE DRIVER TO STOP THE BUS...
...I'VE GOT A *PROPOSAL* I WANT TO RUN PAST YOU.

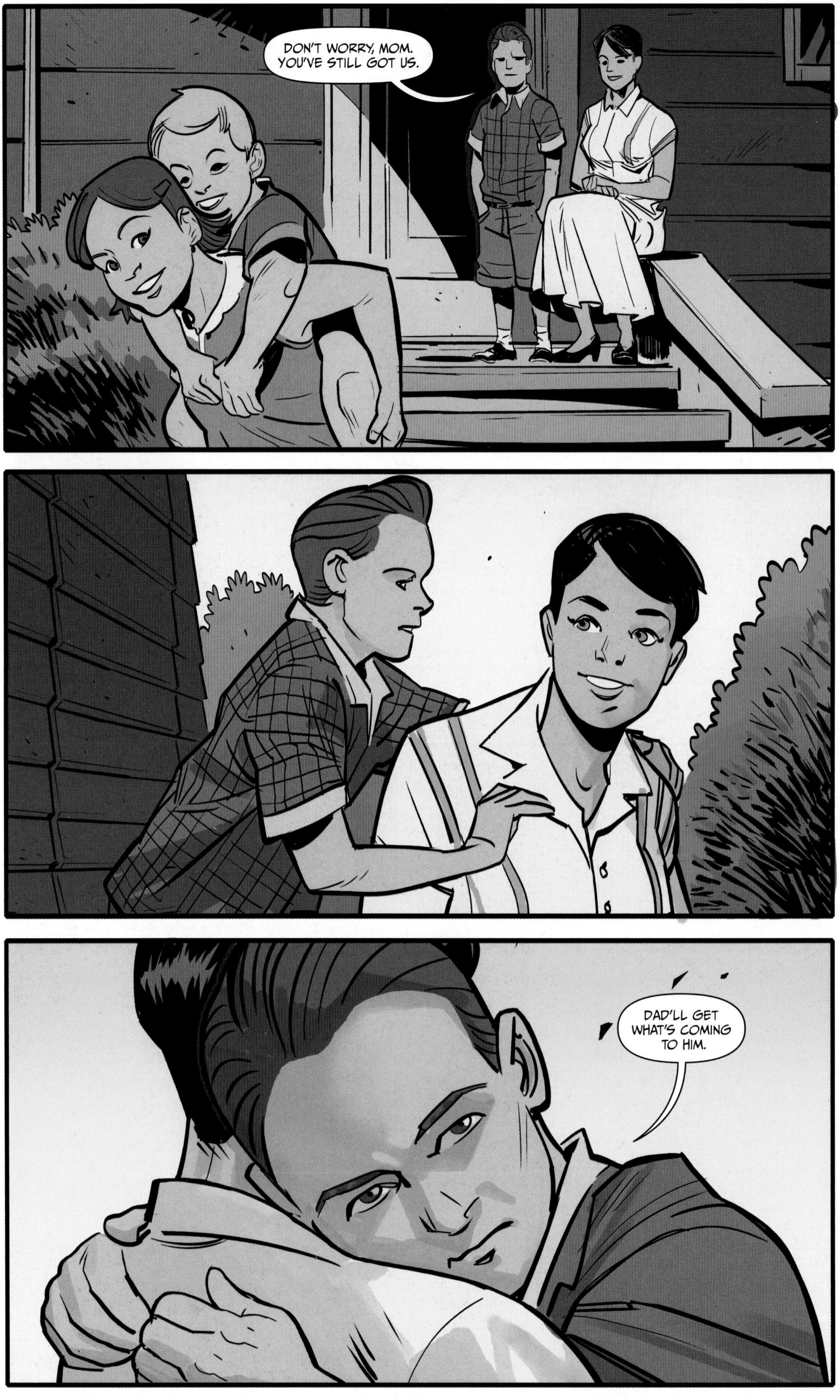
DON'T WORRY, MOM. YOU'VE STILL GOT US.
DAD'LL GET WHAT'S COMING TO HIM.

CHAPTER 4

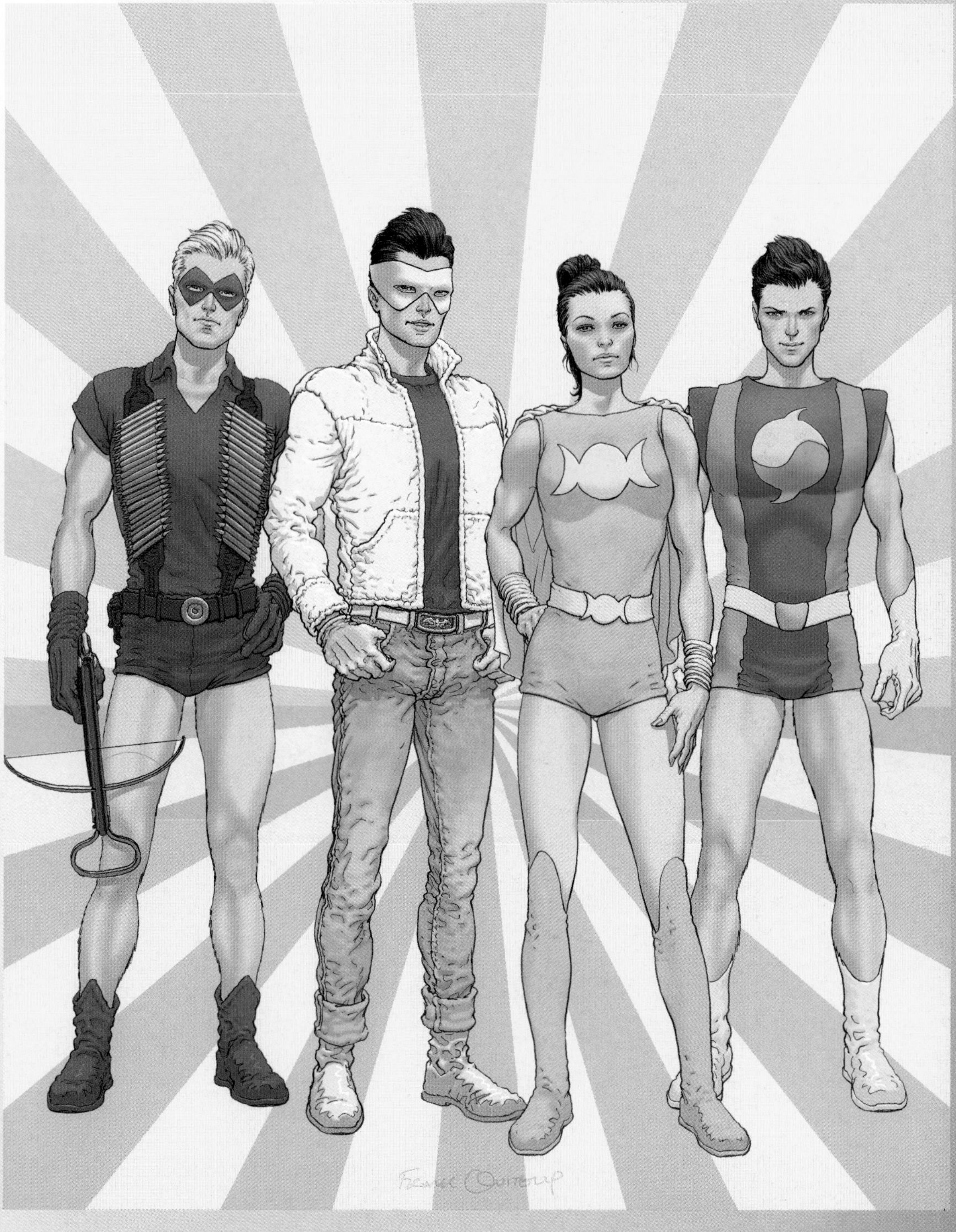

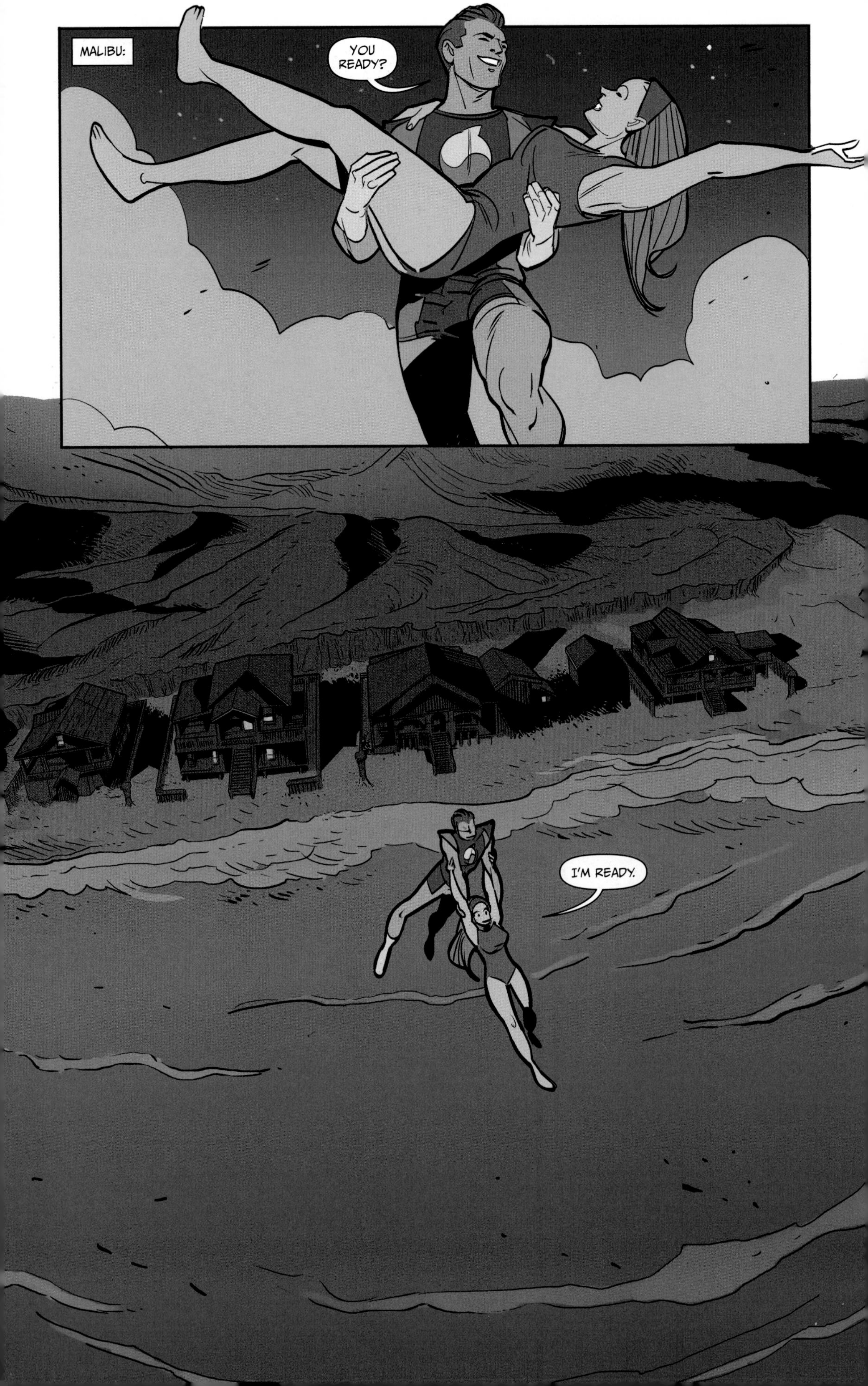
MALIBU:
YOU READY?
I'M READY.

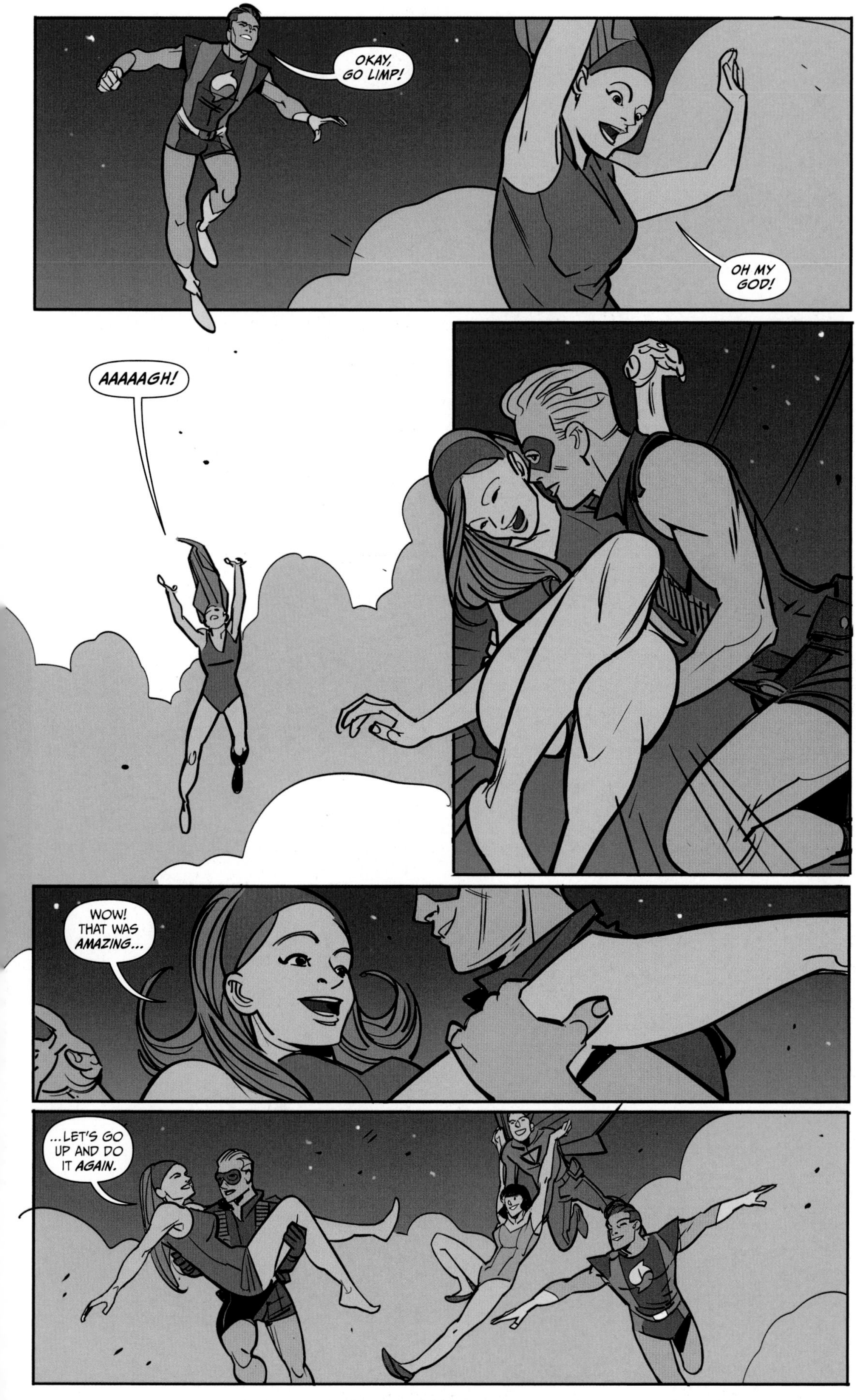
OKAY, GO LIMP!
OH MY GOD!
AAAAAGH!
WOW! THAT WAS AMAZING...
...LET'S GO UP AND DO IT AGAIN.

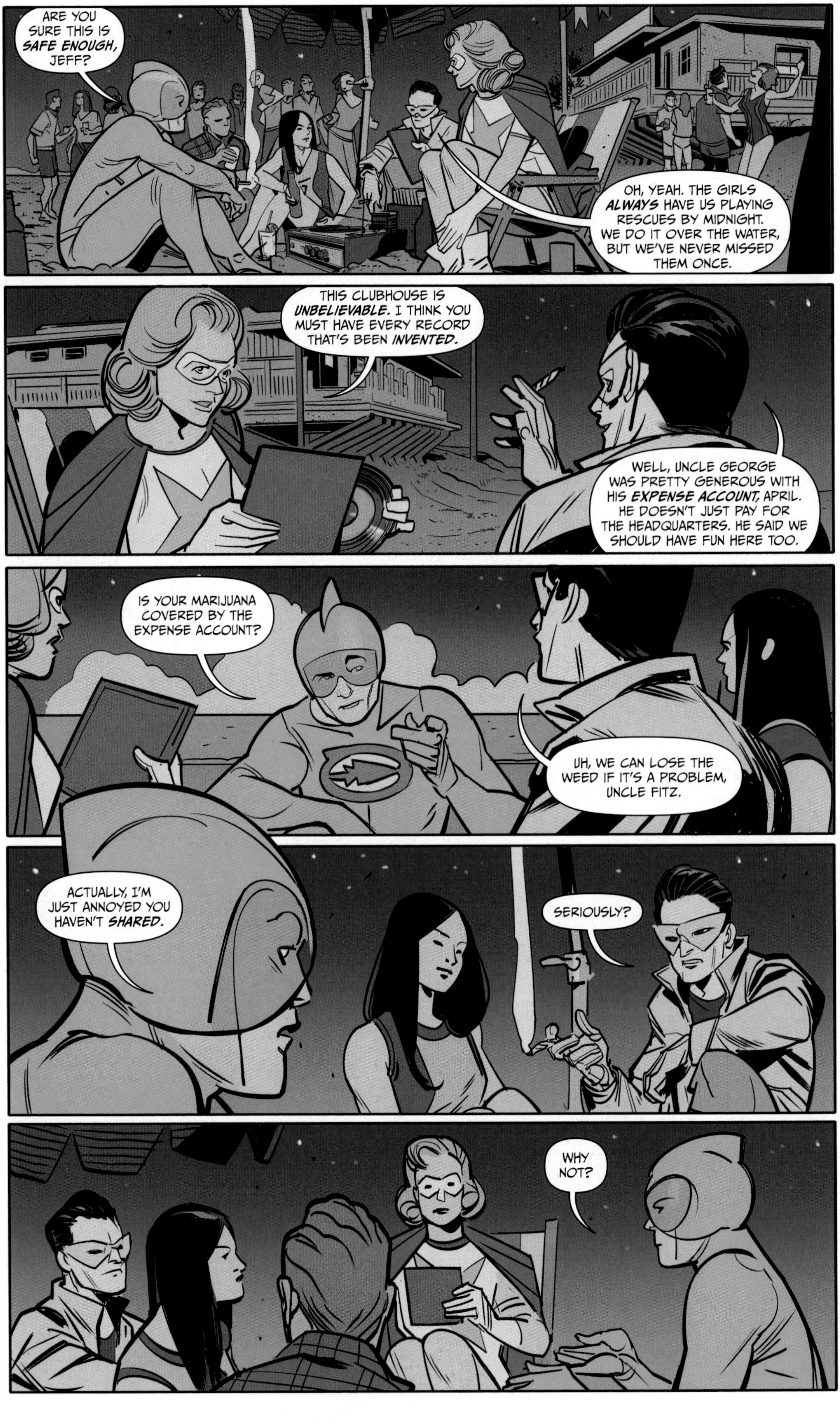
ARE YOU SURE THIS IS SAFE ENOUGH, JEFF?
OH, YEAH. THE GIRLS ALWAYS HAVE US PLAYING RESCUES BY MIDNIGHT. WE DO IT OVER THE WATER, BUT WE'VE NEVER MISSED THEM ONCE.
THIS CLUBHOUSE IS UNBELIEVABLE. I THINK YOU MUST HAVE EVERY RECORD THAT'S BEEN INVENTED.
WELL, UNCLE GEORGE WAS PRETTY GENEROUS WITH HIS EXPENSE ACCOUNT, APRIL. HE DOESN'T JUST PAY FOR THE HEADQUARTERS. HE SAID WE SHOULD HAVE FUN HERE TOO.
IS YOUR MARIJUANA COVERED BY THE EXPENSE ACCOUNT?
UH, WE CAN LOSE THE WEED IF IT'S A PROBLEM, UNCLE FITZ.
ACTUALLY, I'M JUST ANNOYED YOU HAVEN'T SHARED.
SERIOUSLY?
WHY NOT?

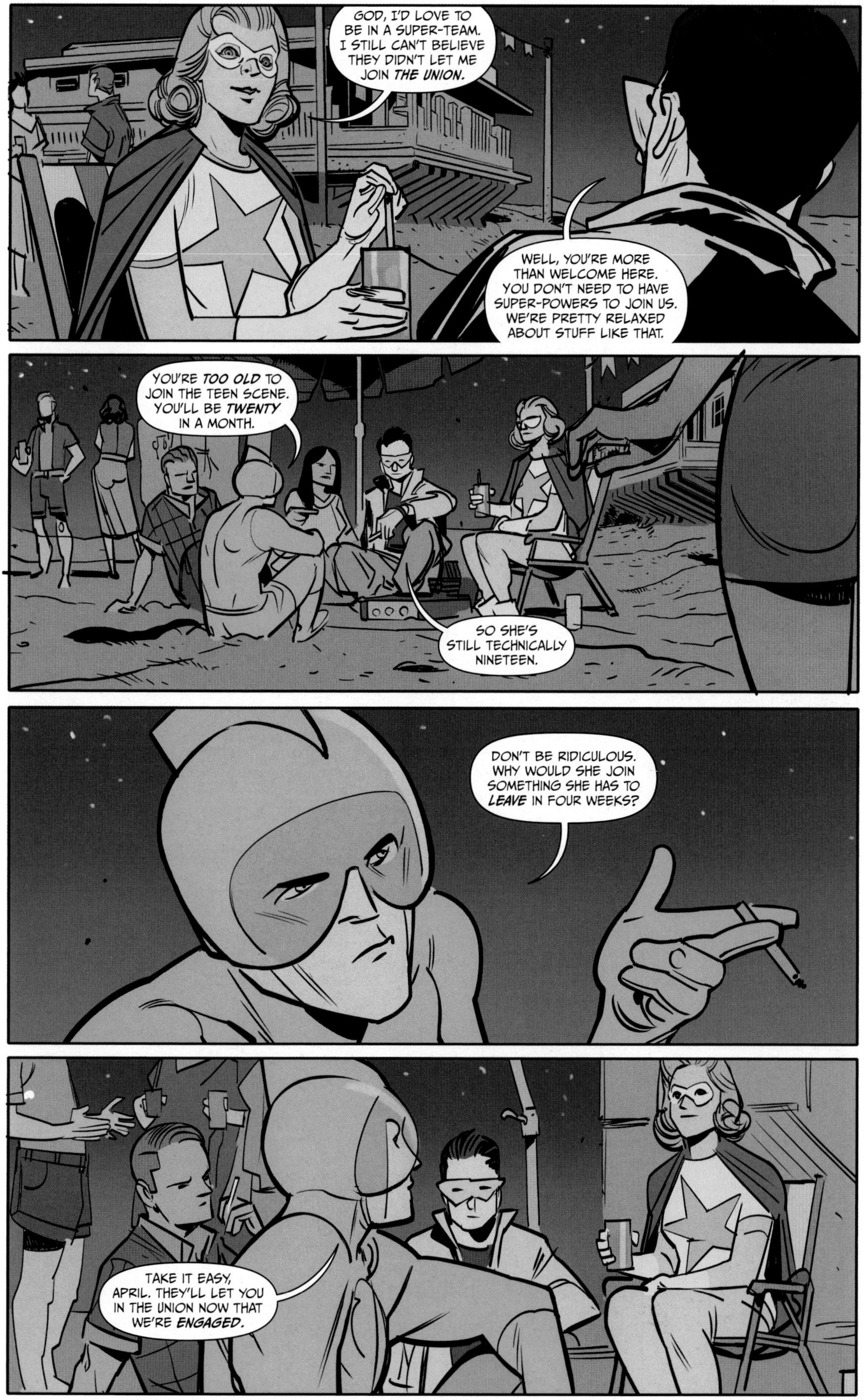
GOD, I'D LOVE TO BE IN A SUPER-TEAM. I STILL CAN'T BELIEVE THEY DIDN'T LET ME JOIN THE UNION.
WELL, YOU'RE MORE THAN WELCOME HERE. YOU DON'T NEED TO HAVE SUPER-POWERS TO JOIN US. WE'RE PRETTY RELAXED ABOUT STUFF LIKE THAT.
YOU'RE TOO OLD TO JOIN THE TEEN SCENE. YOU'LL BE TWENTY IN A MONTH.
SO SHE'S STILL TECHNICALLY NINETEEN.
DON'T BE RIDICULOUS. WHY WOULD SHE JOIN SOMETHING SHE HAS TO LEAVE IN FOUR WEEKS?
TAKE IT EASY, APRIL. THEY'LL LET YOU IN THE UNION NOW THAT WE'RE ENGAGED.

SO HOW ARE THE KIDS?

THE LITTLE ONES ARE CONFUSED. PETER'S JUST ANGRY.

I DON'T THINK FITZ REALIZES WHAT A FOOL HE'S MAKING OF HIMSELF. SHE'S *HALF HIS AGE,* GRACE.

AREN'T THEY *ALWAYS?*

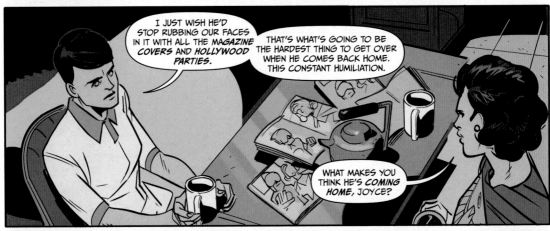

I JUST WISH HE'D STOP RUBBING OUR FACES IN IT WITH ALL THE *MAGAZINE COVERS* AND *HOLLYWOOD PARTIES.*

THAT'S WHAT'S GOING TO BE THE HARDEST THING TO GET OVER WHEN HE COMES BACK HOME. THIS CONSTANT HUMILIATION.

WHAT MAKES YOU THINK HE'S *COMING HOME,* JOYCE?

I'VE KNOWN HIM SINCE WE WERE TWENTY-ONE YEARS OLD. I KNOW FITZ BETTER THAN HE KNOWS *HIMSELF.*

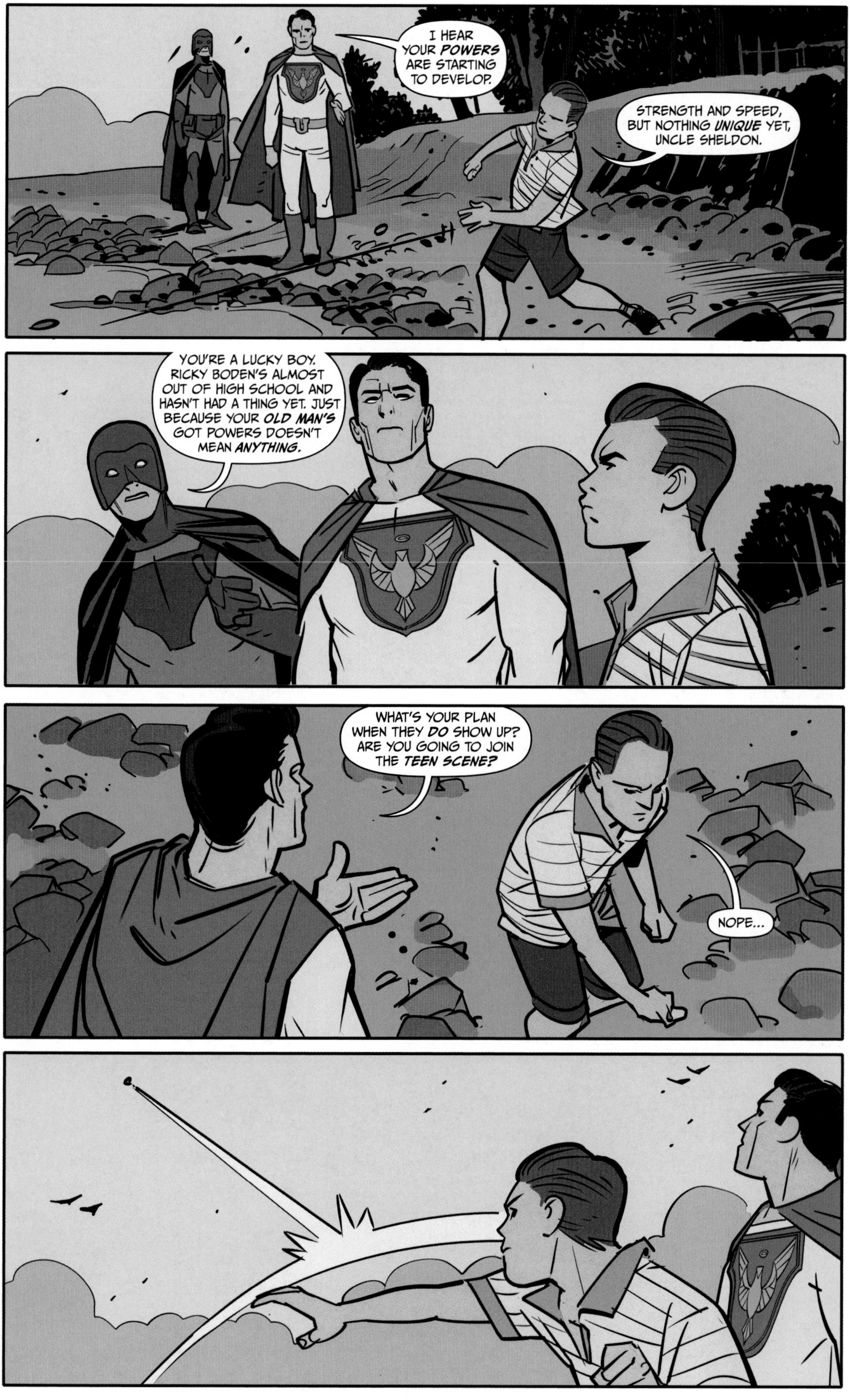
I HEAR YOUR POWERS ARE STARTING TO DEVELOP.
STRENGTH AND SPEED, BUT NOTHING UNIQUE YET, UNCLE SHELDON.
YOU'RE A LUCKY BOY. RICKY BODEN'S ALMOST OUT OF HIGH SCHOOL AND HASN'T HAD A THING YET. JUST BECAUSE YOUR OLD MAN'S GOT POWERS DOESN'T MEAN ANYTHING.
WHAT'S YOUR PLAN WHEN THEY DO SHOW UP? ARE YOU GOING TO JOIN THE TEEN SCENE?
NOPE...

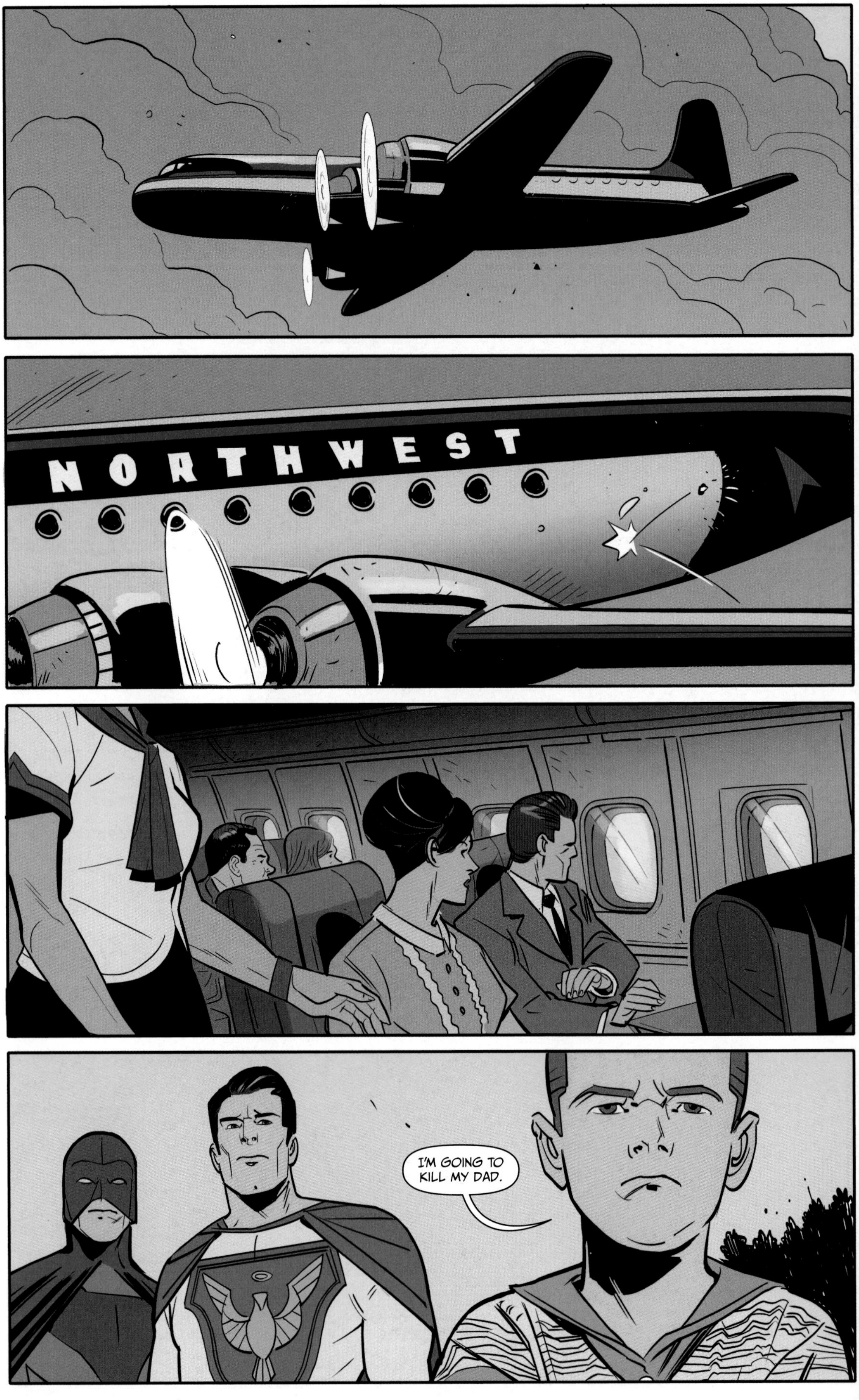
NORTHWEST
I'M GOING TO KILL MY DAD.

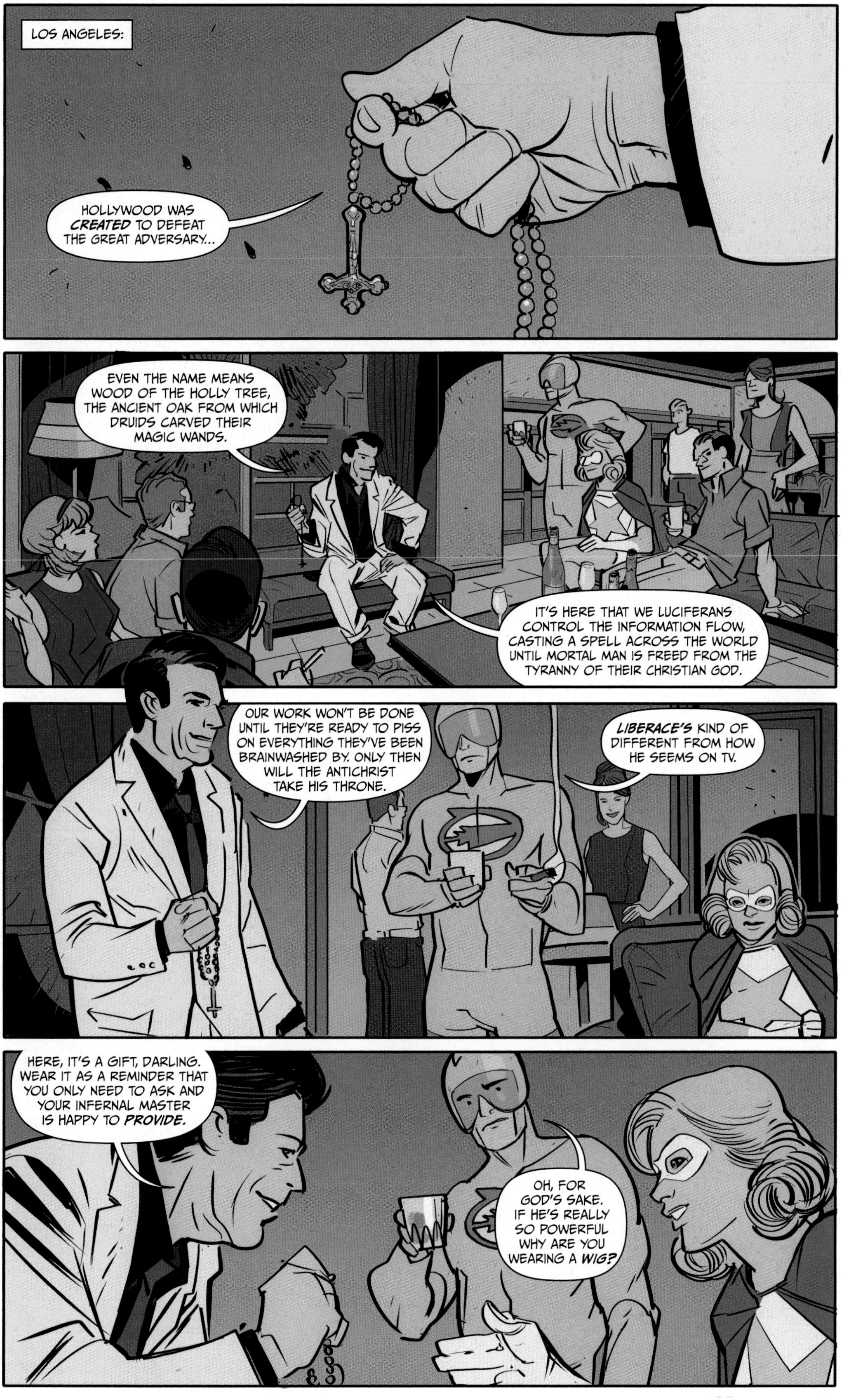
LOS ANGELES:
HOLLYWOOD WAS CREATED TO DEFEAT THE GREAT ADVERSARY...
EVEN THE NAME MEANS WOOD OF THE HOLLY TREE, THE ANCIENT OAK FROM WHICH DRUIDS CARVED THEIR MAGIC WANDS.
IT'S HERE THAT WE LUCIFERANS CONTROL THE INFORMATION FLOW, CASTING A SPELL ACROSS THE WORLD UNTIL MORTAL MAN IS FREED FROM THE TYRANNY OF THEIR CHRISTIAN GOD.
OUR WORK WON'T BE DONE UNTIL THEY'RE READY TO PISS ON EVERYTHING THEY'VE BEEN BRAINWASHED BY. ONLY THEN WILL THE ANTICHRIST TAKE HIS THRONE.
LIBERACE'S KIND OF DIFFERENT FROM HOW HE SEEMS ON TV.
HERE, IT'S A GIFT, DARLING. WEAR IT AS A REMINDER THAT YOU ONLY NEED TO ASK AND YOUR INFERNAL MASTER IS HAPPY TO PROVIDE.
OH, FOR GOD'S SAKE. IF HE'S REALLY SO POWERFUL WHY ARE YOU WEARING A WIG?

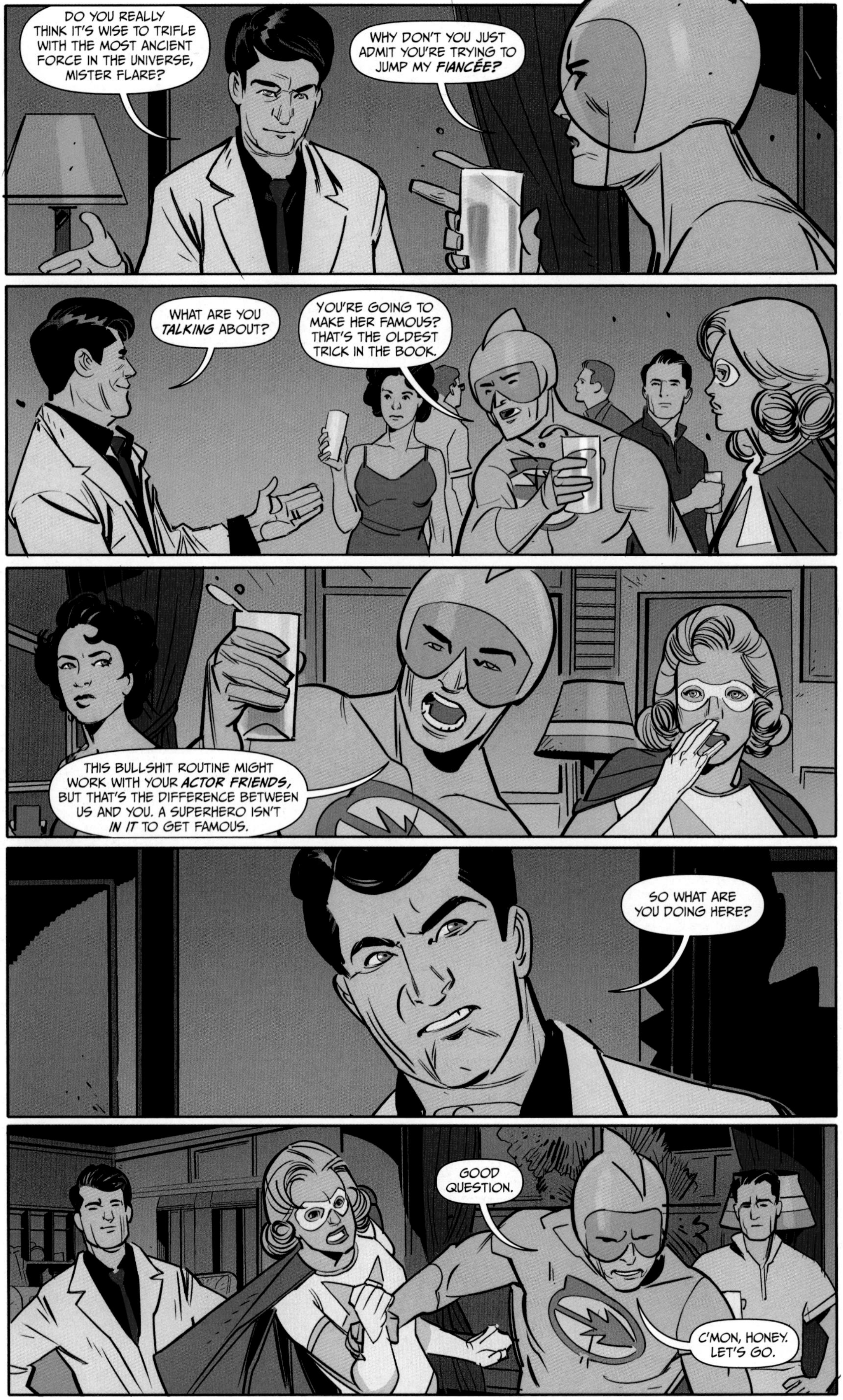
DO YOU REALLY THINK IT'S WISE TO TRIFLE WITH THE MOST ANCIENT FORCE IN THE UNIVERSE, MISTER FLARE?
WHY DON'T YOU JUST ADMIT YOU'RE TRYING TO JUMP MY *FIANCÉE?*
WHAT ARE YOU *TALKING* ABOUT?
YOU'RE GOING TO MAKE HER FAMOUS? THAT'S THE OLDEST TRICK IN THE BOOK.
THIS BULLSHIT ROUTINE MIGHT WORK WITH YOUR *ACTOR FRIENDS,* BUT THAT'S THE DIFFERENCE BETWEEN US AND YOU. A SUPERHERO ISN'T *IN IT* TO GET FAMOUS.
SO WHAT ARE YOU DOING HERE?
GOOD QUESTION.
C'MON, HONEY. LET'S GO.

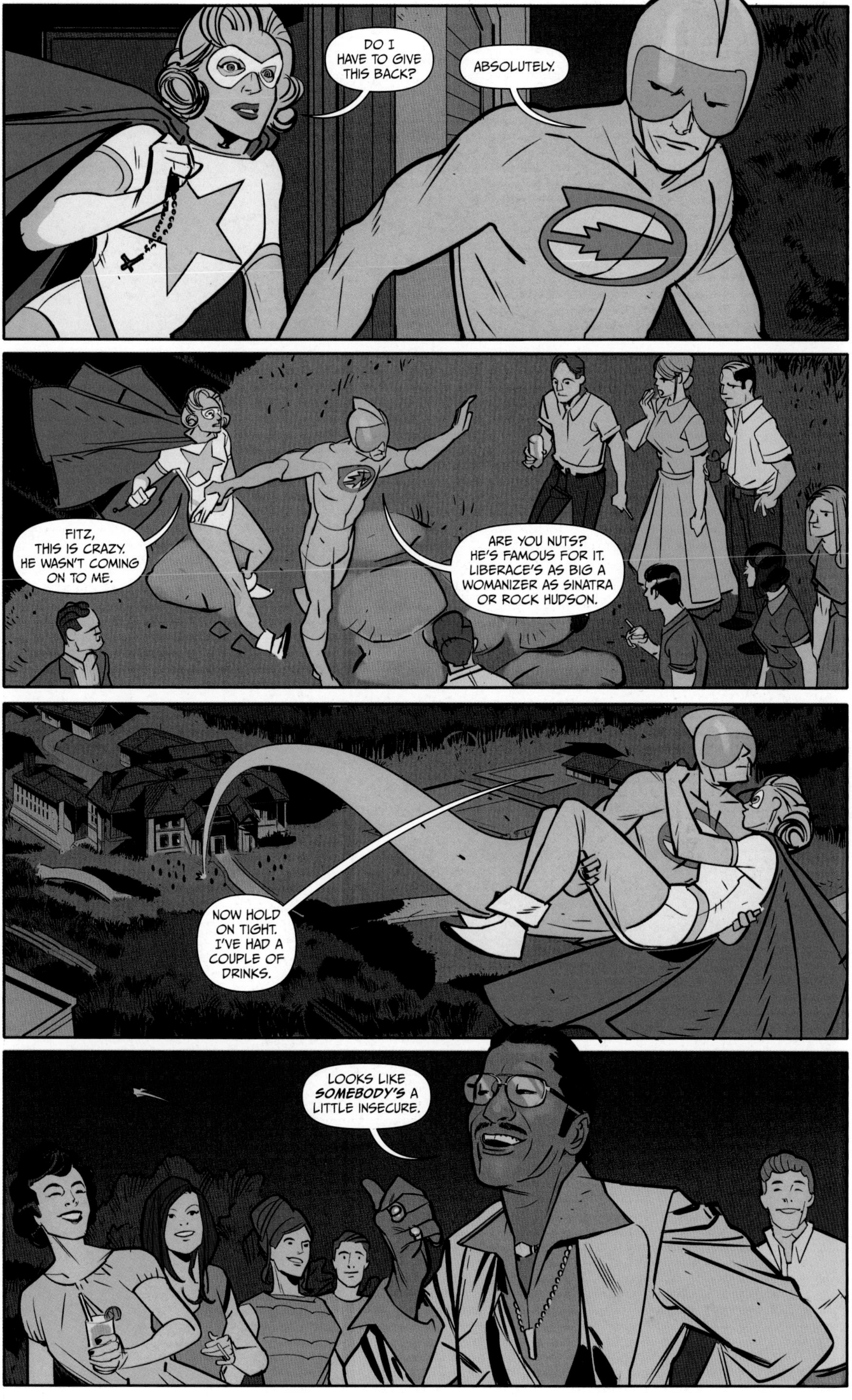
DO I HAVE TO GIVE THIS BACK?
ABSOLUTELY.
FITZ, THIS IS CRAZY. HE WASN'T COMING ON TO ME.
ARE YOU NUTS? HE'S FAMOUS FOR IT. LIBERACE'S AS BIG A WOMANIZER AS SINATRA OR ROCK HUDSON.
NOW HOLD ON TIGHT. I'VE HAD A COUPLE OF DRINKS.
LOOKS LIKE *SOMEBODY'S* A LITTLE INSECURE.

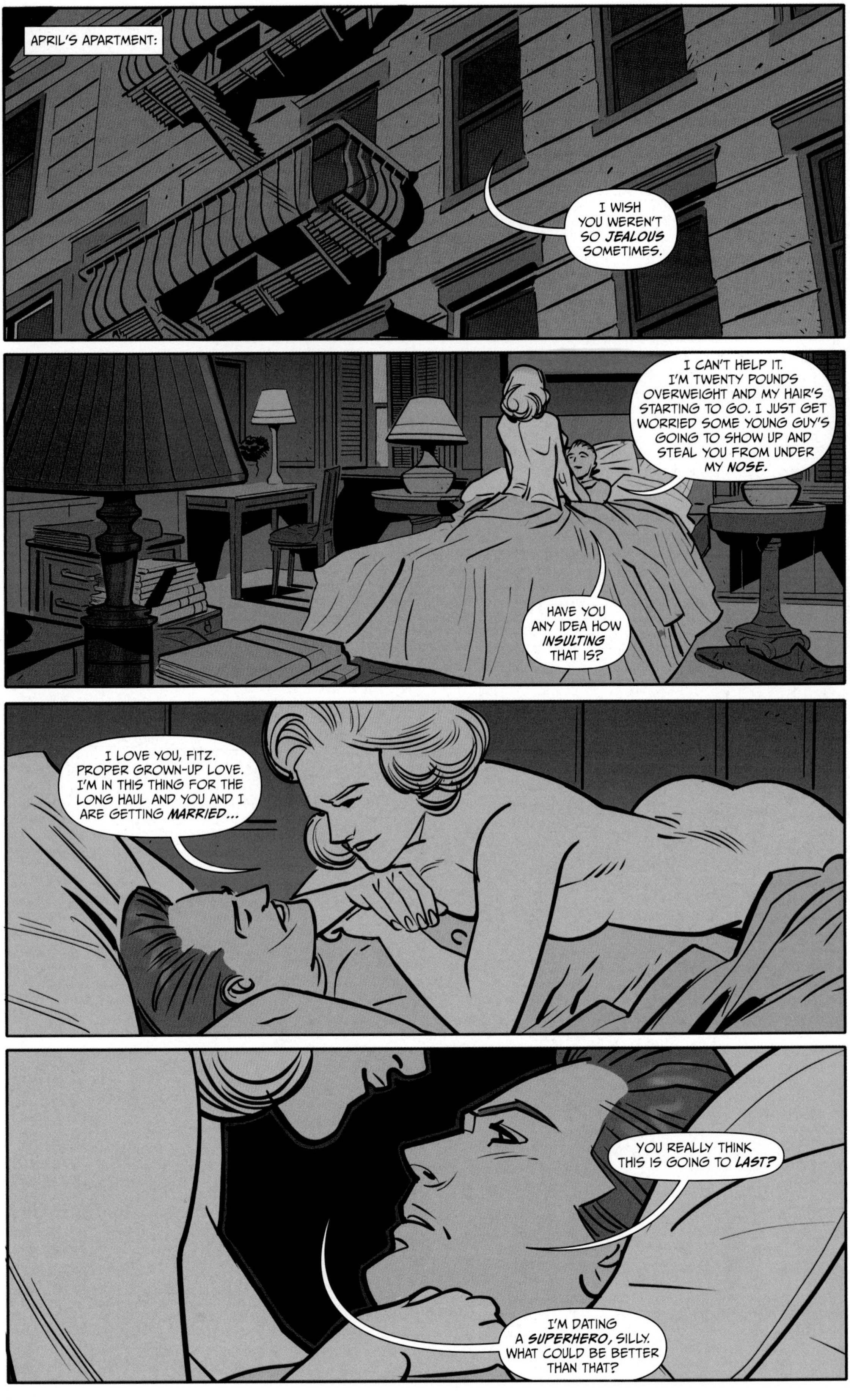
APRIL'S APARTMENT:
I WISH YOU WEREN'T SO JEALOUS SOMETIMES.
I CAN'T HELP IT. I'M TWENTY POUNDS OVERWEIGHT AND MY HAIR'S STARTING TO GO. I JUST GET WORRIED SOME YOUNG GUY'S GOING TO SHOW UP AND STEAL YOU FROM UNDER MY NOSE.
HAVE YOU ANY IDEA HOW INSULTING THAT IS?
I LOVE YOU, FITZ. PROPER GROWN-UP LOVE. I'M IN THIS THING FOR THE LONG HAUL AND YOU AND I ARE GETTING MARRIED...
YOU REALLY THINK THIS IS GOING TO LAST?
I'M DATING A SUPERHERO, SILLY. WHAT COULD BE BETTER THAN THAT?

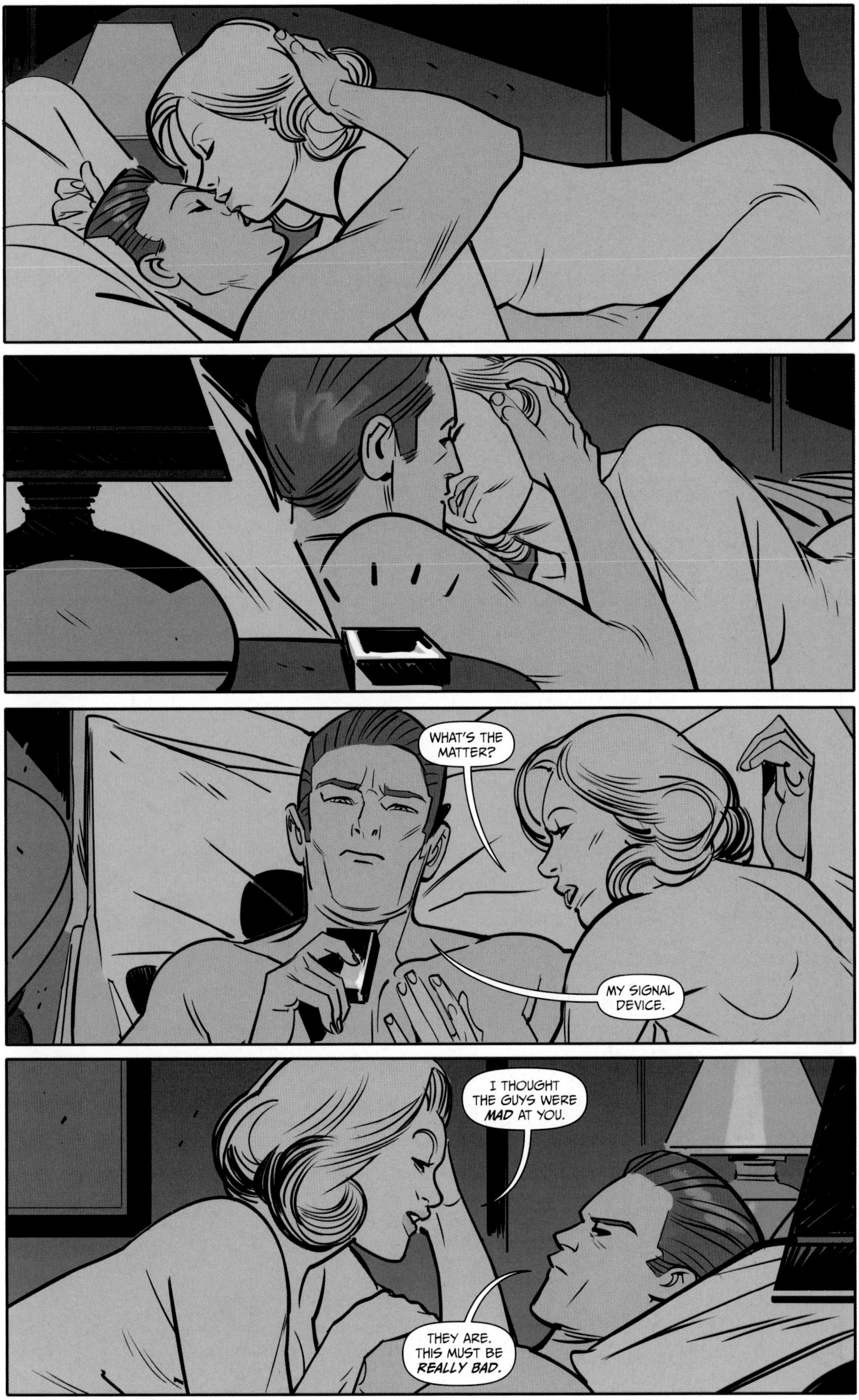
WHAT'S THE MATTER?
MY SIGNAL DEVICE.
I THOUGHT THE GUYS WERE *MAD* AT YOU.
THEY ARE. THIS MUST BE *REALLY BAD*.

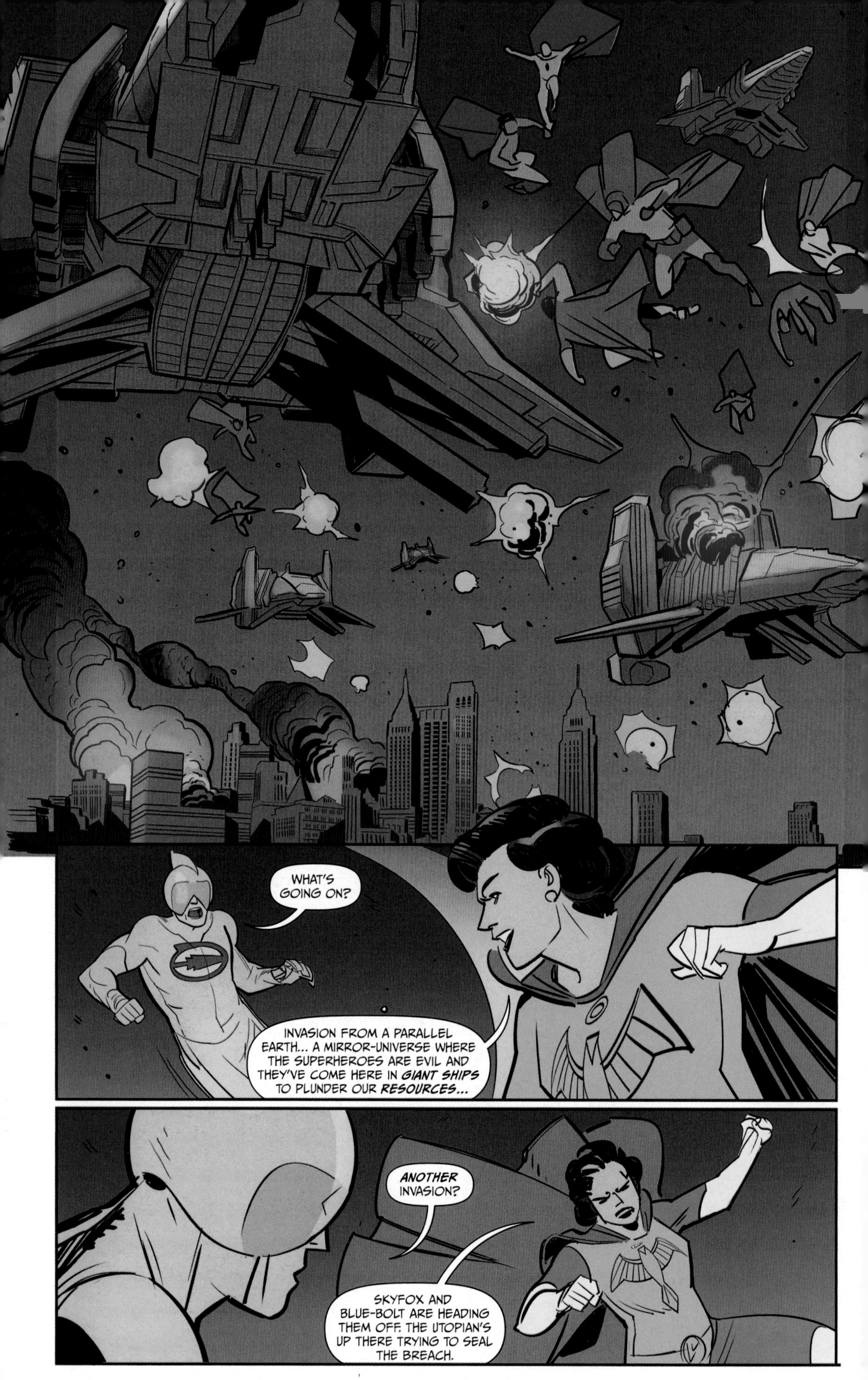
WHAT'S GOING ON?
INVASION FROM A PARALLEL EARTH... A MIRROR-UNIVERSE WHERE THE SUPERHEROES ARE EVIL AND THEY'VE COME HERE IN *GIANT SHIPS* TO PLUNDER OUR *RESOURCES*...
ANOTHER INVASION?
SKYFOX AND BLUE-BOLT ARE HEADING THEM OFF. THE UTOPIAN'S UP THERE TRYING TO SEAL THE BREACH.

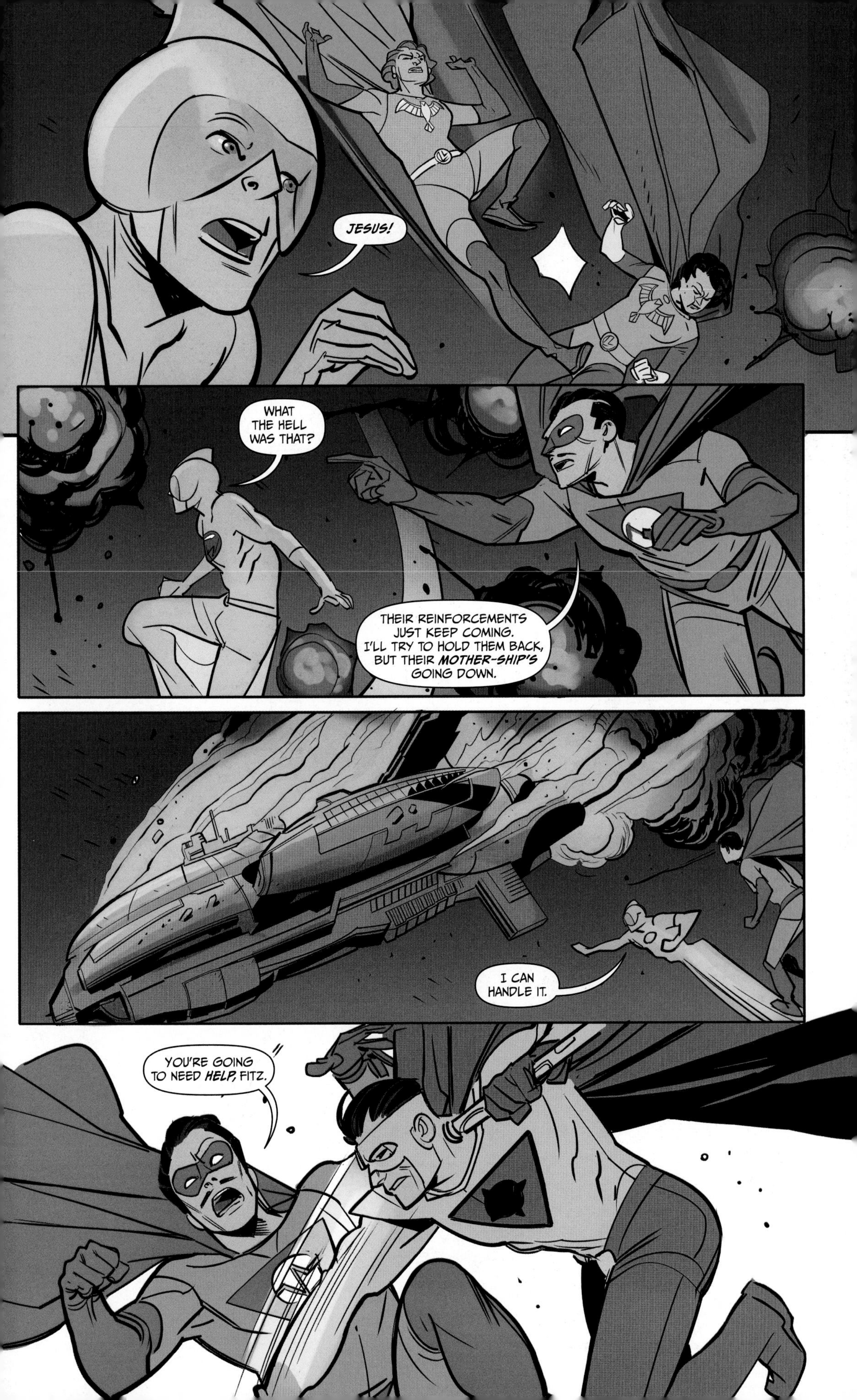
JESUS!
WHAT THE HELL WAS THAT?
THEIR REINFORCEMENTS JUST KEEP COMING. I'LL TRY TO HOLD THEM BACK, BUT THEIR MOTHER-SHIP'S GOING DOWN.
I CAN HANDLE IT.
YOU'RE GOING TO NEED HELP, FITZ.

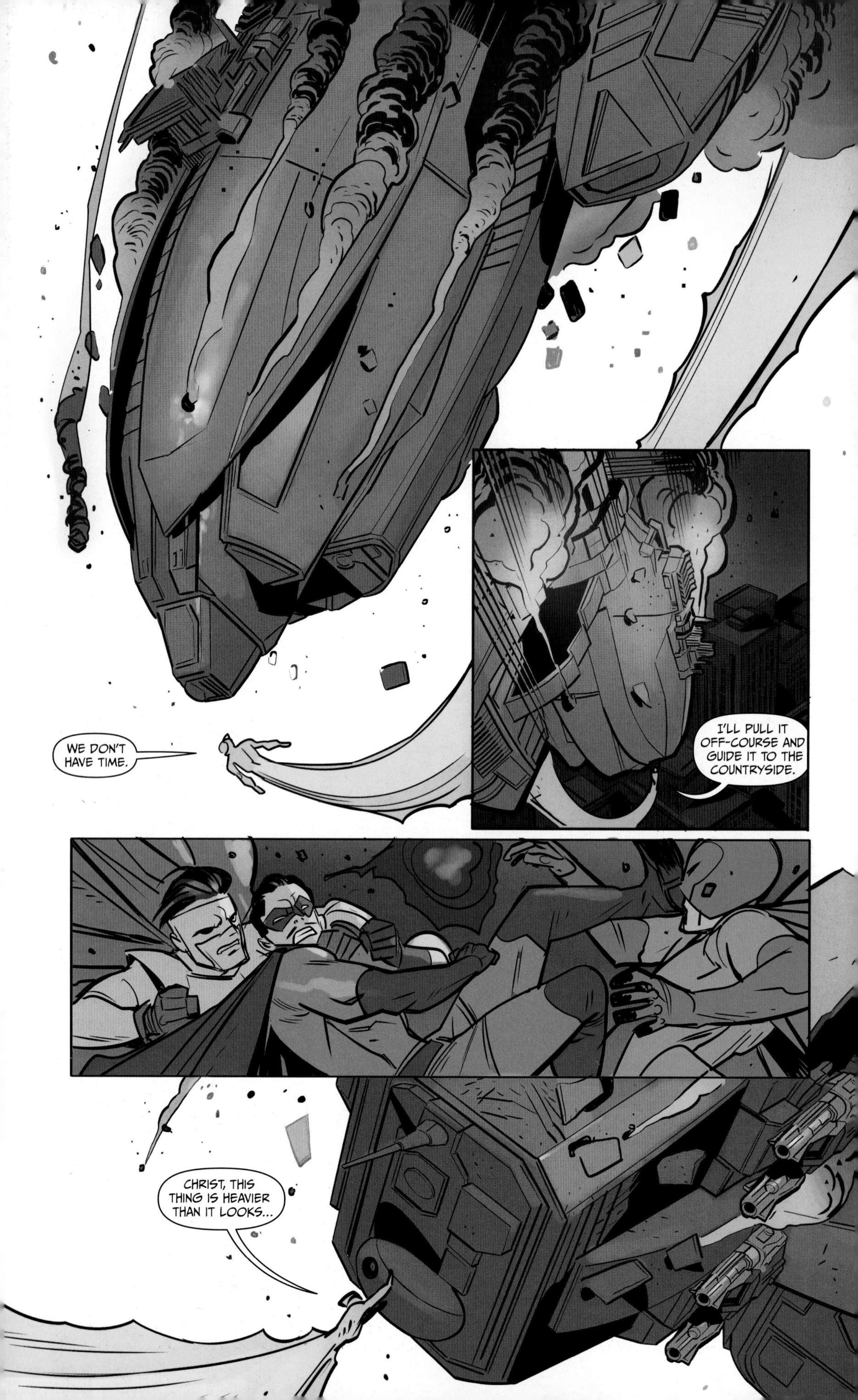
WE DON'T HAVE TIME.
I'LL PULL IT OFF-COURSE AND GUIDE IT TO THE COUNTRYSIDE.
CHRIST, THIS THING IS HEAVIER THAN IT LOOKS...

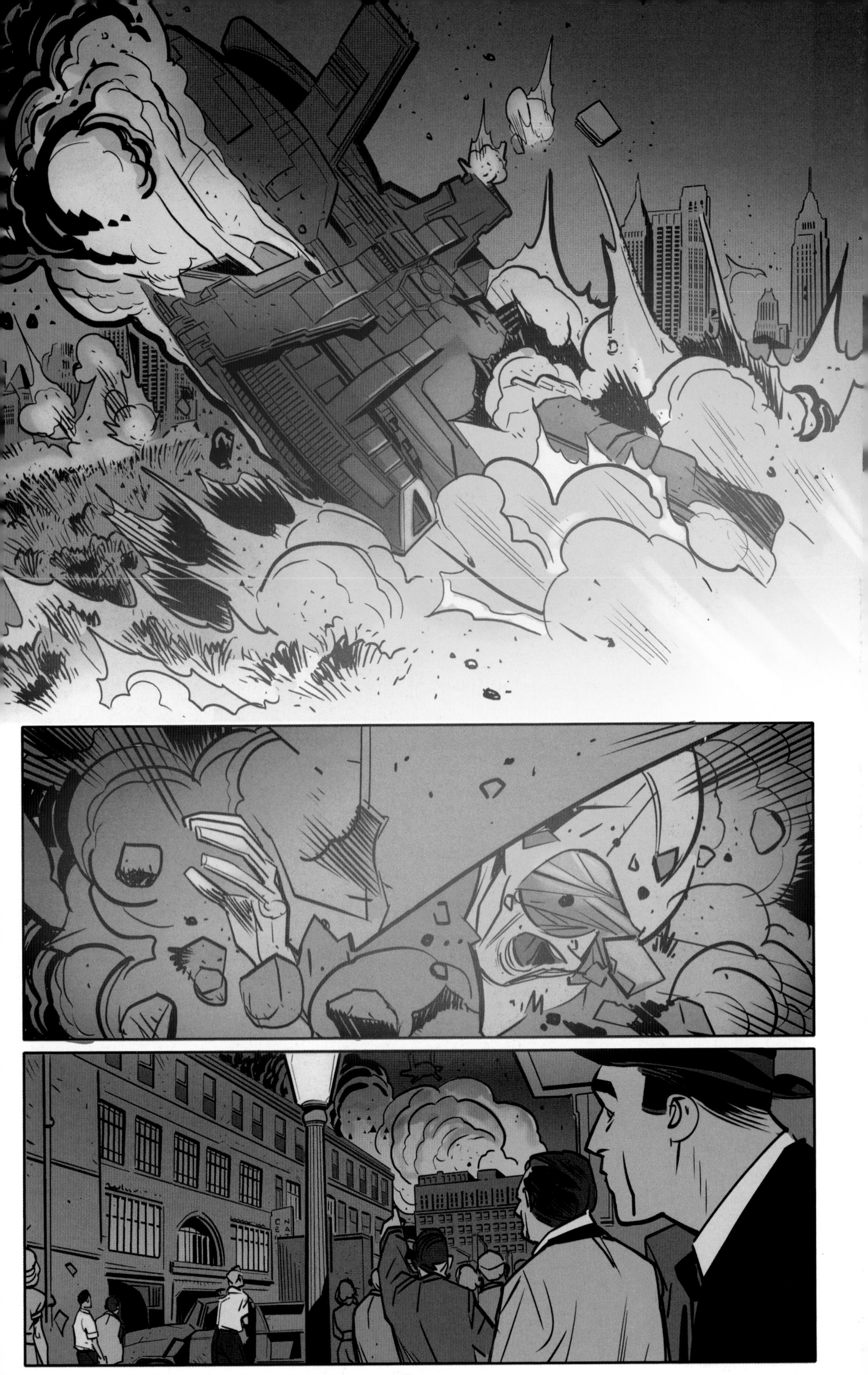

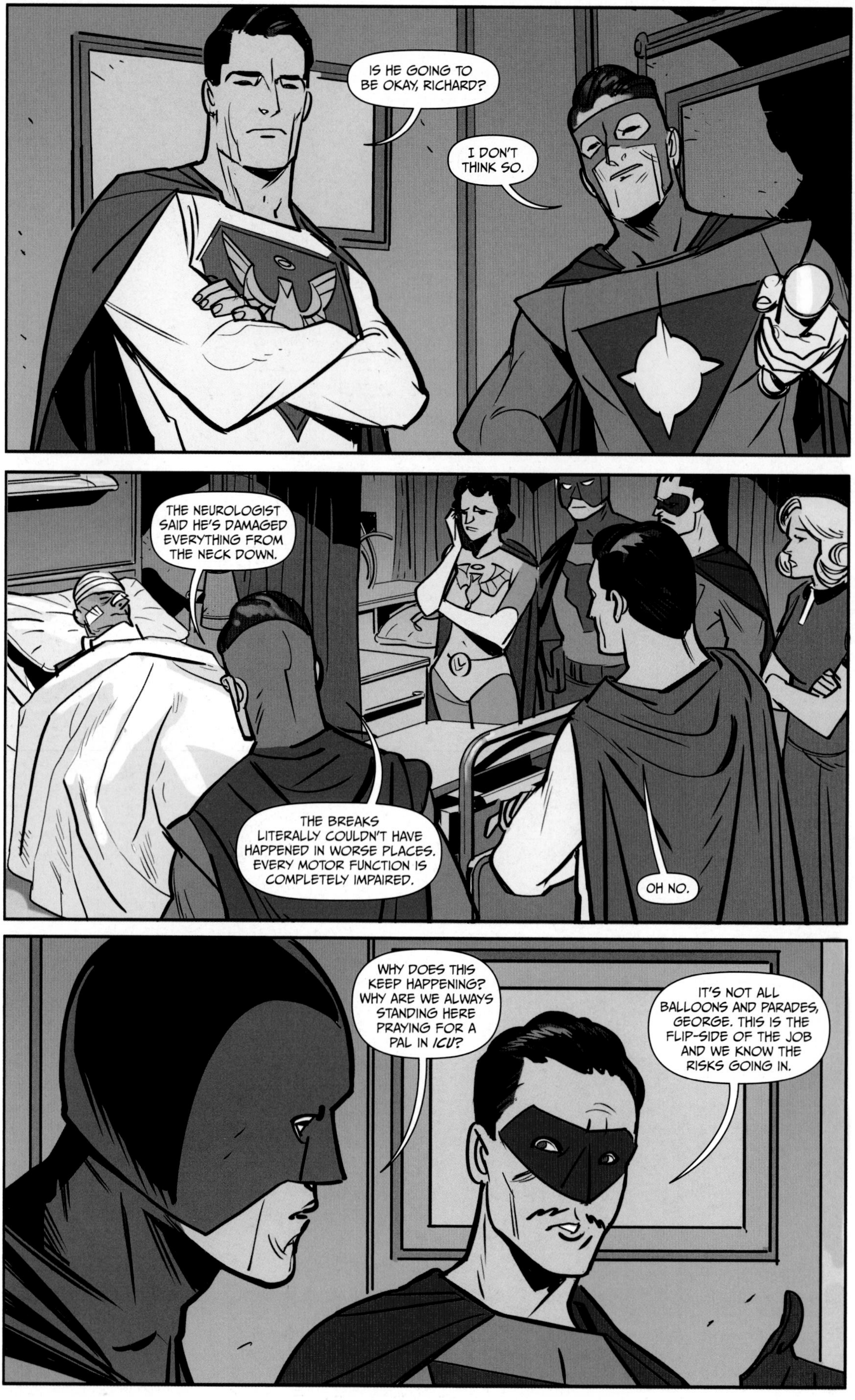

IS HE GOING TO BE OKAY, RICHARD?
I DON'T THINK SO.
THE NEUROLOGIST SAID HE'S DAMAGED EVERYTHING FROM THE NECK DOWN.
THE BREAKS LITERALLY COULDN'T HAVE HAPPENED IN WORSE PLACES. EVERY MOTOR FUNCTION IS COMPLETELY IMPAIRED.
OH NO.
WHY DOES THIS KEEP HAPPENING? WHY ARE WE ALWAYS STANDING HERE PRAYING FOR A PAL IN *ICU*?
IT'S NOT ALL BALLOONS AND PARADES, GEORGE. THIS IS THE FLIP-SIDE OF THE JOB AND WE KNOW THE RISKS GOING IN.

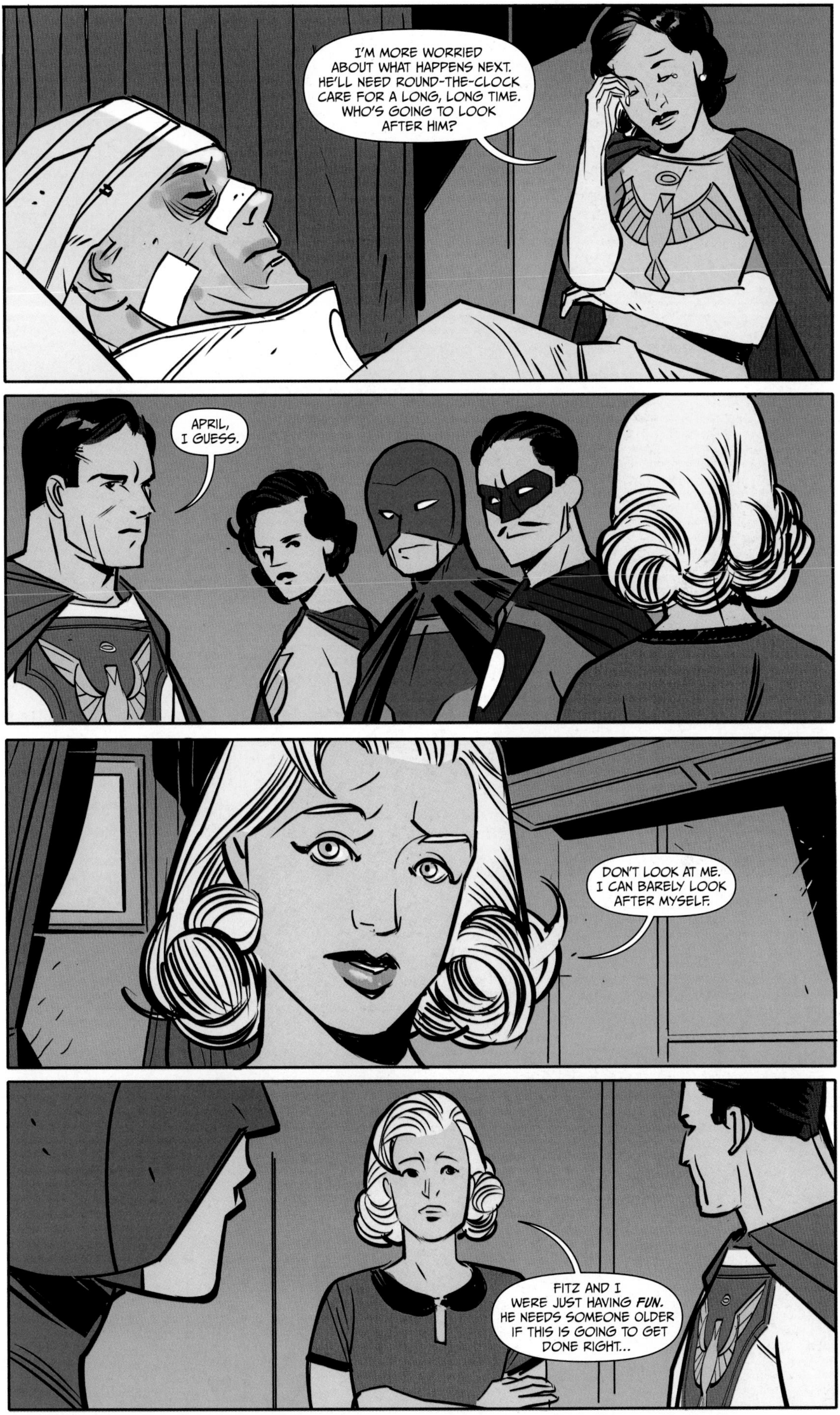
I'M MORE WORRIED ABOUT WHAT HAPPENS NEXT. HE'LL NEED ROUND-THE-CLOCK CARE FOR A LONG, LONG TIME. WHO'S GOING TO LOOK AFTER HIM?
APRIL, I GUESS.
DON'T LOOK AT ME. I CAN BARELY LOOK AFTER MYSELF.
FITZ AND I WERE JUST HAVING *FUN*. HE NEEDS SOMEONE OLDER IF THIS IS GOING TO GET DONE RIGHT...

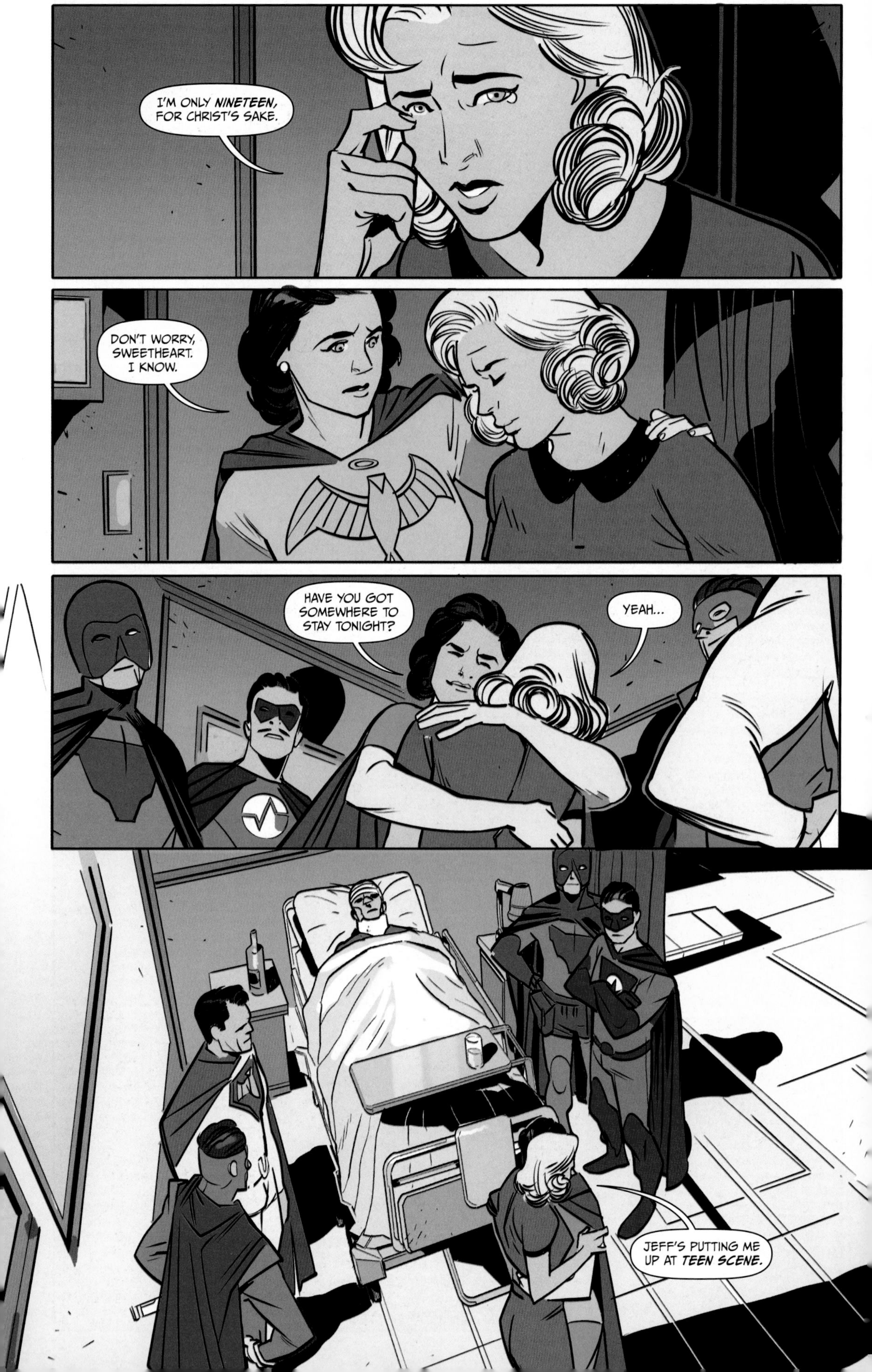
I'M ONLY *NINETEEN,* FOR CHRIST'S SAKE.
DON'T WORRY, SWEETHEART. I KNOW.
HAVE YOU GOT SOMEWHERE TO STAY TONIGHT?
YEAH...
JEFF'S PUTTING ME UP AT *TEEN SCENE.*

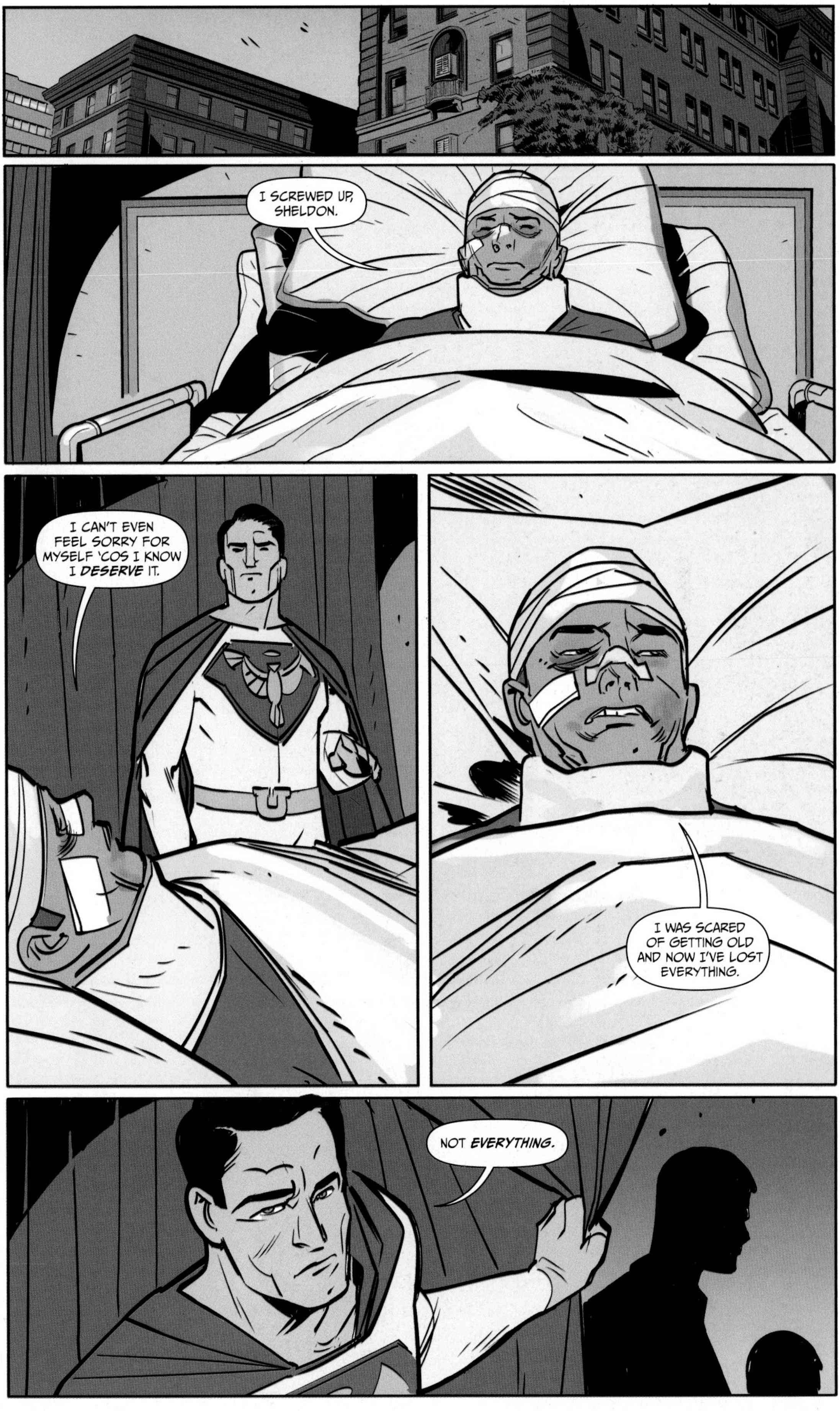
I SCREWED UP, SHELDON.
I CAN'T EVEN FEEL SORRY FOR MYSELF 'COS I KNOW I *DESERVE* IT.
I WAS SCARED OF GETTING OLD AND NOW I'VE LOST EVERYTHING.
NOT *EVERYTHING*.

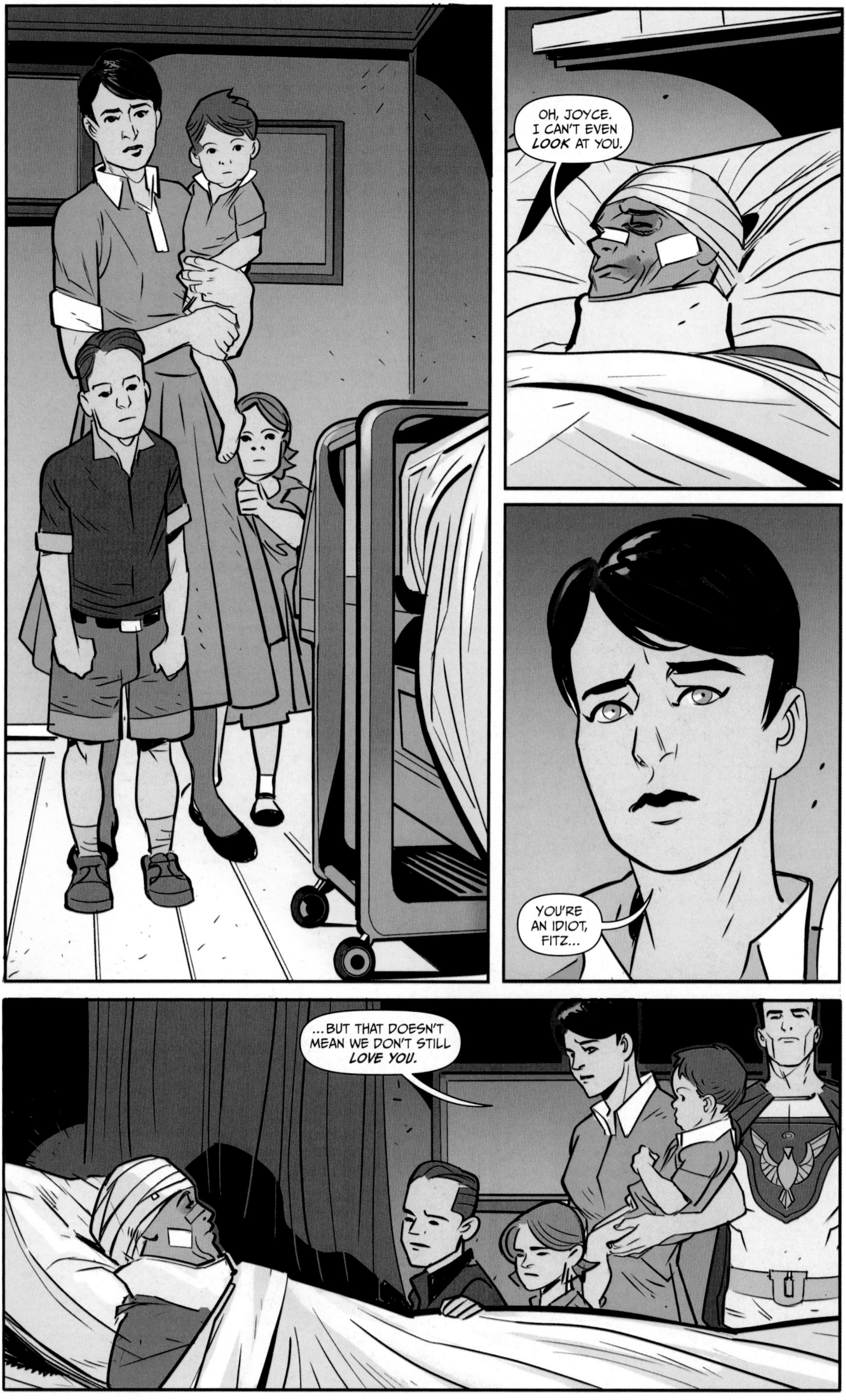
OH, JOYCE. I CAN'T EVEN LOOK AT YOU.
YOU'RE AN IDIOT, FITZ...
...BUT THAT DOESN'T MEAN WE DON'T STILL LOVE YOU.

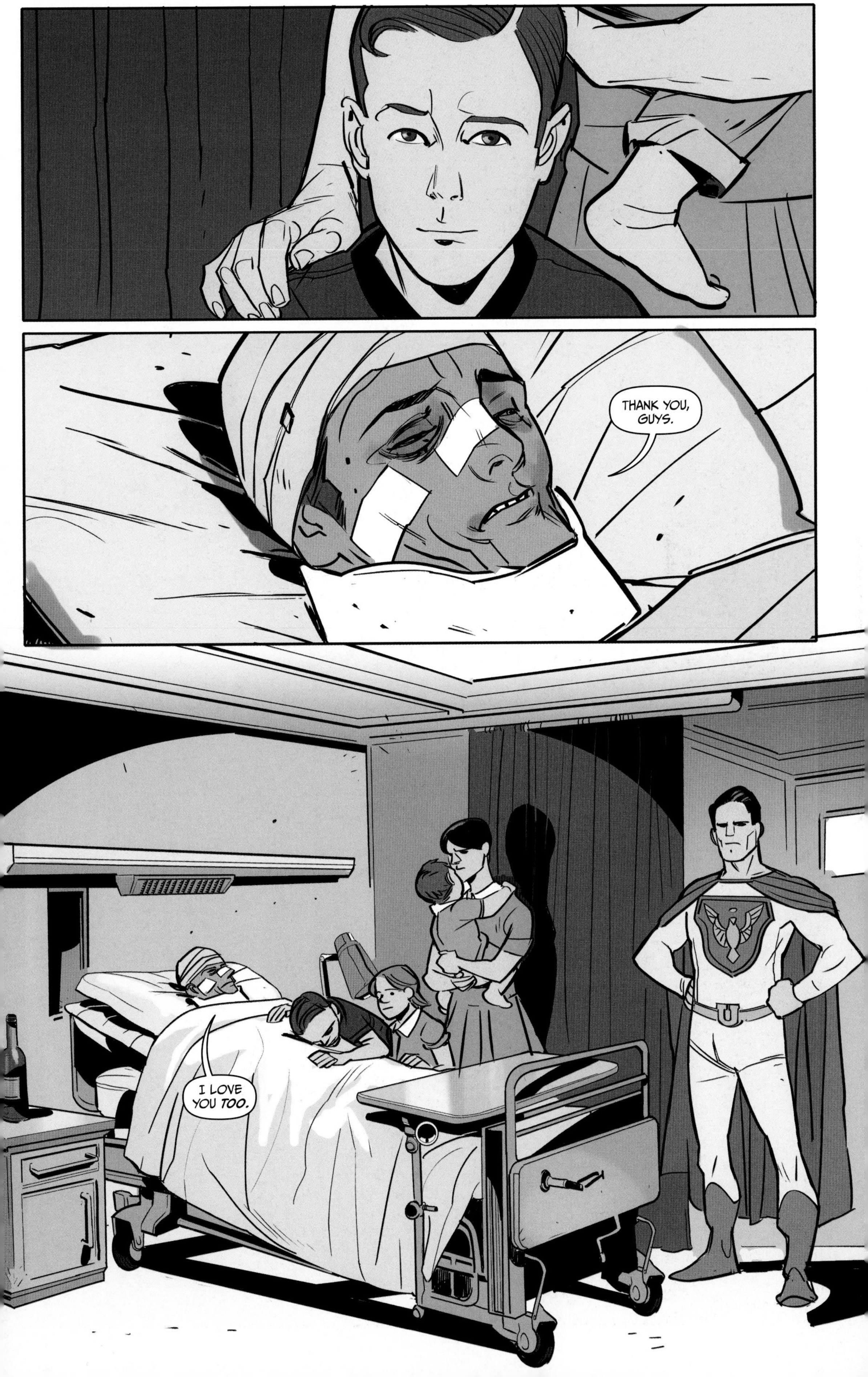
THANK YOU, GUYS.
I LOVE YOU TOO.

CHAPTER 5

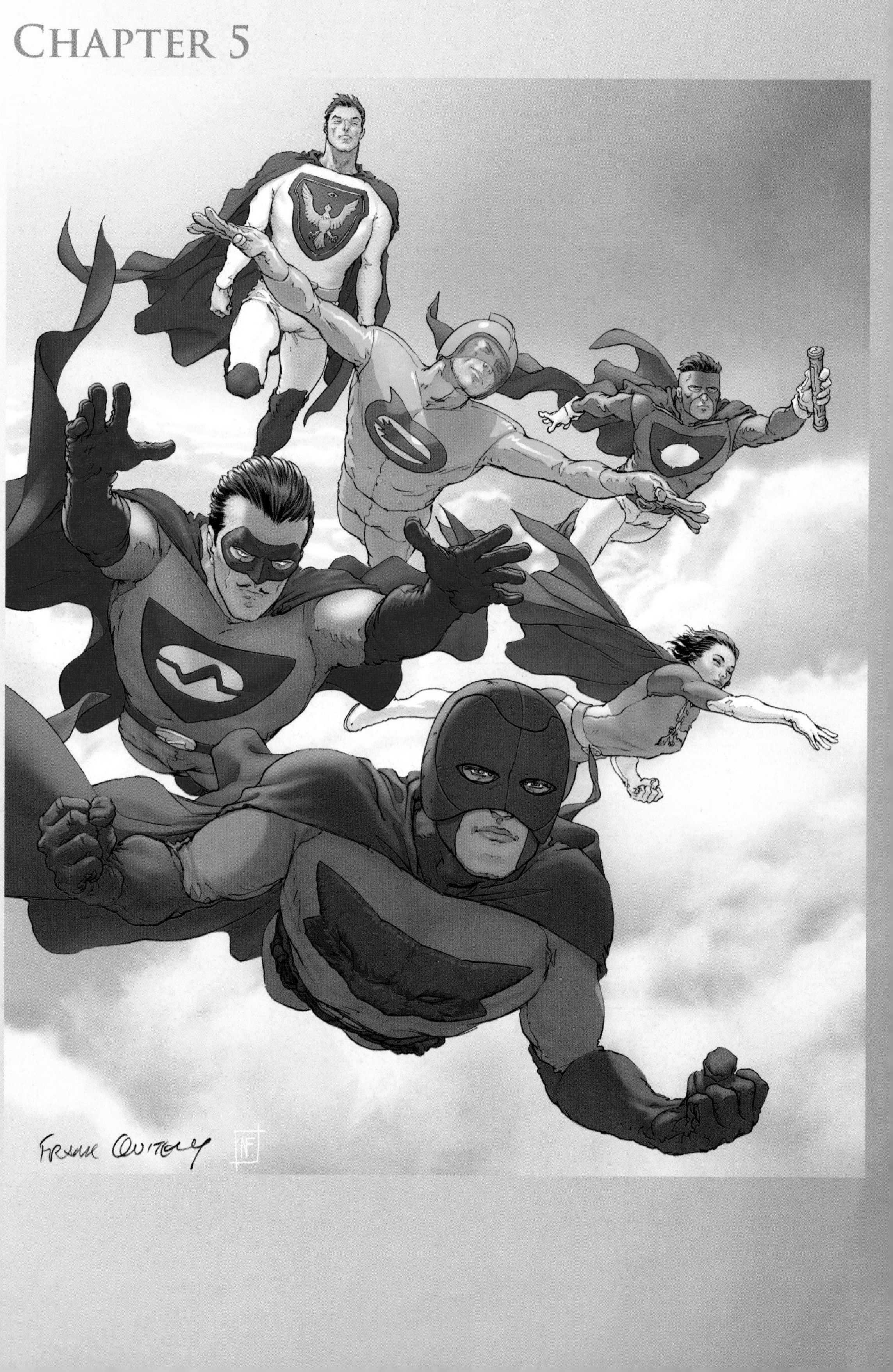
FRANK QUITELY

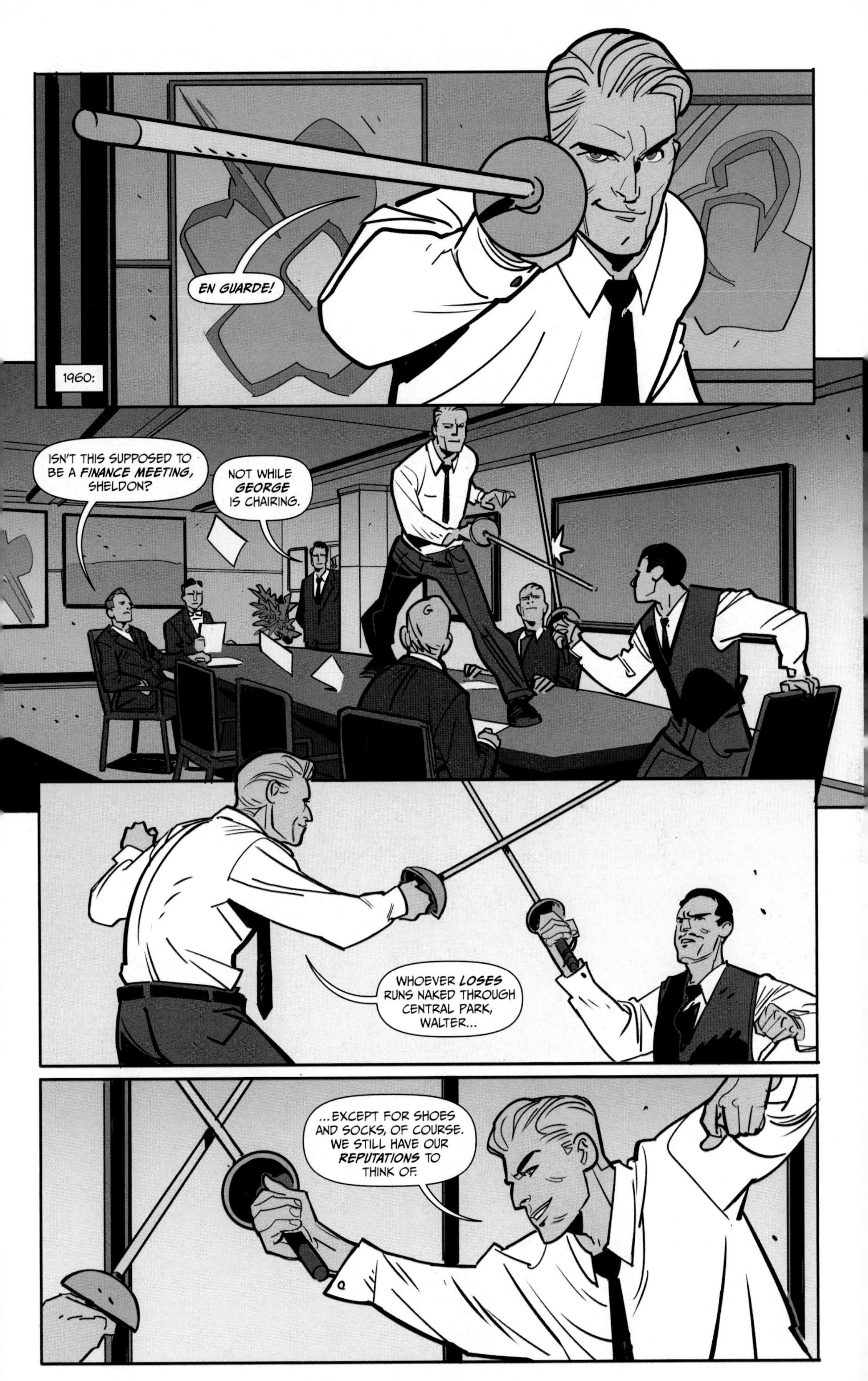
EN GUARDE!
1960:
ISN'T THIS SUPPOSED TO BE A FINANCE MEETING, SHELDON?
NOT WHILE GEORGE IS CHAIRING.
WHOEVER LOSES RUNS NAKED THROUGH CENTRAL PARK, WALTER...
...EXCEPT FOR SHOES AND SOCKS, OF COURSE. WE STILL HAVE OUR REPUTATIONS TO THINK OF.

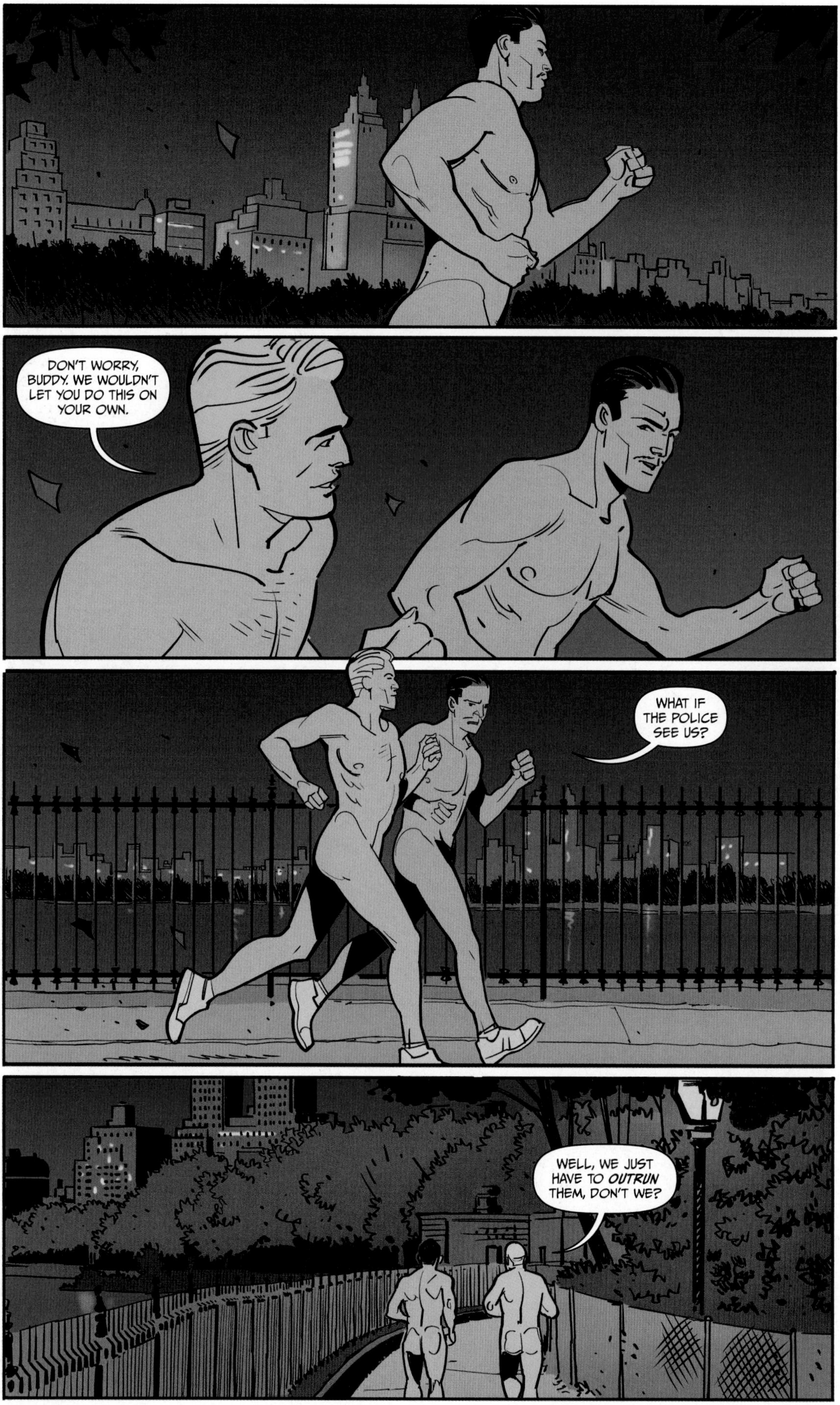
DON'T WORRY, BUDDY. WE WOULDN'T LET YOU DO THIS ON YOUR OWN.
WHAT IF THE POLICE SEE US?
WELL, WE JUST HAVE TO *OUTRUN* THEM, DON'T WE?

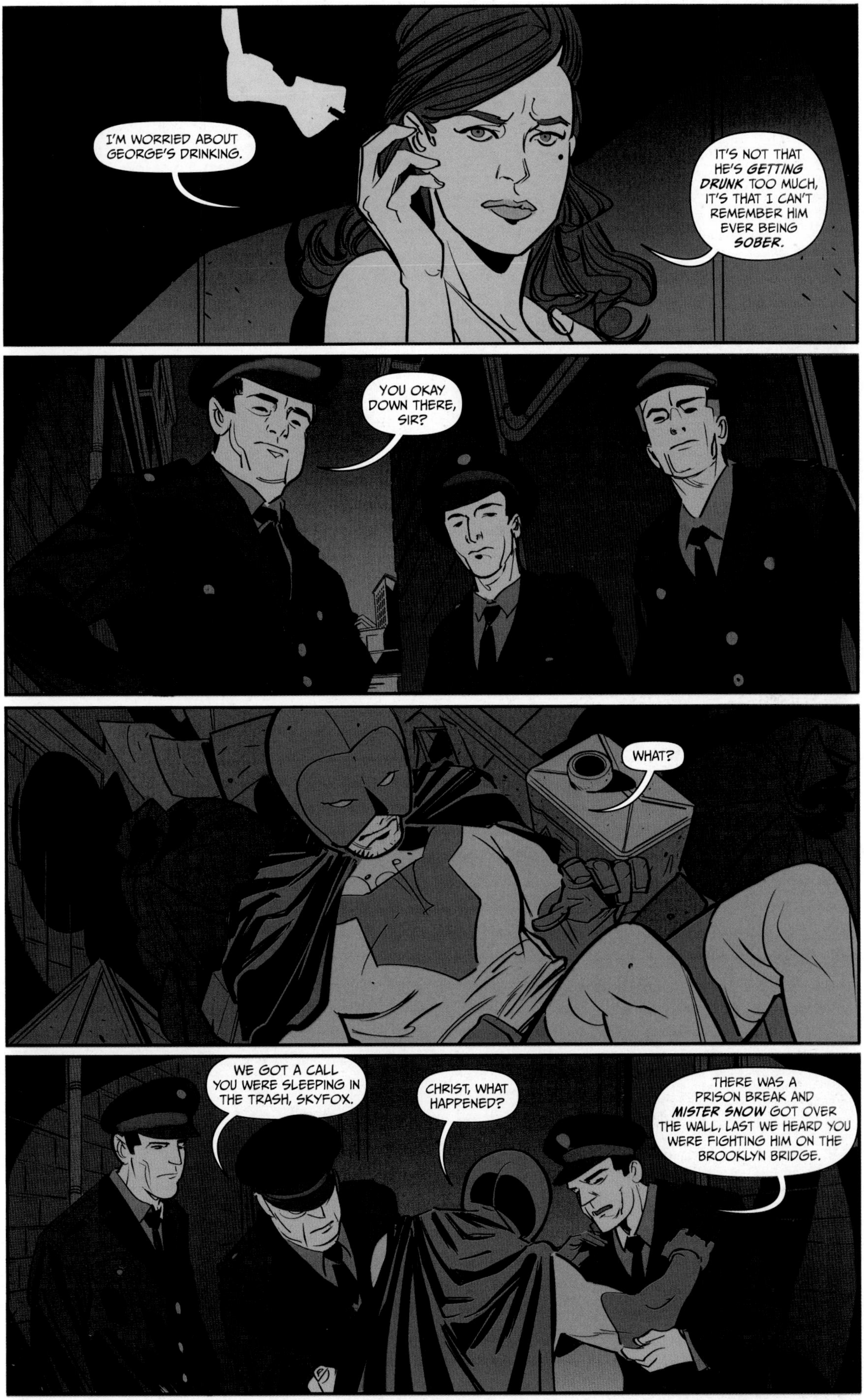
I'M WORRIED ABOUT GEORGE'S DRINKING.
IT'S NOT THAT HE'S ***GETTING DRUNK*** TOO MUCH, IT'S THAT I CAN'T REMEMBER HIM EVER BEING ***SOBER***.
YOU OKAY DOWN THERE, SIR?
WHAT?
WE GOT A CALL YOU WERE SLEEPING IN THE TRASH, SKYFOX.
CHRIST, WHAT HAPPENED?
THERE WAS A PRISON BREAK AND ***MISTER SNOW*** GOT OVER THE WALL, LAST WE HEARD YOU WERE FIGHTING HIM ON THE BROOKLYN BRIDGE.

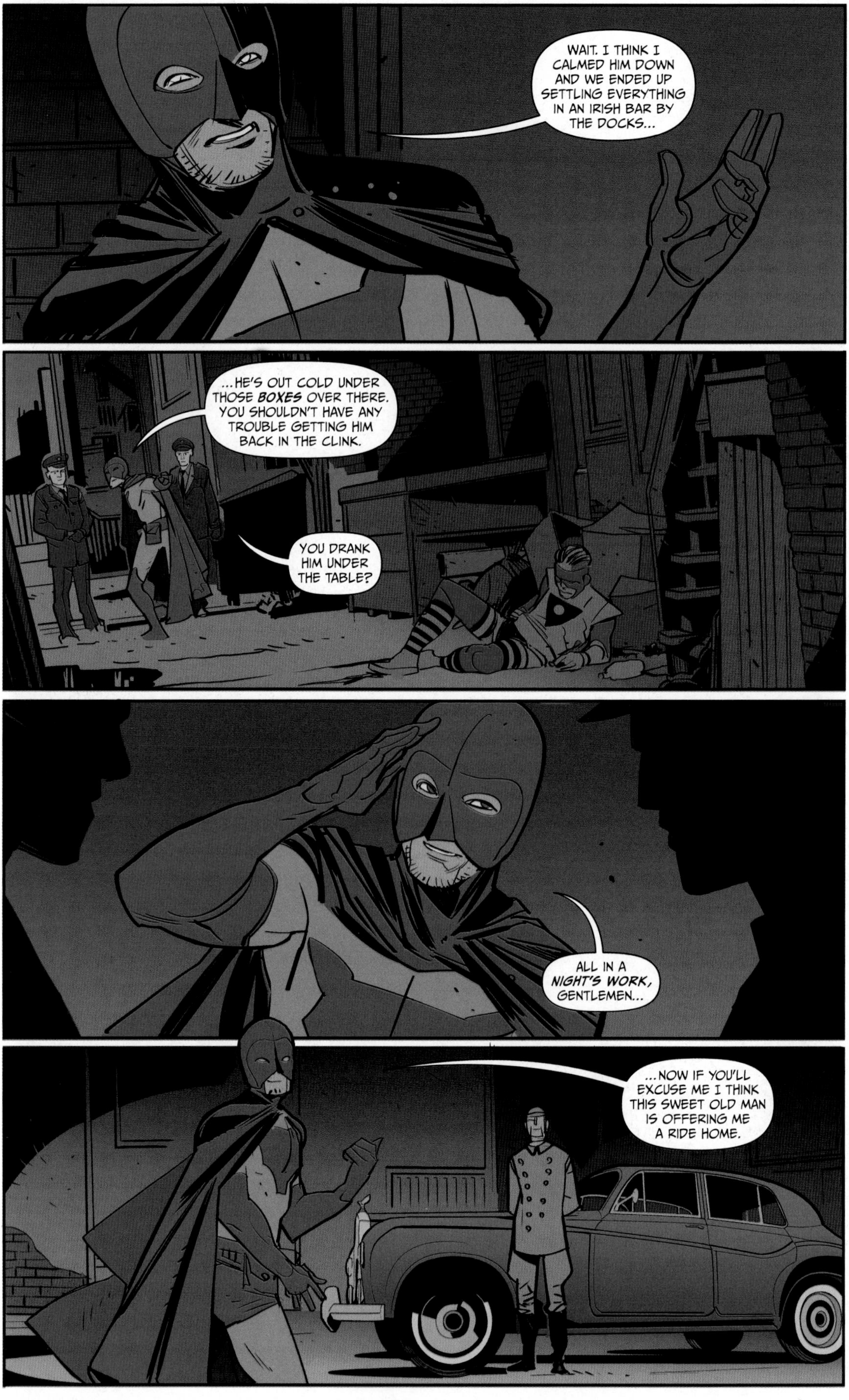
WAIT. I THINK I CALMED HIM DOWN AND WE ENDED UP SETTLING EVERYTHING IN AN IRISH BAR BY THE DOCKS...
...HE'S OUT COLD UNDER THOSE BOXES OVER THERE. YOU SHOULDN'T HAVE ANY TROUBLE GETTING HIM BACK IN THE CLINK.
YOU DRANK HIM UNDER THE TABLE?
ALL IN A NIGHT'S WORK, GENTLEMEN...
...NOW IF YOU'LL EXCUSE ME I THINK THIS SWEET OLD MAN IS OFFERING ME A RIDE HOME.

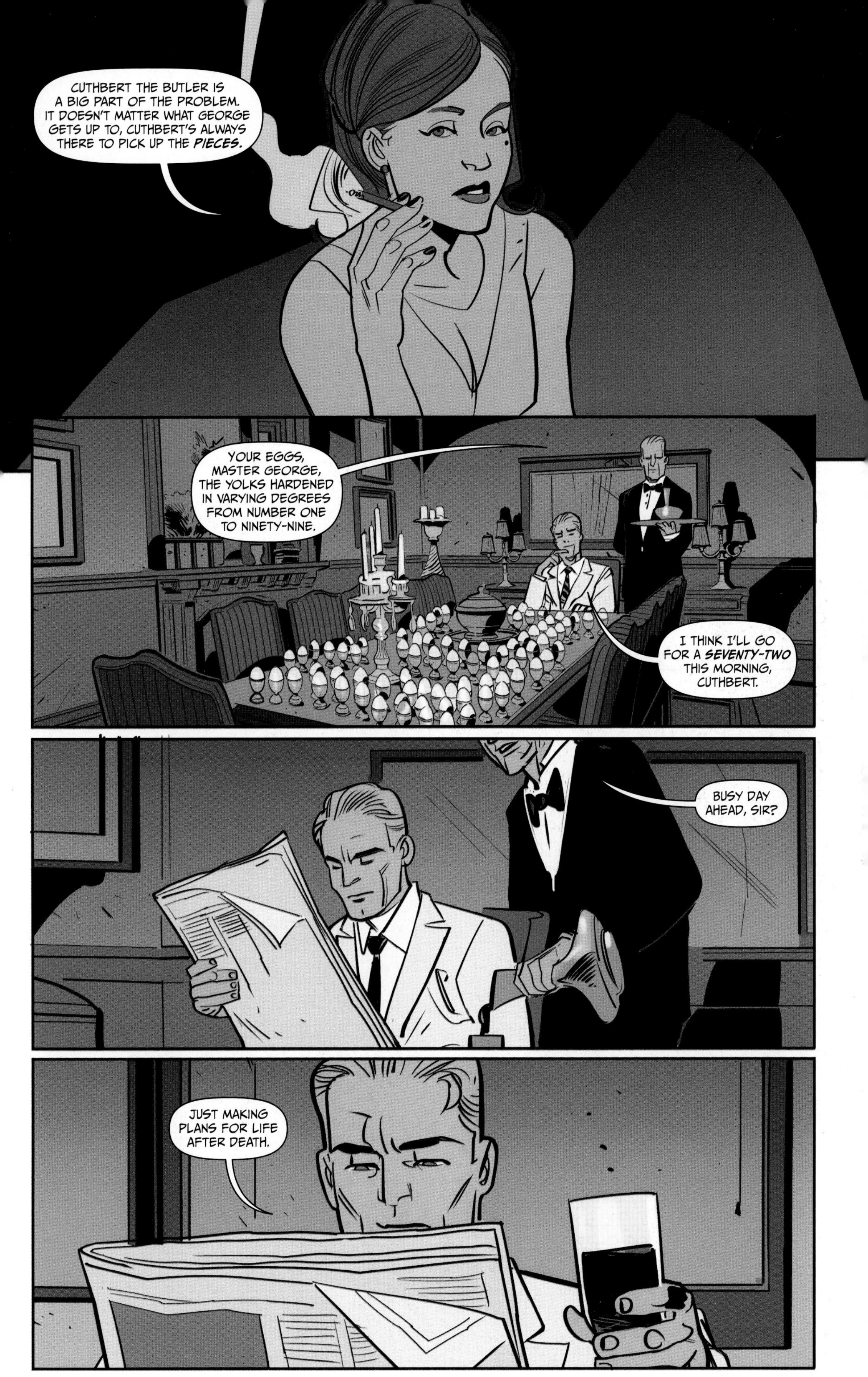
CUTHBERT THE BUTLER IS A BIG PART OF THE PROBLEM. IT DOESN'T MATTER WHAT GEORGE GETS UP TO, CUTHBERT'S ALWAYS THERE TO PICK UP THE *PIECES.*
YOUR EGGS, MASTER GEORGE, THE YOLKS HARDENED IN VARYING DEGREES FROM NUMBER ONE TO NINETY-NINE.
I THINK I'LL GO FOR A *SEVENTY-TWO* THIS MORNING, CUTHBERT.
BUSY DAY AHEAD, SIR?
JUST MAKING PLANS FOR LIFE AFTER DEATH.

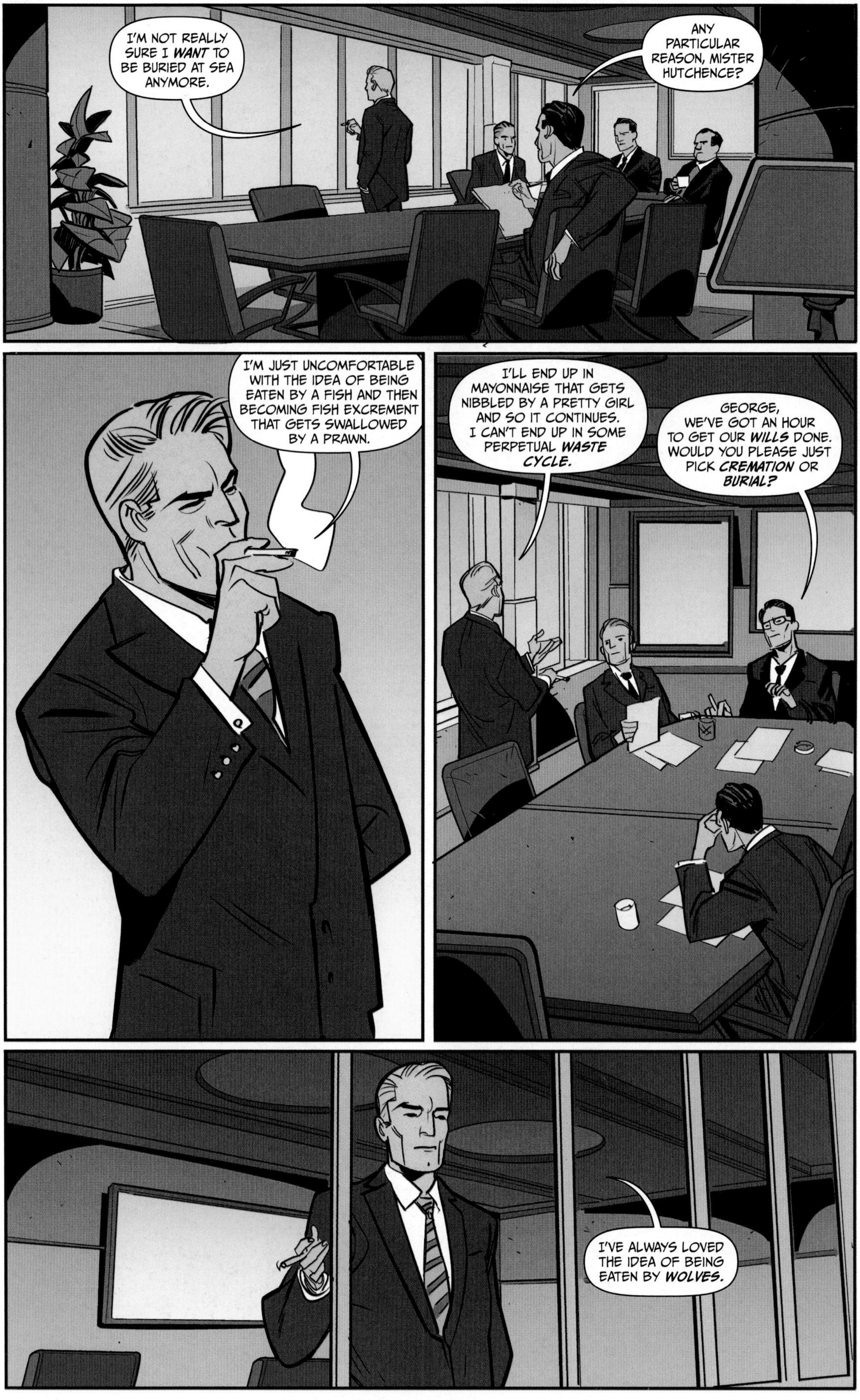

I'M NOT REALLY SURE I WANT TO BE BURIED AT SEA ANYMORE.
ANY PARTICULAR REASON, MISTER HUTCHENCE?
I'M JUST UNCOMFORTABLE WITH THE IDEA OF BEING EATEN BY A FISH AND THEN BECOMING FISH EXCREMENT THAT GETS SWALLOWED BY A PRAWN.
I'LL END UP IN MAYONNAISE THAT GETS NIBBLED BY A PRETTY GIRL AND SO IT CONTINUES. I CAN'T END UP IN SOME PERPETUAL WASTE CYCLE.
GEORGE, WE'VE GOT AN HOUR TO GET OUR WILLS DONE. WOULD YOU PLEASE JUST PICK CREMATION OR BURIAL?
I'VE ALWAYS LOVED THE IDEA OF BEING EATEN BY WOLVES.

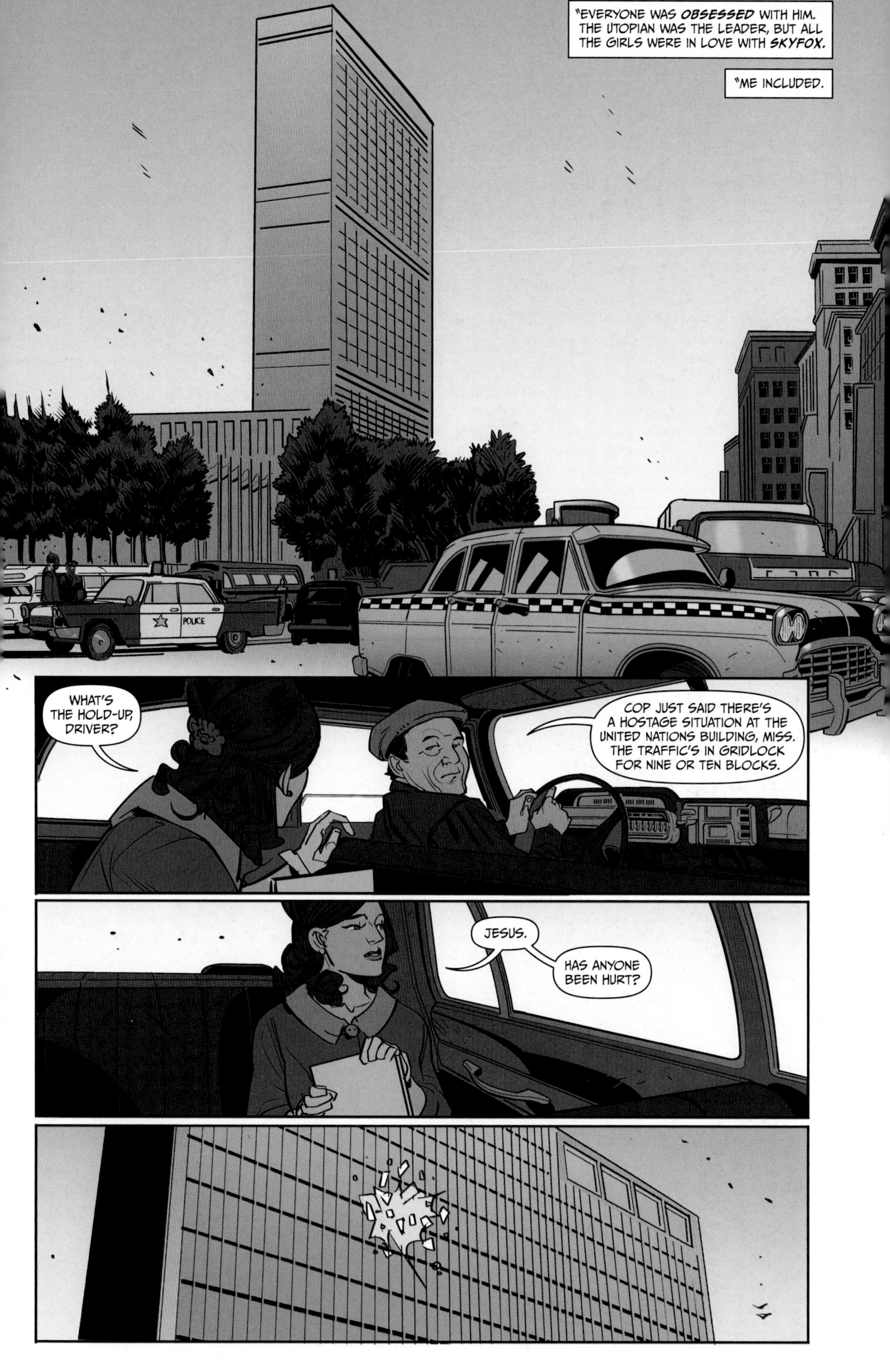
"EVERYONE WAS OBSESSED WITH HIM. THE UTOPIAN WAS THE LEADER, BUT ALL THE GIRLS WERE IN LOVE WITH SKYFOX.
"ME INCLUDED.
POLICE
WHAT'S THE HOLD-UP, DRIVER?
COP JUST SAID THERE'S A HOSTAGE SITUATION AT THE UNITED NATIONS BUILDING, MISS. THE TRAFFIC'S IN GRIDLOCK FOR NINE OR TEN BLOCKS.
JESUS.
HAS ANYONE BEEN HURT?

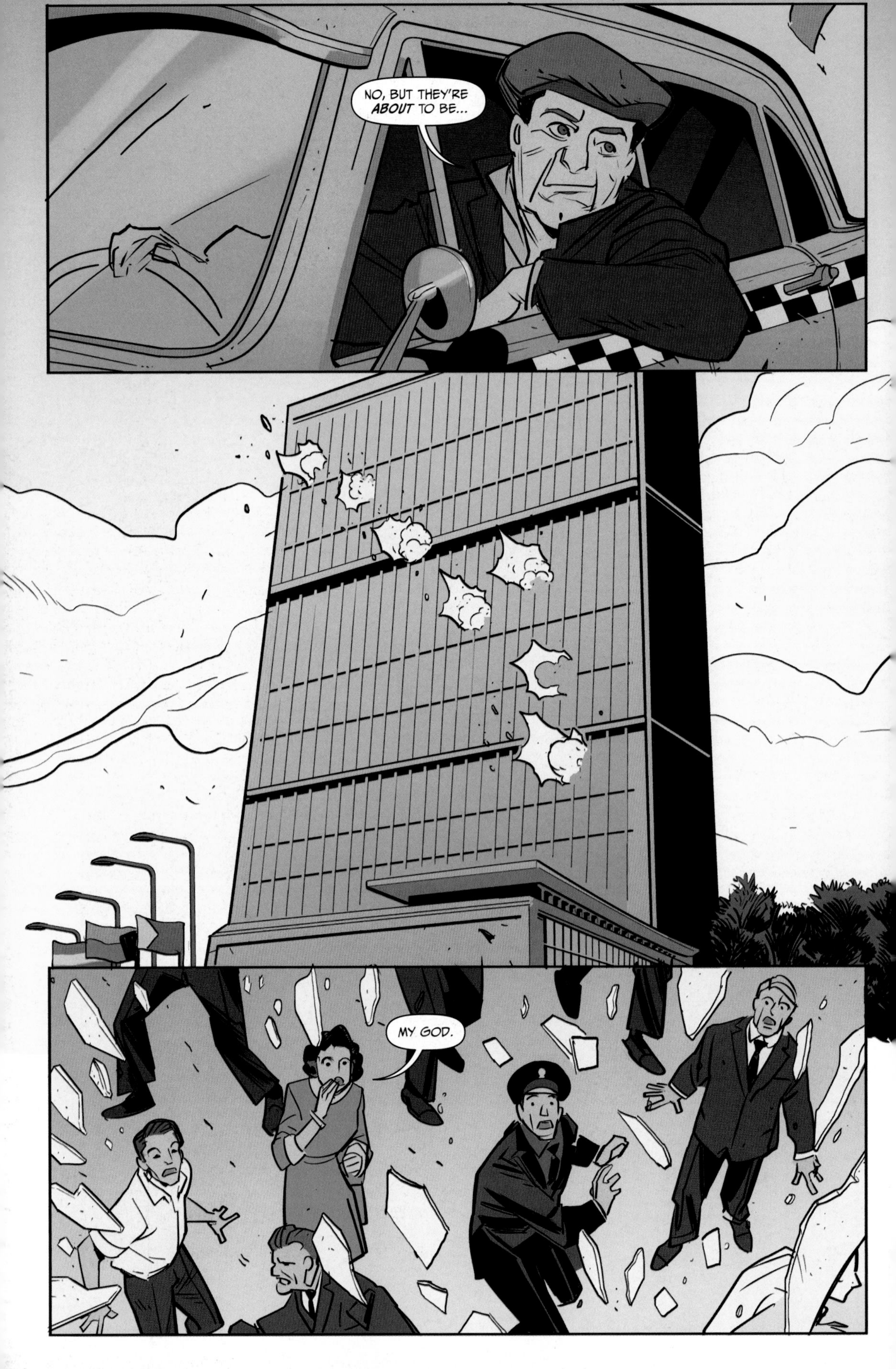
NO, BUT THEY'RE *ABOUT* TO BE...
MY GOD.

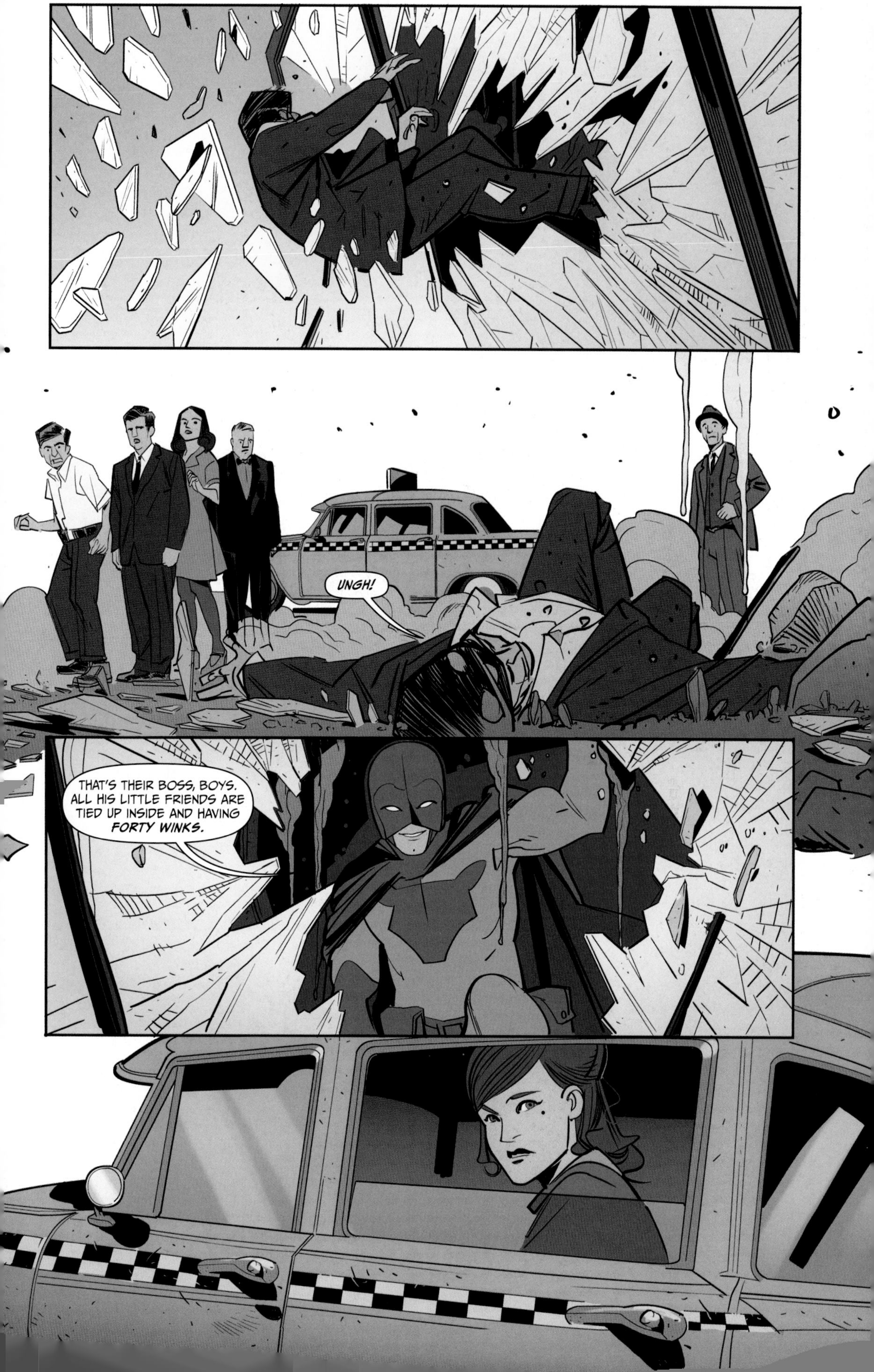
UNGH!
THAT'S THEIR BOSS, BOYS. ALL HIS LITTLE FRIENDS ARE TIED UP INSIDE AND HAVING FORTY WINKS.

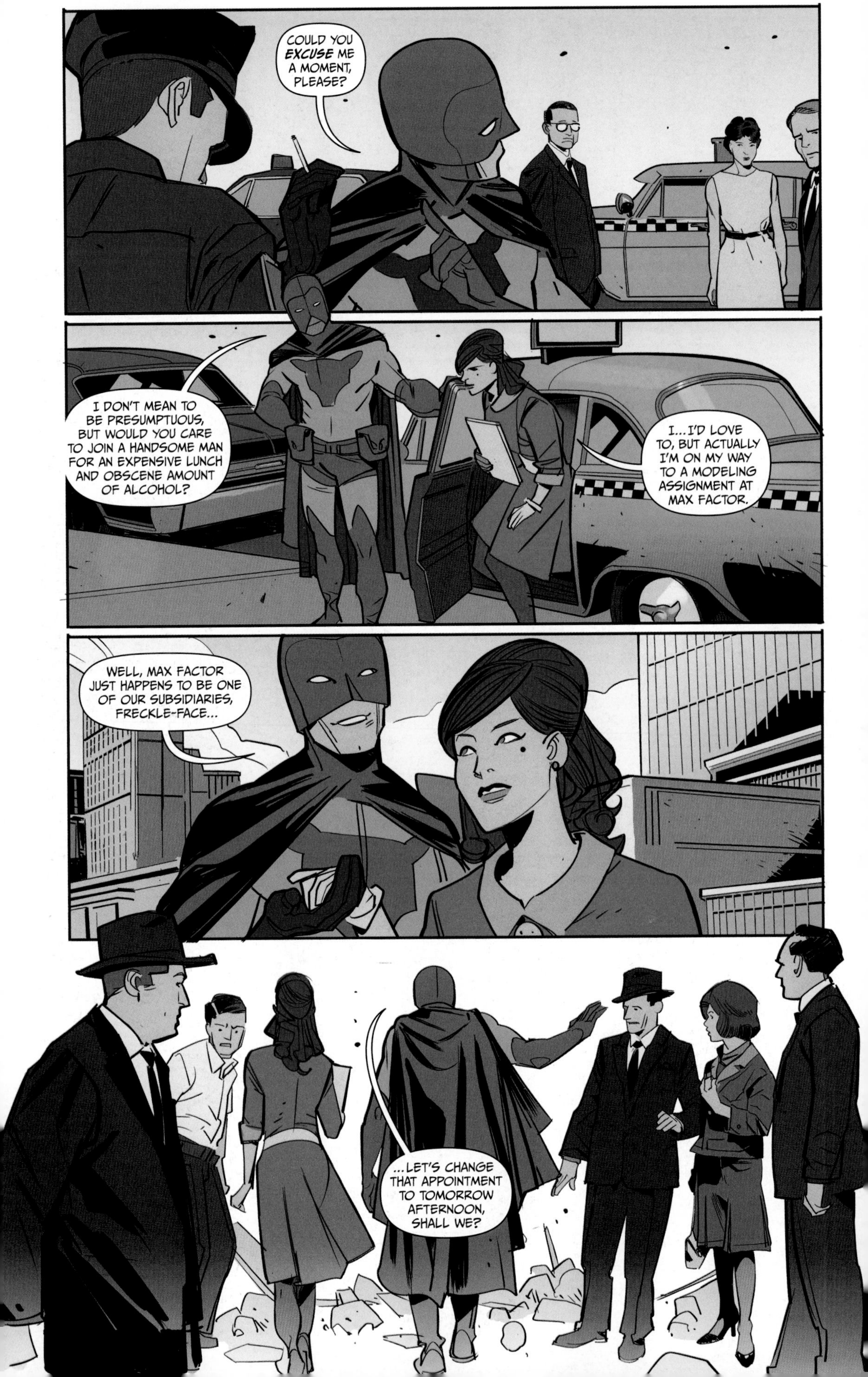
COULD YOU EXCUSE ME A MOMENT, PLEASE?
I DON'T MEAN TO BE PRESUMPTUOUS, BUT WOULD YOU CARE TO JOIN A HANDSOME MAN FOR AN EXPENSIVE LUNCH AND OBSCENE AMOUNT OF ALCOHOL?
I...I'D LOVE TO, BUT ACTUALLY I'M ON MY WAY TO A MODELING ASSIGNMENT AT MAX FACTOR.
WELL, MAX FACTOR JUST HAPPENS TO BE ONE OF OUR SUBSIDIARIES, FRECKLE-FACE...
...LET'S CHANGE THAT APPOINTMENT TO TOMORROW AFTERNOON, SHALL WE?

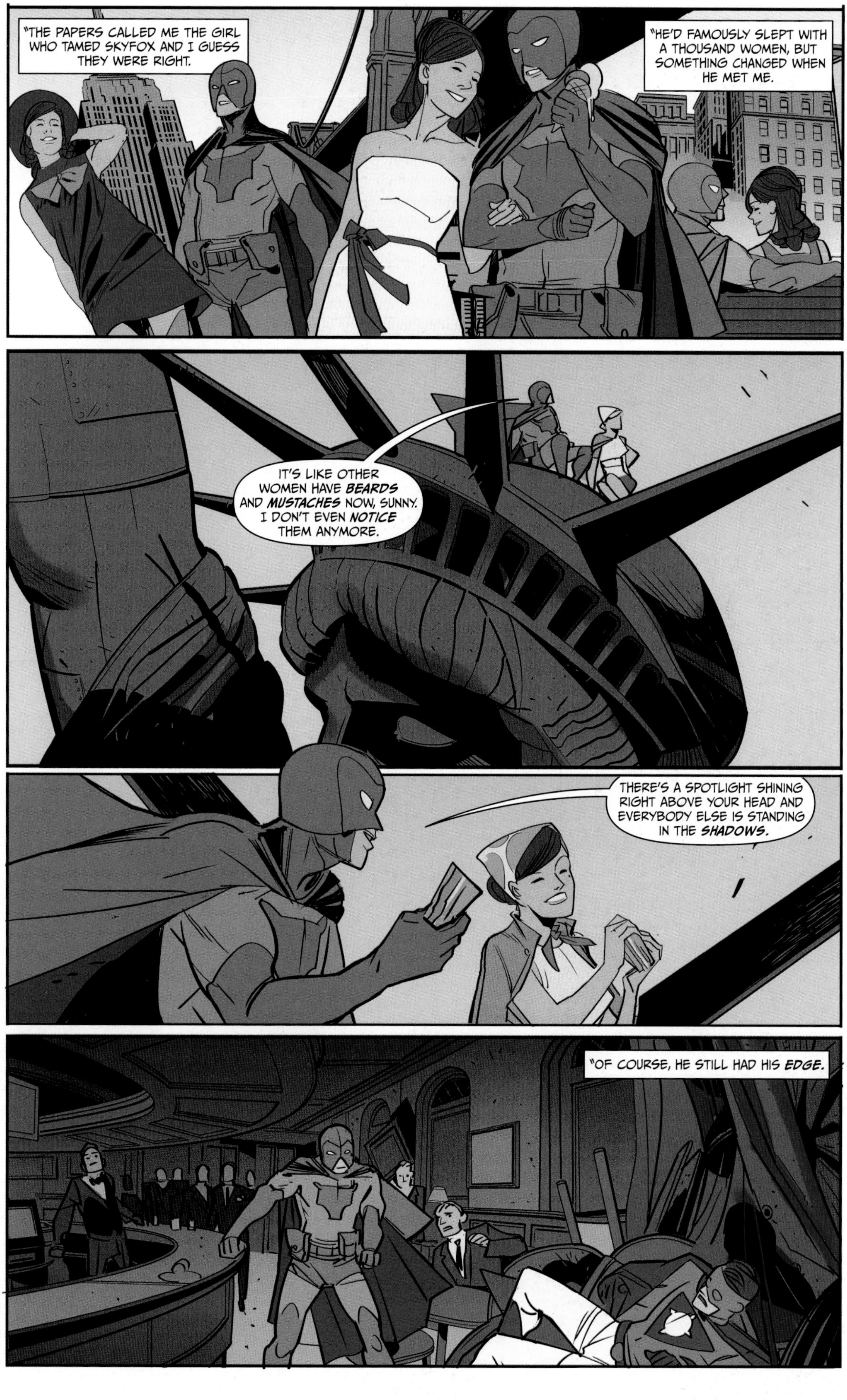
"THE PAPERS CALLED ME THE GIRL WHO TAMED SKYFOX AND I GUESS THEY WERE RIGHT.
"HE'D FAMOUSLY SLEPT WITH A THOUSAND WOMEN, BUT SOMETHING CHANGED WHEN HE MET ME.
IT'S LIKE OTHER WOMEN HAVE BEARDS AND MUSTACHES NOW, SUNNY. I DON'T EVEN NOTICE THEM ANYMORE.
THERE'S A SPOTLIGHT SHINING RIGHT ABOVE YOUR HEAD AND EVERYBODY ELSE IS STANDING IN THE SHADOWS.
"OF COURSE, HE STILL HAD HIS EDGE.

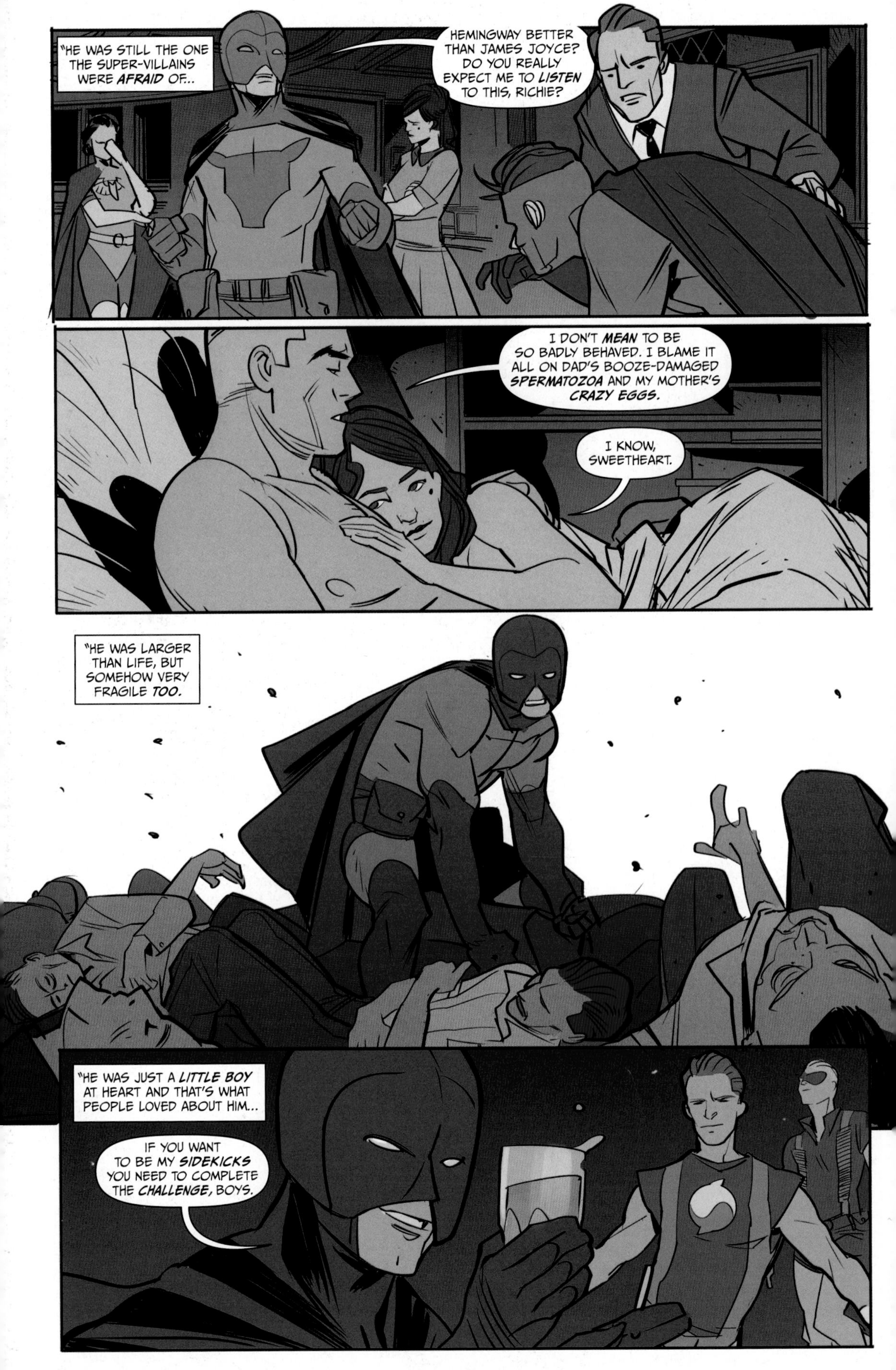
"HE WAS STILL THE ONE THE SUPER-VILLAINS WERE AFRAID OF...
HEMINGWAY BETTER THAN JAMES JOYCE? DO YOU REALLY EXPECT ME TO LISTEN TO THIS, RICHIE?
I DON'T MEAN TO BE SO BADLY BEHAVED. I BLAME IT ALL ON DAD'S BOOZE-DAMAGED SPERMATOZOA AND MY MOTHER'S CRAZY EGGS.
I KNOW, SWEETHEART.
"HE WAS LARGER THAN LIFE, BUT SOMEHOW VERY FRAGILE TOO.
"HE WAS JUST A LITTLE BOY AT HEART AND THAT'S WHAT PEOPLE LOVED ABOUT HIM...
IF YOU WANT TO BE MY SIDEKICKS YOU NEED TO COMPLETE THE CHALLENGE, BOYS.

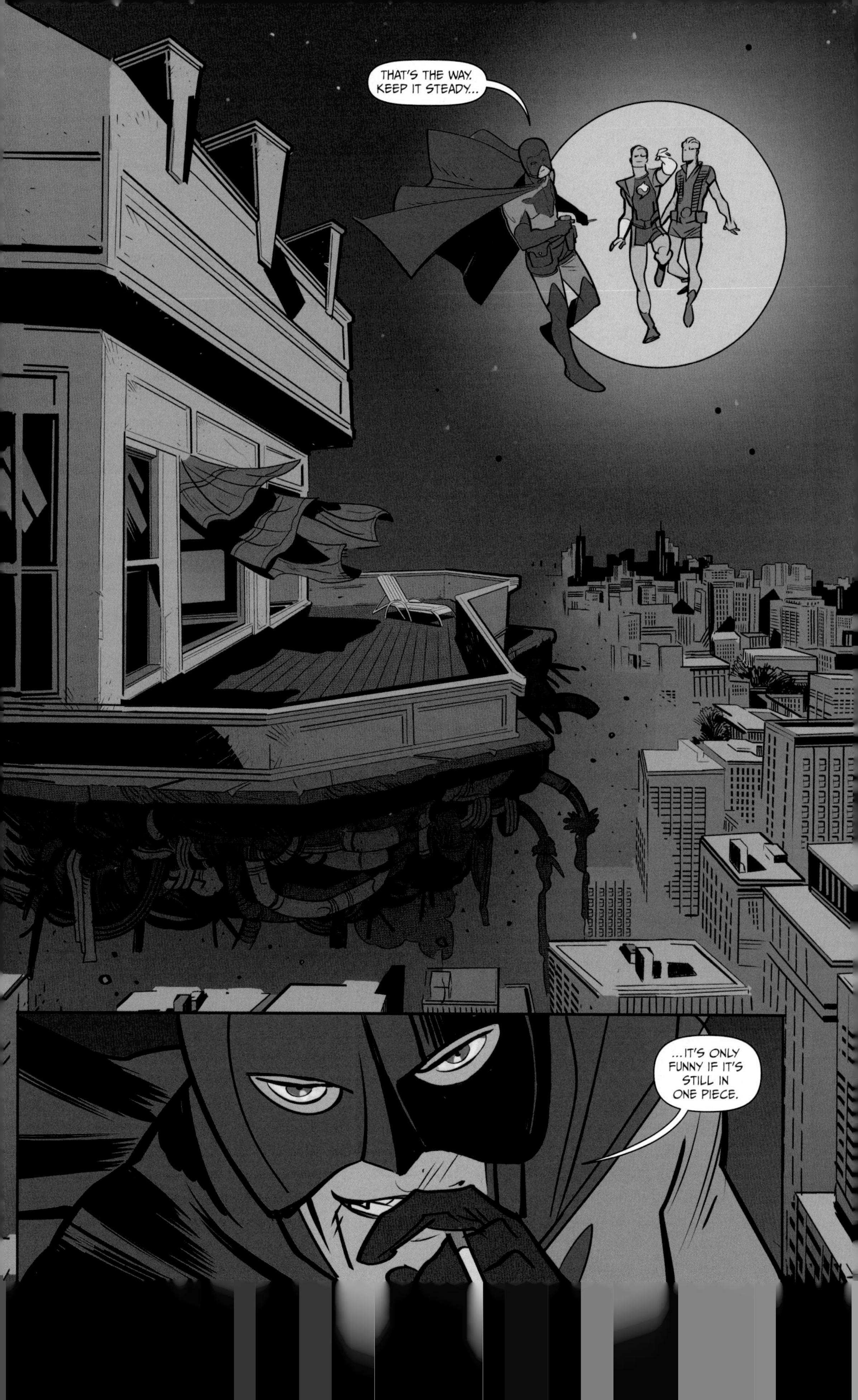
THAT'S THE WAY. KEEP IT STEADY...
...IT'S ONLY FUNNY IF IT'S STILL IN ONE PIECE.

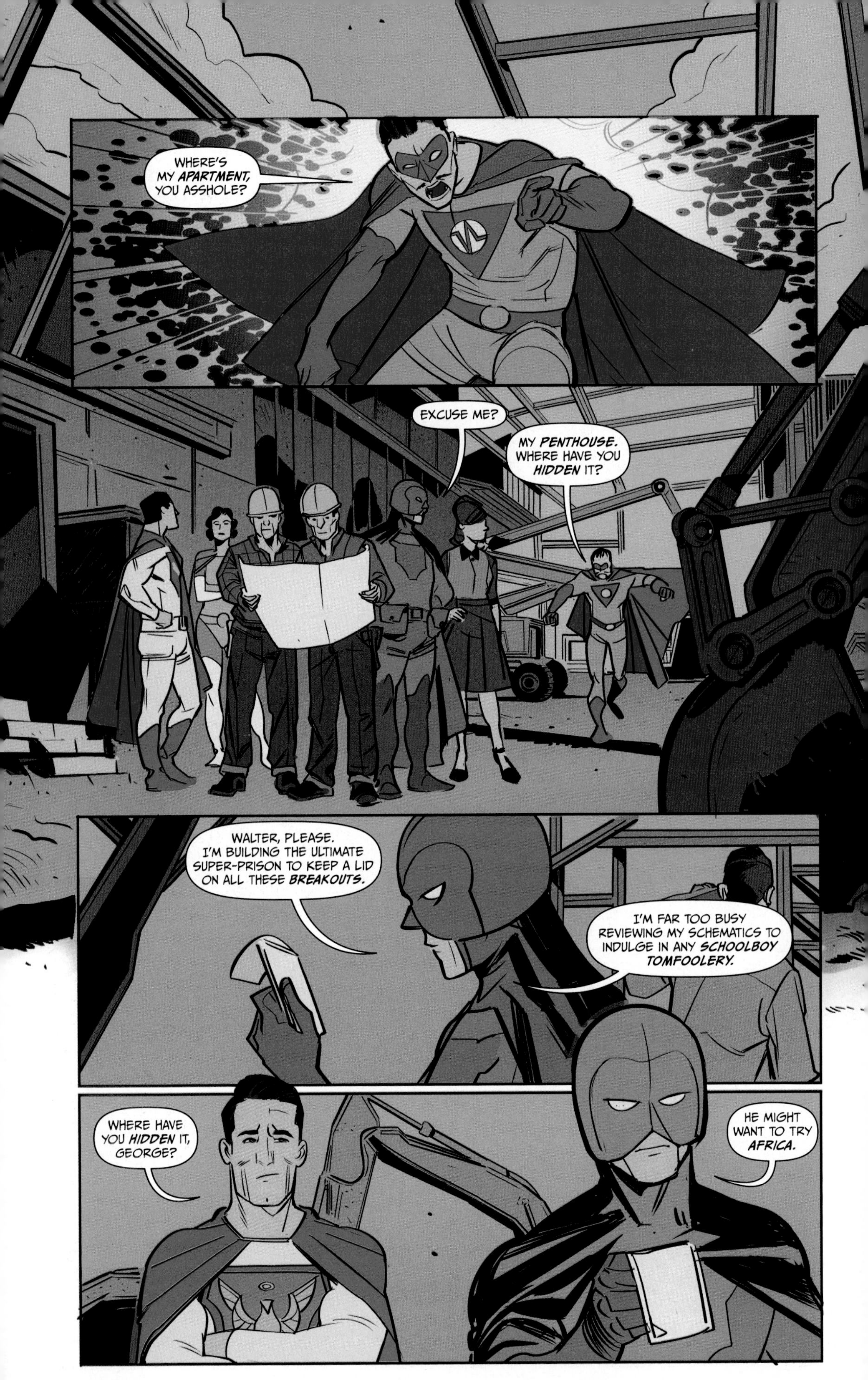

WHERE'S MY *APARTMENT,* YOU ASSHOLE?
EXCUSE ME?
MY *PENTHOUSE.* WHERE HAVE YOU *HIDDEN* IT?
WALTER, PLEASE. I'M BUILDING THE ULTIMATE SUPER-PRISON TO KEEP A LID ON ALL THESE *BREAKOUTS.*
I'M FAR TOO BUSY REVIEWING MY SCHEMATICS TO INDULGE IN ANY *SCHOOLBOY TOMFOOLERY.*
WHERE HAVE YOU *HIDDEN* IT, GEORGE?
HE MIGHT WANT TO TRY *AFRICA.*

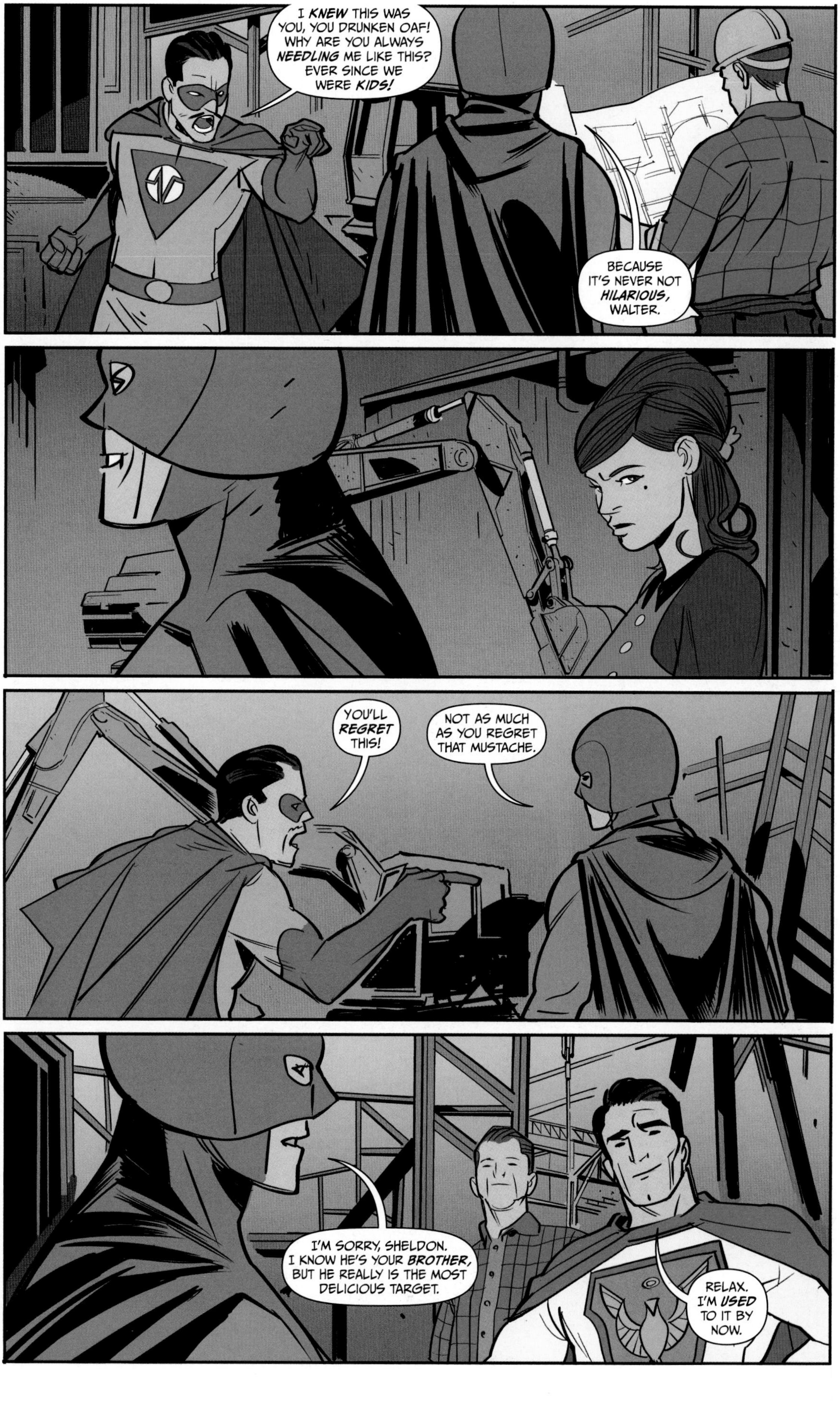
I KNEW THIS WAS YOU, YOU DRUNKEN OAF! WHY ARE YOU ALWAYS NEEDLING ME LIKE THIS? EVER SINCE WE WERE KIDS!
BECAUSE IT'S NEVER NOT HILARIOUS, WALTER.
YOU'LL REGRET THIS!
NOT AS MUCH AS YOU REGRET THAT MUSTACHE.
I'M SORRY, SHELDON. I KNOW HE'S YOUR BROTHER, BUT HE REALLY IS THE MOST DELICIOUS TARGET.
RELAX. I'M USED TO IT BY NOW.

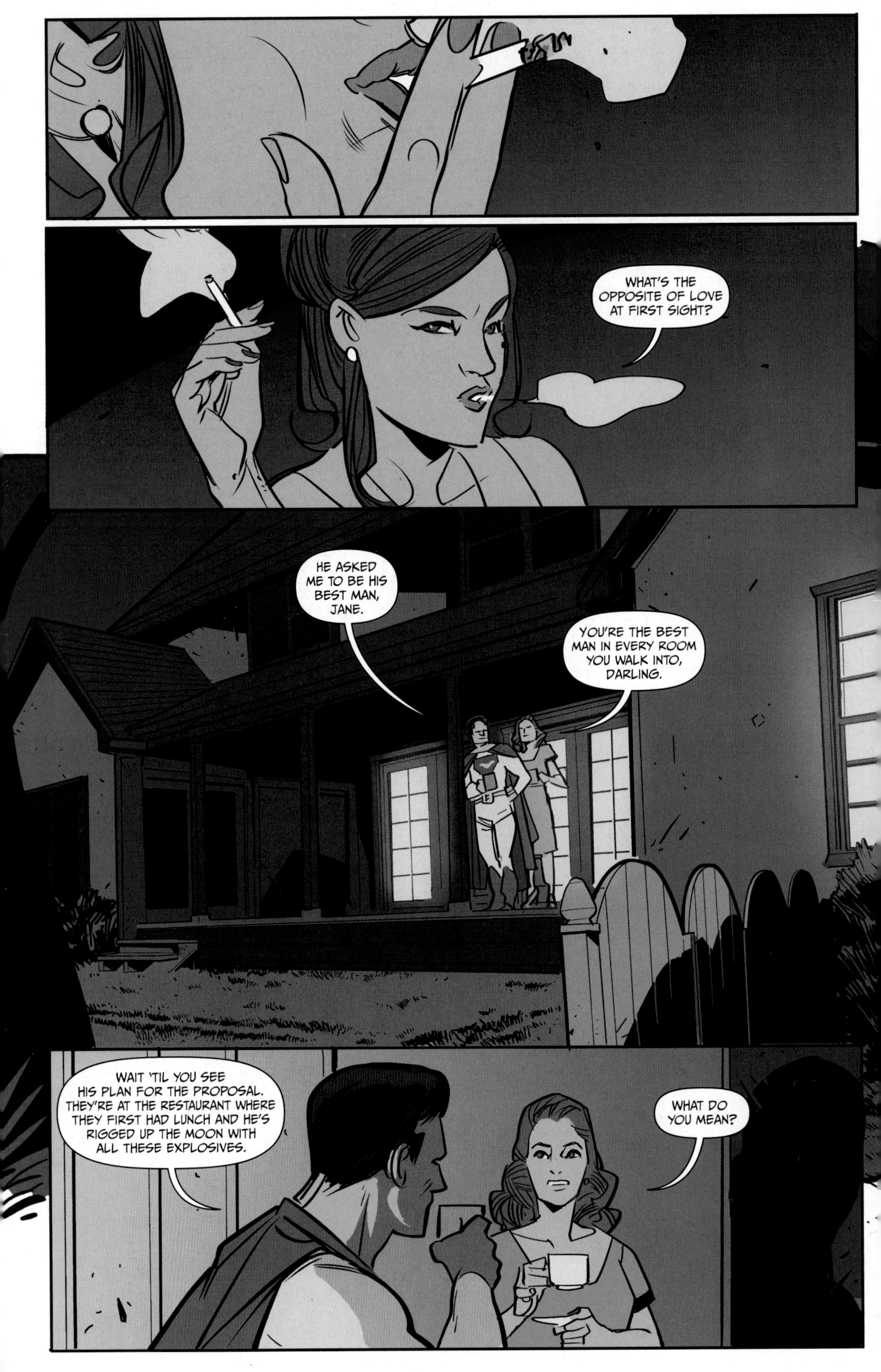
WHAT'S THE OPPOSITE OF LOVE AT FIRST SIGHT?
HE ASKED ME TO BE HIS BEST MAN, JANE.
YOU'RE THE BEST MAN IN EVERY ROOM YOU WALK INTO, DARLING.
WAIT 'TIL YOU SEE HIS PLAN FOR THE PROPOSAL. THEY'RE AT THE RESTAURANT WHERE THEY FIRST HAD LUNCH AND HE'S RIGGED UP THE MOON WITH ALL THESE EXPLOSIVES.
WHAT DO YOU MEAN?

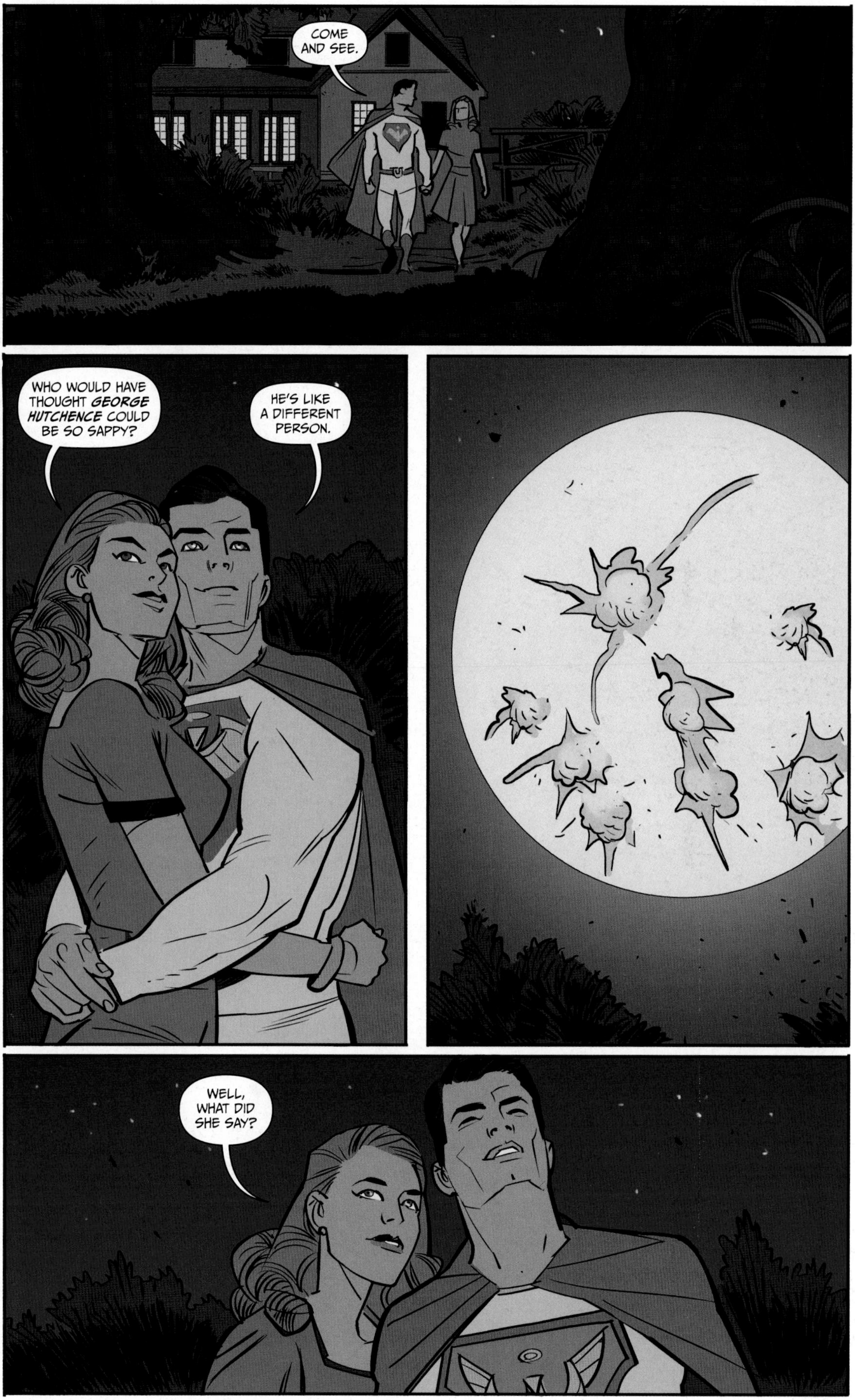
COME AND SEE.
WHO WOULD HAVE THOUGHT GEORGE HUTCHENCE COULD BE SO SAPPY?
HE'S LIKE A DIFFERENT PERSON.
WELL, WHAT DID SHE SAY?

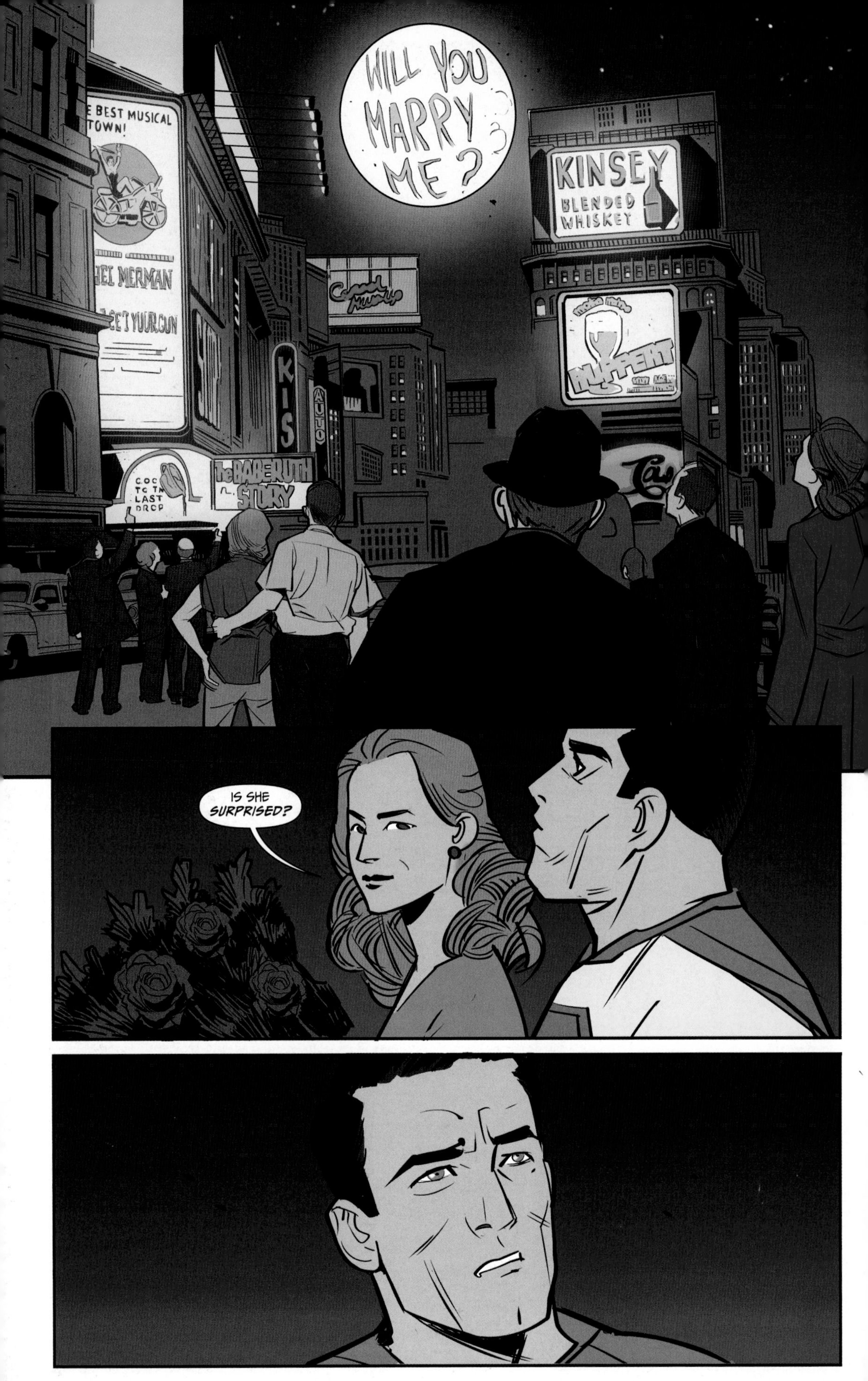
WILL YOU MARRY ME?
E BEST MUSICAL
TOWN!
KINSEY
BLENDED WHISKEY
The BABE RUTH STORY
IS SHE SURPRISED?

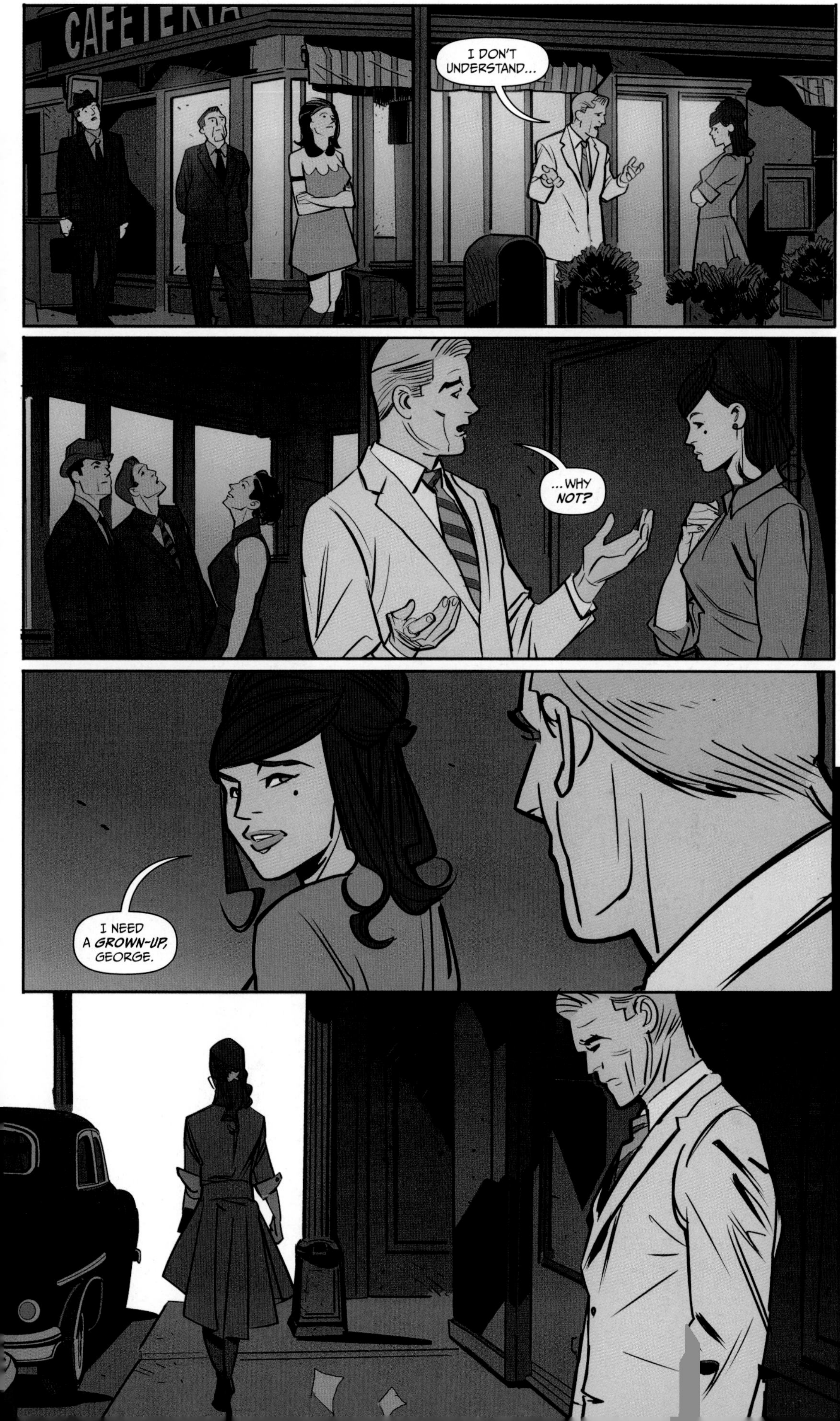
CAFETERIA
I DON'T UNDERSTAND...
...WHY NOT?
I NEED A GROWN-UP, GEORGE.

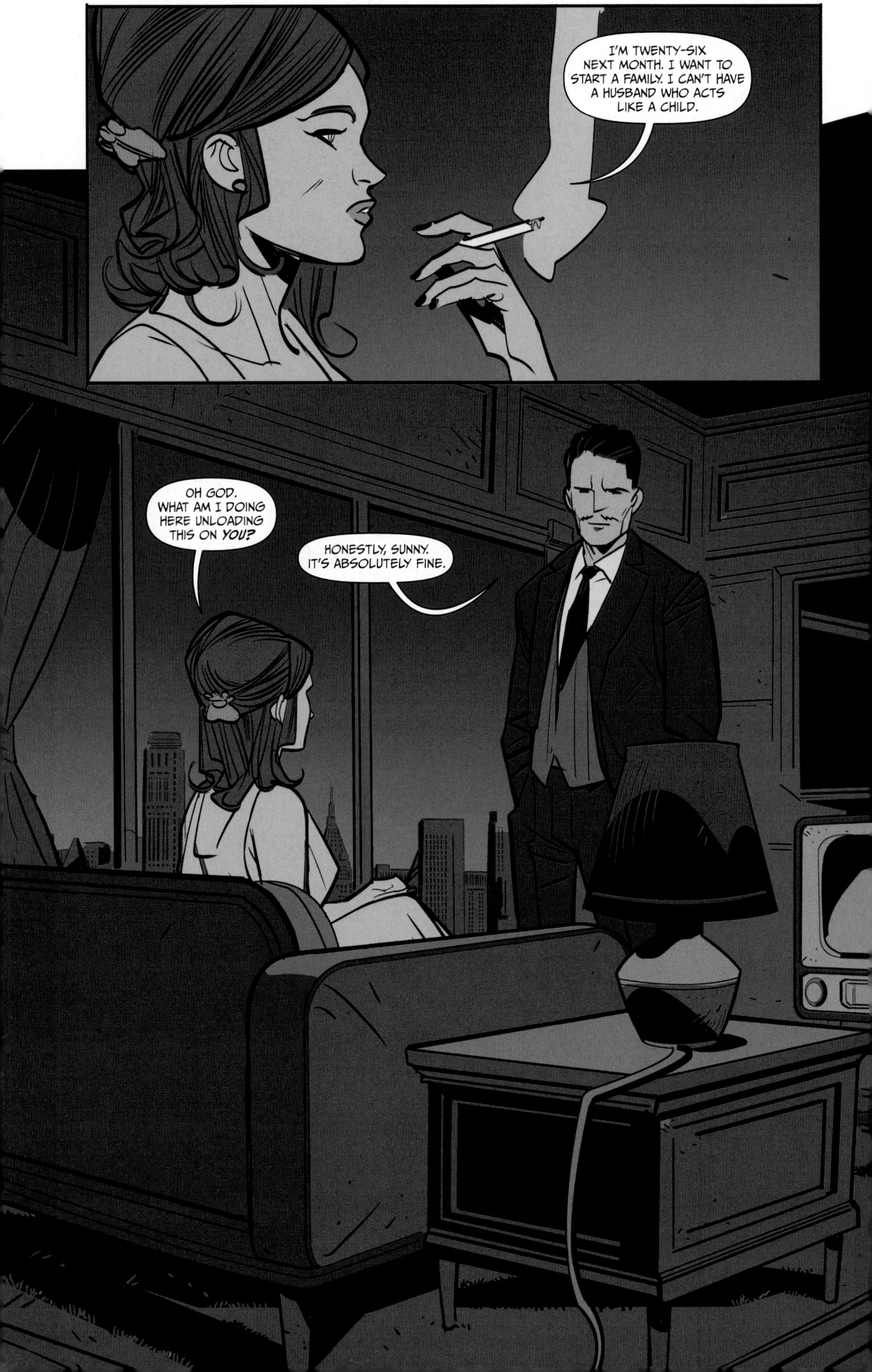
I'M TWENTY-SIX NEXT MONTH. I WANT TO START A FAMILY. I CAN'T HAVE A HUSBAND WHO ACTS LIKE A CHILD.
OH GOD. WHAT AM I DOING HERE UNLOADING THIS ON ***YOU?***
HONESTLY, SUNNY. IT'S ABSOLUTELY FINE.

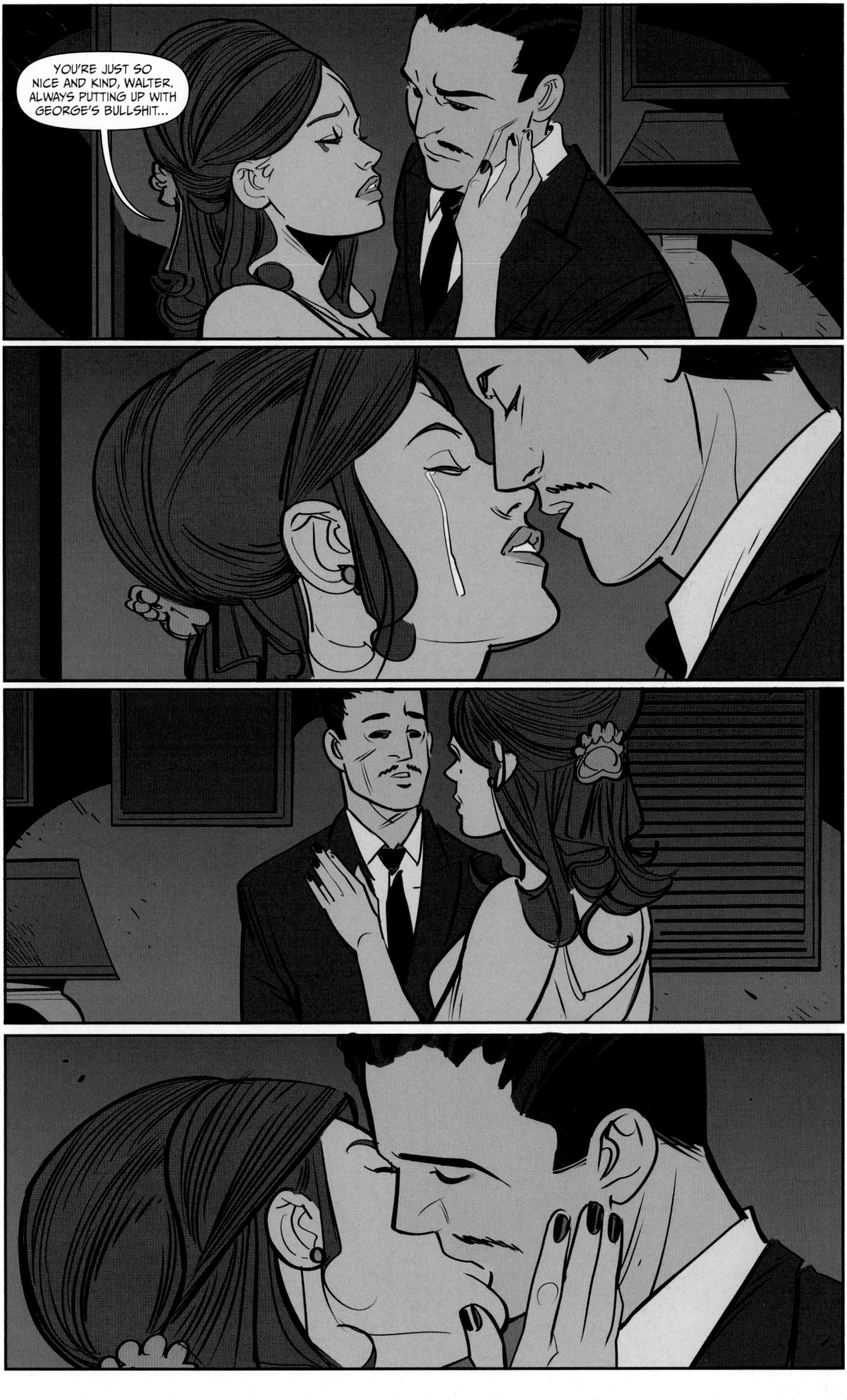
YOU'RE JUST SO NICE AND KIND, WALTER. ALWAYS PUTTING UP WITH GEORGE'S BULLSHIT...

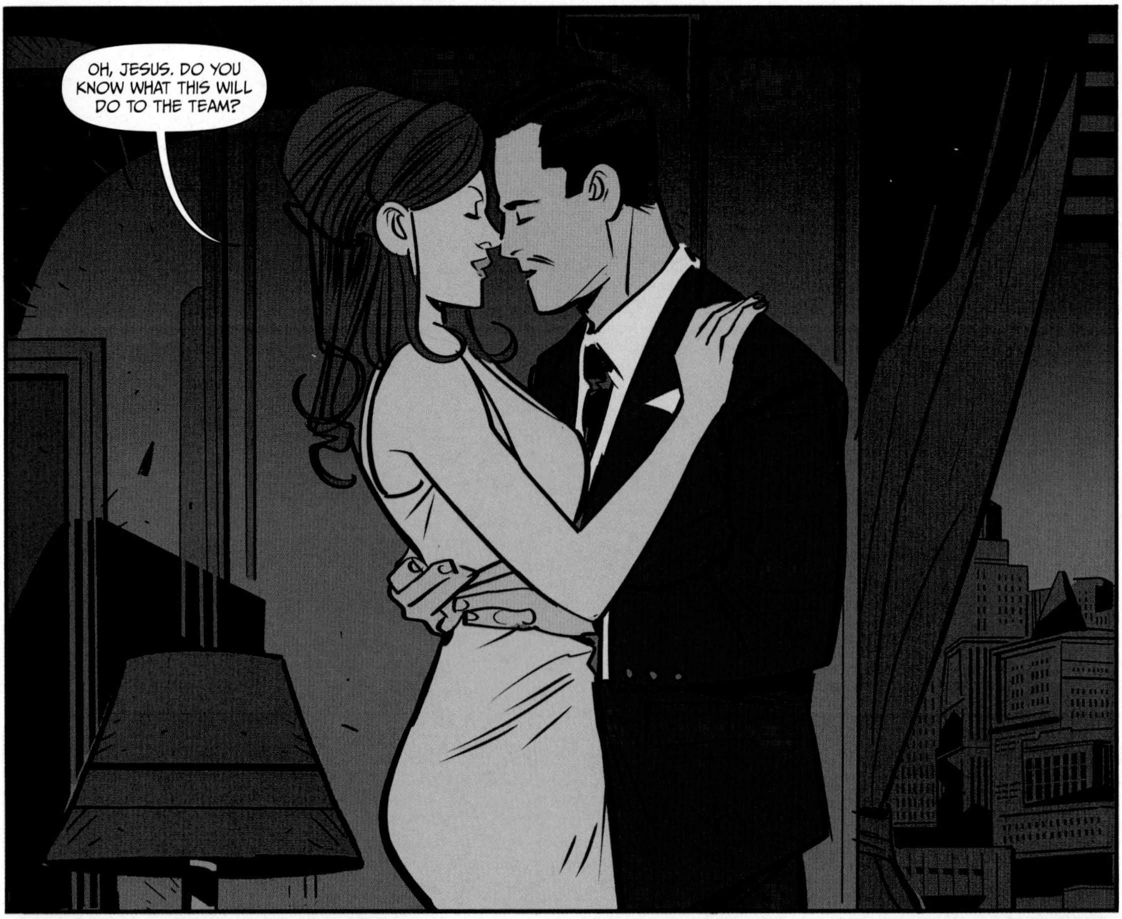
OH, JESUS. DO YOU KNOW WHAT THIS WILL DO TO THE TEAM?

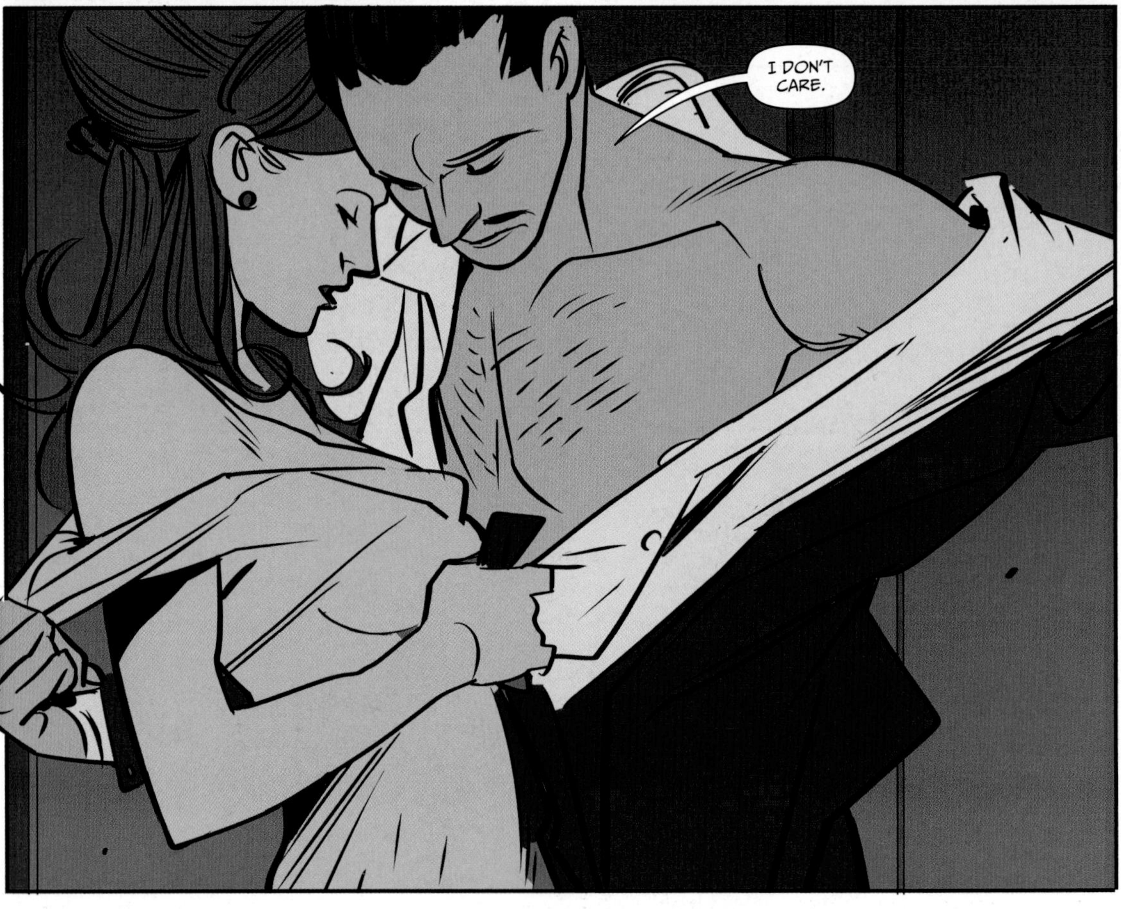
I DON'T CARE.

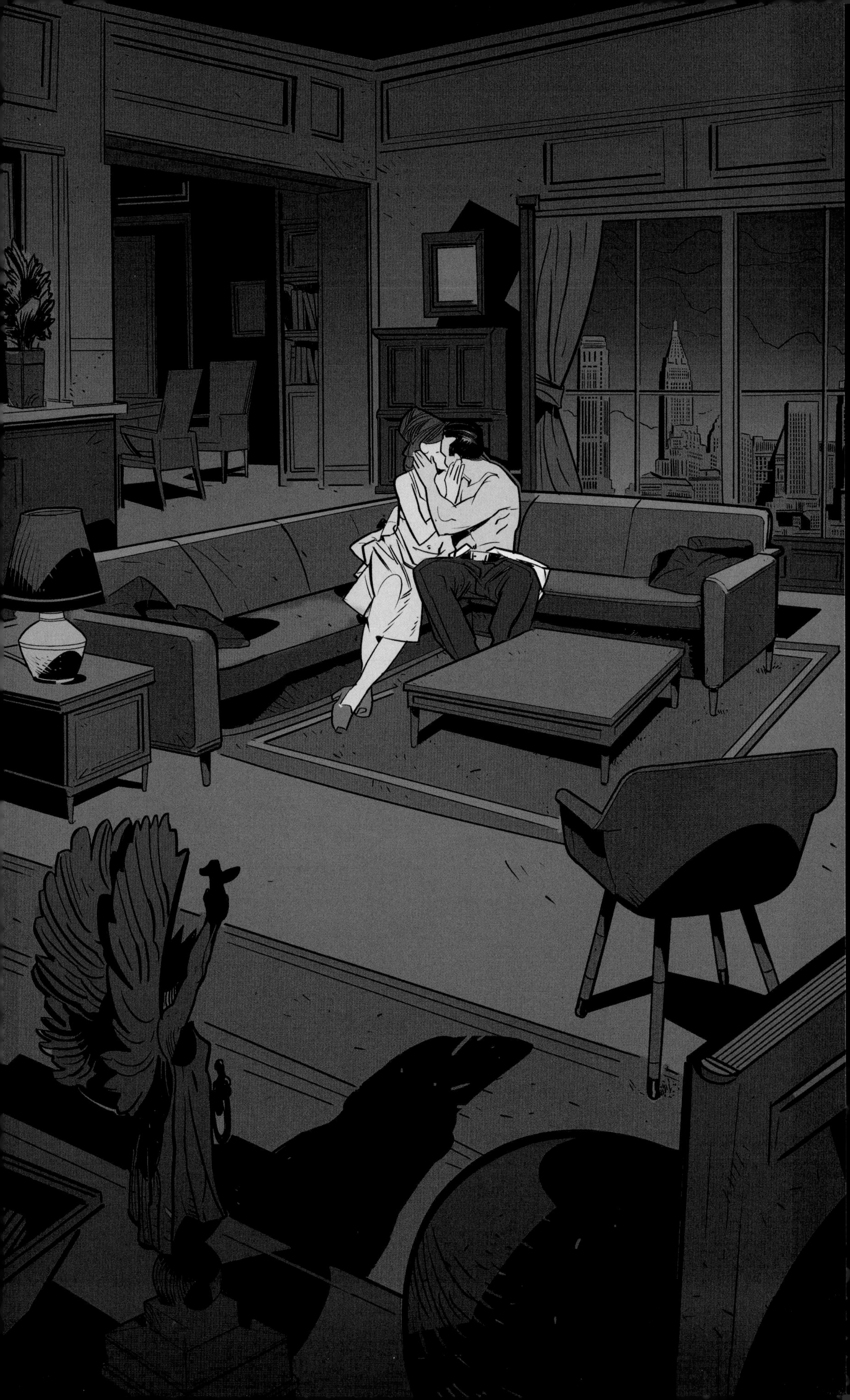

CHAPTER 6

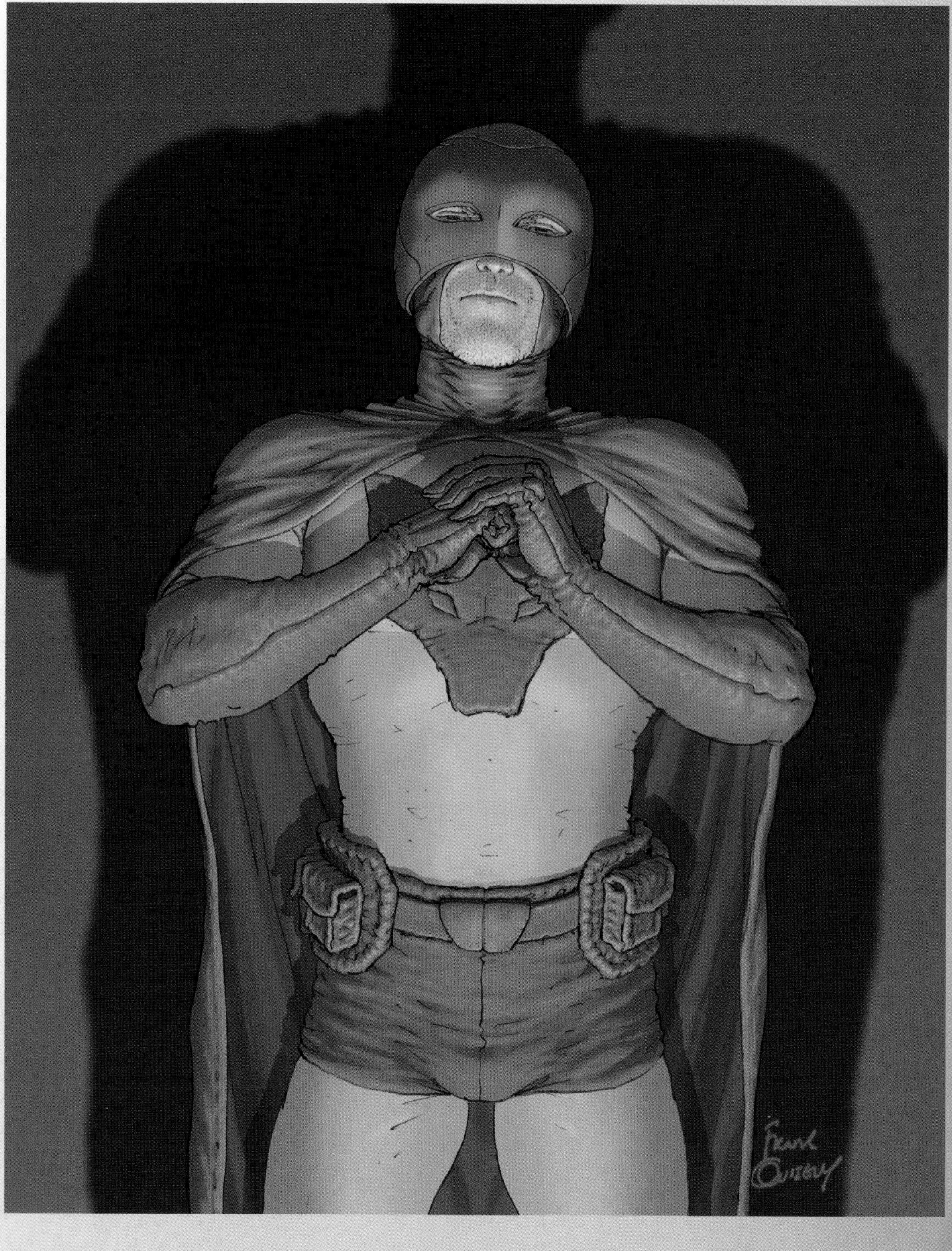

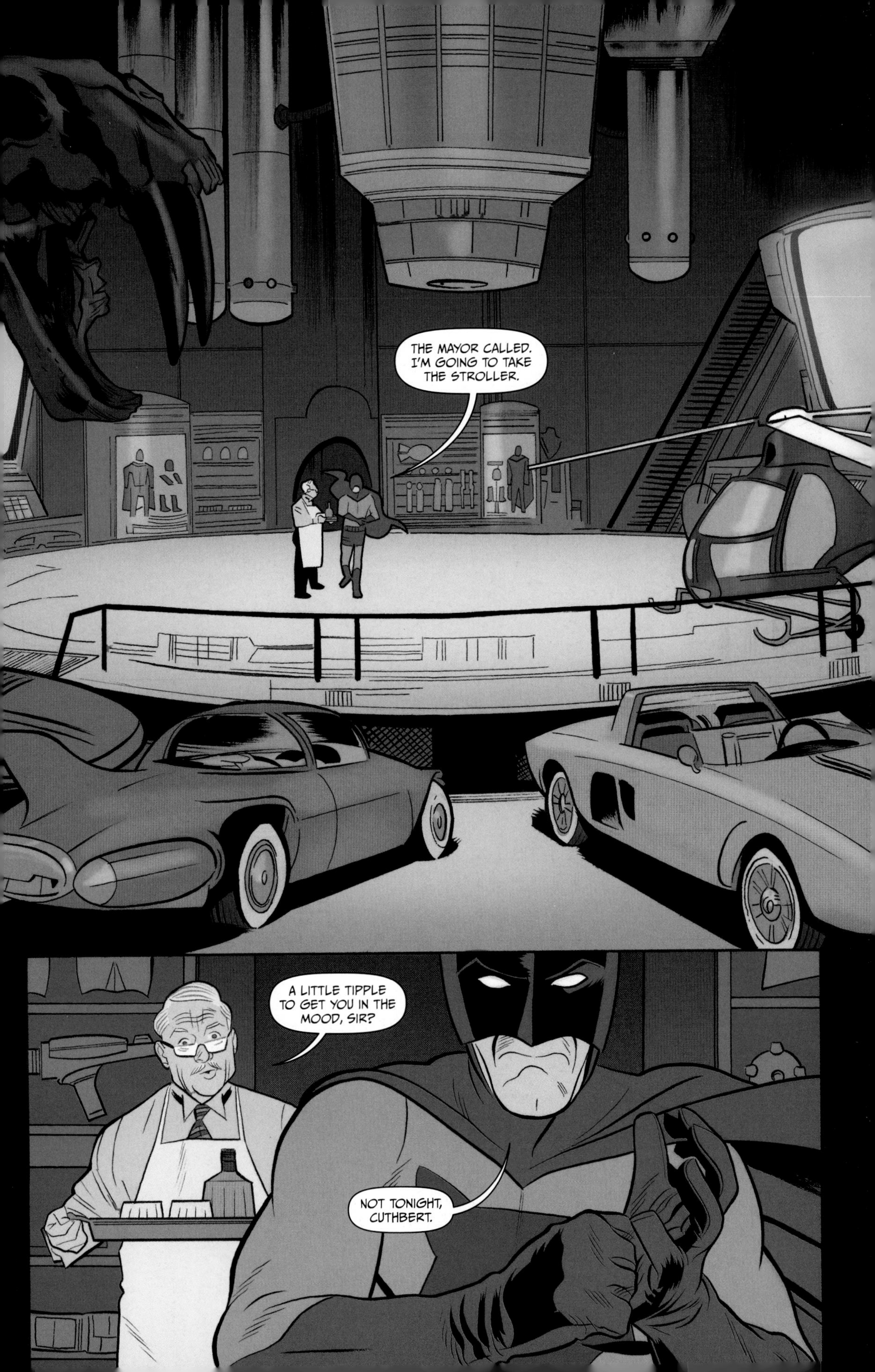
THE MAYOR CALLED. I'M GOING TO TAKE THE STROLLER.
A LITTLE TIPPLE TO GET YOU IN THE MOOD, SIR?
NOT TONIGHT, CUTHBERT.

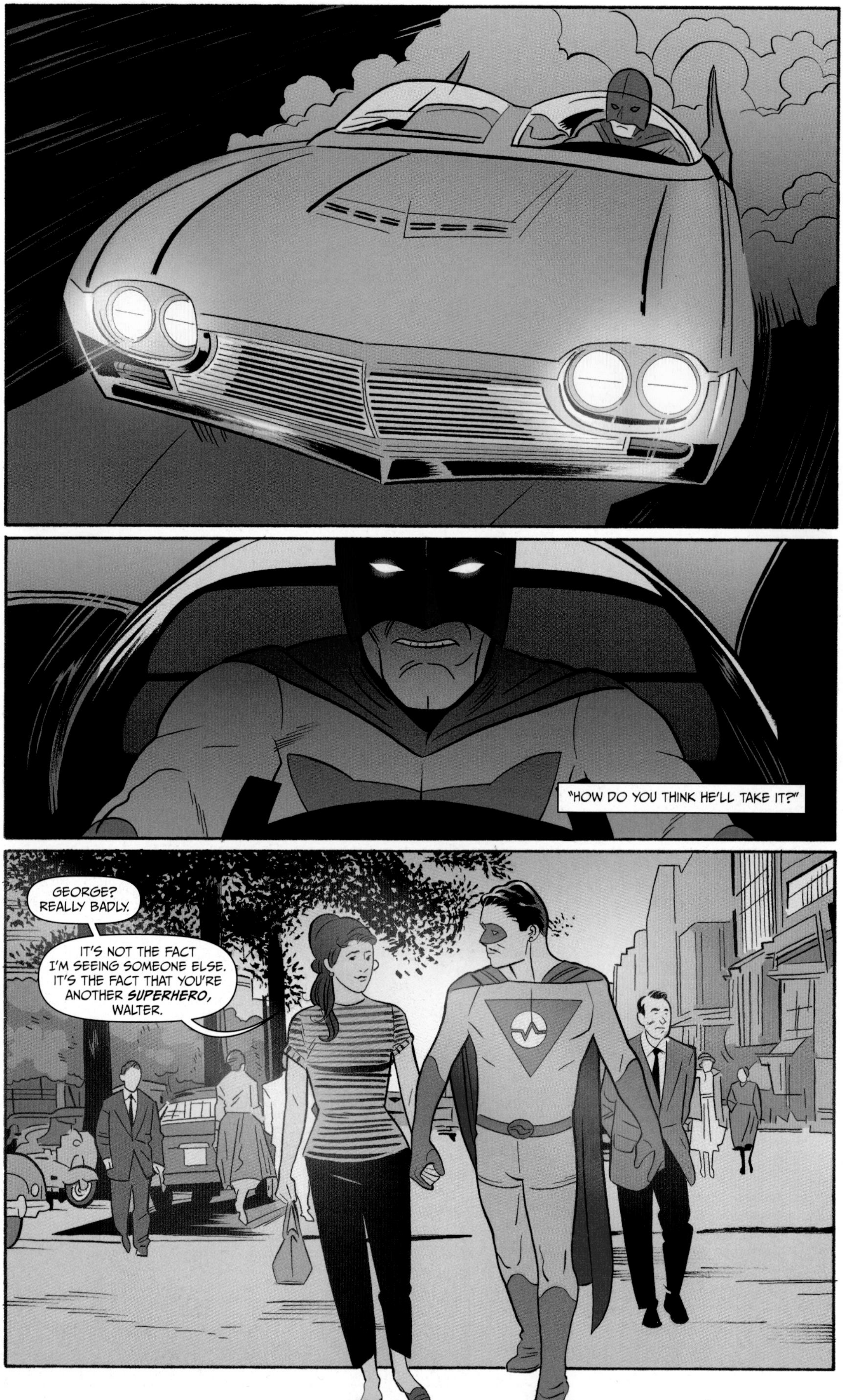
"HOW DO YOU THINK HE'LL TAKE IT?"
GEORGE? REALLY BADLY.
IT'S NOT THE FACT I'M SEEING SOMEONE ELSE. IT'S THE FACT THAT YOU'RE ANOTHER SUPERHERO, WALTER.

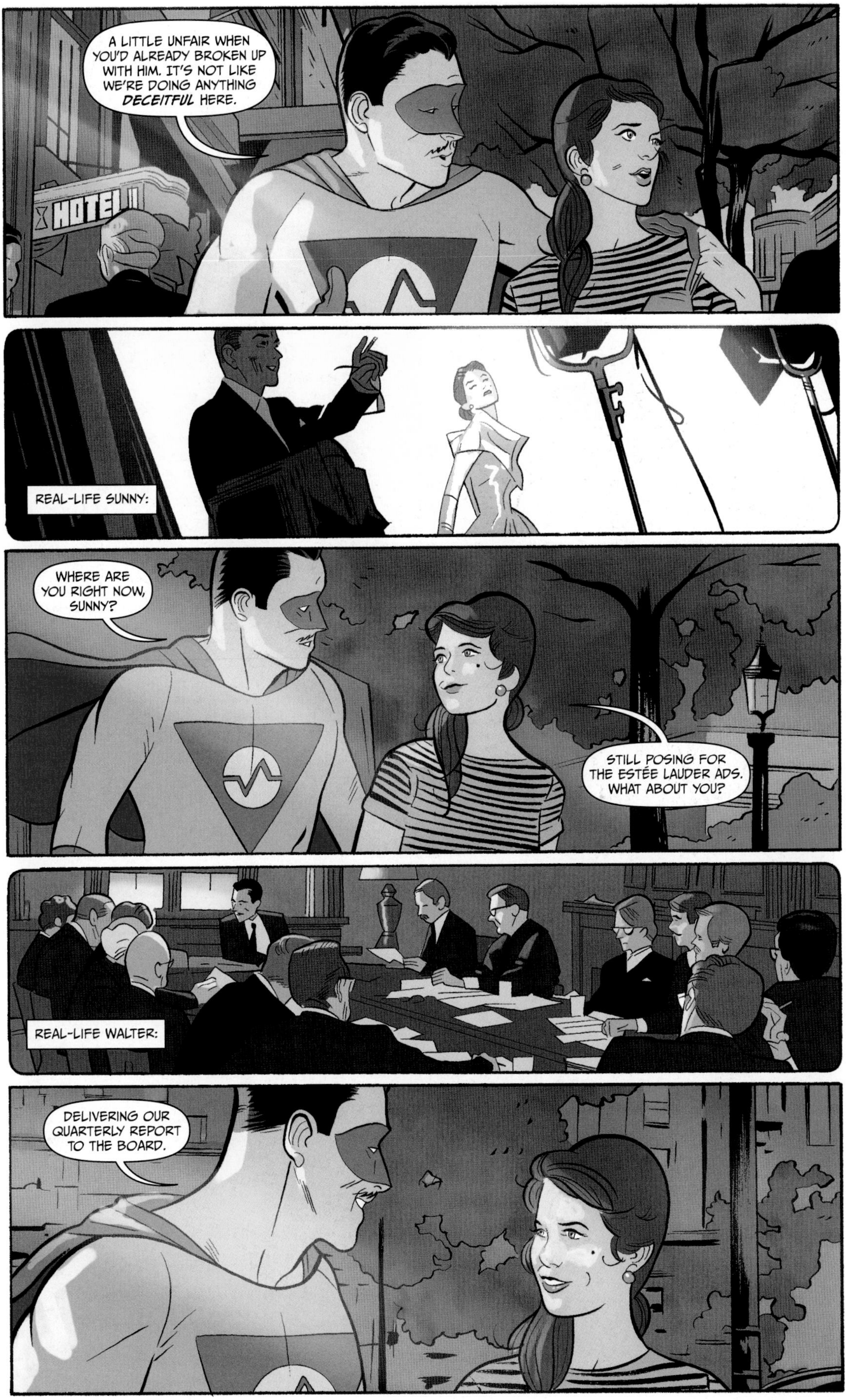
A LITTLE UNFAIR WHEN YOU'D ALREADY BROKEN UP WITH HIM. IT'S NOT LIKE WE'RE DOING ANYTHING *DECEITFUL* HERE.
HOTEL
REAL-LIFE SUNNY:
WHERE ARE YOU RIGHT NOW, SUNNY?
STILL POSING FOR THE ESTÉE LAUDER ADS. WHAT ABOUT YOU?
REAL-LIFE WALTER:
DELIVERING OUR QUARTERLY REPORT TO THE BOARD.

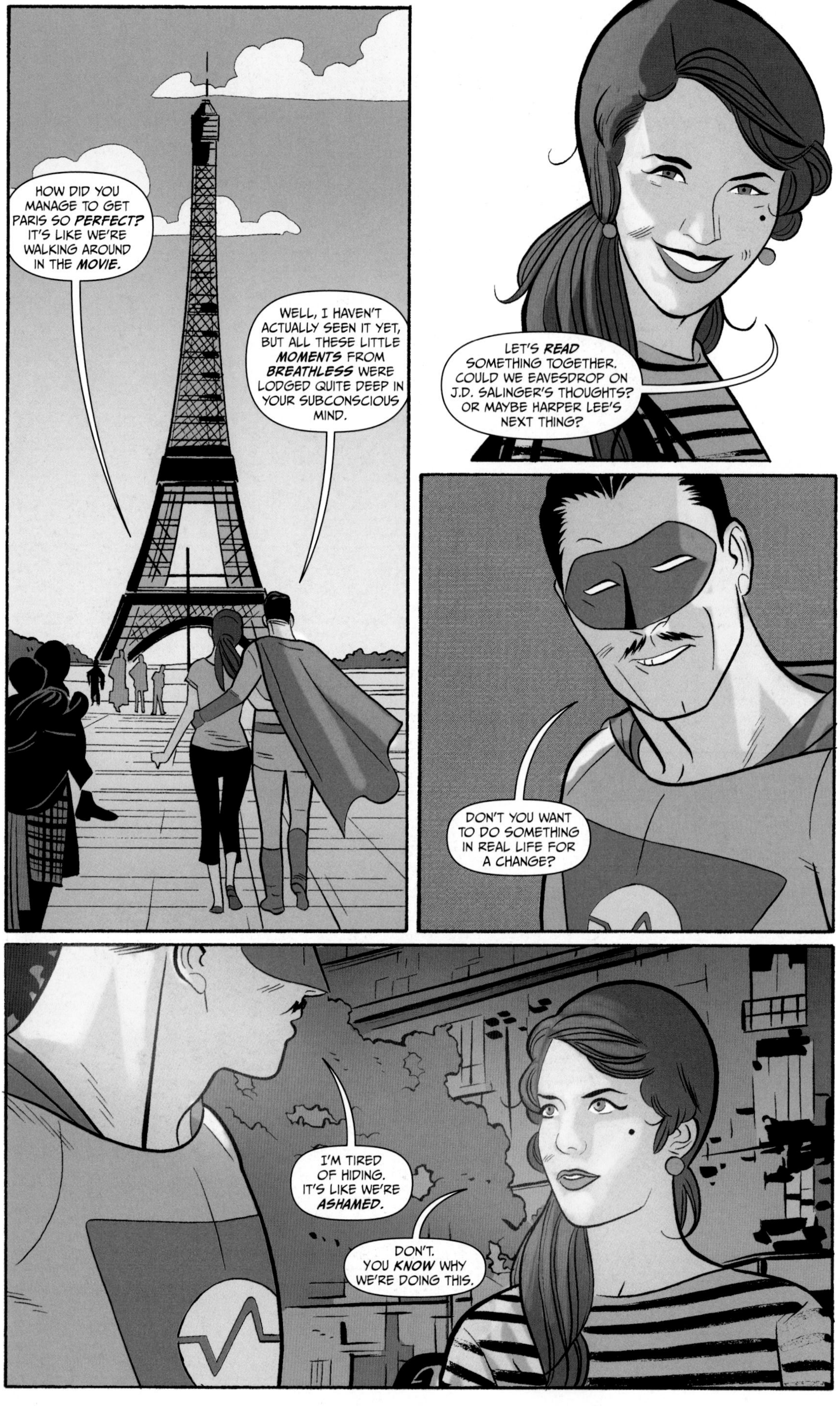
HOW DID YOU MANAGE TO GET PARIS SO *PERFECT?* IT'S LIKE WE'RE WALKING AROUND IN THE *MOVIE.*
WELL, I HAVEN'T ACTUALLY SEEN IT YET, BUT ALL THESE LITTLE *MOMENTS* FROM *BREATHLESS* WERE LODGED QUITE DEEP IN YOUR SUBCONSCIOUS MIND.
LET'S *READ* SOMETHING TOGETHER. COULD WE EAVESDROP ON J.D. SALINGER'S THOUGHTS? OR MAYBE HARPER LEE'S NEXT THING?
DON'T YOU WANT TO DO SOMETHING IN REAL LIFE FOR A CHANGE?
I'M TIRED OF HIDING. IT'S LIKE WE'RE *ASHAMED.*
DON'T. YOU *KNOW* WHY WE'RE DOING THIS.

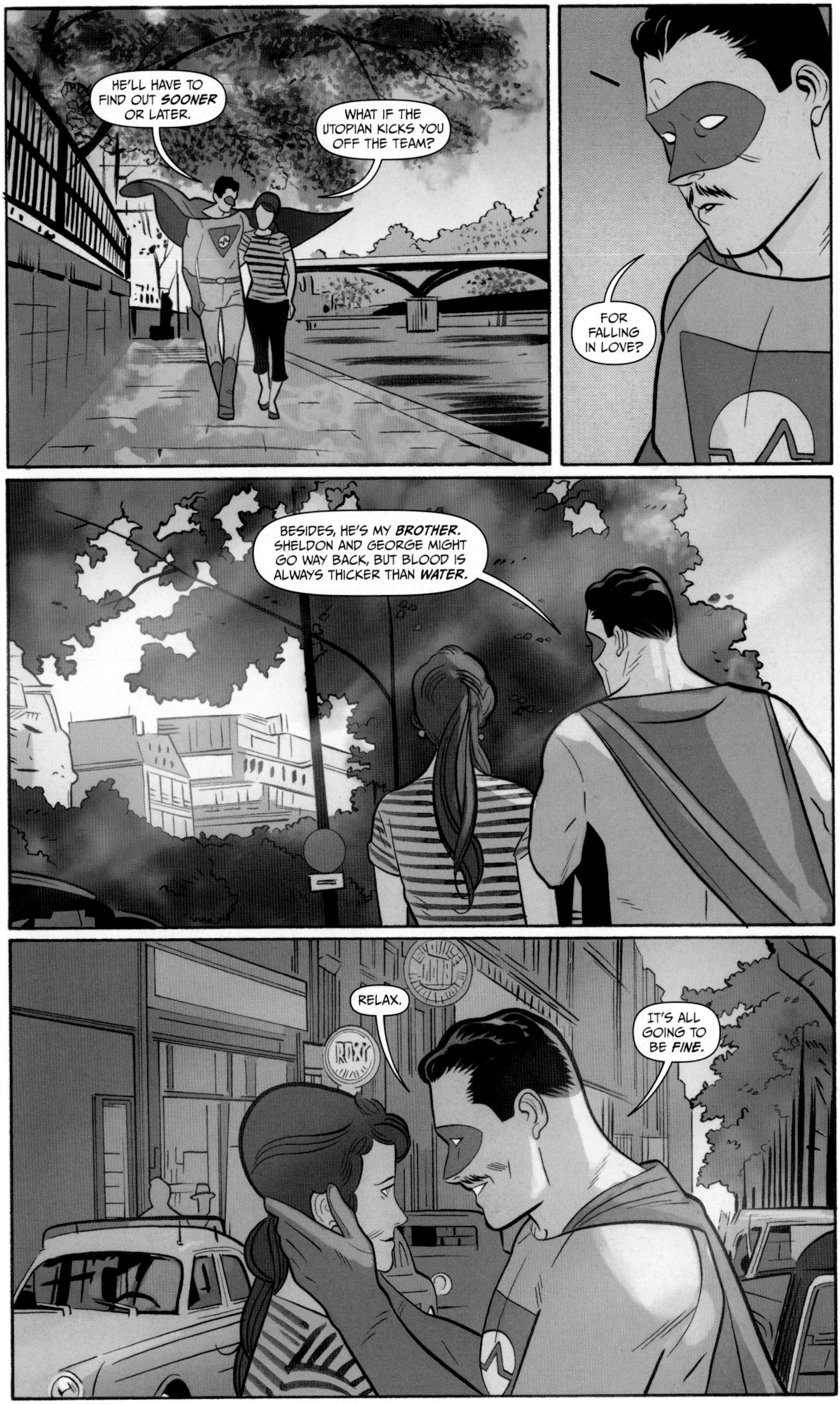
HE'LL HAVE TO FIND OUT SOONER OR LATER.
WHAT IF THE UTOPIAN KICKS YOU OFF THE TEAM?
FOR FALLING IN LOVE?
BESIDES, HE'S MY BROTHER. SHELDON AND GEORGE MIGHT GO WAY BACK, BUT BLOOD IS ALWAYS THICKER THAN WATER.
RELAX.
IT'S ALL GOING TO BE FINE.

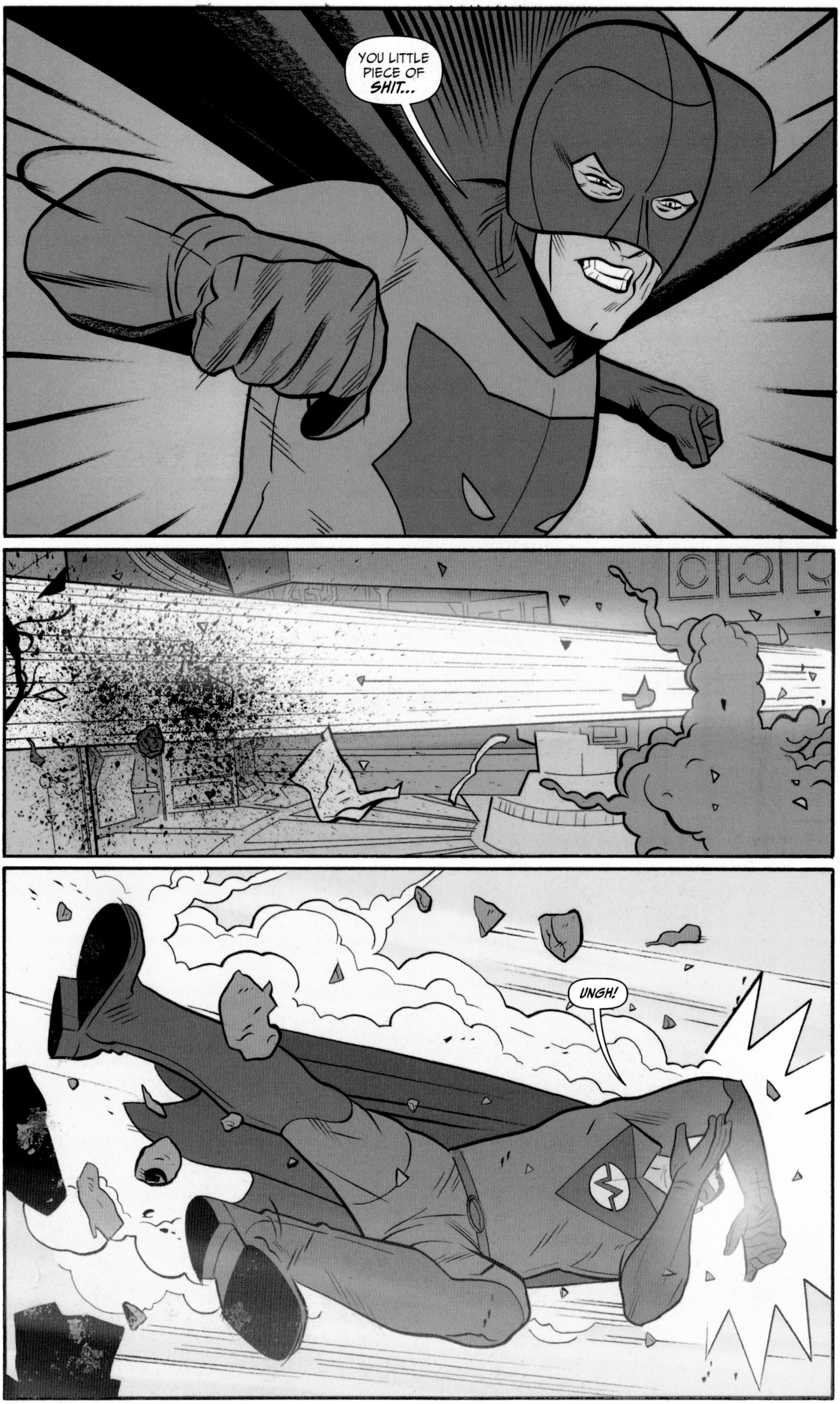
YOU LITTLE PIECE OF SHIT...
UNGH!

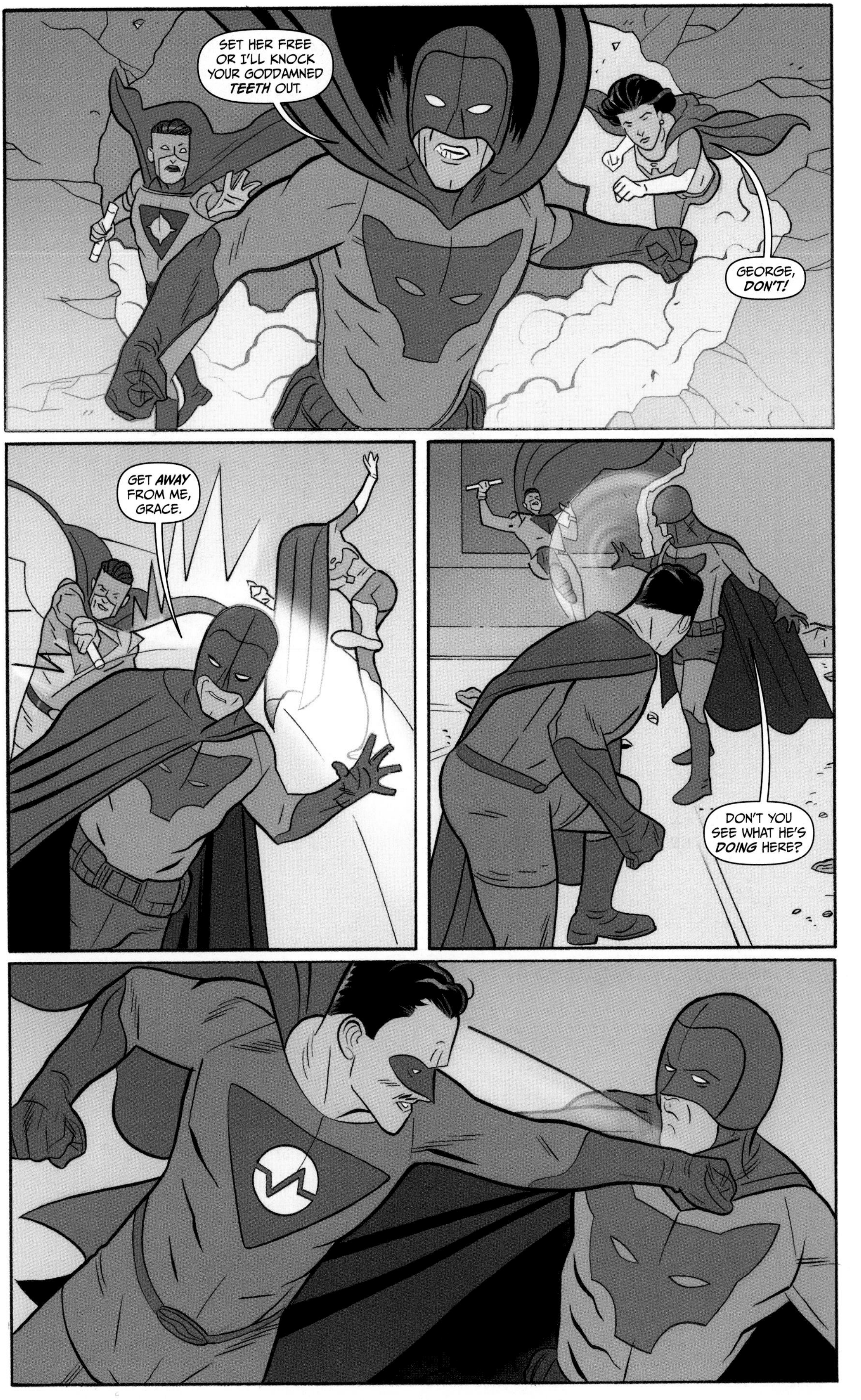
SET HER FREE OR I'LL KNOCK YOUR GODDAMNED TEETH OUT.
GEORGE, DON'T!
GET AWAY FROM ME, GRACE.
DON'T YOU SEE WHAT HE'S DOING HERE?

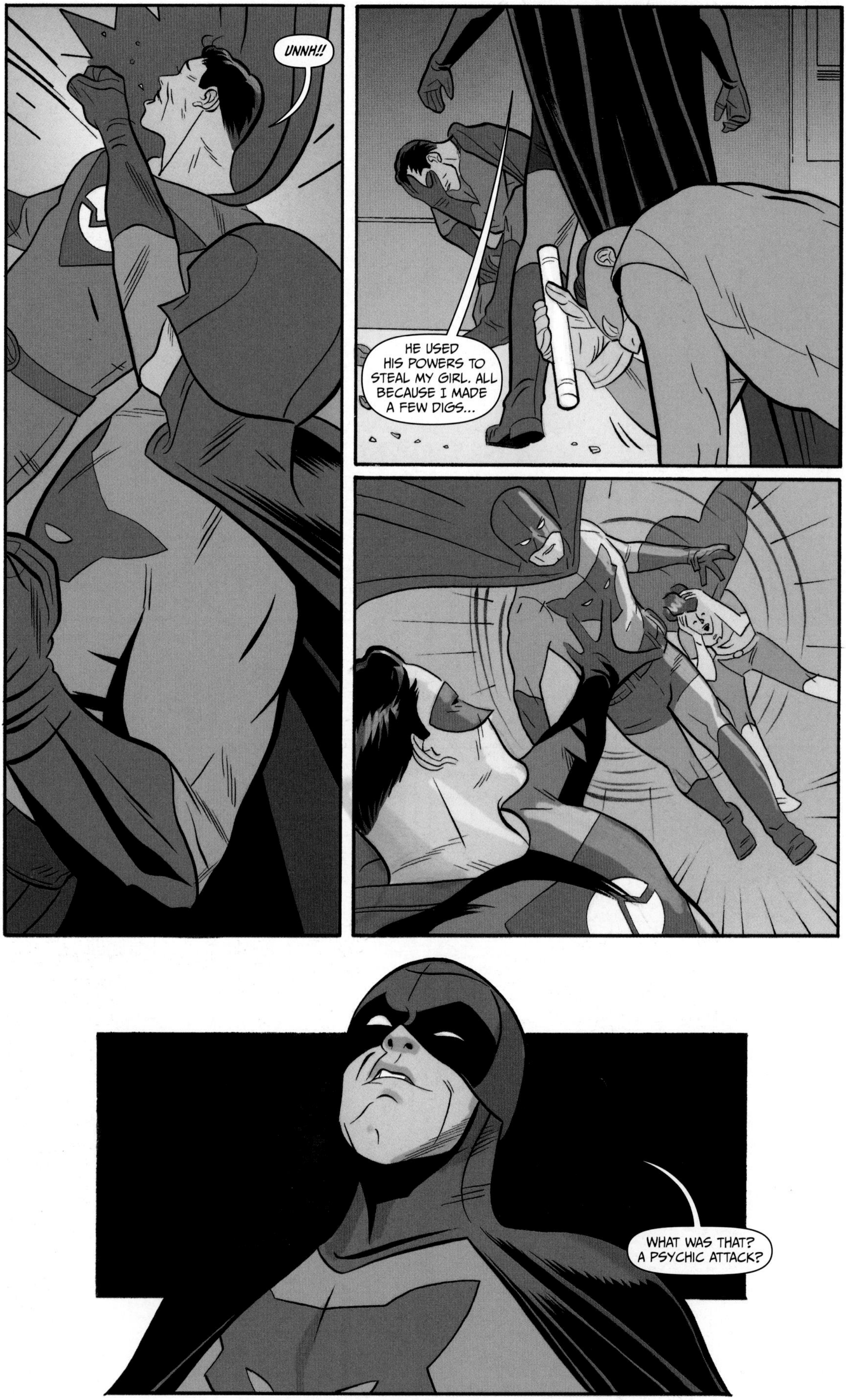
UNNH!!
HE USED HIS POWERS TO STEAL MY GIRL. ALL BECAUSE I MADE A FEW DIGS...
WHAT WAS THAT? A PSYCHIC ATTACK?

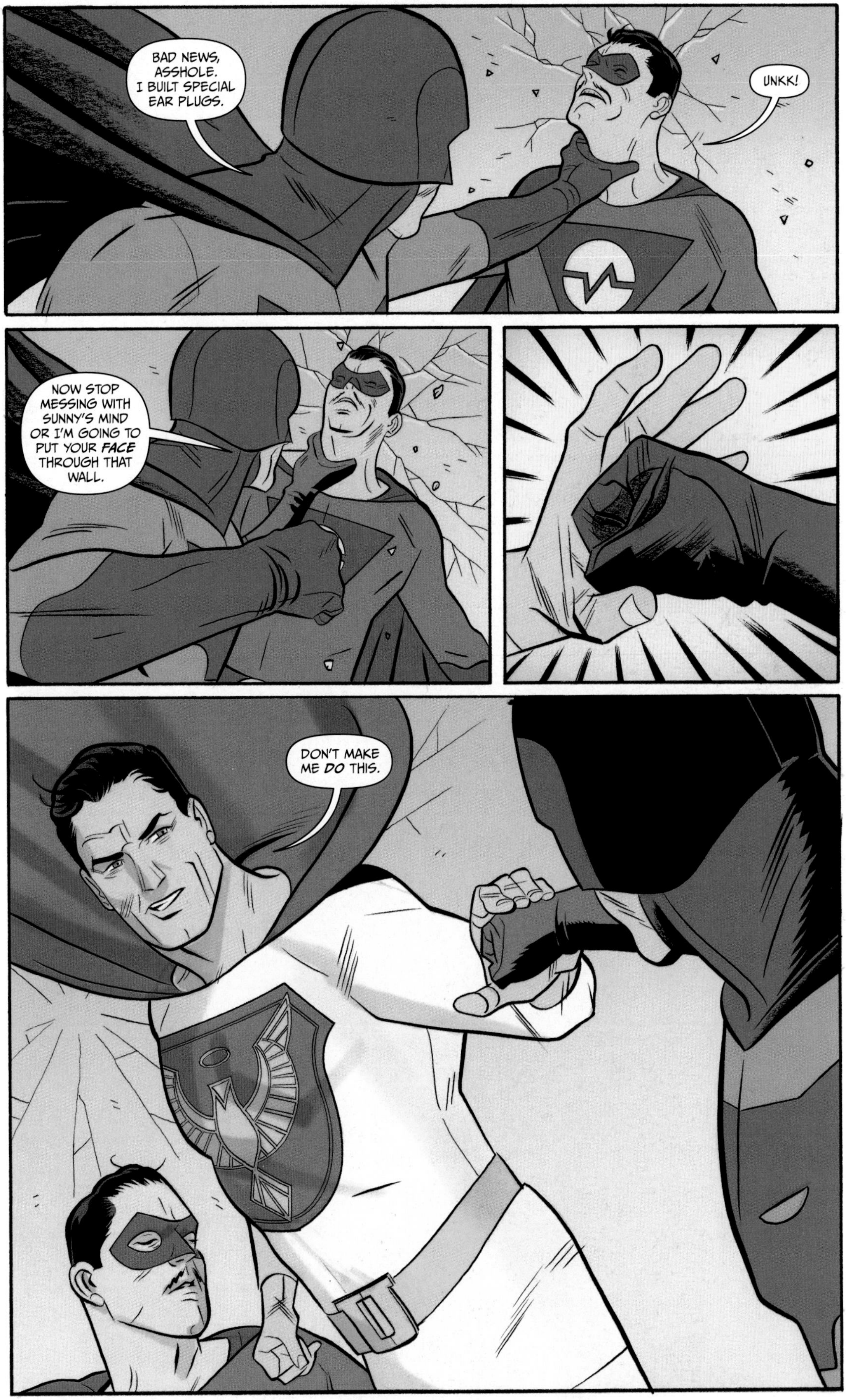
BAD NEWS, ASSHOLE. I BUILT SPECIAL EAR PLUGS.
UNKK!
NOW STOP MESSING WITH SUNNY'S MIND OR I'M GOING TO PUT YOUR *FACE* THROUGH THAT WALL.
DON'T MAKE ME *DO* THIS.

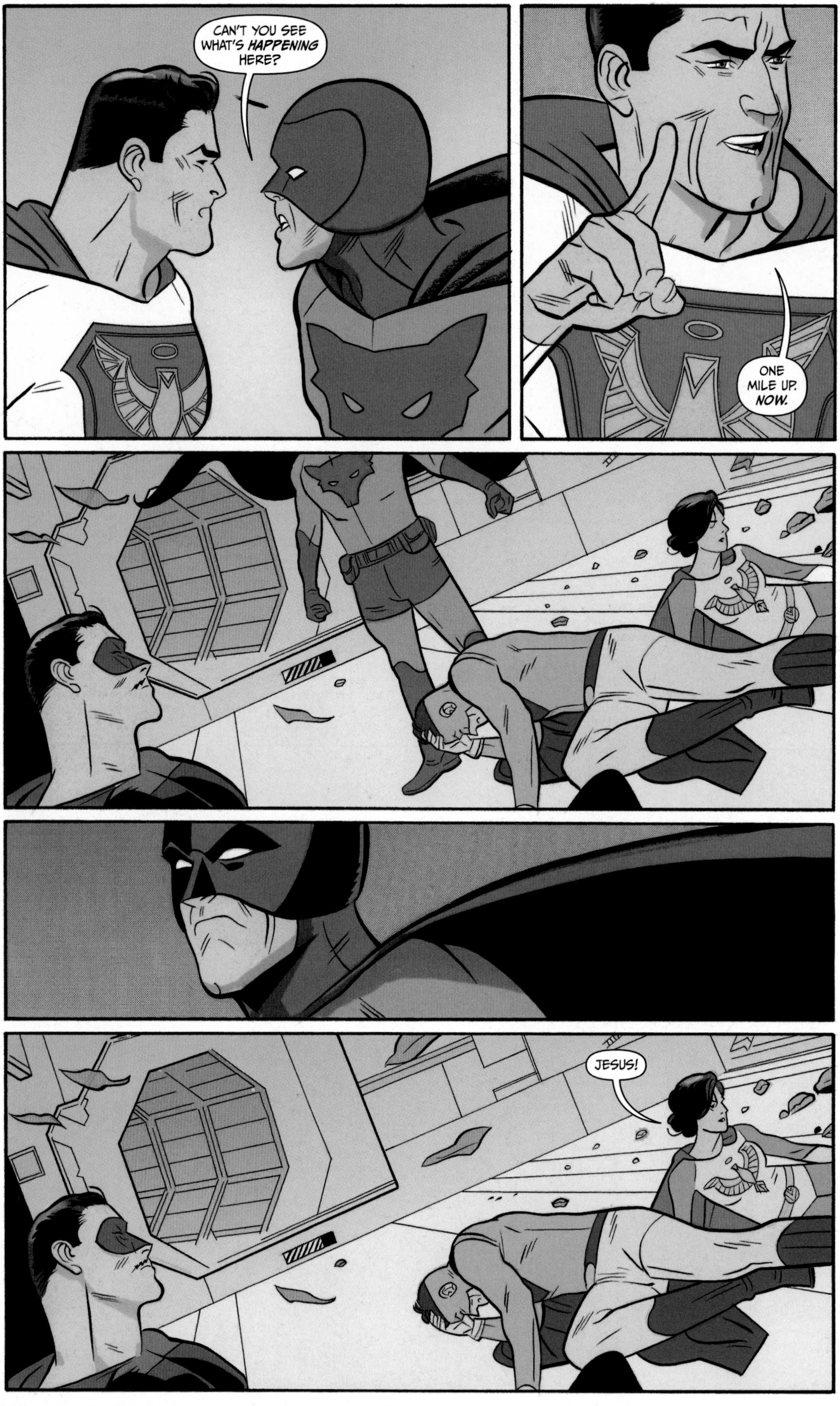
CAN'T YOU SEE WHAT'S *HAPPENING* HERE?
ONE MILE UP. *NOW.*
JESUS!

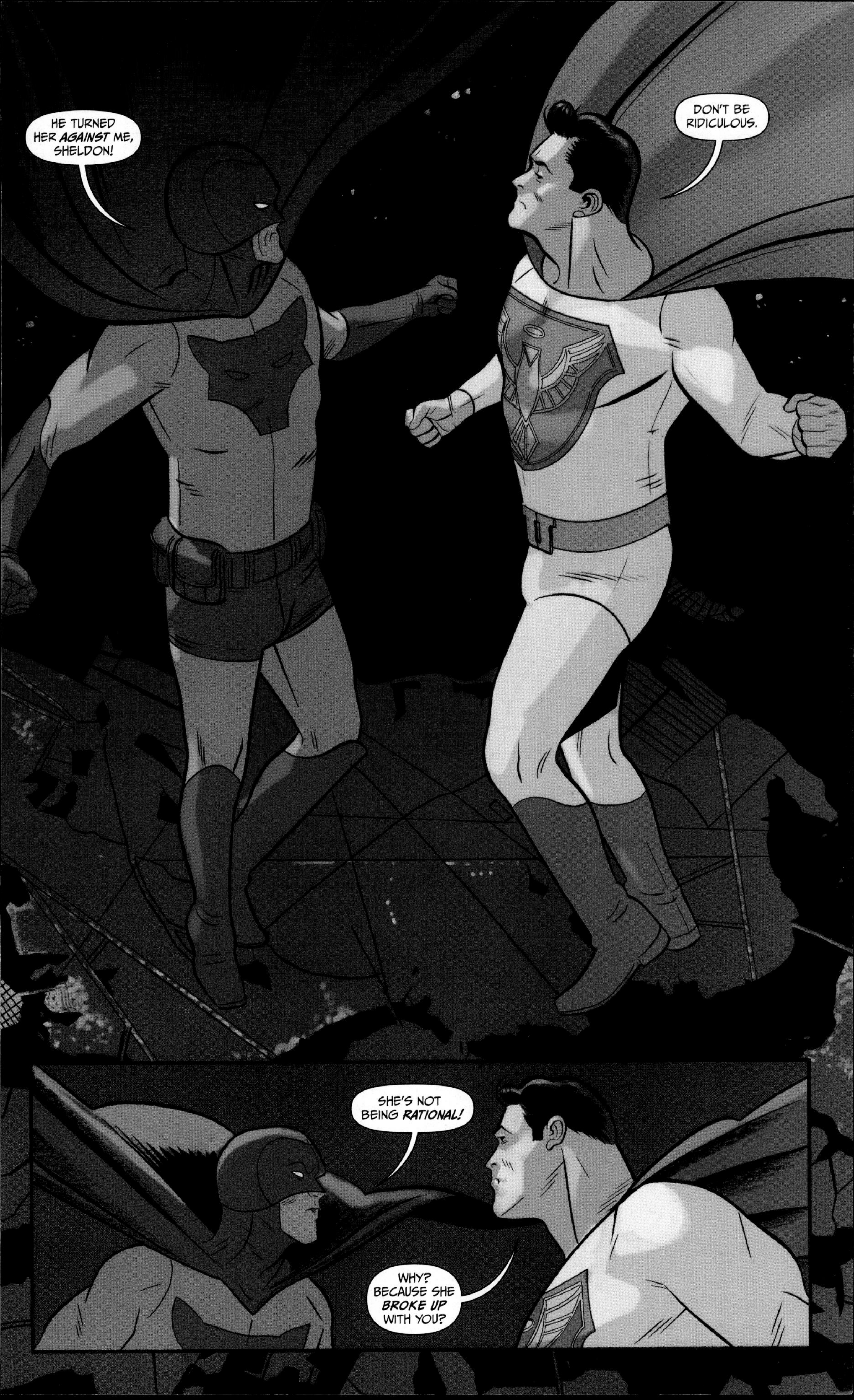
HE TURNED HER *AGAINST* ME, SHELDON!
DON'T BE RIDICULOUS.
SHE'S NOT BEING *RATIONAL!*
WHY? BECAUSE SHE *BROKE UP* WITH YOU?

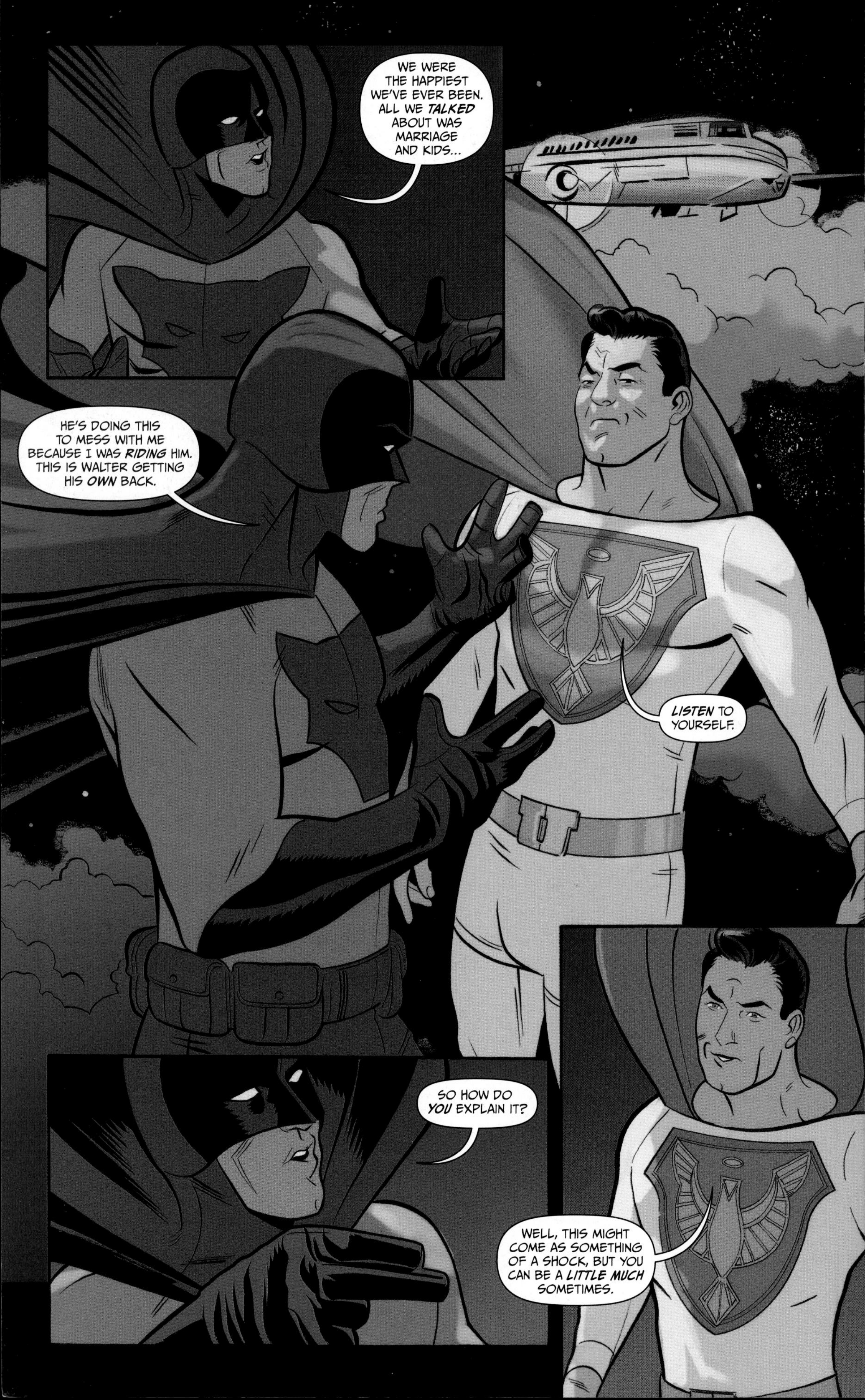
WE WERE THE HAPPIEST WE'VE EVER BEEN. ALL WE *TALKED* ABOUT WAS MARRIAGE AND KIDS...
HE'S DOING THIS TO MESS WITH ME BECAUSE I WAS *RIDING* HIM. THIS IS WALTER GETTING HIS *OWN* BACK.
LISTEN TO YOURSELF.
SO HOW DO *YOU* EXPLAIN IT?
WELL, THIS MIGHT COME AS SOMETHING OF A SHOCK, BUT YOU CAN BE A *LITTLE MUCH* SOMETIMES.

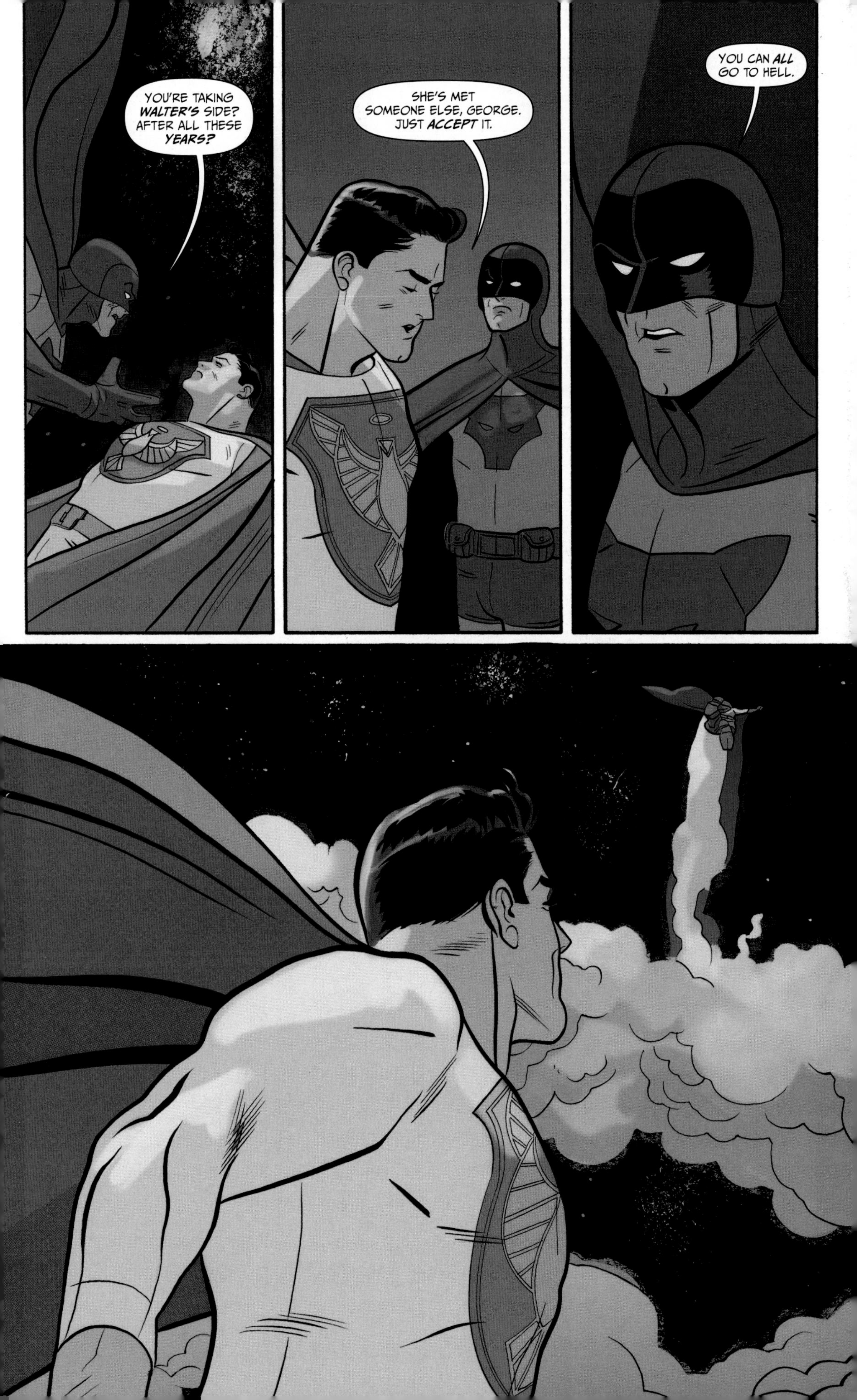
YOU'RE TAKING WALTER'S SIDE? AFTER ALL THESE YEARS?
SHE'S MET SOMEONE ELSE, GEORGE. JUST ACCEPT IT.
YOU CAN ALL GO TO HELL.

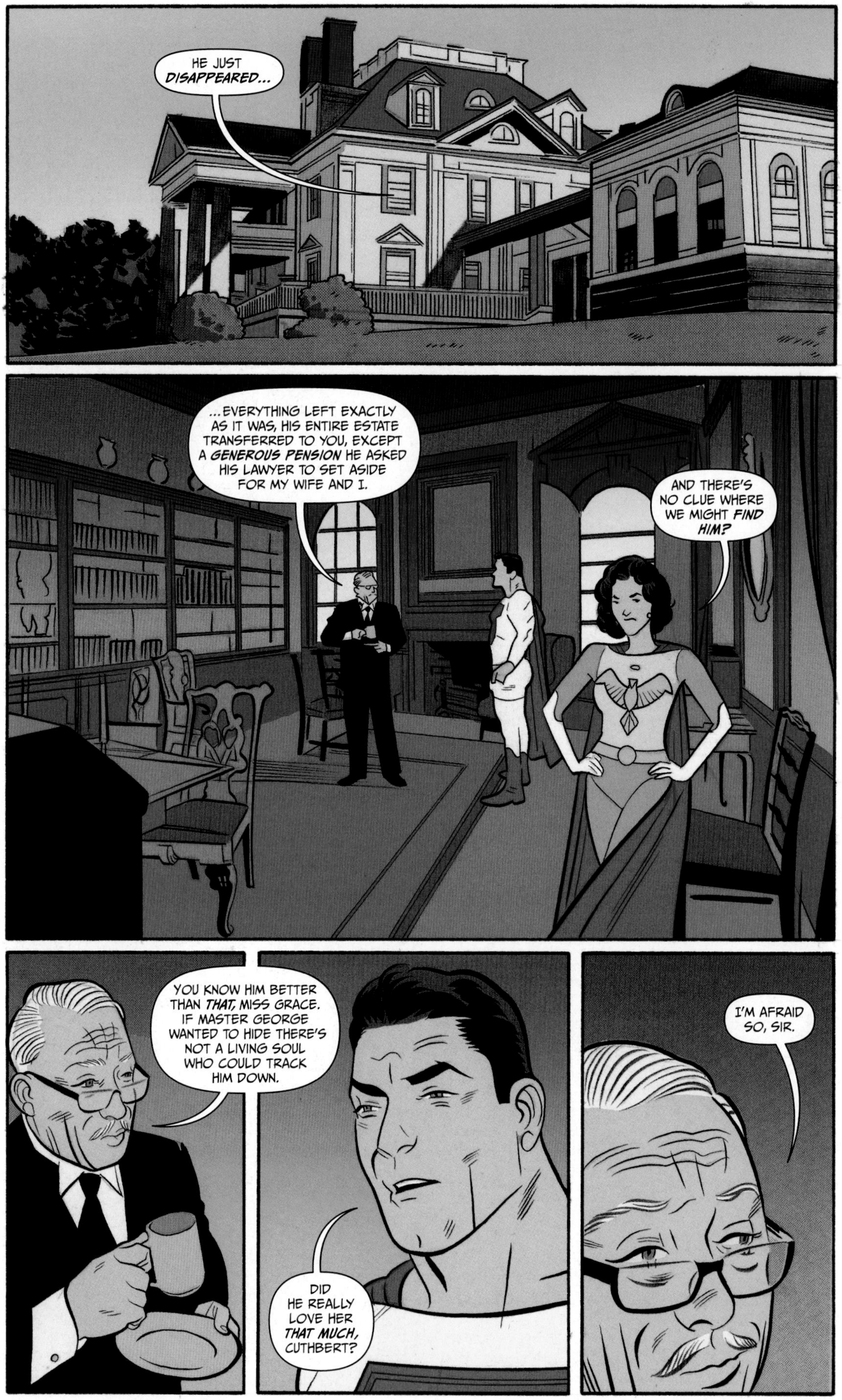
HE JUST DISAPPEARED...
...EVERYTHING LEFT EXACTLY AS IT WAS, HIS ENTIRE ESTATE TRANSFERRED TO YOU, EXCEPT A GENEROUS PENSION HE ASKED HIS LAWYER TO SET ASIDE FOR MY WIFE AND I.
AND THERE'S NO CLUE WHERE WE MIGHT FIND HIM?
YOU KNOW HIM BETTER THAN THAT, MISS GRACE. IF MASTER GEORGE WANTED TO HIDE THERE'S NOT A LIVING SOUL WHO COULD TRACK HIM DOWN.
DID HE REALLY LOVE HER THAT MUCH, CUTHBERT?
I'M AFRAID SO, SIR.

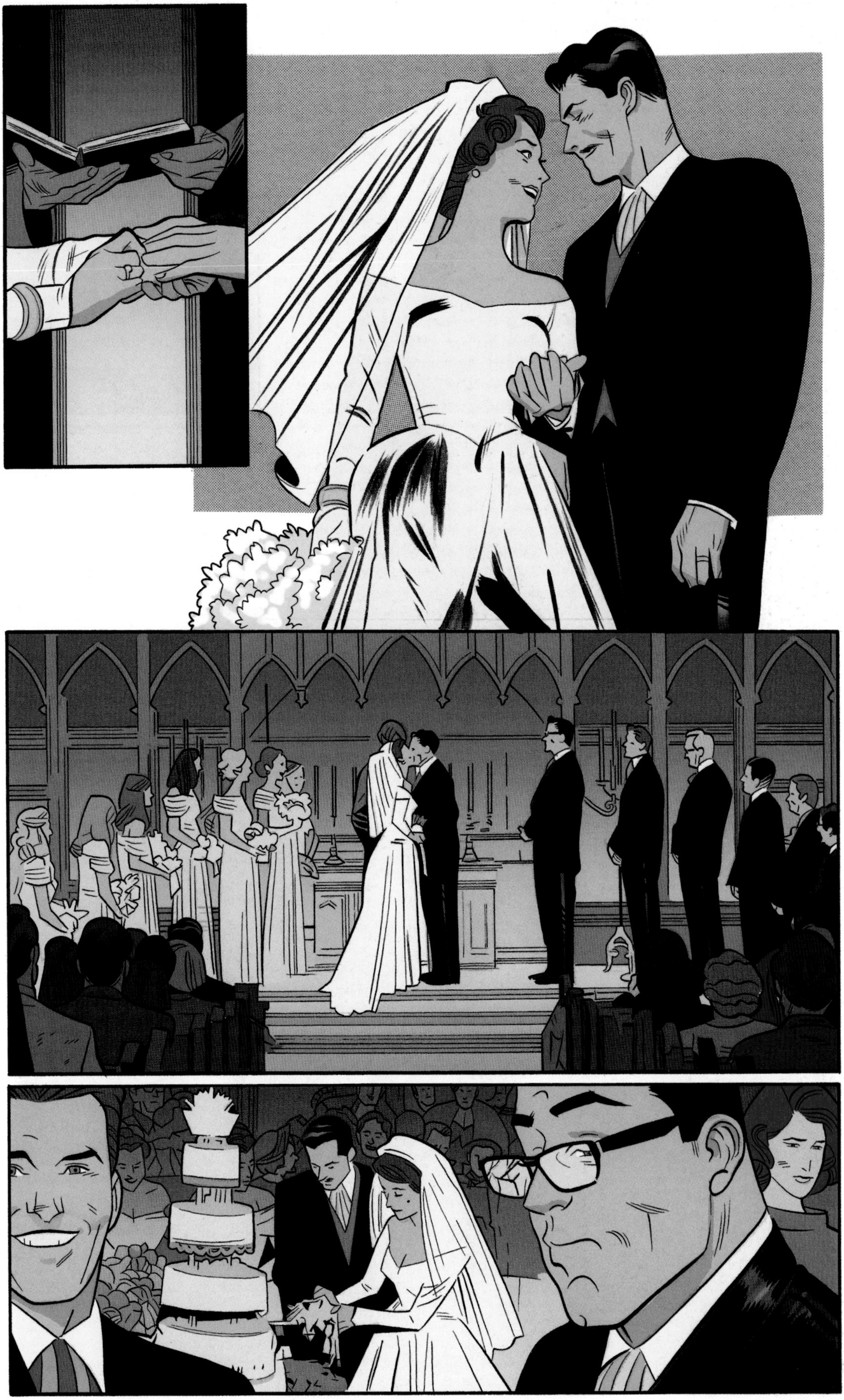

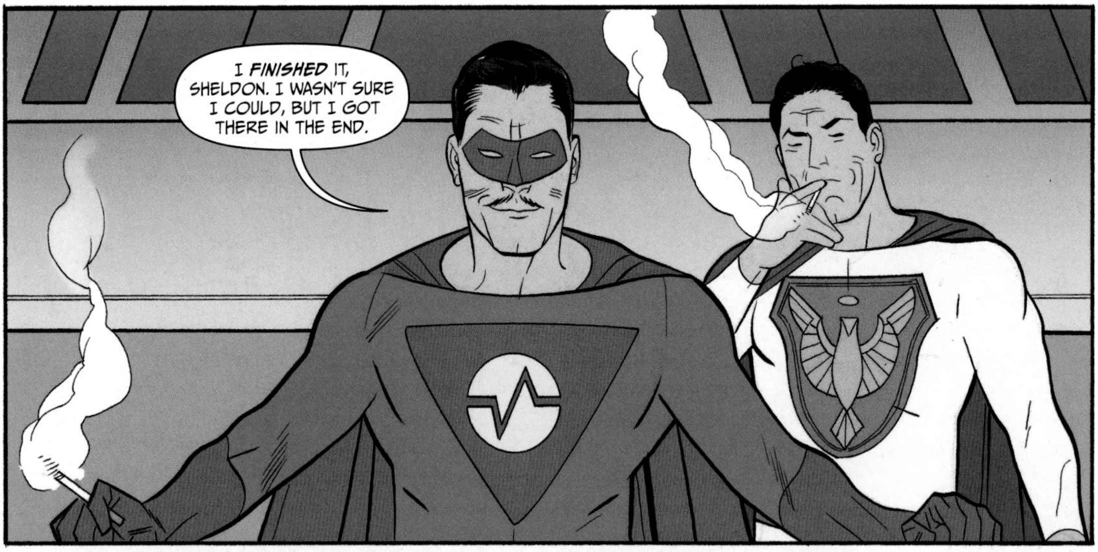
I *FINISHED* IT, SHELDON. I WASN'T SURE I COULD, BUT I GOT THERE IN THE END.

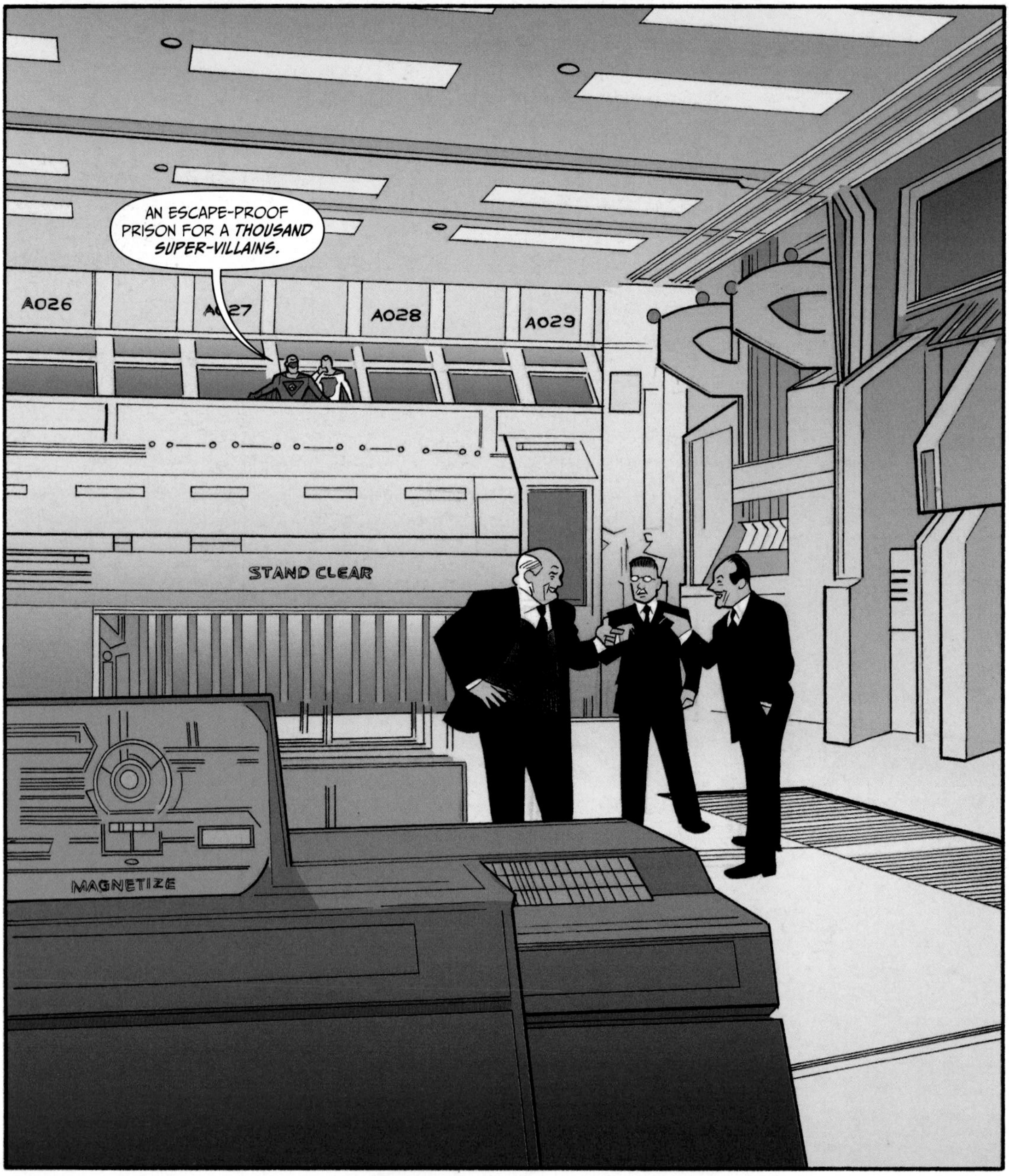
AN ESCAPE-PROOF PRISON FOR A *THOUSAND SUPER-VILLAINS.*
A026
A027
A028
A029
STAND CLEAR
MAGNETIZE

SEEMS A LITTLE PARANOID WHEN THERE ARE BARELY FIFTY *ACTIVE* OUT THERE.

BUT THEY *BREED*, DEAR BROTHER. A WISE MAN ALWAYS THINKS AHEAD.

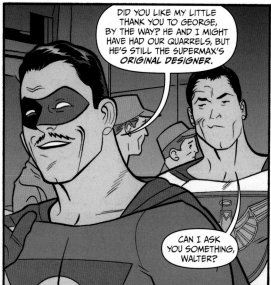

DID YOU LIKE MY LITTLE THANK YOU TO GEORGE, BY THE WAY? HE AND I MIGHT HAVE HAD OUR QUARRELS, BUT HE'S STILL THE SUPERMAX'S *ORIGINAL DESIGNER.*

CAN I ASK YOU SOMETHING, WALTER?

FEEL FREE.

THAT FEELING GEORGE HAD THAT YOU USED YOUR PSYCHIC POWERS TO BREAK UP HIM AND SUNNY...

...IT ISN'T *TRUE*, IS IT?

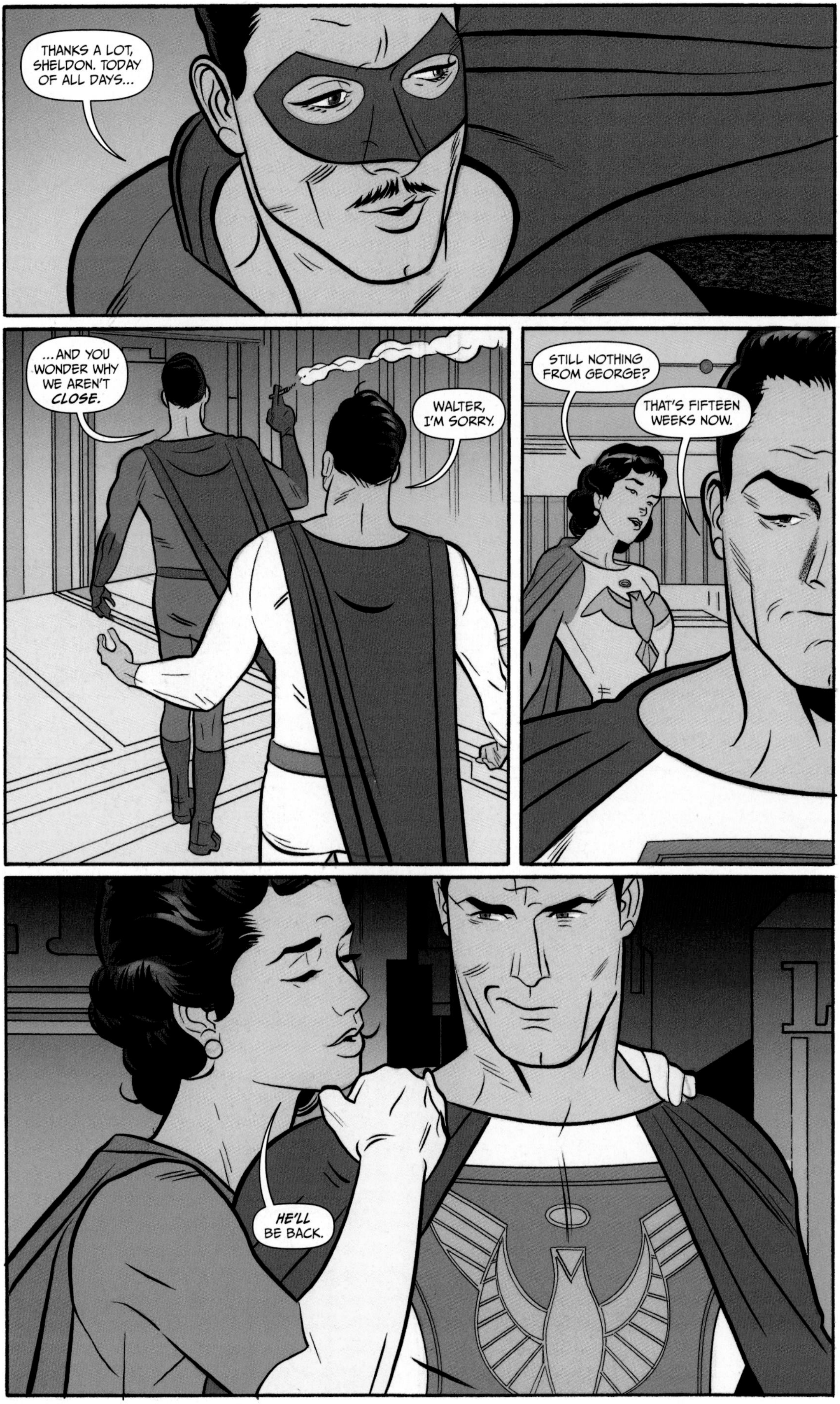
THANKS A LOT, SHELDON. TODAY OF ALL DAYS...
...AND YOU WONDER WHY WE AREN'T *CLOSE*.
WALTER, I'M SORRY.
STILL NOTHING FROM GEORGE?
THAT'S FIFTEEN WEEKS NOW.
HE'LL BE BACK.

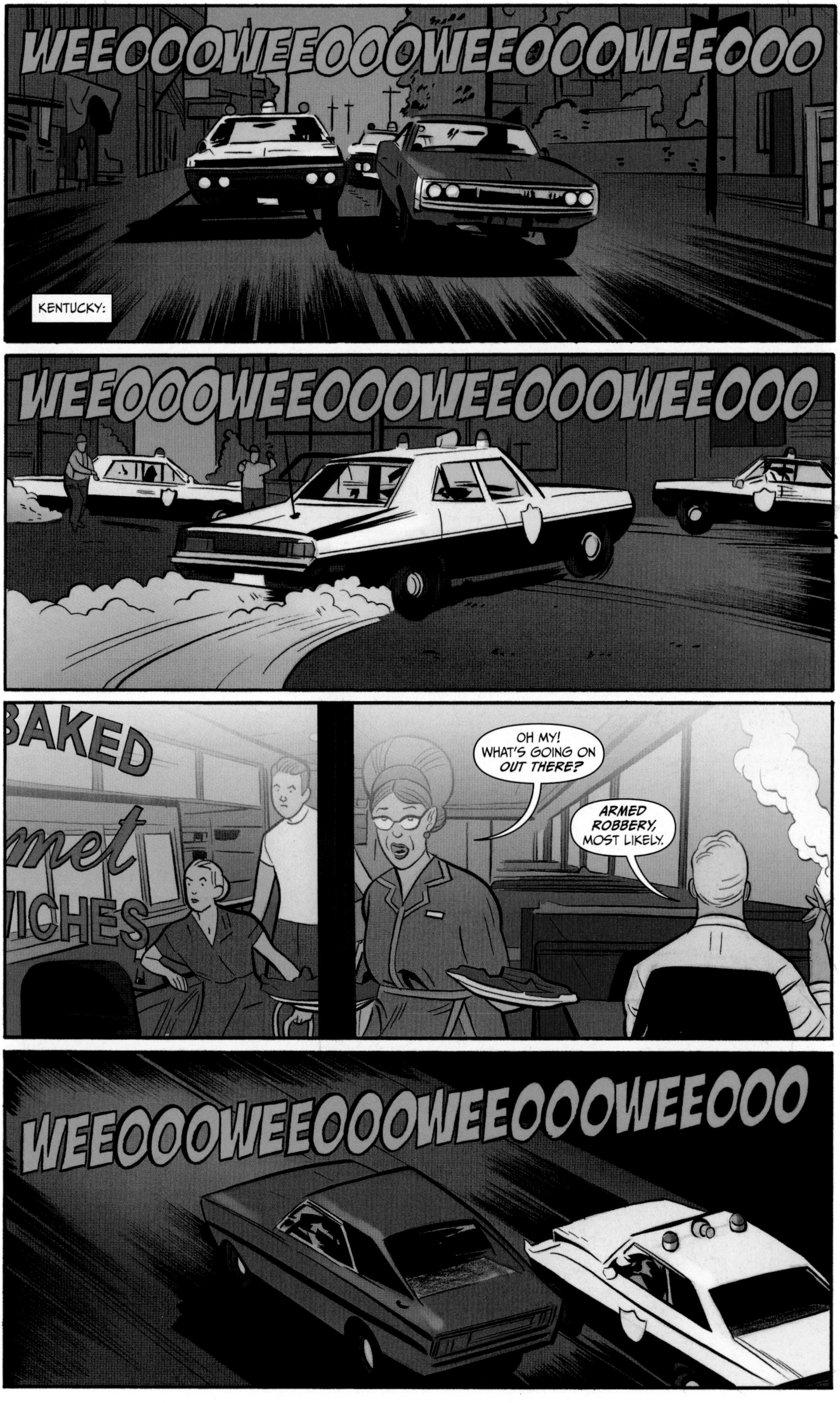
WEEOOOWEEOOOWEEOOOWEEOOO
KENTUCKY:
WEEOOOWEEOOOWEEOOOWEEOOO
BAKED
met
ICHES
OH MY! WHAT'S GOING ON OUT THERE?
ARMED ROBBERY, MOST LIKELY.
WEEOOOWEEOOOWEEOOO

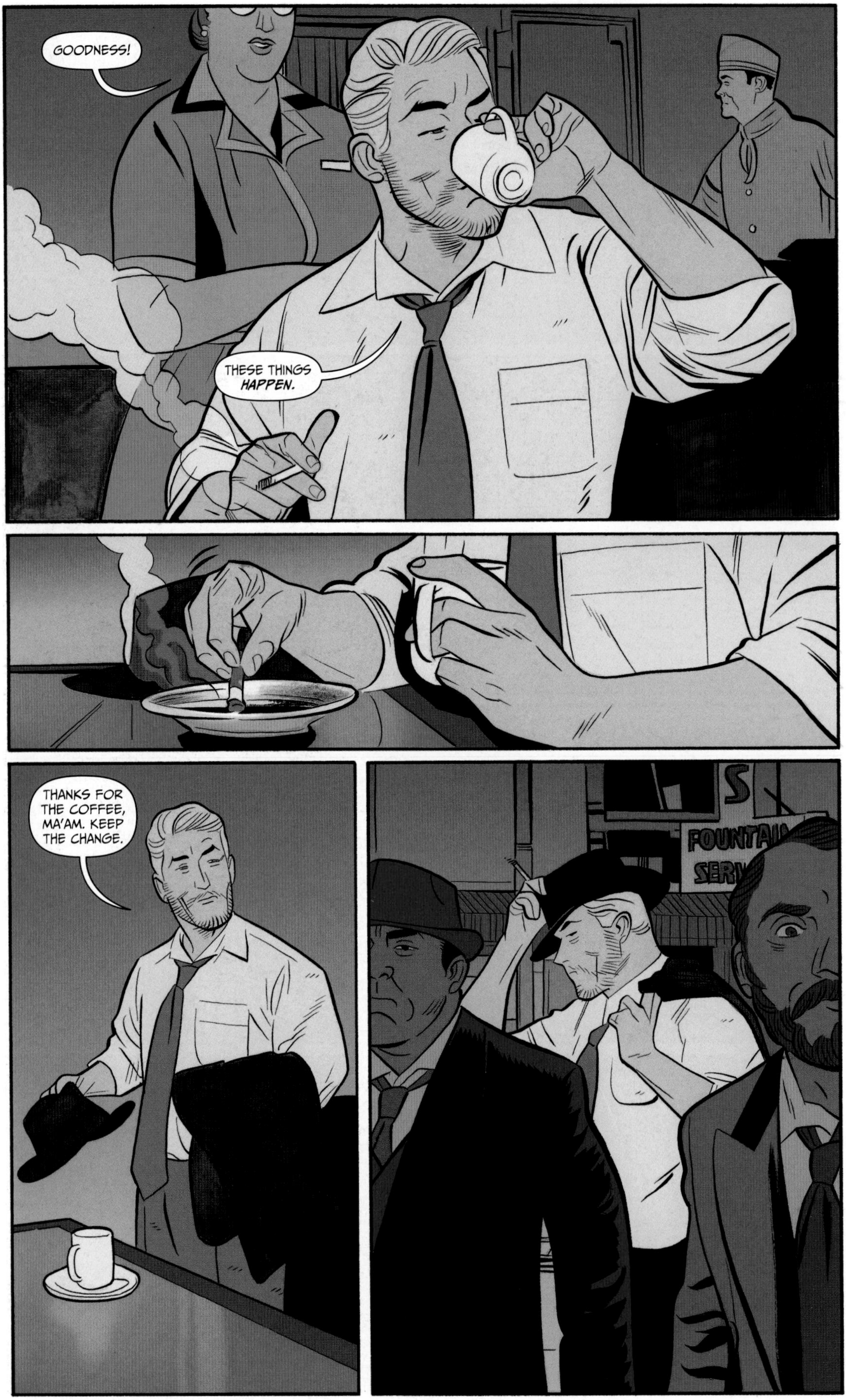
GOODNESS!
THESE THINGS *HAPPEN.*
THANKS FOR THE COFFEE, MA'AM. KEEP THE CHANGE.
FOUNTAI
SERV

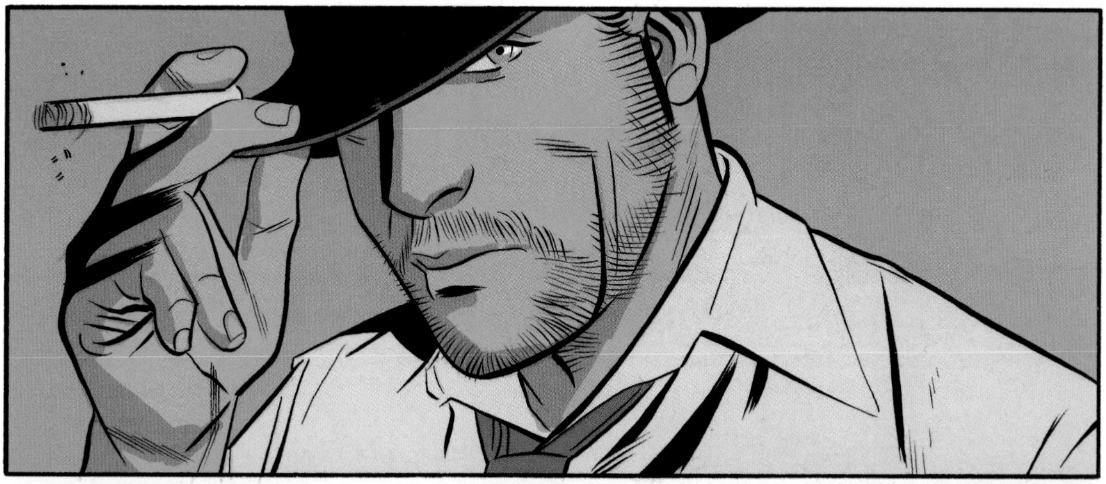

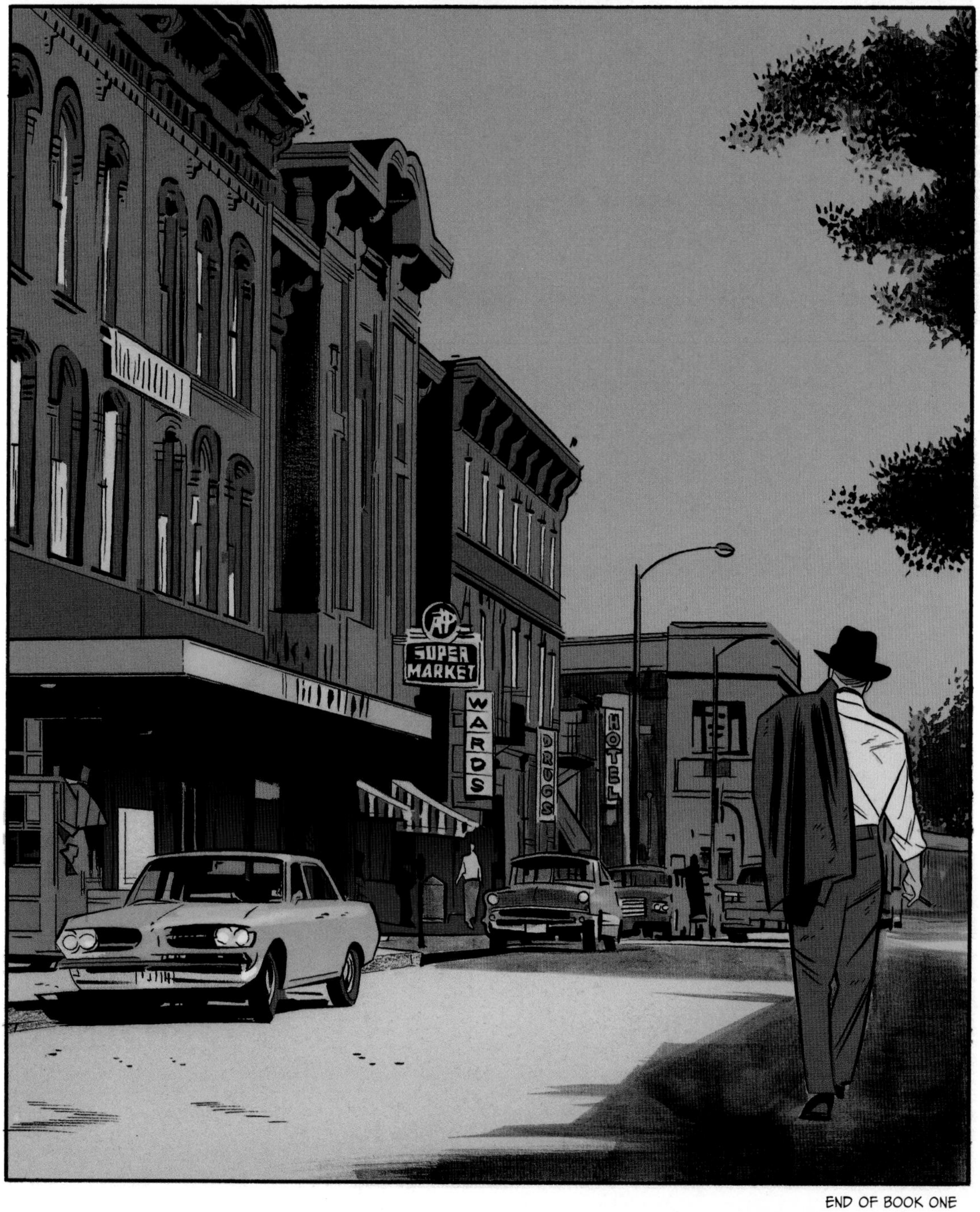

A&P
SUPER MARKET
WARDS
DRUGS
HOTEL

END OF BOOK ONE

MARK MILLAR

Mark Millar is the *New York Times* best-selling writer of *Wanted*, the *Kick-Ass* series, *The Secret Service*, *Jupiter's Legacy*, *Nemesis*, *Superior*, *Super Crooks*, *American Jesus*, *MPH*, *Starlight*, and *Chrononauts*. *Wanted*, *Kick-Ass*, *Kick-Ass 2*, and *The Secret Service* (as *Kingsman: The Secret Service*) have been adapted into feature films, and *Nemesis*, *Superior*, *Starlight*, *War Heroes* and *Chrononauts* are in development at major studios.

His DC Comics work includes the seminal *Superman: Red Son*, and at Marvel Comics he created *The Ultimates*, selected by *Time* magazine as the comic book of the decade; *Wolverine: Old Man Logan*, and *Civil War*, the industry's biggest-selling superhero series in almost two decades.

Mark is an Executive Producer on all his movie adaptations and is currently creative consultant to Fox Studios on their Marvel slate of movies. His autobiography, *In His Eyes Rest The Stories*, will be published next year.

WILFREDO TORRES

Wilfredo Torres is a self-taught American comic book artist and illustrator. He has been working as a professional freelancer since 2007. Before his work with Mark Millar on *Jupiter's Circle,* Wilfredo was best known for his work on *The Shadow: Year One* (Dynamite Entertainment), *Batman '66* (DC Comics), *Lobster Johnson: Prayer of Neferu* (Dark Horse Comics), and *Quantum & Woody* (Valiant Entertainment). Wilfredo redesigned and provided covers for *The Shield* (Archie Comics/ Dark Circle).

Wilfredo is a process junkie who enjoys sleeping, pictures of puppies, home improvement shows, beer, long walks, and drawing people who wear their underwear over their clothes.

DAVIDE GIANFELICE

Davide Gianfelice was born in Milan, Italy in 1977. Before his collaboration on *Jupiter's Circle*, he worked for Vertigo on the acclaimed first run of *Northlanders* and *Greek Street*. His work for Marvel comics can be seen in *Daredevil: Reborn, Wolverine: Weapon X*, and *Six Guns*.

With Dark Horse he collaborated on a run of *Conan the Barbarian*, and with Skybound he provided art for *Ghosted*. In his spare time he enjoys cooking Italian food and has a passion for photography.

FRANCESCO MORTARINO

Francesco Mortarino was born in 1978 in Milan, Italy. After graduating from the Comics School of Milano, he started working for Italian publishers like Edizioni BD in 2008.

In 2014 he started to work with Sergio Bonelli Editore on the *Nathan Never* comic book.

In 2015 he was very proud to collaborate with Davide Gianfelice on the art for *Jupiter's Circle*.

He lives in Milan with his wife and their two terrific children.

IVE SVORCINA

Ive was born in 1986 on a small island in the Adriatic Sea, Croatia. Being self-taught, he somehow managed to start his professional career in 2006, and since then he has worked for such publishers as Marvel, Delcourt, Image Comics, and smaller publishers in Croatia.

Notable achievements include getting kicked out of the computer science college and getting nominated for an Eisner award for his work on *Thor*.

Currently he resides in Zagreb, and is thinking about moving somewhere warmer and sunnier.

PETER DOHERTY

Peter's earliest work in comics was during 1990, providing painted artwork for the John Wagner-written *Young Death: The Boyhood of a Super-fiend*, published in the first year of the *Judge Dredd Megazine*.
For the next few years he painted art for a number of Judge Dredd stories.

Over the intervening years he's worked for most of the major comics publishers, and also branched out into illustration, TV, and movie work.

Over the last decade he's worked on projects both as the sole artist and as a coloring/lettering/design collaborator with other artists, including Geof Darrow on his *Shaolin Cowboy* project, and most recently Frank Quitely and Duncan Fegredo, on the Millarworld projects *Jupiter's Legacy* and *MPH,* respectively.

Peter lives locally, in the Yorkshire countryside.

NICOLE BOOSE

Nicole Boose began her comics career as an assistant editor for Harris Comics' *Vampirella,* before joining the editorial staff at Marvel Comics. There, she edited titles including *Cable & Deadpool, Invincible Iron Man,* and Stephen King's *Dark Tower* adaptations, and oversaw Marvel's line of custom comic publications.

Since 2008, Nicole has worked as a freelance editor and consultant in the comics industry, with editorial credits that include the Millarworld titles *Superior, Super Crooks, Jupiter's Legacy, MPH, Starlight,* and *Chrononauts.* Nicole is also Communications Manager for Comics Experience, an online school and community for comic creators.

Born in Philadelphia and a long-time New Yorker, she now lives near Cleveland, Ohio with her family.

MILLARWORLD®

THE COLLECTION CHECKLIST

KICK-ASS
MARK MILLAR
JOHN ROMITA JR.

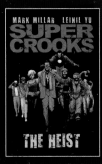

KICK-ASS
Art by John Romita Jr.

- [ ] Kick-Ass #1-8

KICK-ASS 2 PRELUDE:
HIT-GIRL
MARK MILLAR
JOHN ROMITA JR.
TOM PALMER and DEAN WHITE

HIT-GIRL
Art by John Romita Jr.

- [ ] Hit-Girl #1-5

KICK-ASS 2
MARK MILLAR
JOHN ROMITA JR.

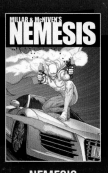

KICK-ASS 2
Art by John Romita Jr.

- [ ] Kick-Ass 2 #1-7

KICK-ASS 3
MARK MILLAR
JOHN ROMITA JR.

KICK-ASS 3
Art by John Romita Jr.

- [ ] Kick-Ass 3 #1-8

MILLAR MURPHY
CHRONONAUTS

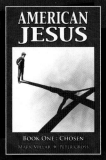

CHRONONAUTS
Art by Sean Gordon Murphy

- [ ] Chrononauts #1-4

MARK MILLAR DUNCAN FEGREDO
MPH

MPH
Art by Duncan Fegredo

- [ ] MPH #1-5

MARK MILLAR · GORAN PARLOV
STARLIGHT
The Return of Duke McQueen

STARLIGHT
Art by Goran Parlov

- [ ] Starlight #1-6

MARK MILLAR DAVE GIBBONS MATTHEW VAUGHN
KINGSMAN
THE SECRET SERVICE

KINGSMAN: THE SECRET SERVICE
Art by Dave Gibbons

- [ ] The Secret Service #1-6

MILLAR·TORRES·GIANFELICE
JUPITER'S
CIRCLE
BOOK ONE

JUPITER'S CIRCLE
Art by Wilfredo Torres

- [ ] Jupiter's Circle #1-6

MARK MILLAR·FRANK QUITELY
JUPITER'S
LEGACY

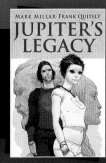

JUPITER'S LEGACY
Art by Frank Quitely

- [ ] Jupiter's Legacy #1-5

MARK MILLAR LEINIL YU
SUPER
CROOKS
THE HEIST

SUPER CROOKS
Art by Leinil Yu

- [ ] Super Crooks #1-4

MARK MILLAR & LEINIL YU
SUPERIOR
FROM THE
WRITER OF
KICK-ASS

SUPERIOR
Art by Leinil Yu

- [ ] Superior #1-7

MILLAR & McNIVEN'S
NEMESIS

NEMESIS
Art by Steve McNiven

- [ ] Nemesis #1-4

WANTED
MARK MILLAR • JG JONES • PAUL MOUNTS
UNIVERSAL PICTURES

WANTED
Art by JG Jones

- [ ] Wanted #1-6

AMERICAN
JESUS
BOOK ONE : CHOSEN
MARK MILLAR ✦ PETER GROSS

AMERICAN JESUS
Art by Peter Gross

- [ ] American Jesus #1-3